Strell d_____ ground to_____ the Hold._____ eyes, it wa_____ open, and snow had collected against the thick, rough timbers . . .

It had been left to the decorative set of doors to keep the Hold secure. Between the two sets of doors hung a huge bell. Shrugging, Strell grasped the frayed cord and gave a firm tug.

Even expecting it, the harsh clank made Alissa jump. The snow seemed to swallow the sound, and she fidgeted as her pulse slowed. It seemed to take forever until the doors opened and they were greeted by a pale figure clenched with cold under a long, elegantly trimmed housecoat.

"Burn me to Ash," Alissa whispered, her eyes going wide and her knees threatening to give. Her papa's memory hadn't been a dream.

first truth

dawn cook

ACE BOOKS, NEW YORK

THE BERKLEY PUBLISHING GROUP
Published by the Penguin Group
Penguin Group (USA) Inc.
375 Hudson Street, New York, New York 10014, USA
Penguin Group (Canada), 90 Eglinton Avenue East, Suite 700, Toronto, Ontario M4P 2Y3, Canada
(a division of Pearson Penguin Canada Inc.)
Penguin Books Ltd., 80 Strand, London WC2R 0RL, England
Penguin Group Ireland, 25 St. Stephen's Green, Dublin 2, Ireland (a division of Penguin Books Ltd.)
Penguin Group (Australia), 250 Camberwell Road, Camberwell, Victoria 3124, Australia
(a division of Pearson Australia Group Pty. Ltd.)
Penguin Books India Pvt. Ltd., 11 Community Centre, Panchsheel Park, New Delhi—110 017, India
Penguin Group (NZ), 67 Apollo Drive, Rosedale, North Shore 0632, New Zealand
(a division of Pearson New Zealand Ltd.)
Penguin Books (South Africa) (Pty.) Ltd., 24 Sturdee Avenue, Rosebank, Johannesburg 2196,
South Africa

Penguin Books Ltd., Registered Offices: 80 Strand, London WC2R 0RL, England

FIRST TRUTH

An Ace Book / published by arrangement with the author

PRINTING HISTORY
Ace mass-market edition / June 2002

Copyright © 2002 by Dawn Cook.
Cover art by Jerry Vanderstelt.
Cover design by Rita Frangie.
Interior text design by Julie Rogers.

ISBN: 978-0-441-00945-9

ACE
Ace Books are published by The Berkley Publishing Group,
a division of Penguin Group (USA) Inc.,
375 Hudson Street, New York, New York 10014.
ACE and the "A" design are trademarks of Penguin Group (USA) Inc.

PRINTED IN THE UNITED STATES OF AMERICA

17   16   15   14   13   12   11   10   9   8

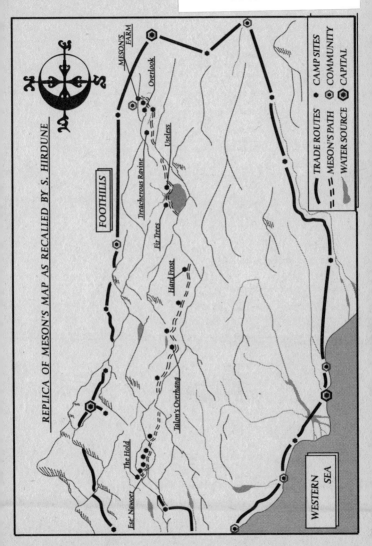

REPLICA OF MESON'S MAP AS RECALLED BY S. HIRDUNE

*For Tim, who not only loosed the beast,
but gave it wings and a heckuva strong updraft.*

acknowledgments

I would like to thank those who helped me bring this work up from its first scratchings:

My husband, Tim; my dear neighbor, Natalie; and the many friends who were kind enough to read the works in progress and offer encouragement. Your criticisms fanned the spark of creativity rather than put it out.

The core members of my writers group: Misty Massey, who showed me the back roads to everywhere; Norman Froscher, who kept the red ink and libations flowing in equal proportions; Craig Faris, who agreed we could all kill him on paper; Todd Massey, whose questions always pulled something out I had forgotten; Virginia Wilcox, who showed me it was possible to put poetry into prose; and of course, Gwen Hunter, without whose business savvy and forceful critiques nothing would have moved from the kitchen table. Thank you for your honest criticism and friendship.

I would also thank my agent, Richard Curtis, for giving me the incredible opportunity to bring my work to light and for being so generous with his time. And my editor at The Berkley Publishing Group, Anne Sowards, whose willingness to explain rather than demand made the difference in keeping the joy of creating alive.

Dawn Cook

"There's no such thing as magic," he protested, clutching his thin coat closer, shivering in the cold.

"That's what they all believe."

"And the only way to insure our survival," said a third, "is to be certain that it stays that way."

The meeting was over. With the scrape of a claw and the downward pulse of a leathery wing, he was alone.

I

"You were up late again last night," she said into the morning quiet. "I don't recall hearing you come in."

Alissa cringed. Ashes, she thought. Her mother hadn't heard her come in because she had fallen asleep in the garden. Again. "I was out on the rock watching the night," she admitted, trying to sound as if it meant nothing. "The big one in the squash patch."

Standing before the sink, her mother sighed, gazing out the window as she continued to clean the pumpkin seeds she had put to soak last night.

"I wasn't alone," Alissa protested weakly. "Talon was with me."

Her mother's shoulders drooped, but she said nothing. Alissa knew her mother's opinion wasn't very high when it came to her one and only pet. That Talon flew at night only made it worse. Kestrels generally didn't, but no one had told Talon that, and the small oddity was easily overlooked. At least, Alissa thought, she could overlook it.

Alissa's mouth twisted as she scraped her knife across her toast, rubbing off the burnt parts with a stoic acceptance. It had been toasted only on one side. At least half of it was edible. She glanced up as her mother slumped at the harsh, repetitive sounds. Breakfast was invariably well-done. Alissa had taken over the kitchen in self-defense years ago, but her mother refused to let go of their morning meal.

It didn't matter how much she scraped at it, Alissa thought. Burnt is burnt. And she pushed the plate with its crusty, black char away with an all too familiar resignation. Slouching on her stool, she stretched until her boots reached the patch of sun that made it into the kitchen. The sound of dripping water slowed. Her mother's shadow lay long behind her. A frown stole over Alissa as she realized it wasn't moving. She looked up, straightening in unease. Her mother was still washing the same handful of seeds as when Alissa had come in. Something was up.

"So, what are your plans this morning?" her mother asked, her gaze never shifting as the water dripped unnoticed from her fingers.

"Um," Alissa grunted, forcing herself to be casual. "I thought the side vegetable patch. The beans are about done. I was going to clear them out, give what's left to the sheep. Oh! That reminds me," she blurted, glad to have some bad news that couldn't possibly be her fault. "I think a dog is about. The sheep have gotten skittish. Even Nanny won't let me touch her."

"M-m-m," was the distant answer, worrying Alissa all the more. Her mother stared out the window, her gaze seeming to go all the way to the unseen plains. The silence grew uneasy. Alissa watched her mother take her eyes from the hills, turning to her hair ribbon draped on its hook next to the sink.

Oh, no! Alissa thought with a tight stab of alarm. Her mother only tied her hair back when she was planning something strenuous like a spring-cleaning, or meting out punishment. And Alissa hadn't done anything wrong lately—she thought. Alissa's eyes widened as the pumpkin seeds fell back into the slop her mother had been rinsing them free of and she absently dried her fingers on her skirt. "Don't do it," Alissa breathed, but her mother's fingers twitched, and reached, and grasped the thin, coppery band of fabric. With a determined abruptness, she gathered her long, dark hair.

Alissa took a shaky breath. She was still all right. If her mother wrapped it about her hair once, she was all right. Once is no problem, twice is lots of work, three, and she was in trouble.

Alissa swallowed hard as her mother wrapped it four times, tying it with a severity Alissa had never seen before. "I should have locked her door," her mother said to herself as her fingers worked. "I should have shuttered her windows." Without another word her mother turned, strode into Alissa's room, and shut the door.

"I'm pig slop," Alissa whispered. "That's it. I'm pig slop." Breakfast forgotten, she tip-toed to the door and put an ear to it. The sharp sounds of cupboards opening and shutting met her. There was an annoyed squawk, followed by a muffled, "Then get out of my way!" and Talon joined her, having flown out the bedroom window and back in through the kitchen's.

Chittering wildly, the small bird landed upon Alissa's shoulder. "I don't know," she said. Talon cocked her head at the closed door. With a slight gasp, Alissa flung herself back to the table trying to look nonchalant. Her mother didn't seem to notice Alissa's artful disinterest as she blew out of her daughter's room and into her own, a bundle of cloth in her arms, a determined look on her face. The door crashed shut. Alissa's ear was against it almost before it hit.

"No," Alissa heard her mutter. "She won't need that. Yes. Most definitely yes. That would be nice, but it won't last a week."

"Oh, Ashes," Alissa whispered, and feeling decidedly ill, she sank down on her stool at the table. It had been her spot ever since she could pull herself into a chair. She had a bad feeling it wasn't her spot anymore.

In a flurry of soft, quick steps, her mother burst forth. Talon gave a startled peep and flew out to lose herself in the bitter smell of frost-killed pumpkin vines. Alissa's overnight pack, the one she used when they went to market, was in her mother's hands. "This isn't big enough," her mother said, then turned to Alissa. Her mother wore a tight smile, looking pained and desperate. "Good. At least you're dressed for it."

Alissa's eyes slid to the work-stained trousers tucked into her boots. She usually wore a full-length skirt, but slogging about in the garden demanded something a bit more sturdy.

Not wanting to admit what the pack meant, Alissa hastily shifted her plate as her mother dropped her load on the table. She strode briskly to the storage chest and brought out a larger pack, Alissa's winter coat, and a second set of work clothes. Under them was her mother's treasured pair of cream-colored boots. All of it went on the table.

"Are we going somewhere?" Alissa asked weakly, noticing that almost everything on the table belonged to her.

"Half right, dear. Half right." The oiled tarp hanging behind the door joined the pile.

Alissa's stomach dropped. It was worse than she thought. "Mother," she protested. "I know we talked about this, but you can't send me to the Hold. It's just one of Papa's stories. The Hold doesn't even exist!"

"Yes, it does."

Alissa's brow furrowed. "Have you seen it?" she accused.

As expected, her mother's eyes dropped. "No. He said— he said it wasn't safe." What Alissa thought was fright slipped into her mother's eyes, sending a chill through her. "I'm not supposed to know it's there," her mother said softly.

Taking a quick breath, Alissa pushed her fear away, turning it into something far more familiar. "You're going to send me there, though," she said sharply.

Much to her surprise, her mother didn't tell her to hush, or be still, or even give Alissa that look of hers. Instead, she reached out and ran her hand through Alissa's hair. Her fingers were trembling and she looked worried. "I waited too long to send you on," her mother whispered. "I didn't want to see. Your papa said it was a month's trip, and you'll have to get there before it snows."

"You're going to make me leave because of a bedtime story?" Alissa cried in disbelief.

Silently her mother took from a pocket a small pouch and reluctantly extended it. Alissa had never seen it before, but she was sure it was a piece of her mother's childhood; the initials stitched on it were from her maiden name. Slowly Alissa accepted it, feeling the heavy weight of uncertainty in her hand. It smelled faintly, sort of a rank, back of the throat smell. "What is it?" she asked, grimacing at the stink.

"Your inheritance." Her mother leaned forward, her eyes pinched. "Go on. Open it."

At her encouraging nod, Alissa picked at the knots holding it shut. Finally they loosened and she peered inside. "Oh, Ashes!" she cried, her head snapping back as she struggled not to retch. The stench was a sharp, eye-watering assault that seemed to close off her throat. Fish wrapped in decaying cabbage, summered at the bottom of a wet ditch didn't come close. Alissa couldn't even see what the bag held for the tears streaming down. It was worse than her mother's salve, if that was at all possible. "What is it?" she gasped when she found the breath to speak.

Her mother slumped where she stood. "Bone and Ash," she whispered. "That decides it. Falling asleep in the garden I could dismiss, but this?" She took a deep breath, closing her eyes in a slow blink. Alissa shivered when they opened. Her mother looked old. For the first time, her mother looked old. "You have to go," she said faintly, taking the bag from Alissa and tightening the strings. "Now. It was wrong of me to make you wait."

"But what is it?"

Slowly her mother sank down in a chair. "Dust. Your papa said it was your inheritance."

"My inheritance? A rank bag of dust is my inheritance? Can't I have a goat instead?"

Her mother's lips pursed and she frowned, returning for a moment to the mother Alissa knew. "Don't be flippant, Alissa. It's from your papa. He said it would free you from the guilt of obligation. He kept it in that jar I store my salve in, but he said you should carry it on your person after you leave, and I thought the bag would be easier."

Alissa lifted her chin defiantly. "I'm not going."

"Here." Her mother made a loop of the drawstring and put the bag around Alissa's neck.

Alissa looked down at the unfamiliar bump. The bag was well-made. With the drawstring tightened, she couldn't smell a thing. "Mother," she protested, starting to take it off. "I'm not a Keeper. Papa wasn't a Keeper. There is no such thing as Keepers or Masters or the Hold. And I'm not wearing this. It stinks!"

Her mother's hands covered hers, stopping her. "I can't smell anything, Alissa. But your papa could."

The first faint stirrings of panic began to swirl through Alissa, and she swallowed hard. "This is ridiculous. *I'm not going.*" She felt her throat catch. "If you don't want me anymore, I—I'll leave, but don't expect me to believe *this!*"

Her mother's eyes grew wide. "Of course I don't want you to go, but you belong to the Hold. For almost twenty years you were mine, but look at you." Her brow furrowed, and she brushed her hand through Alissa's hair again, trying to arrange it. "I can't ignore it anymore. Up all night, staring at the sky. The Hold is calling to you as strongly as it used to call to your papa. Always, just before he would leave, he would lie awake at night until he thought I was asleep, then slip out to the garden. He never knew I watched him, sitting on that same rock. . . . Oh, Ashes!" Biting her lip, she turned away.

"I can't pretend anymore," her mother said to the floor. "Curse you, Meson, you warned me this might happen if we had a child, but I didn't want to believe. You promised me I wouldn't be alone, but I'm going to lose her just like I lost you. . . . And it's not my fault!"

"Mother?" Alissa reached out. She had never seen her mother like this. It was scaring her.

Taking a ragged breath, her mother seemed to steady herself. "It's not your fault either. Come on." She smiled her eyes shining with a hint of tears. "Let's raid the kitchen. You'll need more cooking tools then you have. The mortar you chipped out last year is large enough for a cooking pot. Let's start with that."

Alissa's thoughts went terrifyingly blank as her mother took her elbow and led her unresisting to the cupboards. She was going to be forced out because of Papa's stories? Had her mother gone mad? It was almost winter. The passes would be closed in a month. She had to do something! But nothing rose to disturb Alissa's wonderfully empty skull.

Sitting numbly on the floor in the patch of sun, Alissa watched item after item disappear into her much larger pack. She hardly heard the patter of her mother's voice as she talked of the importance of the placement of this and that— warning Alissa that she should pay attention or she wouldn't be able to find anything. Her mother's voice was too cheerful, a thin disguise for her growing grief. All too soon the pack was full. The shelves looked bare, though her mother had taken little.

"There," her mother said with a forced brightness as she stood and dusted her hands. "Warm clothes . . . kitchen tools. You've the tarp, extra blanket, water sack, supplies. . . . Oh!

I've something else." Alissa rose as her mother took her papa's fire kit from the mantel. "You will need this for a while," her mother said, blowing the dust from it before handing it to her.

As a child, Alissa hadn't been allowed to touch her papa's fire kit. Now it was hers. "It looks like it hasn't been used," she said, eyeing the unblemished striker rock.

"It hasn't."

Alissa went cold as the fire kit thumped into her pocket. Her mother was serious. Whether or not the Hold was real, she was leaving. Today. Now. Alissa's eyes went wide. "Mother. You can't do this. What if it snows?"

"You've just enough time. Here. Put these on." She extended her cream-colored boots. "Your papa gave them to me when we were traveling." Her voice had begun to tremble. "Wear them out for me?"

"What if I get sick!"

"When have you ever been sick? Put them on. They should fit now."

So Alissa did, too bewildered to appreciate the smooth softness of the fine leather. Her old boots sat abandoned in the patch of sun, looking as if they belonged to someone else.

"What—what if I get hurt!" Alissa threw out desperately.

That seemed to take her mother aback, but she gave herself a little shake and straightened. "I know it's going to be hot, but put on your coat. There's not enough room in your pack for it." She held it up until Alissa obediently put her leaden arms into the sleeves. They struggled a bit; her mother hadn't helped Alissa put on her coat since she was five. They were out of practice. "And here is your bag," her mother said, "and your hat."

"Mother," Alissa said firmly, realizing her excuses weren't working. "I don't want to go."

"Yes, you do." The pack hit Alissa's shoulders, and her floppy hat was placed lopsided on her head. "Otherwise you wouldn't have fallen asleep in the garden. Your papa was the same way. There." Her mother hesitated, looking Alissa over. "By the Hounds of the Navigator, you almost forgot to take a cup."

"What if I promise to not sleep outside anymore?" Alissa cried, but her mother had gone into the kitchen. In a moment she was back with the cup Alissa's papa had carved for her when she was three.

"Take this," her mother murmured, unbinding her hair to use her ribbon to tie the cup to Alissa's pack. "I'd give you a metal one, but this won't be stolen if you run into someone." Her mother's eyes went distant, and a wash of worry crossed her features.

"Mother. Wait!"

"My," her mother interrupted desperately, her eyes wide, "with that hat and pack, you look just like your papa. Even your eyes have darkened to his gray."

Almost of its own accord, Alissa's gaze dropped. "They're blue," she said sourly, knowing they weren't but wishing they were. Everyone born in the foothills had blue eyes, fair skin, and light hair. It was glaringly obvious that Alissa wasn't a proper farm girl. She looked too much like her plains-born mother. And though Alissa's hair and eyes were as fair as her papa's, she had her mother's height and dark skin. Alissa didn't look enough like plains or foothills to be accepted by either, so was scorned and hated by both.

With a gentle, resolute hand, her mother took Alissa's chin and tilted her eyes up to hers. "They are not blue," she said lovingly, "and don't be ashamed of your heritage. You're not a half-breed. You're just—you. You belong to the plains *and* hills, Alissa, not neither of them."

Alissa's eyes dropped. It was an old argument.

"Now, out the door with you," her mother said softly, and Alissa's breath caught.

"It's a wonderfully crisp morning, you should make good progress," she continued, opening the door and gently leading Alissa out. "Here. Don't forget your walking stick." The familiar, smooth length of wood was pressed into Alissa's hand.

"Mother! Don't!" She looked back to see her mother standing in the threshold, her arms tight about herself, looking small and alone.

"Just head west," she said. "That's the way your papa always went. He said you would be able to find the Hold on your own, that it was instinctive, like geese going south. He said those who dwell there will complete your studies. I hope I've done you no disservice in your book learning. Your papa never said what was needful."

The sun streamed down about Alissa, her new boots planted firmly upon the hard-packed dirt in front of the house. Faint over the pasture still damp with dew, came the nervous bleating of the sheep. Their watch goat, Nanny, rattled her bell as if in warning.

"Good-bye, dear," her mother said as she gave Alissa an abrupt hug, filling her senses with the musty smell of pumpkin. "Mind what I taught you. Especially about controlling that temper of yours. It's going to be the end of you someday." Her mother pulled away, leaving Alissa's cheek damp. "I'm sorry," she whispered, taking a quick breath. "I didn't want to lose you. You were all I had left of him."

"Mother!" she cried, grasping her mother's sleeve. "Don't make me go. Papa didn't believe in magic. He said there was no such thing as magic."

Her mother drew back, her face still. "Of course he said that. He didn't know if—if you would be able to do it."

"But I can't!" she protested vehemently. "I can't do anything a Keeper can do in Papa's stories. I can't start a fire, or speak silently without words, or still anyone. I can't even keep a cat from running away from me."

Her mother smiled, a mix of pride and heartache. "You will," she said, wiping her eyes.

"Magic isn't real!" Alissa shouted. "They're just stories!"

"It's real, Alissa. I've seen it." Her mother closed her eyes in memory. "Your papa once stopped the wind for me."

"Then why didn't he ever show me anything? Why didn't he ever do one thing?"

Her mother gestured helplessly. "He said if he did, it might trigger your abilities. It's not his place to teach, and . . ." She hesitated. "He didn't want you to be like him. He wanted you to be like me. He was so sure you would take after me, but at the same time was worried you wouldn't." Her mother bit her lip and her eyes dropped. "He was afraid," she said softly.

"Of what?" Alissa nearly shouted, terrified that this was really happening.

"He was afraid for you. Or of what you might become," her mother whispered. "I was never quite sure which." And the door shut with a frightening sound of finality.

2

"I should have just eaten the *burnt toast!*" Alissa shouted, her voice echoing off the hills before her. Exhausted, she collapsed at the cliff's edge. Her rump hit the dirt, and her breath puffed out. Talon landed with a soft rattle of leaves, her chittering sounding almost abusive.

"Oh, do be still," Alissa said. "I'm not going another step today." Squinting at the low sun, she gestured to the tree-choked valley below them. "It's already dark down there. Do you want to make camp in that? It's not going to start snowing tomorrow."

No, Alissa thought as she bent to loosen the laces of her lovely new boots. It won't snow tomorrow, but soon. And if she was in the mountains when it did, she wouldn't get out.

An aggressive scolding exploded from the pines behind her as a squirrel protested Talon's presence. Together Alissa and her bird turned to see it, dancing on the branch tips in outrage. Talon launched herself after it, and the squirrel fled with a startled chirp. Grimacing, Alissa turned away as the sound of smacking branches filled the air. There was a tiny shriek.

"Talon." She rubbed at her eyes. "Let the squirrel go. I'm not going to eat it, and it's too big for you."

Ashes, she thought miserably. Her feet felt as if they were going to fall off, her neck ached, and her back was sore from the constant rubbing of the pack.

There was a rush of dry leaves as Talon returned to shove a tuft of tail-fluff into Alissa's fist. "Very nice," she dryly praised her bird, tucking the trophy into her hatband. "Now go find yourself a grasshopper." Talon appeared to swell in pride, seeming to know by Alissa's actions that her gift had been accepted.

Together Alissa and Talon looked out over the bluff as the soft, green damp from the valley rose, easing the heat of exertion from Alissa's face. Far below in the shadow of the surrounding hills lay a lake, black and still, not yet hidden by the evening fog. The southern end of the long lake looked the easiest side to traverse. It was as good a direction as any, she thought, tucking her legs up and propping her chin on her knees. Seeing as she didn't know where to go. West, her mother had said. Burn it to ash. What was she doing out here?

Of course she'd go west. North or south would be more foothills, and why go east to the plains? Everything was dull there, up to and including its inhabitants. The last original thought they had entertained was baked out of them by the sun generations ago. Besides, her scandalous mix of hills and plains features was obvious. A plains' encampment would run her out, as would any respectable foothills village, hers included. The only time she was tolerated was market day, when her mixed blood wasn't so obvious.

Alissa pushed her worry aside and rose with a spine-tingling stretch to set up camp. Tomorrow she would make an early start. Wherever she was going, she had to clear the mountains before winter.

But it was hard to keep her thoughts upon snow on such a warm evening, and as Alissa kicked up last year's leaves looking for wood and something to eat, she found herself humming a song concerning an addle-brained lad and his incessant predicaments. She flushed as she realized what she was doing. It was a tavern song. She had often slipped away from her mother at market, drawn by the promise of music and dance, hiding in the shadows to learn the songs and steps her mother deemed improper for a lady. Alissa flushed again. But as there was no one here to find fault with her, she gave up all pretense at decorum and began to sing.

> *"Taykell was a good lad,*
> *He had a hat and horse.*
> *He also had six brothers,*
> *The youngest one of course.*
> *His father said, 'Alas, my boy.*
> *I've nothing more to give ye.'*
> *His name forsook, the path he took,*
> *To go to find the blue sea."*

Talon seemed unimpressed. Shifting her feathers in mild agitation, she preened in the reddening light. The refrain was next, and Alissa bellowed it out as was proper.

> *"Oh, fathers hope for daughters,*
> *Someone light and frilly.*
> *They leave the house, to find a spouse,*
> *A blessing in it really.*
> *The land your father farmed on,*
> *Was split among his sons.*
> *If this goes on much longer,*
> *Soon there will be none!"*

The wintry, accusing voices of wolves rose to challenge Alissa's in a series of low moans, leaving no doubt as to what they thought of her singing. She couldn't help her grin, continuing to gather sticks until there was more than she would likely need. Wolves, she contended, were nothing to be frightened of. But it never hurt having a good blaze to remind them of their place.

The sun had gone down by the time she was settled before her fire scraping the last of the "what's under the leaves that I might eat?" out of her bowl. Setting the empty bowl aside, she dug through her pack, searching for her needle and threads. One of her stockings had a hole, and although she had known about it for several washings, she freely admitted she was never one to appreciate the "finer arts of domestication." She'd have to do something about that someday, she thought as she searched for her sewing kit, frowning as her fingers found the rank little bag her mother had given her. She had hidden the pouch at the bottom of her pack her first day out, thinking she could punish her mother in some small fashion by disobeying her by not wearing it.

"My inheritance," she grumbled to Talon, holding it between two fingers as if it were a dead rat. "Where did Mother find something that reeks so wonderfully?"

Perched on the firewood, Talon shifted her feathers, giving the impression of a shrug.

Alissa tightened the strings and went to shove it back to the bottom of her pack, but she hesitated. Silently she stared at the small sack, her fingers seemingly loath to let it go. It didn't feel right to put it back anymore. Reluctantly she looped the cord over her head. The Hounds take her, she thought. What if the seams tore? She would stink like a cart of rotted potatoes.

"Papa's stories of the Hold," she scoffed nervously, feeling the unfamiliar weight about her neck. The Hold was synonymous with Masters, and Masters with Keepers, and Keepers with magic, and magic? Alissa harrumphed. Magic was slop for pigs. There was no such thing as magic. Feeling foolish and self-conscious, she glared down at the bag of ill-smelling dust, finally tucking it behind her shirt and out of sight.

"What am I doing out here, Talon?" she asked softly, reaching to ruffle her bird's feathers. "I ought to be bringing the sheep into the paddock now, not watching the stars rise from behind the mountain they used to set behind." She slumped further into the dirt. Perhaps her papa had been a Keeper. It didn't follow she had to be one. And asking her to believe they could do magic was ridiculous. Her papa must have been embellishing his tales of the Hold to make it more exciting.

She had spent a lot of time with her papa before he left. He always had the most interesting answers to her questions, and she missed their early-morning chats. A smile quirked the corners of Alissa's mouth. She imagined if he were still alive, his answers would make more sense now than when she was five. She should go to the Hold if only to find a piece of her papa. Once she saw it, she could go back home. And it did feel right to be moving. She had been unusually restless since the lace flowers bloomed.

Asking her to believe in magic, though, was ridiculous. Magic was for babies and ignorant coastal folk. Her belief in magic and happy endings died when her papa hadn't come home. Although, she admitted as she scuffed her boot into the leaf litter, there were several, hard to explain talents that occasionally cropped up. They were real. She'd *read* about them.

Alissa knew she wasn't a shaduf. Hot tempered as she was, it wasn't from knowing the circumstances of her own death. Being a septhama was completely out of the question. Alissa had never *seen* a ghost, much less get rid of one. And as for a matchmaker? Auras were mysterious, never-seen conjectures to her. The only thing she had seen hovering about her mother's silhouette was the occasional bad mood. Besides, Alissa thought crossly, there were ways to foster such bizarre quirks of human nature. None involved being cast out from one's home to find a mythical fortress.

Alissa shuffled through her belongings looking for her pipe. Despite her pleadings otherwise, her mother had insisted a proper lady knew how to play an instrument, claiming it soothed the sheep and made Nanny give better milk. Alissa was painfully aware she wasn't any good at piping. But it was a reminder of home, and it would help ease her lingering melancholy.

A tentative note drifted out, echoing softly off the far peaks in the evening's rising damp. Pleased with the effect, Alissa sent another note to follow it. Slowly a halting melody emerged. The echo made a gentle counterpoint, odd and surreal, scarcely audible over the crickets. It was the lullaby her mother had sung Alissa to sleep with when she was a child. It seemed fitting.

The stars slowly brightened. They were unusually sharp, as the moon was only a sliver that wouldn't show itself until nearly sunrise. She found herself relaxing, the music and quiet hush working together to soothe her worries. Or at least allow her to forget them for a time.

A thin, eerie whine from Talon split the night, pulling the

pipe from her lips with an awkward peep. Alissa stared at her kestrel in astonishment. The bird was tense and alert, her head cocked at the stars, looking as unnerving as the time she warned Alissa and her mother about the twister last spring. Deciding the echo must be bothering her, Alissa chuckled and slumped back. Something, though, wasn't quite right. Music was still coming from the valley.

Her breath escaped in a small hiss. That wasn't an echo. Someone was mimicking her!

The wind rose, ruffling Talon's feathers and scattering the coals from the edge of the fire. Her heart pounded as she squinted into the night, searching for the missing twinkle of a fire in the valley. Talon's eyes, though, were on the sky. The music continued, unearthly and disturbing. Now that Alissa had stopped, it steadily gained in complexity until she hardly recognized it. It came faintly through the blackness sounding better, its ghostly notes rising out of the valley.

The crickets' song vanished as if blowing out a candle, pulling a tight gasp from Alissa and raising gooseflesh. Talon's head swiveled in a tight arc, and then, drawn by the whoosh of cutting air, Alissa saw it. A huge shadow slashed an unmistakable silhouette against the stars.

By the Navigator's Hounds, it's a raku! she thought in terror. Yanking back her first, deadly impulse to run into the woods, she shrank into her blanket. Hardly daring to breathe, she watched the monster pivot on a graceful wing tip and drop into the valley. Ashes, Alissa thought in fear and wonder. It was larger than six horses. Just its magnificent tail was thicker than she. Rumor said they had powerful haunches ending in claws as long as her arm, teeth like shattered glass, and skin as tough as snake hide. This was all hearsay. No one had ever seen a raku close enough to verify the stories and return. Three heartbeats later, the music ceased with a startling squawk.

Alissa forced herself to move, unclenching her fingers from about her pipe and wedging it into her inner coat pocket. Steadfastly ignoring the shaking in her fingers, she built up the fire until the light billowed forth like a watch-beacon. Somewhere she had heard that rakus didn't like fire.

It seemed a good bet it was true. Alissa knew rakus might be about—she was in the mountains, their preferred hunting grounds—but she had never seen one before.

Up until recently they were said to have been a daily hazard of farming in the foothills. Even now when a sheep went missing, it was blamed on the leathey-winged hunters, never on the thief who probably took it. Her papa claimed they had once been as common as beggars on market day, and that he used to have long conversations with one in particular. That, Alissa scorned, was ridiculous. Everyone knew rakus were no more than wings and appetite.

The beast had dropped into the valley, but unless it was going for a swim, there was nowhere to land. It was probably already gone, a possibility she emphatically hoped was true. She was bigger than a sheep, but rakus weren't known for their discriminating taste. They were the most feared predators of the mountains, said to be behind many a lost traveler.

Easing her blanket closer to Talon, Alissa settled herself to try and sleep, shunning the cover of the pines for the more certain safety of the fire. The crickets had returned full force, and her small falcon's grip was again loose. Talon's feathers were fluffed for sleep, and she wasn't even looking at the sky. Her bird, Alissa realized, spotted the beast long before she had. If Talon was calm, she would be, too. "Brave words, Alissa," she whispered, "but rather impractical."

As she gazed sleeplessly into the night with her blanket clutched about her, she considered the uncomfortable fact that she wasn't the only one watching the sky. The realization left her uneasy in a way the raku hadn't. Someone else was out here. Traveling alone wasn't smart, and though Alissa knew her fire made her safe from wolves and rakus, nothing could guarantee her safety from her fellow human beings. There was a small comfort in that whoever it was would probably be headed east out of the mountains. Only an idiot such as herself, she contended, would start the crossing this time of year. If she made it through tomorrow without seeing anyone, she could forget the entire incident.

Sighing, Alissa turned from the fire to the moonless skies. It was going to be a long night.

3

Strell reached up, straining as the sweat trickled into his eyes, his fingers searching for the lip of the rock face. Pebbles and dust sifted over him as he found the edge. Immediately it crumbled. Eyes wide, he scrambled for another hold, his heart pounding as he felt his grip slip.

He flung his hand higher, and this time the earth held. Blowing in relief, he clung to the rock face and risked a glance down. Strell swallowed hard. "Bone and Ash," he whispered. "Why am I doing this?" Because, he answered himself, if you don't catch up with whoever was on top of this bluff last night, you'll never find anyone who'll believe you saw a raku. Only mad men and fools claimed to have seen a raku that close and lived to tell of it.

Strell looked down again and closed his eyes against the fall. "It's not worth it," he breathed, pressing himself tight to the rock face. But the skills he had gained as a boy, tagging after his brothers as they climbed about the walls of their desert ravine, served him well. His muscles tensed, and as he found a new toehold, he levered himself up, wedging an elbow over the edge. With a groan and a scattering of rocks, he hauled himself over the lip of the cliff.

Flat on his back, Strell lay at the edge of the cliff and laughed weakly at how foolish it had been to try to climb straight up. "But I made it," he said with a breathless chuckle. Whoever he was following must have gotten up another way, but he couldn't see how.

High in the southwest, a falcon rode the thermals. Strell's eyes followed it as it stooped after something by the lake. As

if its disappearance was a signal, he rolled to his feet and untied the thin rope from his belt. Peering down the cliff face,
he pulled his pack and coat up. The rope was carefully coiled
and placed into his pack before he turned to investigate the
abandoned camp.

His fellow traveler was alone, he decided, as there was
only one smoothed area by the fire where a bedroll had been.
The firepit held a staggering amount of half-charred wood,
still smoldering with the dusky scent of security. He smiled,
imagining he would have used more if he sighted a raku
from here. They were solitary hunters, shunning mankind
but for the occasional raid when the cold bit deep, vanishing
like wolves into the cursed fog the mountains were afflicted
with.

Strell's hope rose as he saw the beginnings of a trail
headed east into the heavy woods. He would have to set a
fast pace to catch up with his fellow traveler before he
reached the plains and the trail became confused. The traveler had to be headed to the plains. Only a fool would risk
crossing the mountains this late. Strell was a passable
tracker, and he was anxious to ask him about not only the
raku but the music. It had been a long time since he'd played
a tune so hauntingly beautiful, and he wanted to hear it
again. He hadn't caught all the nuances last night.

Strell ran a hand over the thick bristles on his chin with a
sudden thought. Perhaps he should get rid of his beard first.
He was nearing familiar territory. It would be symbolic, he
thought, taking off his hat and digging through his pack for
his soap and mirror. He would leave his barbaric beard behind with the barbaric mountains. It wouldn't take long, he
rationalized. The person he was trailing might be someone
he knew—and he did have a reputation to uphold.

With a soft sound of satisfaction, Strell took a fold of
cloth woven with the likeness of seaweed from his pack, un-
folding it to find his mirror. The unusual fabric was for his
mother. For his father he had a packet of salt. It had taken
him a week to convince the salter to teach him how, but he
made it himself. Also hidden among the folds of cloth was a
blunt knife, jar of ink, packet of wax, a pair of dice made out
of fish bones, and a new kind of knot. They were for his

brothers. For his sisters he had a satchel of dry, purple glaze, an anklet bell, two evenly matched shells, and a tightly wrapped slab of soap reeking of flowers. Surprisingly enough, the bell had been the most expensive of the lot, costing even more than the mirror.

Strell took the cracked glass from its box, propping it up reverently before him. The coast was the only place glass was still common enough one could trade for it. Hills pox claimed the sole clan in the plains that had known the art of molding glass. Glass, in any form, was almost nonexistent east of the mountains.

Setting his souvenirs aside, Strell poured a portion of the sun-warmed water from his water sack into a bowl and lathered up his thin sliver of soap. He slipped his shaving knife from his boot sheath and began to remove the thin foam. Only the faint noise of the wind in the pines, the scrape of his blade, and the rustle of a raggedy squirrel in last year's leaves destroyed the hush. Strell soon finished, and he gazed at his reflection wondering what his parents would think.

Staring back at him were plainsmen-brown eyes set above a sharply angled nose, bent from being broken one too many times. His cheeks were pink from his shave, but the rest of him was tan from long exposure. Strell shifted his jaw from side to side. His chin was cleft, and if he wasn't careful, he missed a spot there. Satisfied, he ran his hand through his dark, gently curling hair to try and arrange it somehow.

As the youngest son, he had always been smaller than his brothers. But the travel had done him good. I bet I could look Sarmont eye to eye now, he thought. Sarmont was the eldest, and he took great pains to be sure everyone knew it. Strell rubbed his nose in remembered hurt. In all fairness, he chuckled, he had deserved it—every single time.

Strell tossed his shaving water over the edge of the cliff, packed everything away, and put his coat on against the chill of the trees. His coat was nearly brand-new, still sporting the rich, dark color of oiled wood. It went down to the tops of his boots, covering every finger-width of his long legs, and he was quite proud of it.

"One more week at that last town," he said ruefully, "and I could have bought one brushing the ground." Or a new hat, he added soundlessly as he looked his over. It was a fine hat six years ago, but it had been trampled, soaked, and otherwise abused until it was a shadow of its former self. But if he had stayed a week longer, he might not have made it home before the snow.

Thoughts of home and family were foremost in Strell's mind as he placed the sorry-looking hat comfortably on his head and returned his pack to his shoulders. He was eager to see the colorful tops of his family's tents poking up like mushrooms from their ravine. The site of their holdings had been chosen by his grandfather Trook with much care. In the far past, a strong river had carved a canyon deep into the hard, clay soil. The water had long since gone, making the land useless for farming even if his father would stoop that low. But it was perfect for his family's profession of clay works.

Eyeing the faint signs of passage, Strell turned his back on the tracks and the mountains to stride into the woods toward his still-distant home. He wasn't going home to stay—it was a visit—but he wouldn't brave the mountains again. Now that he had all the stories and songs the coast could give him, he would remain where he belonged, deep within his beloved, arid plains.

S trell hesitated under the chill shade of the pines, reluctant to step into cultivated fields. Beyond grazed a small flock of sheep. No, he decided as an alert head with sharp horns oriented on him. There was one goat, too. Farther on stood a pretty little house tucked under the trees.

Yesterday Strell had tried to track the unknown traveler through the woods scrub, his hopes of catching up with him evaporating immediately. It hadn't taken long to realize the fool was headed *into* the mountains, not out. Somehow they had passed each other unknowingly. Strell wished him well, wondering what could be so urgent it was worth risking his life over.

Earlier that morning Strell had stumbled across what was obviously a farm's irrigation works. The craftsmanship of those lines, he grudgingly admitted, had been exceptional for a farmer. And now those lines had led him here.

Strell eyed the quiet farm and shifted his pack uneasily, weighing his need to know where he was against the possibility of snarling dogs and angry young farmers with pitchforks. Plainsmen weren't welcome in the foothills. He ran a quick hand through his hair in worry. Whatever he was going to do, he'd better do it quickly. That goat was staring at him.

"Hello-o-o-o!" he shouted through cupped hands. He waited, listening. "Hello? Anyone about?" Strell eyed the goat now casually moving his way, its bell clanking softly.

A shutter at the house thumped open amid a billow of smoke, and a woman leaned out, coughing violently. Strell waved to catch her attention. Pointing to the flock, he shouted, "Is that your goat?" The woman ducked inside. Immediately the brightly painted door opened and she stepped out.

"Nanny!" she scolded, her pleasant voice coming faint over the fields. "Leave the young man alone." The goat turned, appearing to understand as it paused in its threatening advance. "Nanny won't chase you now," the woman called, waving him closer. "Come on down."

Strell picked his way through the field, prudently giving the grazing animals plenty of space despite the lady's assurances. As he drew close, his eyebrows rose at the house's deceptively simple lines, and his estimation of its inhabitants went up a bit more. This was no shack in the hills, he decided. It obviously belonged to a family of means. True, he had never actually *seen* a foothills homestead before, but everyone knew they were nothing like this!

The woman stood and waited, motioning him to a simple but well-sanded bench set against the front of the house. "I would invite you in," she apologized, "but the house needs to air." Sitting down, she gestured again for Strell to do the same. "My name is Rema," she said, leaving her last name unspoken. It was unusual but not impolite under the circumstances.

"Strell," he answered, declining her invitation to sit. She was, he decided in confusion, from the plains despite her thick hills' accent. Dark hair and eyes were a combination to be found only on the arid flatlands, and her skin was as dark as his. Hills people were invariably fair, pasty-looking things. A woman of such stately presence had no business among the ignorant farmers. They would run her out as soon as speak to her, yet here she was as if she belonged.

"You're coming from the coast then?" Rema's hands folded graciously in her lap. Her accent had shifted to deep plains.

"Yes." Strell was suddenly conscious of his travel-stained clothes. "I'm going home. I've been away these past six years."

She smiled knowingly. "Goodness, that's a long time. You must be the youngest son."

Surprised, Strell nodded. "How did you know?"

She pointed to his feet. "Although old, your boots are well-made, as is your coat, which, by the by, is new and specially tailored. Your background is excellent as betrayed by your accent, and you're the youngest of a large family, or you wouldn't have been allowed to leave. Only a young son has any chance to choose his profession, and only the youngest is allowed to go wandering into the wilds for six years! I'd say you're a traveling poet or bard, or your coat would have been cut to the style on the coast and not the plains." She smiled. "How did I do?"

Strell closed his mouth with a snap. "Uh, yes. Musician, actually."

Laughing lightly, Rema looked up at the gently soughing branches. "I'm sorry," she apologized, all trace of her hills' accent gone, "but it's been a long time since I've seen such a charming mismatch of styles and outdated clothes. They suit you very well."

"M-m-m," Strell said, eager to change the subject. "Do you know how far the Hirdune valley is from here?"

"Hirdune. . . ." Rema's eyes went distant. "You mean the Hirdune potters?" She rose, cutting off his next words. "Let's look at my maps," she said over her shoulder, and went inside.

Rocking forward to his toes, Strell followed her in, carefully wiping his feet on the doorsill. This lady demanded the very best of a person, and he wanted to leave her with a good impression. He silently took in the well-swept floors, the wide windows, and the artful placement of household goods to display a modest show of wealth. There was even a book by the hearth, used by the look of it, not just for show.

Rema was standing at a table in what was obviously the kitchen. Light poured in to make the low-ceilinged room seem bright and airy. The acrid smell of burnt bread hung in the air. A thick stack of supple leather sheets was piled before her, and she was shuffling through them, shifting each one gently. Strell stepped closer. This wasn't what he had expected. They were in vibrant color with an astonishing artistry. "Where did you get these?" he whispered. They were the most gorgeous maps he had ever seen, and there were dozens of them.

"They were my husband's." Rema bit her lip, not looking up.

"Oh-h-h," Strell breathed as his fingers alighted upon a map. It showed the range of mountains he had just crossed. Trails were marked in a vivid yellow, rivers and lakes in blue, and what were probably good campsites were x-ed in red. The coast, too, was shown, and Strell eagerly ran his eyes over familiar landmarks, remembering the people he had left behind.

"See here?" he said, shifting the map to an open spot. "This river here? This is were I rode in my first boat." Strell smiled sheepishly. "I was sick the entire three days it took to get to the delta. I was supposed to entertain the crew in return for passage."

"And you were seasick?" Rema continued her search. "How awful."

"My head was hanging over the side of the boat more often then not. The passengers and crew thought it was amusing. I hadn't any money to pay for my fare, but the captain said I earned my passage, though I hadn't played a note the entire trip."

"How nice of him," the woman said absently.

"Not really. He said I was entertaining enough. They had never seen anyone stay that shade of green for quite so long."

Rema smiled, looking up at him.

"And look here," he said, pointing again. "This is where I spent my first winter. I lived with a smith, pumping the bellows when the wind wasn't blowing from off the water." Strell felt his mouth quirk in a soft smile. The smith's daughter had been a delight.

"And here," he said, almost to himself. "This is where I learned how to fish, and there's the beach where I watched a man walk across live coals."

"You mean fire?" Rema set down her map and peered over his shoulder.

"Yes. Barefoot. They do it every year." Strell pointed out the small bay. His eyes went distant in thought as Rema bent closer to see. Having a map like this would increase the credibility of his stories and bring him a correspondingly higher wage for his tales.

"This," he said slowly, "is a very fine map." He hesitated, feeling a stir of excitement. Plainsmen lived to trade. When the two participants were skilled, it was very like a formal dance. Bargaining with anyone else was like dancing with a goat. He hadn't played the game with his countrymen in what seemed like ages. "It's a little small, though," he added, giving his words the proper cadence to signify he was testing the sands to see if she was willing to part with it.

The woman started, and Strell was sure he heard her breath catch.

"Yes," she said slowly, flicking her eyes to him and away, feigning disinterest. "My husband was always one to skimp on the hide. See how uneven the edge is?"

His pulse increased, and though it meant a small misstep, Strell smiled. Clearly, Rema missed the thrill of a good trade as well. "I understand," he murmured, carefully rolling the marvelous map up and setting it before them. "My mother is the same. I'm bringing her a rude cloth from the coast. Enough to make a scarf, nothing more, but she will undoubtedly try to make a cloak from it." He hesitated, pitching his voice with the proper formality. "Would you like to see it? There's the pattern of an ugly fish woven into it. By far the most ugly weave I have ever seen."

Rema nodded. Her cheeks were flushed. They both knew

the ruder he made the silk sound, the more elegant it probably was. And that, of course, was the game.

Hiding a grin, Strell opened his pack and pulled out the cloth intended for his mother. He would give her his mirror instead. He kept his back to Rema as he unfolded the cloth, spinning quickly to make it furl out across the table, covering all the maps in a glorious wave.

"Oh," Rema sighed, letting her desire show for a brief instant. This was allowed. It was an expansive compliment, carefully ignored by the wise trader. Then the wistful look in her eyes vanished. "Oh," she said again with a false melancholy. "I see what you mean. Such a thin weave. The threads aren't even. The colors have faded." Her hand reached partway out, unable to hide her longing to run the silky fabric through her fingers.

Strell carefully tugged at the silk, making pleats to best show off the tight weave. Rills of light ran across the table as the sun glinted on the tops of the folds. To her credit, Rema put her hands behind her back, never touching the fabric. It showed a strong will and an experienced player. Silently he waited. He had made the first overture to trade, however nebulous it had been, and so it was up to her to openly broach the subject.

"A mother cherishes the rudest of gifts," she said softly, "when it comes from a loving heart." She smiled, a glimmer of loss in her eyes. "Still, the size of it would do nicely for a scarf, as you say. And the green, though faded, will probably go well against her skin." Rema paused, and Strell waited. "I would quite fancy a green like that, if the weave was tighter and there being more to it than the small square you have there. Even so, would you consider trading it to me?"

Strell grinned. The show of emotion was far beyond the rules, but it didn't seem to matter anymore. "This shoddy piece of crafting?" he said, snatching it up to expose the maps underneath. "I couldn't. The council would have me up against the pole for cheating you out of your worthy goods." He hesitated. "Unless you have something equally coarse and ill-made?"

Rema nodded slowly, her eyes on the fabric. "As you say, my husband's map is rather unattractive and badly stained. I would say it's fit only for diapering a child. I've no use for it. Would you consider that?"

"A rag for a rag," Strell mused, looking to the ceiling in apparent idleness. "I think the council would smile upon such a worthless trade. Done and done, if you will?"

"Done and done," Rema repeated. Only now did she touch the silk, taking the fabric from him and holding it up to herself. She smiled, looking ten years younger. The game was over. "It's so beautiful. They weave on the coast?"

"They do everything on the coast," he said. "Most fish, but the craftsmen and farmers live beside each other." Strell shrugged. "It's like the Navigator's garden."

Rema seemed to have hardly heard him. "I never thought I'd ever have anything so fine again. Thank you, Strell."

Embarrassed at her delight with the fabric, Strell reached for his new map, having to unroll it for a last look before consigning it to his pack.

"Here," Rema said, reaching for the tie that bound her hair. "I've clearly gotten the better of the deal. Let me even it out a bit."

Strell's eyes widened as she took the map from his slack fingers and rolled it up, tying it with her hair ribbon. A gift of a lady's ribbon was a token of affection in the plains.

"It's been so long," she said in explanation, flushing. "These farmers don't know how to bargain, and nothing fine ever makes it this far into the foothills. I owe you supper, too. Please stay and tell me the news of the plains."

"My news," he said with a laugh, "is six years old. You probably know more about who has married whom than I do." Strell half turned his back on her and placed the map in his bag, sorry in a way that he was in such a hurry to get home.

Rema straightened. "I suppose," she said with a soft disappointment, draping her silk in a puddle on one of the chairs. "Let me see if I can find that map showing the plains."

Feeling awkward and uneasy, Strell stood in Rema's kitchen as she continued searching through the leather skins. It was obvious she longed to return to the plains. The question of why she hadn't was one he didn't want to delve into.

"Ah, here it is."

Strell stepped close, looking to where a slim finger pointed to an X with the word "home" written next to it. "This is where we are," she said. "And I believe Hirdune was here." Rema pointed again. Her head bent closer to see the light tracings of the more traveled footpaths. "Not too far," she said with a forced brightness. "Is your home near there?"

Again Strell found himself mesmerized by the incredible detail. Even the river that had cut his family's ravine was shown. "Well," he said, grinning, slightly embarrassed, "not exactly. If the truth be told, I'm a Hirdune. We all live there." He bent closer to estimate the distance, holding his breath against the pungent scent of ink. "Just a few weeks away," he said, pleased.

Rema grew still. Slowly she gathered the sheets except for the one he was still pondering and set them aside. "You say your entire family lived there?" she said slowly.

Catching the past tense in her words, Strell looked up, and upon seeing the pity in her eyes, his chest tightened in panic. "What do you mean, *lived there*?"

"Oh, Strell." Rema took his hands and led him to a stool. "I don't want to be the one to tell you this, but five years ago the spring rains came with the snowmelt. There was an unexpected flood wash. The settlement of Hirdune was completely destroyed. No one made it out of the ravine."

4

She was moonstruck, Strell thought as he trudged down the mountain toward the village. Stark raving moonstruck. The idea that his family could be gone without him knowing was ludicrous.

Strell turned, offering a wave to the poor woman before

striding under the trees. He ought to have realized she was mad the moment he had found her here. A plainswoman would have to be crazed to live among farmers. He was willing to bet he would hear a few tales tonight of the mad plainswoman who lived on the hill. Strell smiled faintly. He had asked for it, really, blurting out that he was a Hirdune. His family was well-known for its skill in pottery, and gossip flowed thick and fast. She may have only been harassing him for having laid claim to them. His first wash of panic at her words had quickly vanished, leaving only annoyance.

Still, he mused, pausing to pull a blackberry cane from his sleeve, her eyes seemed to have held true sorrow. She had said she knew what it was like to lose your entire world, and seeing her standing alone in the front yard when he said good-bye, it seemed she did.

His family was fine, he thought as he picked his way through the light underbrush. He would know otherwise. He would have to. How could they be gone and he not know it?

Strell soon found the rutty path leading down and to the east. Rema's thoughts may be addled, but her directions were sound. Feeling more confident now that he was again on a well-traveled road, he strode forward, eager to find the village before the sun set. He hadn't seen a road in over a month. But even without it, he would know he was headed in the right direction. The smoke-stained sky was better than a sign for pointing out the way.

Strell came upon a silent farm, quickly passing with his head lowered in case it wasn't as deserted as it seemed. The yard was neat and clean, the fences painted and the fields weed-free, looking bare from the recent harvest. The next farm was quiet, too, but for a wildly barking dog. The sheep were fenced in close to the barn. He was beginning to wonder what was going on until he met a wagon lumbering up the mountain.

The back was empty of produce, carrying instead a group of adults and children. They seemed well-fed and content, eyeing him with distrust as they passed. Several cloth-wrapped packages made a modest pile behind the driver. Now Strell knew why the farmyards were empty. It was market day, the only occasion when the foothills and plains folk mixed.

Over the ages, an uneasy balance had emerged between their two societies. The foothills had the land to grow and raise food. The plains had the raw materials and time to make goods. They traded, exchanging the skills of the soil for that of weft and weave, clay and carving. Necessity fostered a slow hatred of each other as they gouged prices as deeply as was prudent. But they were careful to never come to blows. It was a truce they dared not upset.

He smiled tightly, ignoring it when one of the men spit in his path. Today, out of all days, he could linger in a foothills village without drawing attention to himself, and perhaps make a little something if he cared to try a few of his newest tunes. There would be plainsmen about, and they would pay to hear his music.

As the sun dipped to the horizon, the fields grew fewer and the fences more numerous until Strell walked between thatched houses instead of trees. The road became slick with mud, and after his weeks in the mountains, the stink of people seemed to catch in his throat. Never meeting the villagers' eyes, he confidently walked down the street, headed for the square where the wagons would be set up. Small homes made up the bulk of what he passed. Hard-packed dirt and weeds made thin strips between the buildings. It was nothing like the clean sands of his homeland. Strell's thoughts went distant in anticipation. There was space in the plains. You could see the horizon wherever you looked.

Strell passed a house where two poorly-dressed children hung by the door, watching him go by, whispering behind their hands. His jaw clenched. He had almost forgotten what the foothills were like. His six years at the coast had been a blessing. Everyone looked different there. No one could tell where you came from until you opened your mouth. Even then they were eager for news. The coastal people might be superstitious and odd, but they had accepted him as an equal, and he wasn't eager to slip back into old patterns and expected behaviors.

Strell tugged his pack up, his anger welling. He'd better

remember to watch his step. Market day or not, he wasn't welcome. The sooner he got to his plains, the better.

A heavily loaded wagon stopped short before him, and Strell slipped as he tried not to run into it. He barely caught himself before going down in the mud. Three foothills girls, pallid and white, giggled behind their hands. Face burning, Strell adjusted his pack. Their clothes would be used for rags in the plains. But they were well-fed, and Strell felt a flush of jealousy. He had never gone hungry as a boy, but not many in the plains could say that.

The sounds of market became louder, and Strell's anger slowly diminished, pushed aside by feelings of remembrance. He had grown up taking his father's wares to the foothills, and anticipation brought back fond memories. They never left empty-handed, trading their bowls and clay tiles for wheat and fruit. After an exceptionally good market, they might even manage to buy potatoes. Strell hesitated as he passed the last house bordering the open field at the center of the village. He'd been alone for so long, it was odd to be among the press of people again.

"Strell?" called a deep voice, thundering over the babble of commerce. "Strell Hirdune? By the Navigator's Wolves, it *is* you!"

Strell half turned, a grin breaking over him as he spotted a familiar face, head and shoulders over most of the crowd. It was Petard, the only man who had ever come close to besting his father's skills at the potter's wheel.

"Get out of my way, ash-covered, know-nothing, dirt scratchers!" the man bellowed, elbowing the shorter farmers out of his path. "Strell Hirdune. I'd recognize that bent nose anywhere."

Strell clasped the man's arm as he came close, only to find himself yanked off his feet and into a back-slapping, jaw-snapping hug. Petard smelled like clay chips and glaze, and Strell felt his tension ease as he breathed in the familiar scent.

"I never thought to see you here!" Petard said as he put Strell at arm's length. His wind-scarred face wrinkled in pleasure. "World traveler on your way back to civilization, eh?"

Strell rubbed his jaw, wondering if all his teeth were still there. "Something like that. What brings you this deep into the foothills? Isn't this west for you?"

Petard draped an arm over Strell's shoulders and began leading him through the crowd, ignoring the farmers' muttered curses and ill looks. "The trade routes have shifted. Moving west, following the outskirts of the foothills instead of the oases. I have to drag my aching bones halfway to the mountains now to get a good price."

"It's good to see you," Strell said. "Somehow I'm not surprised the first face I recognize in six years would be *yours*."

Petard pointed out the wagon laced with his silk banners of yellow and black. A young woman was tending the front, showing a couple a nest of bowls. Strell could see they were second-rate even from here, but the farmer's wife was flushed in excitement at the coming purchase. Strell smiled. Some things never change. Why show the best when common will do?

"You were gone so long, everyone thought you'd taken up with a coastal beauty to make fishing pots the rest of your days," Petard said, motioning him to come around to the back.

Strell followed him, eyeing Petard's daughter with more than a casual interest. She was tall and dusky, a true plainswoman, something he hadn't seen in *far* too long. Her thick black hair nearly reached the small of her back. Petard must be doing well, he thought, to allow her to keep it that long. Their eyes met as he slipped behind the wagon, and she flushed demurely. "No," he said absently. "I'm back. For good." He hesitated. "Is that Matalina?"

Petard's dark eyes glinted. "Matalina!" he shouted over the wagon.

Strell's mouth dropped open in surprise. "Let her close the deal," he said in earnest, knowing how precious a customer was.

"Matalina!" Petard cried again. "Tell them to come back tomorrow. It's almost time to leave for the night. Strell Hirdune is here. Back from the coast—for good. Bring the water." He turned to Strell, making him sit down on the largest, rolled-up rug beside the small fire. "You remember

Matalina, eh?" he said, bursting with eagerness. He brought two cups from the wagon and handed one to Strell.

Strell looked it over with a critical eye as Petard made a show of settling himself across the fire. He adjusted the thin robe he wore over his trousers, clearly giving Strell time to evaluate his skill. Here in Strell's hands was Petard's true level of crafting, and Strell was impressed. The canny plainsman had always given his father a run for the more affluent customers. This, apparently, hadn't changed either.

There was a soft noise at his elbow and Strell started, surprised to find Matalina behind him. She had a waterskin in her thin hands. Her even, white teeth made a startling contrast with her dark skin, and Strell suddenly found himself flustered. "Thank you," he said softly as she filled his cup. She was dark, modest, and exotic after the coastal women.

"Go. Go on," Petard grunted, shooing her away. Strell watched her slip around the end of the wagon.

"Eh?" Petard half whispered, pulling Strell's attention back to the fire. "You like her? Me too. She works harder than any three sons I could've had." He shifted closer, warming his hands. "You knew I had no sons, Strell?"

Strell froze, a whisper of alarm drifting through him. "Um, yes. I'm sorry."

"No need!" Petard shouted. "I have my daughters." Pride filled his eyes as he looked over the wagon to see Matalina helping another customer. They had a basket of apples, and Petard's expression grew shrewd. Strell watched him force his eyes away from the infant deal being struck and back to him.

"Don't mind those rags she has on," Petard said softly. "I make her wear them here, or the dirt scratchers would raise the price of corn."

"Petard," Strell said awkwardly. "How is my family?"

The tall man abruptly stood. "Water? Why are we drinking water? We should be drinking wine. A Hirdune returns to us. We should drink wine!"

Strell covered his cup with his hand. "Petard. My family? Are they here in the foothills?"

Petard sank down, resting the wineskin between his knees. He ran a hand under his nose.

"Petard?" Strell said, suddenly afraid. What if that mad woman at that farm was right?

"I'm sorry, lad," Petard said, his voice softer than Strell had ever heard it. "I don't know how to tell you this."

Strell's breath hissed in over his teeth. A dog barked the next wagon over, and a child laughed. His mind went to nothing, and he heard himself say, "She said there was a flood."

"She?" Petard fixed him with sharp look. "You already know?"

"A woman on a farm told me. I didn't believe her."

Petard's head bobbed. "I wouldn't have either. But she told you the truth. There was a flood to rival the Tears of the Navigator. Scoured the sand down to stone in places. The first oasis was destroyed. That's what shifted the trade routes."

Strell swallowed hard. He was cold, and he set his cup down before Petard could see the trembling of his fingers. His breath came faster. "She said they got caught in it." He looked up, desperate to see a sign of hope in Petard's eyes, but there was only sympathy. The tall man reached around the fire with his foot and tipped Strell's cup over. Water seeped into the ground. Silently Petard filled the cup with wine.

Almost frantic, Strell whispered, "My family?"

Petard's eyes closed in a long blink. "Bless them who join the Navigator suddenly, for they bring him the purest thoughts."

Gasping, Strell hunched into himself, closing his eyes and raising a hand to his head. No, he thought, feeling ill and light-headed. They can't be gone. It had to be a mistake.

He found himself on his feet, accidentally kicking over his wine. The red stained the soil, covering the clean spill of water. "I have to go," he heard himself say.

Petard rose, his face alarmed. "Whoa, Strell," he said gently. "I know it's soon, and I know you're raw, but don't run off."

"I have to go see!" Strell cried, near to panic.

A strong hand gripped his arm. "There's nothing to see.

Stay until you sort yourself out. I've plenty of food. I know your work. You have a place with us as long as you want."

Strell backed up, panic making his legs weak. How could they be gone and he not know it? He looked at the press of people, familiar, yet made strange by the years. It felt wrong. He was wrong. They all were wrong. He had to go. He never should have come back. Come back to find—this.

"Strell!" The grip was on his shoulder now, and Strell stumbled back, afraid they would force him to stay. "Wait, boy. You can't walk into the desert."

"I have to see," he said raggedly.

Petard shook his head. "Spare yourself, lad. The canyon was scrubbed clean to rock. There's nothing left to go back to. I know. As soon as I heard, I went to look for anything of value that might have been spared." He winced. "I meant, *anyone* spared," he finished lamely.

Anger flared, an easy outlet for his pain. "Scavengers!" Strell spat. "You could hardly wait until my father was dead before ransacking his shops."

Petard's face went red, the scars from sand-burn showing white against his thick skin. "Grief has made you careless, boy," he said darkly. "Watch your tongue. I loved your father as much as any man. He had a skill. Some say he gave it to you."

Strell turned to face the crowd, not seeing it.

"The desert took them, Strell. They're gone."

Strell spun, looking dazedly into Petard's eyes. They were as dark as his father's. "Father," he whispered, a stab of loss nearly doubling him over.

"Stay with us," Petard said softly. Matalina was behind him looking sad and welcoming. Her hair was as long and thick as his sisters'. Strell tore his eyes from her. His sisters, drowned in the flood while he dallied on the coast. They were buried in the sand like animals without mourning, without notice. There had been no fire to light their way, no flames to free their spirit.

"Where will you pitch your tent in the cold season?" Petard asked persuasively. "Who but another potter will even consider to take you in, a man not of their blood?"

"No one," Strell whispered, knowing it was true. Without his family, he was dead.

Petard took a breath. "I have no sons. Stay with me. I will give you my name."

Strell's head came up. His pulse pounded. "No!" he gasped, then caught himself. "No," he said again, softer. His name. The desert had taken his family. Now it wanted his name.

Petard drew back, clearly affronted. Matalina shifted nervously. Though Strell knew he was being inexcusably discourteous by refusing Petard outright, grief allowed no other answer. A part of him marveled at Petard's foresight. Such a trade would save both of them. Strell needed the support of a family to survive in the desert, and Petard needed a male heir to keep his family from dying out. To say yes would save both of them. His cold, logical plains sense said take it, but his plainsman's heart refused. They wanted to take *his name*.

"No?" the tall man said shortly, his anger held in a tight check.

"I won't return to the plains," Strell breathed, unable to focus on either of them. To see the shadows of his mother and father everywhere. The desert took his family. How could he return to it? He hated the sand, the flatness, everything.

"Well, you can't stay in the foothills," Petard said sharply. "They will be on you before you can starve." The man's eyes softened. "See reason, lad. It's a good trade for both of us."

Strell slumped down to sit upon the ground, his head in his hands. How could they all be dead and he not know it?

There was a small scuff as Petard moved, laying a fatherly hand on Strell's shoulder. "I'm sorry, lad. perhaps there was a better way to tell you, but I don't know it." He shifted awkwardly. "I'll look past your hasty words because of your grief. It's almost dark. Come with us to the edge of this smelly little dirt-square of a village for the night. Think my offer over. Give me your answer tomorrow."

Strell said nothing, sinking deeper into himself. Thinking it over would lead to him saying yes as logic overcame heartache. He would accept a half-life with Matalina and

Petard. He would lower himself to live a lie. He would say yes. He didn't want to.

Strell felt a faint stir of purpose flicker among the shadows of his pain. If he couldn't survive in the foothills, he would return to the coast. Strell knew Petard would disagree. The proud man would probably knock Strell unconscious and forcibly take him back to the plains. But there was nothing left for him there, his future buried in the sand. "Give me a moment," Strell whispered, knowing Petard wouldn't leave him unless thinking Strell would accept his offer.

As expected, that seemed to satisfy the tall plainsman as he gestured for his daughter to tighten the harness of the horses. "But, Papa . . ." Matalina whispered, her smooth, dusky voice bringing memories of his sisters crashing down upon him.

"Let him be," Petard said gruffly. "He needs to get drunk or in a fight, or both. Either way, I don't want to be there. We'll find him in the morning."

Strell sat like a stone as they packed up and left, never acknowledging their good-byes. He stifled a tremor as Matalina laid a gentle hand upon his shoulder in parting. A small part of him realized he was no longer in the shadow of the wagon. Slowly the fire died from neglect. The dew rose, and it grew quiet as the square emptied. The comforting sounds of blowing horses and jangling harnesses subsided.

He stirred as the sky darkened and the children were called to supper. Petard's offer was frighteningly generous, but even if he accepted it, he would still be an outsider. They weren't his kin. It would drive him mad, the almost belonging but not quite. He had to return to the coast. He knew people there, knew how to fit in. It wouldn't be home, only a place to be. But it was dangerously late to start back.

Strell stood and hiked his pack up. But now he had a map. With it, he might traverse the passes before the mountains were locked down with snow. He had traded better than he could have guessed, exchanging a bit of silk for his sanity.

He slunk through the streets, the only light and noise coming from the open door and windows of a tavern. The houses became fewer and finally disappeared altogether. Stumbling in a night with an unrisen moon, he traveled the way he had come, lost in a haze, trying to outdistance his grief. He blindly followed the path he had taken out of the mountains, as if going back could erase what he found at its end.

5

Alissa's pack slid to the ground with a muffled thump. She soon followed, collapsing into an exhausted heap on the hard, thin soil that even the wind deemed too poor to claim. The evening wind whistled eerily through the pass up ahead. Now that she had stopped moving, the icy chill bit deep, drying her sweat unsettlingly fast to a cold whisper upon her forehead. It wouldn't be long before the sun was gone. She would have to hurry to set up camp. But she couldn't bring herself to move for anything right now.

Put bluntly, today had been an ordeal of self-torture. At dawn by her lakeside camp, she had come to the realization that she was *still* going too slow. Her mother claimed the Hold was a month in, but that was at her papa's pace, not Alissa's. And he knew the way. Looking over her progress, it seemed as though she was on a pleasure jaunt, not a desperate bid to find a mythical fortress before the mountains locked down with snow. And so today she had halved her breaks and quadrupled her aches.

Alissa lolled her head back in an effort to ease the soreness in her shoulders. Shooting pains raced down her neck as she gazed desperately up. The evening's first star stared accusingly back at her. With an ill-mannered groan, she got to her feet, promising herself a warm dinner and maybe a wash.

The stiffness began to settle in earnest as she squinted down the slope at Talon. The small bird was quite a ways back, fidgeting in indecision on the nearest tree. Grass was scarce in this windswept spot, much less trees. But there was a pile of half-rotted wood stacked up by a past traveler, and because Alissa knew herself to be basically lazy, this was where they would camp whether Talon liked it or not.

Muscles protesting, she knelt to light the fire. It leaped into existence with the wind's help, snapping at the shadows until they fled into the night, consuming the dry wood a bit too fast for her taste. Alissa looked for Talon. She hadn't moved. "Come on, Talon!" she coaxed at the top of her lungs. Fire or not, she thought, it was cold, and she still had the water to fetch. But Talon only called mournfully, fluttering her wings and refusing to budge. "Silly bird," she grumbled, knowing Talon didn't like being in the open, but Alissa was too cold to care.

Her lips pursed in worry as she glanced up at the darkening sky, then to the peaks tall about her. The sun was gone, but it still shone on the higher reaches, and they glowed an unreal pink and red. She dropped her eyes to the small, miserable shadow that was Talon, silhouetted against the sky. "Come on," she called again. "You can sit on the firewood."

She gave the pile a tiny kick, stumbling as her foot broke through the dry-rotted wood. Grubs and other wigglies fell out as she yanked her foot free with a shudder, shaking it violently to get them off her.

"It's just a bunch of crawlies!" she shouted, but Talon didn't move. "Fine!" Alissa yelled. "Be that way. Stay there all night for all I care!" Grabbing her water sack, she stalked out of camp, picking her way through the scree to the stream she had found earlier. It wasn't far, but it was at the bottom of a steep ravine.

The thin light had faded to a bare hint as Alissa found the lip of the drop-off and looked uneasily over the edge. She could hear the water bubbling as it slipped through its rocky bed, and the last of the light reflected off its shimmering skin to reveal the bottom of the gully. The short walk had done nothing to cool her temper, and she eyed the sheer descent darkly. It hadn't looked that bad earlier.

Alissa paced the edge looking for an easier way down. Her eyes strayed to the darkening heavens, wondering if it was worth all this. "Hot tea," she muttered, gathering her scattered resolve. "Warm bath."

Her foot skidded on the loose gravel. Arms swinging wildly, she struggled to catch her balance. With a muffled shriek, she toppled over the edge of the ravine to roll and tumble all the way to the bottom, finding it with a final, terrifying thud. Stunned, she lay in a disheveled heap as a sprinkling of small stones and pebbles showered down. There was a tiny, ridiculous clink as the last rock found its new resting place.

Silence. The gurgling of the stream seemed to rise loud. "Aw, Blood and Ash," she gasped, gingerly shifting her elbow out of the freezing water. All her hurts clamored for attention. "Ow," she moaned. "Ow, ow, ow . . ." she continued, unable to think of anything more creative. Easing herself up in stages, she rubbed her raw hands and took stock of the situation. Her ankle was the worst, and she tentatively felt it through her boot. Dull throbs exploded into shimmering waves of white-hot knives. Alissa's breath whooshed out in a sharp surprise. "Wolves," she gasped through clenched teeth as soon as she found her breath. But for all the pain, she didn't think her ankle was broken. The rest of her was sore, but not bad considering she had just fallen three bodylengths.

Alissa slowly levered herself up, keeping all her weight off her right foot. Swallowing hard, she lowered it. Pain lanced through her ankle, hammering spikes all the way to her skull. A feeling of tight nausea was close behind. Shocked, Alissa clutched her middle, struggling to sit and keep her noon meal down all at the same time.

"Oh! Wolves take you!" she shouted, angrily wiping away the tears the pain had drawn out. She sat with her head on one knee, taking shallow breaths until the pain lessened. How, she thought miserably, was she going to get out? Maybe she could crawl up using only one foot?

The stone was cold, and it seemed to bite deep into her hands as she searched the rock face for a handhold in the dark. Pebbles and dirt slipped and rattled from under her to vanish soundlessly into the water. Her foot hit an outcrop, and Alissa's eyes widened as she struggled not to cry out.

Admitting only a temporary defeat, she sat with her back to the wall of the ravine and began to shiver in earnest. She savagely pulled her hat tight over her ears and clutched her arms about her legs, cursing herself for having allowed her temper to make her careless. The thought of her fire, probably out from neglect, made her even more wretched. She was stuck at the bottom of the proverbial well.

6

Gone. Everything was gone. The house—gone. His father's shops—gone. *His family*—gone. The words hammered at Strell with each step. The previous night he had walked until fatigue brought him down like a beggar by the side of the road. He had woken at daybreak to the creak of a passing wagon and a half-rotted beet hitting him. Too miserable to eat, he had turned west, heading up the mountain before the birds finished greeting the day. Rema's farm was nearly a day behind him now. He gave her fields a wide berth, afraid if she saw him, she might try to reason with him. He didn't want to be reasonable.

The day passed in a blur of motion. Never stopping to eat or rest, he stoically hiked upward, careful to keep his mind blank and his thoughts empty, trying to outdistance his pain. To face the truth when the sun was in the sky was too much to ask.

Only now as the dusk fell and the chill wind swept down the mountains did he shake his heartache enough to notice his surroundings. It was past his usual time to make camp, but the long twilight the mountains were afflicted with gave him enough light to make his way. So he continued, finding a false peace in motion. If he stopped, his memories would catch him.

Strell forced his way uphill through the dusk, all but oblivious to the sharp sting of the brambles. He thought he was on the same trail he had come down on. According to Rema's map, a good portion of the trails through the range began from the cliff he had scaled yesterday. If he could find it again, he would be a long way to starting a successful return trip.

The brush suddenly thickened before him, and Strell paused, putting a hand to his side, his lungs laboring. His stomach hurt. It couldn't be hunger. How could he be hungry when his family was dead. They had been dead for five years.

Strell closed his eyes and clenched his fists, savagely pushing his grief aside. He wouldn't think. He couldn't afford it. With a determined abruptness, he forced his way through the low scrub to find his path fall to nothing. He had found the bluff.

His feet stopped of their own accord, halted by the lack of clear direction. Trembling, he stood in the cool breath of the night and looked out over the valley with vacant eyes. Exhaustion took him, and he sank down beside the ash-covered leavings of another's fire. It remained unlit; his hands lay still. Rebelling against the abuse, his body refused to move, and so his mind took over, racing, running, struggling to find a way to make sense of it. He began to shake from exertion and lack of food, and still he did nothing as the stars turned and the dew rose.

A sudden gust blew the ash from the wood below, laying open the black, twisted remnants of a tree. He shuddered at its sight, and a glimmer of awareness crept back into him. Cocooned by the concealing dark, his thoughts returned to his brothers, buried in the sand like beasts. His eyes closed in pain as he remembered his sisters. The image of them lying in the earth where the flood carelessly dropped them was almost too much to endure. And then his parents, unwavering in their unusual conviction that Strell had to find his own way, although they would never say why. They were all gone. He should be punished for being alive when his family was dead.

Gritting his teeth, he tensed, struggling for control. His

breath grew ragged and his fingers clenched with a white-knuckled strength. "Nooooo!" he howled into the night, pounding his fists into the earth. "It isn't right! It can't be true," he cried as a rush of unwelcome emotion burst forth. But he knew it was. His entire life was gone.

The crickets sang as Strell quieted, but he was too raw to find solace. Even the silvery, disturbing song of the wolves did little to stir him. They took up his lament when he faltered, filling the night with his pain for him. The beasts knew well the suffering of loss, found cold and alone in the quiet depths of winter, and he welcomed their grieving, elegant and refined in their feral honesty.

Strell huddled by the unlit fire, his arms wrapped tightly about his knees, alone in his thoughts, and now alone in the world. Fingering his pipe as if it were the only thing left that was real, he wondered which trail he should take in the morning. Glad for a distraction, Strell turned to his pack to find his map. A frown crossed his face as his fingers found something round and hard. It was an apple. Strell closed his eyes in misery. Matalina had probably put it there without her father's knowledge. There was a wedge of cheese, too.

He set the apple aside, shocked to find his fingers trembling as he tried to light a fire in the ashes of the old. Perhaps he ought to eat whether he was hungry or not. Soon the new fire lit the bluff, and by its bright flickering, he slipped the copper ribbon from his map and shook the supple leather out. He ate Matalina's apple as he squinted at the map to look over the possibilities.

Without willing them, his eyes went to find the canyon he had once called home. Mercifully, the map didn't chart that far into the plains, and he pushed his sorrow aside. Next he looked for the X that marked Rema's farm. Strell drew the map closer, squinting in the dim light. Next to the X was a tiny squiggle he didn't recognize.

Strell listlessly glanced over the rest of the map and found that all the writing, if that's what it was, was unfamiliar. The intricate forms didn't even look like proper words, but they must be, situated like labels next to lakes and prominent peaks. Leaning close enough to the fire to warm his fingers,

Strell studied the unusual characters, wondering what language it was.

The spoken word was similar everywhere Strell had traveled. Accents were common and sometimes so severe as to seem like a different tongue, but one could usually muddle through. The written word, however, was reserved for the affluent families, and they prided themselves on keeping it pure and unchanged through the centuries. It was the same no matter how far one traveled. Unlettered folk, whether from the hills or plains, relied on pictures to get by.

Strell could read; all his family could. It was part of his sisters' dowries, and the thought of them brought another resurgence of his grief. He took a ragged breath, holding it, ignoring the tightness in his chest, concentrating upon the insect walking down the edge of his map. Slowly he exhaled, shocked at how his breath seemed to shake. Would the ache ever lessen, he wondered, or would he just have to learn how to live with it?

He rolled his map up, retied it with the copper ribbon, and tucked it away. There was a path that headed east around the lake below, and that looked like a good place to start. He would have to abandon the trail halfway across the range and strike out on his own to reach the coast before the snow, but he could do it.

With a new, faintly pessimistic sense of purpose, Strell rested by his fire. It was all but out again from neglect. The moon wasn't up, and so the stars were unusually bright and numerous, as yet unfettered by the mountain's nightly fog. He gazed into the black, searching for solace in finding the Navigator. It was one of the brightest stars and the hub of the night sky, the lodestar, so to speak. Easy to see. He squinted, trying to find all of the eight stars clustered about it, aptly named The Navigator's Hounds. Some people called them wolves, some puppies, but mostly hounds. The darker and clearer the skies, the more of them could be seen.

There was a child's rhyme that said: "Fair weather will hold / When six hounds are bold." Another boasted: "Your heart will be lost to a maiden / Under skies with eight hounds a bayin'." How many hounds, he wondered, were hunting among the stars tonight? And would they find his brothers and sisters in the sand to lead them home?

The first six stars were unmistakable, clustered at their master's heel. The last two were much more difficult to find, being some distance from their pack mates and so close together, they often looked like one star. Sinking down onto his sleeping roll, Strell gazed into the heavens and began to count. "Eight," he murmured sleepily, and then much later, "No, there's only seven . . . I think." With that, he rolled onto his side as his frantic pace caught up with him and he fell into a deep, exhausted sleep.

7

"Hello?" Strell called. There was no answer. The camp was empty. There was no fire.

Preoccupied with his grief, Strell had blindly followed his map, trusting it to think for him. Shunning rest and food, he circled the lake and climbed to the next pass, covering in one day what took most people two. Now as the sun slipped away, he had stumbled upon another traveler.

Strell strode forward, jerking himself to a halt just shy of the pack set against the huge boulder. The situation was just too odd, reminiscent of the many coastal tales he had spent the last six years learning: tales of courtly men and women with long-fingered hands and eyes as yellow as the sun, meeting under the pretense of friendship only to spirit away the unwary. A fox barked, sounding so much like one from his homeland, it pulled a gooseflesh from him.

Grinning at a sudden thought, he scooped up a fistful of scree and jiggled it in his hand. He had learned a charm to ward off such risks. Bought it, really, from an old woman with no teeth who didn't believe him when he said there existed a place where it never rained.

"Rock in the east, keeps away the beast." He chuckled, embarrassed he was doing this, and tossed a rock over his shoulder. "Stone in the north, spirits won't come forth," and another went to his right. "Pebble in the south, seals the raku's mouth." A stone clattered to his left. "Sand in the west, will protect you best," he finished, blowing the dust toward the setting sun.

Laughing, Strell entered the camp and crouched by the small arrangement of firewood. His fingers went carefully among the sticks to find they were cold. The wood was half burnt, as if abandoned before fully alight. A frown crossed him, and he wondered if he ought to walk away. It could be a trap, but if it was, why put the fire out? There were easier ways to take a traveler.

He stood, placing his hands on his hips and looking up to the pass. If someone was looking for trouble, Strell would rather meet it here than up the trail where he might not be as wary, thinking he had left them behind. Besides, there was only one pack.

Strell's face went slack in thought. That raku he saw three nights ago might be the reason for the abandoned camp. Stifling a shudder, he bent down and quickly restarted the fire before it became any darker. It would be a large fire. The last thing he wanted was to find a raku in the dark. Perhaps he ought to make a habit of having a fire until he was out of the mountains.

Strell put a large log on the new flames, surprised at how fast it caught. The darkness beyond the fire seemed all the deeper, and he stood back up, glancing over the badly situated camp. It was right under the pass to the next valley. The wind would be blowing all night. But at least it was high enough so he wouldn't have to wake up to that cursed fog.

There was a small depression next to the boulder where the wind had deposited a fair amount of soil over the years. What little grass existed was there. That was where the pack and tall staff lay. Farther out past the fire, the ground grew rocky again, not the ideal spot for a bedroll, but Strell placed his pack here, not wanting to have his back against the boulder just yet.

With a small sigh, he sank to the ground, stretching his legs to the fire. He leaned over and snagged the staff, pulling it closer. It had a marvelous ivy design carved into it. Strell ran his thumb across it, catching himself on a small nick at the top. If no one claimed the staff by morning, he would take it as his own. He set the staff possessively next to him, wondering if he ought to see what was in the pack.

His stomach rumbled, and as it was the first time he had been hungry in two days, he resolved to wait. Thoughts of food instantly made him ten times more hungry. Strell tugged open his pack, pulling out all his food to check for spoilage. His eyes flicked to the fire, and he decided he might as well make something warm. Returning to his pack, Strell dug all the way to the bottom for his tripod. The unwieldy metal poles were often more trouble than they were worth, and he struggled to get them arranged without burning his fingers.

As he worked, he found himself humming a dancing tune. Frowning, he stopped, but as soon as his attention wandered, he found himself doing it again. Strell rolled his eyes but then straightened. Faint on the wind was the same tune, played upon a pipe—badly.

Strell's eyes slid to the abandoned pack. The fire snapped for his attention, and he absently put a stick on it as he stood and dusted his hands. His foot edged out, and he nudged the staff away from him. Maybe the camp wasn't as deserted as he thought. Perhaps the wood never caught, and so went cold sooner than he guessed. Whoever it was played music, and another minstrel would make pleasant company. But the tune faded to silence. In a moment he heard fragments of another. It wasn't getting any louder, so he decided to investigate.

"Hello?" he shouted. "Who's piping on such a cold night?" Again, there was no answer. Mindful it still might be a ruse, Strell carefully wove his way between the rocks. The music grew louder, and with a short laugh he recognized it. It was "Taykell's Adventure," a tavern song sung by big drunken farmers and skinny plains merchants alike. Everyone knew it from the smallest child who could speak to the oldest grandmother who no longer could.

The barest hint of a smile drifted over him as he slipped his instrument from his coat pocket and began to play along, the lyrics running through his mind.

> *"Taykell met a maiden,*
> *Fair as a summer's day.*
> *He told her he was homeless.*
> *She asked if he would stay.*
> *Pleased to find a wife and home,*
> *He quickly then said, yes,*
> *And then too late, he learned his fate.*
> *How could he have but guessed?"*

He was at the refrain now. The other player had stopped, and Strell continued on alone.

> *"Oh, fathers hope for daughters,*
> *Someone small and frilly . . ."*

"Watch out!" came a muffled voice, seeming to come from the ground. "The drop-off is right in front of you!"

Strell jerked to a halt. He looked down, his eyes widening. The earth disappeared at his feet. "By the Hounds," he whispered, "I almost walked off the edge."

"I can't believe anyone else is out here," the voice shouted up. There was a pause. "Do you have a rope?"

Shaking off his astonishment, Strell tucked his pipe away and squinted to the bottom of the ravine. Down below was the faint glint of starlight upon water. Suddenly everything became clear. "This is your camp up here, isn't it," he blurted.

"Yes. I've been down here all day," the voice said, a tinge of exasperation creeping into it. "Do you have a rope?" Her accent was odd. Not plains or foothills, but somehow both.

"Uh, it won't hold you. I'll be right there." Strell sat down and slipped over the edge.

"No! Wait!" the voice shouted up in panic.

Strell found himself out of control as he bumped and jos-

tled to the small river, halting with a suddenness that jarred
his teeth. Rocks and dirt continued to fall, and he covered his
head to wait the small avalanche out. Finally it stopped, and
he looked up into a young woman's shadowed face.

"You'll bring the entire slope down on me," she finished
dryly.

"Sorry." Strell gingerly stood, his foot slipping into the
stream. Yanking it out, he bent to check his boots. They were
well-oiled and newly soled, but seams tore and knots frayed.
His toes remained dry, and he puffed a sigh of relief. He
wouldn't walk in wet boots. It was too easy to blister your
feet, and then a longer camp would be required as the painful
sores healed.

He glanced sheepishly at the girl, then peered up at the
rock face. Even steep as it was, the cliff should pose no problem. Spotting a few handholds in the starlight, he nodded
sharply.

The girl was sitting with her back against a river-
smoothed boulder, her knees drawn up to her chin, a full
water bag next to her. It was obvious what had happened, he
thought. She had slid down for water and couldn't get back
up with the heavy load.

"Can I take that up for you?" Strell asked, trying to make
up for nearly burying her.

"That'd be nice," she said shortly, proffering the bag.

Slinging the bag over his shoulder, he pulled himself up
to his first handhold and stopped. Puzzled, he looked down
at the girl. She hadn't moved. "Aren't you coming?"

"I can't stand up," she whispered, looking away to the
river. "I told you I've been down here all day." Her voice got
sharp. "Don't you think I would've gotten out of here if I
could?"

Strell stared at her. He would have thought someone stuck
at the bottom of a ditch would be a little more conciliatory.

Seeing his expression, the girl dropped her eyes. "I'm
sorry," she said softly. "But I'm half starved and frozen, and
my foot hurts. I think I may have"—she hesitated—"broken
it," she finished with a slight quaver. "It's not getting better
very fast."

Immediately Strell relaxed. She was scared. His youngest

sister had been like that. The more frightened she had been, the more arrogant and snippy she was. He dropped his eyes, surprised to find his grief muted by a pang of sympathy. Perhaps he ought to start over.

Strell stepped off the incline and set the water bag down. Taking off his hat, he crouched so he could see her face to face. "My name is Strell," he said formally, offering his hand palm up, the traditional greeting in any situation no matter how unusual. "May I be of assistance?" he said, tilting his head to the slope.

"Alissa Meson," the young woman said, taking his hand for the barest instant. It was so cold, it made his fingers tingle.

"Meson?" Strell repeated warily. That sounded like a farmer's name. He squinted, leaning forward to see the small, furred shape on the rock next to her. "What *is that*?" he asked.

Alissa glanced at it and away. "A vole. Why? Do you want it?"

Strell frowned. "It's dead."

"I would hope so."

He waited for an explanation, but she wasn't offering one, and it was just too odd to delve into at the bottom of a ditch.

"I would be grateful," she said quietly with a stilted formality, "if you could help me out of here." She smiled with what was clearly a forced pleasantness. "I seem unable to do it myself."

"Let's see your foot." Strell reached out, freezing as she cleared her throat in warning. Embarrassed, he drew back. Handling a woman's foot was rather a delicate situation, even a booted one. "May I see," he asked meekly.

"Of course," she said. "It's the *other* one."

He looked down. The foot in question was tucked up under her, hidden by her coat. She had taken off her boot, and he felt himself redden until he realized she wore stockings. A small part of him relaxed. She was from the plains. Only farmers were uncouth enough to go without stockings. He himself had three pairs.

"This one?" he asked, determined to not overstep his bounds again.

"Please," she said with a smile. At least Strell thought it was a smile. She might have been baring her teeth at him for all he knew. It was really dark down here, and so cold!

Her breath hissed through clenched teeth as he shifted her foot. "Sorry," he murmured. He was no healer, but he had dealt a lot with sprains and strains, and he wasn't completely without skill. He ran his fingers lightly over the swollen foot. "It would have been better had you left your boot on, but since it's off, we should probably see if your ankle is broken before I move you. You should be able to travel on it in about three or four days if it's only a sprain."

Alissa's brow was pinched. When she nodded hesitantly, he lowered his gaze and firmly probed the bone and tissue, glancing up as she closed her eyes and thumped her head back against the rock face. Strell felt his knot of worry ease as he decided it was a sprain. "Nothing broken," he said cheerily, then blinked in surprise. Alissa hadn't heard him. She had passed out!

"Just as well," he whispered as he stood up and looked down at her. "You won't like the way I'm going to get you out of here."

The water bag went over his shoulder and her boot slipped into his coat. He decided to leave the vole behind. It was an easy climb, and Strell left her things at the top before carefully descending to sling the unconscious woman over his shoulders, catching her outlandish hat as it fell off. He frowned at the wide, floppy brim and the tuft of red fur stuck in the band. It wasn't a plains' hat, and her hair was hacked short in the foothills' fashion.

It was too dark to see more, and so with a silent plea she remain unconscious, he started up, huffing and puffing at the extra weight. Much to his relief, she didn't wake. Not stopping for her boot and water bag, he carried Alissa to her camp and gently laid her by the fire. Curious, he crouched beside her, no longer convinced she was from the plains.

Pale hair fell unusually short over wide-set eyes. Beneath them was a small nose, snubbed up at the end. She was thin and wiry, and would probably come up to his chin, maybe more. Her voice had given her the illusion of being nearly a child, but once in the firelight, Strell could tell her age was probably close to his own.

She was dressed in traveling clothes. A smudge of dirt was on her chin, and he stifled an urge to smooth it away. Her skin was dark, but the heel poking from the hole in her stockings was several shades lighter. Strell chewed on his lip, uncomfortable with not knowing where he stood. She had the short, fair hair of a farmer, but her skin tone and height were much as his own. Wherever she was from, it obviously wasn't the coast; her jawline wasn't angled sharp enough, and her hair wasn't the thick, luxuriant wave all the coastal people were blessed with.

Abruptly embarrassed by his scrutiny, Strell placed her staff on her side of the fire and returned to the dark for her things. By the time he returned, she was sitting up, struggling with the knots holding her blanket to her pack.

"Ah," she sighed as the last knot loosened, "this will help." Giving him a quick glance, she shook out her blanket and drew it over her head like a tent so only her nose showed. "Thanks for getting me out of that pit," she said, shifting closer to the fire. "I'm sorry I snapped at you, but I was beginning to think I was going to have to spend another night down there."

"It wasn't a problem." Strell sat down, the fire safely between them. "I don't think your foot is broken. How long were you down there?"

"Since last night." She fussed with the coals until the heat and light billowed forth. An uncomfortable silence began to grow.

"Here's your boot," Strell said, glad to find something to say, "and your water. Would you mind if I warmed some up? I could use a cup of tea."

She straightened, pulling the blanket from her head. "That sounds wonderful. Could you pass me my water bag?" Alissa started to dig in her pack.

Strell leaned around the fire to set it next to her. He watched her bring out a stone bowl, and when she stretched to put it in the fire, he made a small motion of dismay. "Oh. . . . Let me see first?" he asked boldly, his professional curiosity sparked.

Shrugging, she handed it to him. It *was* made of stone, he decided, but it had never been clay. He tapped it smartly, and a clear, bell-like tone was sounded. Strell smiled faintly upon hearing it, remembering the countless times he had spun a bowl in his father's shops only to smash it later if it lacked that same clear ring. Angling the vessel toward the fire, he was startled to see the shadow of a flame through its wall. This bowl was a splendid example of craftsmanship. He had never seen its like. "You were going to put this in the fire?" he asked quizzically.

"When you're done with it. You like it?" she added shyly.

"M-m-m-m . . ." he grunted, handing it back. "I bet it cost a fortune at market."

"I wouldn't know," she said lightly, "but thank you. It was rather tedious to make." With a faint smile, she filled it with water and placed it in the outer coals.

"You made that?" Strell exclaimed, now satisfied she was from the plains despite her questionable looks. "It's wonderful," he gushed. "I should know. My family used to make them. Well," he admitted, "not exactly like that, but out of clay." Ignoring the sudden tightness of his throat, Strell dug through his pack for his dwindling supply of tea leaves. "Sorry," he muttered. "For a moment I thought you were from the foothills."

"I'm sorry?" Alissa murmured.

Strell bobbed his head and continued his search. "Your fair hair and eyes. I thought you might have been a foothills bast—uh—squatter. Beg your pardon. Every family in the plains has an occasional throwback. But someone who can make such a marvelous piece of work has *got* to be from the desert."

"Oh," Alissa said faintly. "So you're of the opinion that smoothing a stone bowl is far beyond the capabilities of those *poor*, ignorant farmers?"

Deep into his bag, Strell shrugged. "I've never seen its like. A bowl polished out of stone so well, it looks as if it came from the Navigator's table itself! I have yet to meet the *farmer* who has the skill to make anything nice, much less something that exquisitely pure and beautiful."

"Why, you . . ." sputtered Alissa.

Startled, Strell looked up.

"I have *never* . . ." she said, her face a bright red.

"How can you sit there . . ." This time she got a little further. Eyes flashing, she took a deep breath and explosively let it out, shaking in anger.

"Now you look here," she said, her voice soft and dangerous. "Those so-called ignorant farmers are the only thing between your kind and *starvation*. Do you think it's easy trying to win a harvest from the foothills? Weather claims it often. Occasionally there's a surge of pestilence, and that takes its share. If you're lucky, the growing season isn't too hot or cold, and the snows of last winter are enough to last through the summer. You put by what you need and take the rest to market where some stuck-up, ignorant, self-righteous, *plainsman* fingers it with a sneer before offering you half of what you're asking!"

Alissa stopped to find her breath. Strell sat and stared in shock. She was a *farmer*?

"Then," she shouted, "when we look to buy some simple thing from you, all we hear is, 'You may want to look at this section, it's more in your price range.'" Livid, Alissa flung an angry hand toward the steaming water. "That bowl is nothing!" she yelled. "It's not fit for the table. It's not even a bowl. It's a kitchen mortar!"

Strell began to slowly edge backward.

"I was willing to suffer your company considering you hauled me out of that ravine, but you insult me too far. I'm a *throwback*, am I? A *foothills squatter*? Get out of my camp!"

Too stunned to move, Strell watched Alissa's attention shift high above his head. He felt a prickling on the back of his neck as her face changed from anger to dismay, then horror. "Talon! No!" she shouted, trying to get up. The blanket tangled about her. With a small cry, she almost fell into the fire.

Strell instinctively moved to catch her, drawing back at a sudden pain in his neck. "By the Hounds," he said, finding himself under attack by something feathered, sharp, and more determined than a beggar camped outside a rich man's tent.

Alissa was shouting again, but not at him, something he

was oddly grateful for. He couldn't quite make out what she was saying, as his head was between his knees with his arms covering it. Tiny claws and a wickedly pointed beak raked him, ripping at his coat. Hard thumps beat against his back. "Talon!" he heard Alissa shriek. "Stop it. Stop it now!"

The barrage of blows ceased, and Strell cautiously raised his head. Alissa was sitting before the fire with her blanket bunched about her. She was cooing and shushing to a ruffled bird perched on her knee. As Strell moved, the small bird opened its wings and chittered. "Hush," Alissa whispered to the small falcon, coddling and caressing the agitated bird, trying to pacify it.

A rock was jabbing him, and he shifted. The bird whipped her head around and hissed.

Still using her gentle tone, Alissa half sang, "I wouldn't move yet if I were you." Her eyes never left the bird.

Strell froze, and only the fire snapping and Alissa cooing broke the stillness. That tiny thing attacked him? he thought. It was smaller than a blue jay.

He had seen kept birds before and admired them greatly. Most had been hooded and tied, firmly under their owner's control. Being attacked was more than annoying, it was humiliating. He shifted again and the bird glared, but at least he'd gotten that stone out from under him.

Ceasing her soft murmur, the girl set the bird on the stack of firewood. "Are you all right?" she asked in a bland voice, not smiling at all.

Strell angrily brushed his coat. "I'm sweet as potatoes," he said sarcastically.

The bird and Strell regarded each other warily as he removed his hat. A small sound of disgust slipped from him. It was worse than he imagined. The rear top and brim were in tatters. Appalled, he threw it down. The bird chittered but remained at her perch. "If you can't control a falcon," he said tightly, "you shouldn't have one." Where, he thought, was he going to get a new hat? His was useless now.

Alissa silently looked at the mass of shredded leather. As if reading his mind, she cleared her throat and said in a quavering voice, "I'm sorry about that. You can have mine." Covering her face, she turned away.

Strell felt his lips curl in disgust at the very thought. No wonder he hadn't recognized the style of her hat. It was a *farmer's* hat. Not trusting her vicious bird, Strell slowly removed his coat. It wasn't as bad, but it was a mess. There was a ragged tear from the left shoulder to nearly halfway down the back. Scratches marred the dark leather, crisscrossing the shoulders and sleeves like fractures in new ice. Furious, Strell dropped his coat into a crumpled heap. The hat was old; the coat was new. It had been especially costly, as it was made to his specifications and not the tailor's.

"I'll sew it together," came Alissa's muffled words. Her hands were still over her face, and she had begun to shake.

How typical, thought Strell. Here he was scratched and bleeding, and all she could do was cry. Well, he wasn't going to pat her on the head and say it was all right, because it wasn't.

Taking one of the cloths he used for cleaning his instrument, Strell doused it in the cold water from his water bag. He wasn't about to ask to use the warm water in her bowl to clean the scratches on his shoulders. It wasn't his fault, he thought, savagely wringing his rag out. It's that half-witted farm girl's. Can't even control a tiny bird. Talon, she called it. Strell snickered. At least she got the name right.

Strell pulled off his shirt and tossed it aside, not caring if he set the beastly carnivore off again. He glared across the fire. The bird was oddly at peace, considering her mistress was rocking back and forth with her hat pulled over her face. No, he thought sullenly, it was his hat now. Burn him to ash. What if someone he knew saw him with a *farmer's* hat.

His eyes narrowed, and Strell looked closer at the girl. She wasn't crying. She was laughing! "That does it!" he exploded.

The bird gave a startled squawk but remained where she was.

"I'm sorry," Alissa gasped, her eyes bright with tears. "Talon is a good bird. She's never done anything like that before." She laughed, trying to stifle it, failing miserably. "You looked so funny. Cowering as if . . ." And she collapsed, giggling as the tears ran down her face.

Strell sat and stiffly dabbed the scratches on his wrists

and neck, wanting nothing more than to leave. But there was
nowhere to go, and he refused to do anything that might give
her the notion he was accepting any of the blame for this.

There was a last hiccup of laughter from the far side of
the fire, and Alissa tossed him a small stone jar. It landed on
his ruined coat with a thud. Strell ignored it. "I said I was
sorry," she tittered. "You don't have to like me. I know all
too well what plainsmen think of *my* kind, but your scratches
will fester if you don't put something on them."

Strell took the jar with a nasty look, noting with a trained
eye that it was worked the same way as the bowl. He sniffed
suspiciously, detecting nothing from the creamy white salve.
It was probably some folk remedy, he thought patronizingly,
but it was better than nothing, and he dabbed it on his
scratches.

His spare shirt hadn't been washed yet, and he refused to
put it on, having to content himself with wrapping up in his
coat and blanket. Carefully watching the bird, he leaned forward and set the jar next to the silent girl with a firm thump.
He retreated to his side of camp and sank into a cold silence.

The fire snapped and popped, and by an unspoken agreement they let it die down to coals. Alissa crumpled something into her steaming cup, and it smelled delicious. She
kept her eyes on the fire as she held her ankle in one hand
and her cup in the other, taking slow, methodical sips. "I
meant it when I said I would fix your coat," she said into the
long silence. Her voice was cold and emotionless.

"M-m-m," Strell grunted, chewing on his dried meat. It
was tough and stringy, but he wasn't about to bring out his
cheese and fruit.

"If you hand it to me, I'll fix it now," she said, seeming
not to care one way or the other.

Strell silently removed his pipe from its pocket and stiffly
handed his coat to her, tensing in the sudden cold.

The evening passed very slowly. Alissa kept herself bent
low over her work, and he occupied himself with clearing a
spot to sleep. Every time he thought he had all the rocks, a
new one would surface to jab at him. Realizing he could
never make a comfortable bed between the stones and his
scratchy blanket, he gave up and stared at the stars, dis-

creetly watching her out of the corner of his eye. He didn't expect much of a job from her—she was only a farmer's daughter and hardly had the skill to lace her own boots—but anything would be better than that gaping tear. The grease he kept for his boots would help disguise the scratches, but his fine new coat would never be the same.

The fire settled and shifted, sending sparks up to vanish suddenly in the dark. Alissa steadfastly ignored him. Lulled by the steady, rhythmic flow of her needle, Strell fell asleep. His last conscious thought was how comforting it was to be sharing the fire with another human being, no matter how insensitive, irritating, and thoughtless that person was.

8

Meson brushed the sweat from his brow and adjusted the chisel. Three firm taps, and the shape of an ivy leaf took form on the walking stick. Last fall he had caught Rema sighing over a set of bowls at market. They were Hirdune-made; far beyond their means. He was hoping that with a fine bit of worked wood, he might persuade the stingy flatlander to part with at least one of their like. It was to be a surprise. Rema assured him she was content with the life he could provide for her here in the foothills, but it tore at him. She was accustomed to so much more.

"Papa!"

"Just a moment, sweetheart," he mumbled, the handle of a second chisel between his teeth.

"Papa!" it came again, urgent and muffled.

"Alissa?" Meson looked toward the pines to where she had been making pies out of birch seeds and mud. The grove was empty.

"Help me, Papa! I'm slipping!"

Slipping? he thought, and his gaze shot to the well. *"Wolves!"* he swore, his chisel falling forgotten to the ground. The three heartbeats it took to get to her seemed an eternity. Meson reached the well, grabbed his daughter by the back of her dress, and pulled her to safety.

His heart pounded as he clutched her close, cursing himself for being so inattentive. Then he put her at arm's length. *"How many times have I told you to stay away from the well!"*

Pale blue eyes filled with tears, and her chin began to quiver. *"I'm sorry, Papa. But—"*

"No." He gave her a little shake. *"It's not safe. You could have broken your neck!"*

"But, Papa—"

"No." Meson frowned, and Alissa collapsed in on herself. *"I'm sorry,"* she whispered, and his heart melted.

"Come here, Lissy," he said softly, and she fell into him, weeping for having displeased him. *"Hush,"* he said, breathing in the warm scent of her hair, smelling of meadow and sun. *"It's not your fault. I've been promising to put a wall about the well for five years now. I'm the one who deserves a good scolding."* Alissa looked up, snuffing and hiccuping. *"Let's not tell your mother about this, hmm? It will only get me into trouble."* He tweaked her nose, winning a soft, hesitant smile. *"Tomorrow we will go to the rock slide and get enough stone to put a few rings up around that hole in the ground."*

"But then I won't be able to reach it," she protested.

Halfway to a stand, Meson froze. Slowly he lowered himself to sit on the ground. *"Reach what?"* he distantly heard himself say.

"I won't know until I see it." Alissa leaned to look down the well. *"But it's there. I can feel it. Will you get it for me?"* She beamed, plying her five-year-old charms upon him.

Meson swallowed hard. *"Yes. I'll get it."*

Alissa's eyes grew round. *"You know what's down there?"*

"M-m-m-m. I always hide my treasures in a well. I always have; I always will. But you're not to touch it. Understand?"

Her head bobbed, and Meson took her chin in his hand,

turning her to look at him. "You are not to touch it," he repeated sternly, and she dropped her gaze.

Lying flat upon the ground, Meson leaned over the lip of
the well, grinning as two small hands clamped upon his ankles. His smile quickly faded as he sent his fingers to brush
the rough walls of earth, searching for the feel of leather
among the dirt and stones. Recognizing the binding, he carefully slipped the book from its hiding place and sat up. Again
he wondered why his teacher, Talo-Toecan, had given it to
him for safekeeping. The Master knew things of power made
him uncomfortable, always seeming to attract misfortune. It
appeared as if the book's bad luck had finally seeped up out
of the ground to find him.

"That's it!" Alissa cried, jumping up and down. "I knew
something was down there!"

It was as if the summer sun had turned to ash as he
watched his daughter dance in delight among the pines and
yellowing birches. Alissa had lost the gamble of birth. He
could no longer deny his child was a latent Keeper. Cursing
himself for a fool, his eyes went distant and unseeing upon
the ancient tome. His Lissy had found it. It would have to go
back. For her to find it again could prove deadly, and there
was nowhere on his small farm he could hide it where her
sensitive soul couldn't ferret it out. Oh, she would never willingly disobey him, but she couldn't help herself. Even now he
had to clear his throat as her eager hands reached to take it
from him. "Lissy . . ." he warned, and she flushed.

"Here." He smiled with a bittersweet understanding.
"You can look at this." From between the binding and spine,
he wiggled free a thin gray oval about the size of a coin. He
put it into her grasp, and she held it up to the sun and
squinted through it.

"What is it?"

"I don't know. A teacher of mine gave it to me on the
wager I could recognize the whole of a thing by seeing a part
of it." Meson chuckled. "I guess he won."

Alissa shifted eagerly. "Can—can I have it?"

Immediately he shook his head.

"You never let me have anything!" she wailed.

"Absolutely not. I don't know what it is—yet." He gave her a quick, sorrowful squeeze to soften his words.

"All right," she conceded and handed it back, her eyes widening as she realized its gray color was gone; the warmth of her hand and the noon sun had turned it a luminescent gold. Meson hid a smile, wondering if her astonishment would win out over her desire to appear cavalier over its color shift. Deciding by her silence that pride had won, Meson wedged the disk back in the book, and they both sighed. He stood and tucked the book under an arm and took his daughter's fingers. "Come on. Let's have our noon meal. Then you can help me pack."

"Pack?"

"Yes," he said, ignoring the sudden tightness in his chest. "I need to map out another part of the mountains."

"Oh." Alissa snatched up the walking stick in passing, peering at its end far over her head. "Is this for Mother's bowls?" she asked, stretching to run a finger over the small nick where the falling chisel had marred it.

Meson started. "No," he lied. "It's for you."

"Thanks," she breathed, thumping it in time with her steps.

"It's a going-away present," he said, gazing about his small farm as if he would never see it again. "A going-away present."

The dream faded with the scent of gritty fingernails and dry pine needles. Alissa clenched her eyes shut and held her breath, struggling to rebury old wounds. Slowly she exhaled.

Wolves take her, she thought miserably. She hated it when she dreamed of Papa. This time, though, it seemed as if it had been real, like she was reliving it, almost as if—as if it was a memory. She had smelled the dry curls of worked ash, felt the cramped pinch of his right boot he used to complain about, and even now, her throat was as tight as his had felt that afternoon. He had known, Alissa thought bitterly. Burn him to ash. He'd known he might not come back.

She felt the beginning of tears and gave herself a mental

shake. This was daft. No one dreams memories, especially not their own. She would just forget it. Besides, something was cooking. It actually smelled good, and the novelty of *that* was irresistible.

Cracking her eyelids, she saw Strell scraping the last of his breakfast from his bowl, studying a piece of leather on the ground before him. His mended coat lay untouched where she had left it after he fell asleep last night. Her hat was on his head. Recalling how he shamelessly spied on her sewing last night, Alissa decided turnabout was fair play and didn't move.

His shirt clung to him, still damp from its obvious laundry. He didn't seem at all cold for it, which she thought terribly unfair. Oblivious to her scrutiny, he ran a hand over his head and squinted up at the pass. She could almost see what was on the ground before him. If he would only shift a bit. . . .

Talon dropped from the sky to startle them both with her scrabbling claws and loud complaints. Alissa could feign sleep no longer. Strell glanced at her and away as she sat up. Safe in Talon's tenacious grip was a grasshopper, and the small bird danced impatiently for Alissa's attention. From the day they had made their acquaintance, Talon insisted on offering Alissa her catches, not eating until Alissa refused whatever the kestrel had caught. But this morning Talon would have to wait. Alissa wanted to know what Strell was busy rolling up and tucking away.

"Good morning," she said cautiously, pretending to stretch as she tried to get a good peek. She felt she could manage civility despite his slurs last night.

"Morning," he grunted, eyeing Talon warily as he stuffed the leather back in his pack.

Unsure if he was still angry about last night or if he was simply not a morning person, Alissa turned to Talon. "What a fine grasshopper you caught," she cooed. "I'm not very hungry right now," she lied. "You eat it."

There was a snort of scorn from the opposite side of the fire, which Alissa carefully ignored. As if sharing Alissa's sudden unease, Talon refrained her usual dramatic—and utterly false—display of diffidence, meekly accepting the large insect as Alissa gingerly proffered it back. Fluttering to the woodpile, Talon began to meticulously dissect her meal. The silence grew.

Not knowing what to say, Alissa picked up her "new" hat and looked it over. Talon's tuft of squirrel fur was wedged into one of the tears, and she felt her eyes narrow, not knowing whether to be pleased or affronted. Strell's hat, she decided, was a mangled mess of ancient leather. She had done him a favor in taking it off his hands. Still, it was well-oiled, and if she wanted a hat, she would have to mend it. Alissa let it fall to the ground. Just the thought of the work involved to make it usable again made her fingers ache. How, she wondered, could Talon do so much damage in so little time?

Strell continued to fuss with the tin pot hung over the fire on a shaky-looking tripod. He hadn't acknowledged her except for that wonderfully expressive grunt. Looking for her water bag, Alissa found it full and within her reach. Strell must have filled it. Her bowl, too, was clean. Strell must have washed it. Huh, she thought. She hadn't expected that.

"Thanks for the clean bowl," she said as she poured some water in it to heat. "Would you like some tea?"

Strell eyed her with a sullen wariness. "Why so nice?" he said bluntly. "I thought you wanted me gone."

"Uh," Alissa stammered, surprised at his frankness. "You did get me out of that ravine, and you're entitled to your own opinions, no matter how idiotic and backward they are. Besides"—she flushed—"after today, you won't be anything but a nasty memory."

He stiffened, taking this with the expected bad grace. "Alissa, you may be Mistress Death herself, but I'm not leaving until you can walk out of these blessed mountains on your own." Clearly disgusted, he threw a stick on the fire. "Just my luck," he muttered. "The snows are less than a month off, and I'm out in the middle of nowhere playing nursemaid to an ignorant farmer who doesn't know to keep her eyes on the ground where they ought to be."

"So now I'm Mistress Death?" Alissa said. What was it with this . . . this . . . dirt-eater! she fumed. "I don't need a nursemaid. And I don't need your help."

"You did last night."

"I would have gotten out eventually."

"In the belly of a wolf, maybe."

Alissa felt her cheeks warm. "I don't ever recall asking for your help."

Strell simpered at her. "Yes, you did."

Her lips pursed. She had. "Well, I don't need it now. Why don't you take your wretched coat and go back where you belong?" Angry, she rose and limped to his side of camp. Strell's frown shifted to astonishment as she snatched his coat. It was obvious what was going through his mind, she thought. Up and around in three days. Ha! Maybe for a milk-sop of a flatlander.

"Here!" Her ankle gave a twinge, and she felt herself go ashen. Feeling ill, she threw the coat in his lap instead of his face, where she wanted to. "I spent half the night on it so you could go, leaving me debt-free."

"But . . . your ankle," he stammered. "I saw it. It was the size of a duck's egg."

"It looks fine to me!" she said, embarrassed to have his eyes on her foot, even if it was in a stocking. Her ankle was still swollen, but it could bear her weight.

Strell's mouth opened in protest. Then his face hardened. "Fine!" he barked, and he began shoving things into his pack.

Sullen, Alissa returned to her side of camp and dumped her water on the fire. She'd skip breakfast. It wouldn't be the first time, she thought crossly as the fire sizzled, sending a billow of acrid smoke into the dawn-still air. Thumping down by the blackened, wet wood, she snatched her boots. The tension was almost palpable as they both worked furiously to part ways.

Strell muttered something and reached for his tripod. At the same moment, Alissa unthinkingly tried to jam her swollen foot into her boot.

"Ah-h!" they simultaneously cried. The pain in Alissa's ankle ebbed to a dull throb. Annoyed, she looked at Strell, wondering what *his* problem was. Seeing him kneeling by the fire, her face went pale and her stomach churned. In his anger, he had forgotten the tripod had been sitting over the flames all morning. Stunned, he stared at the angry burn blossoming across his palm.

"Here!" Alissa tossed her mortar to the ground and dumped her water bag into it. Water splashed over the edge as Strell broke from his shock and plunged his hand into the bowl. Taking Strell's water bag, she slowly added more, making a muddy slurry where the fire had been.

"No, don't take it out," she said, pushing his hand down as he tried to do just that.

"Of all the idiotic . . ." he began bitterly.

"Uh-huh," Alissa agreed. "That was kind of daft."

He stiffened. Their eyes locked, and Alissa met his glare with a wide-eyed innocence. "Well, it was!" she protested, and he turned away.

The wind gusted, sending a chill through her. Ashes, she thought, what if he was really hurt? "All right," she said, meekly, sorry for having agreed with him so quickly. "Let's see it."

His jaw clenched as he raised his hand. Drops of water plunked back into the bowl. Taking a deep breath, his eyes rose to hers. "Will—will I be able to play?" he said.

"Play?" Alissa started at him blankly.

"You know . . . music?" With one hand, he pantomimed blowing into a pipe.

"Oh." Alissa looked at the long, angry blister. It didn't seem as bad as she had first thought. "Yes." She winced. "I suppose so." A faint stirring of unease slipped through Alissa. He was a piper? she thought. He couldn't be the same one she heard the night the raku flew over her. He would be halfway to the plains by now.

"How long do you think?"

She blinked, jerked back to present. "I don't know."

"You don't?"

His voice carried a hint of alarm, and Alissa glanced at him. "The only thing I ever tended was Talon, and all she needed was food." Together they turned to her, and Talon chittered happily under their gaze.

"Who made that salve then?" he asked. "It worked well on my scratches."

"My mother," Alissa said shortly, reluctant to talk about

her. Alissa awkwardly stood up. "It would probably do your burn some good."

Leaving him to cradle his hand, Alissa went to her pack and upended it. She glanced back at Strell as everything spilled out in a sliding mess, but it was the fastest way for her to find anything. Apparently Strell had discovered his manners and was at least pretending not to watch as she stuffed everything else away. She wondered if all plainsmen were that nosy or just him.

Strell held out his hand as she sat down before him. At his hesitant nod, Alissa spread the thin, creamy salve over the burn, and with a clean but ratty bit of cloth from his pack, she loosely bound it. "There." She met his eyes, wiping the stinky salve from her. "That should help."

"Thank you," he said. Then his eyebrows rose and he cocked his head, staring at her. "In the morning light, your eyes are gray. I thought they were blue."

Alissa stiffened. "Well, your nose is bent," she said crossly. His eyes were as brown as her mother's, with flecks of gold. Suddenly aware their heads were nearly touching, she drew back and jumped to her feet, scrambling for something to do. There was nothing. He was packed. She was packed. Even the fire was out, extinguished by her flood. She snatched up the jar of salve and jammed it into her bag. Talon took flight, sounding as if she were laughing. Once more at a proper distance, Alissa remembered her boots. Dropping down on the sparse grass, she tightened their laces, wincing at the twinge her ankle gave. Tomorrow it ought to be fully healed.

"Will you be able to travel?" she tentatively asked, concerned that now she would be the one morally obligated to stay and play nanny.

Strell flexed his hand, blanching as the skin pulled tight. "I'll make do. I don't want to risk an early snow."

"I know what you mean." Alissa looked east down the slope toward her unseen home. "But you're farther along than you think. That's the last valley before the foothills."

"Last valley?" he repeated, his eyebrows arching up. "It's the first. I'm heading in."

Alissa stared at him, a curious mix of disgust and panic

stirring in her. Aw, Hounds, she thought. He was going the same way she was. "Are you mad!" she shouted, hoping she could get him to turn around. "It's too late to start across, and now with your hand . . ." She gestured weakly. It was obviously he shouldn't be alone for a few days at least.

"I have to. I have no choice," he said, his face losing all expression.

No choice? she wondered. Everyone has a choice. They just may not like it. Alissa waited, hoping he would say more or tell her she was right and that he would go back to his plains where he belonged. But he didn't. He just sat there, looking at his tired, worn boots, keeping whatever was bothering him to himself.

Well, she thought. If he wasn't going to hoe his row yet, they'd better get going. The snow wouldn't wait for them. And with that, Alissa stood and shouldered her pack.

Strell just sat there.

"Are you coming?" She stood with her staff in hand, thinking the situation was eerily familiar.

He looked up from his obviously very interesting boots. "I told you, I'm headed west."

Exasperated with his sorry attitude, Alissa picked up her staff and frowned at him. With her tender ankle and his burned hand, they had no business being out here. "What makes you think I'm not headed that way, too?"

Strell stared up at her. "You're jesting, right?"

"No."

"What's so important that it can't wait until spring?"

Alissa's eyes closed in a long blink as she struggled to keep her voice level and mild. "None of your concern. Why can't you wait?"

Grunting, Strell lurched to his feet. Too proud or stubborn to ask for help, he wrestled with his pack until Alissa held it up for him. He didn't say thanks, but she really didn't expect him to. How he had planned on traveling alone, Alissa couldn't begin to guess. Strell glanced up at the pass, then behind Alissa and out over the valley. Understanding filled his face, and his eyebrows rose. "That was your music," he whispered. A thin finger pointed accusingly at her. "That was your fire on the bluff the night I saw that raku!"

Alissa's breath caught in dismay. It *was* him! she thought. But that was days ago. How on earth could she have passed him? Maybe she was going faster than she thought. "I see it didn't eat you either," she said, struggling to cover her own surprise. Bone and Ash, she moaned silently. This was worse and worse.

Strell's face darkened. Then he drew himself up and shook his head as if in refusal. Without a word, he turned and began to walk stiffly toward the pass. Alissa watched him go, thinking it was going to be a long, miserable trip. And how could anyone travel slower than she? He must have stopped to butcher some poor animal.

As she turned to follow, the sharp clink of metal against stone drew her eyes down. She crouched to tuck the still-warm tripod into her pack. Whistling sharply for Talon's attention, she rose. With her back to the sun, she hobbled gingerly to catch up. "Hey!" she called. "Wait up!"

9

"Strell?" Alissa wheezed. "Can we stop for a moment?" Flushed, she leaned back against a wide beech, staring desperately up at its yellow leaves. They rattled in the breeze that somehow failed to find her, hot and sticky on the forest floor. Her pack made an uncomfortable bump, and she slid down the smooth bark until her rump hit the dirt. She didn't want to let Strell know she was having trouble keeping up, but Hounds, she felt like she had been whipped.

During one of their frequent breaks yesterday, Alissa had caught him shaking his head in wonder at her needlework on his coat. She suspected his opinion of persons "not of the plains persuasion" might be changing. At least he wasn't treating her like a beggar-come-calling anymore. His attitude was more like that to a relative who visits only when she wants something.

"You'd better not say anything nasty," she muttered under her breath as he pulled up sharp and returned. Alissa knew her face was pink and that sweat was dripping unladylike from her forehead. Trying to hide her fatigue, she bent to tighten her laces.

A pair of dark boots stomped to a crackling halt just within her sight. "Is it your ankle?" Strell said gently.

Startled, Alissa glanced up. He actually looked concerned. Not knowing what to think, she shook her head. She had forgotten all about her ankle. "Tired," she sighed, wondering if perhaps there was a reason her mother had always frowned at how fast she seemed to mend.

Strell slipped off his pack and awkwardly opened it with one hand. Sitting on the leaves, he pulled out a piece of dried meat and offered it to Alissa. She drew back, wrinkling her nose.

"Sorry," he said. "I thought it was a rumor. Foothills people really don't eat meat?"

"Nothing that has feet."

Shifting uncomfortably, Strell pulled a stick out from under him. "Then why do you all keep animals?"

"*You* eat them."

Strell grunted at that, sending the stick into the trees to clatter among the gray branches. "How about some cheese?" Rummaging deeper, he brought out a large wedge and broke off a generous portion. This Alissa accepted with a wan smile, too tired to say anything. Strell, she noticed, had put his meat away, contenting himself with the cheese as well.

"I wish you'd tell me when you need a rest," he said cautiously.

"What do you think I just did!"

"Wait," he said sharply. "Don't untie your tent just yet. If you exhaust yourself, you're more likely to get hurt. I, for one, don't want to wait around for a pulled muscle to mend just because you were too thickheaded to call for a break." He hesitated. "Alissa, please don't make too much of this. It's not that important. I've been traveling since I was fifteen. I didn't expect you to match my pace. I—I just forgot."

Alissa sullenly bit into her cheese. He was right, but it was galling to have to admit it. Talon landed on Alissa's knee, crooning gently. Fine, she thought. It wasn't worth arguing over, and it was painfully obvious she had been pushing herself. "You're right," she said softly. "I'll tell you from now on."

"What's that? I couldn't have heard you right." He actually had the audacity to pretend to be shocked.

"I said you were right!" Alissa snatched her staff and struggled to her feet. Talon took flight with a startled squawk.

Laughing quietly, Strell stood and ineptly shouldered his pack, ever mindful of his sore hand. "There's a lake up ahead," he said. "I don't think it's too far. If you think you can last, would you like to try to reach it before we stop for the night?"

Normally Alissa would have come back with a sharp remark, but this time, instead of saying the first thing entering her head, she thought about it. She was tired, and her back and feet felt like she would be crippled for life, but a bath sounded great. "Not far?" she sighed.

"Don't think so. It's early yet. We can slow up." Strell smiled encouragingly down at her. He had her old hat on to block the sun, and Alissa thought it looked ridiculous on him. The floppy leather was half in his eyes, and she impulsively bent it up so as to please her sensibilities. Strell's eyes widened, and Alissa spun away hoping he hadn't seen her flush. What did she care what he looked like? But before she could take three steps, she froze and pivoted on a slow heel.

"How do you know there's a lake up ahead?" she said carefully. "You said this morning you had come in through a different valley." Alissa's thoughts went back to that mysterious something he had shoved into his pack yesterday. "You have a map? Let me see?"

"'Course I have a map," Strell said. "You think I'd be ignorant enough to risk the mountains this late without one?"

Alissa's eyes narrowed at the implied insult, but she swallowed her anger as he knelt and rummaged through his pack. Silently, almost reverently, he took a roll of leather, untied its ribbon, and carefully laid it out.

Flatlanders didn't generally have maps showing mountain paths. There were rough sketches drawn in haste to illustrate tales, but there wasn't enough traffic through the mountains to warrant anything better. Curious, Alissa unslung her pack again and dropped heavily down beside him. Her eyes widened in recognition. "Where," she said shortly, "did you get this map?"

"I bought it. Why?"

"That's one of my papa's maps!"

"Your father's?" Strell looked her up and down. "You're Rema's daughter?"

Stunned, Alissa stared at him. "By the Navigator's Hounds," she whispered. "How do you know my mother?"

His eyes glinted slyly as he fumbled for his water sack. "You look tired, Alissa. Care for a drink?"

"Of all the . . ." she began, then caught her breath. No, Alissa thought. She wouldn't let him get to her. Calm as a morning in spring, she proffered her cup. "Yes, please."

Strell managed to pour the water one-handed, eyeing her cup's ribbon with far more interest than it deserved. Alissa's eyes flicked to the map. Burn her to ash if its tie wasn't one of her mother's hair ribbons. He hadn't stolen the map; her mother had given it to him!

"It looks as if it will be a clear evening, don't you think?" he drawled, seeming to take a great interest in the sky.

Fine, Alissa seethed. She could play along. "Oh, yes!" she said brightly. "Very clear." Her mind whirled as she sedately sipped at her water, trying to find the sense in it. She hadn't been gone long enough for her mother to go roving about. And why had her mother given him one of Papa's maps? They were too precious to hand out like cookies on market day. Ashes, Alissa fumed. She didn't get one! And as for tying it with a hair ribbon? Ribbons were tokens of endearment in the plains *and* foothills. Why had her mother given him that! "Do you think the weather will hold?" Alissa asked with a pained smile.

Pausing as if this took a great deal of thought, Strell looked up at the clattering leaves. "Oh, I don't know. What do you think?"

"It's hard to say," Alissa murmured. "I do believe there's the chance for a sudden storm—perhaps even a *violent* one."

Her foot began to thump against the ground. The silence stretched. Somewhere in the distance, Talon called. She couldn't stand this, Alissa thought. If he didn't tell her, she would do something she would regret later and Strell would regret right now. Alissa took her empty cup, and with immeasurable restraint, set it down between them with a firm thump.

"All right, all right," he said gaily. "There's not much to tell. I followed your farm's irrigation works out of the mountains. I asked for directions. She showed me the maps. I bought this one for a length of coastal fabric."

Yeah, Alissa snorted, that sounded like her mother. She was a milksop when it came to fabric. Always complaining about the quality. Then Alissa paused, doing a quick calculation. Hounds. That meant Strell had traveled to her home and back again in the same time it had taken her to just get out here. No wonder she was having trouble keeping up. But then another thought stopped her cold. What had Strell done that the plains wouldn't take him back?

Silently Alissa weighed her curiosity against the bliss of ignorance. Curiosity won. "Let me see if I have this right," she said slowly. "You were headed *out* of the mountains, made a trade with my mother, then turned around and came *back*?"

Brushing a bit of dirt from his coat, Strell grunted, "Yup."

Alissa swallowed hard. She was beginning to know that grunt. There was something he didn't want to tell her. "Why didn't you go home?" she asked timidly.

"Because it's gone!" Strell exploded. "Washed away five years ago in some accursed flood! I've nothing left. Nothing!" Lurching violently, he rose and stormed off to stand with his back to her, looking sightlessly through the trees.

Alissa's shoulders slumped in relief. He wasn't a thief or murderer. He was running from the loss of his family. No wonder he had turned around. The ties that bound home and family were far stronger in the plains than in the foothills. It was a matter of survival. He was more alone than even she, Alissa thought, compassion stirring in her. The only reason her mother had left was to escape persecution for her choice in spouses. Foothills and plains do *not* intermarry.

Alissa's relief turned somber as she remembered that spring. It had been hard on everyone. Half their early lambs had died with the shakes. Many settlements had been inundated, but she only knew one that was completely lost.

Her eyes rose to his stiffly held back. "You're a Hirdune potter?" she breathed, well-acquainted with the high regard her mother held that family's work in.

"Not anymore," came his ragged voice.

"I'm sorry, I didn't know," she called, unsure if he would welcome a show of sympathy from her. As she sat in an awkward silence, wondering what to say that wouldn't sound trite, her eyes fell upon the map. She snatched it up, bringing it close. She hadn't seen this one before!

All but forgetting Strell, Alissa oriented the map and found they were, as fate would have it, within easy reach of a lake. Then she scanned the entire map until she found what she was looking for. There in her papa's handwriting were two words that might explain it all. The Hold. "May the Wolves of the Navigator come to earth and hunt me," she whispered. "It really exists."

"Strell!" she shouted. "It's here! The Hold is here, and we can reach it before it snows!"

Slowly Strell turned and came back, his face expressionless and his manner distant. "It's beautiful, isn't it?" he murmured, gesturing to the map.

"Yes," she agreed absently, used to her papa's work. "But look." Her finger stabbed down. "The Hold!"

"The what?"

"The—uh—Hold." She faltered, suddenly unsure if she should say more. Keepers, magic, and a mythical fortress? That ought to go over like a blue-eyed bride at a plains wedding. "That's where I'm going." Alissa frowned. "Only I didn't quite know the way. With this map, I should be able to make it before winter sets in." Alissa stared at the map and bit her lip, her thoughts turning decidedly uneasy. She didn't really want Strell to know about her destination.

Strell looked down at her with his hands on his hips.

"That's my map, and I'm not going to the Hold. I've never even heard of it."

She gritted her teeth. He was a minstrel, she thought darkly. He must have heard of it. "You know," she muttered, not eager to hear him laugh at her. "Masters, magic—"

"There's no such thing as magic," Strell scoffed. He leaned over and yanked the map right out of her hands.

"Then why do you throw rocks around when we set up camp?"

"That's different."

Alissa rolled her eyes. Why was she defending something she didn't believe in? "Fine. No such thing as magic." She snatched the map back and flung it down. "But there's the Hold," she said, pointing, "which means there are probably Keepers at it, and while I refuse to believe they can do magic, they must be of some use."

"Keepers?"

She thought back to her papa's stories. "Yes. They administer to the Masters." Alissa couldn't help her frown. *She* would never be anyone's servant.

A faint grin stole over Strell. "Does Alissa want to be a Keeper?" he teased. "Magic from her fingertips. Oooo. Should I be afraid?"

"Hush your mouth," she muttered. "This wasn't my idea."

He chuckled. "Well, I'm going to the coast." He glanced into the trees.

Alissa's brow smoothed out. "Good," she said. "I'm going to the Hold. I want to see if there's any truth to the stories my papa told me."

Strell nearly jerked himself out of balance, so quick did he turn around. "Stories?" he said. "Wait a moment. You said Masters? As in the Masters of the Hold?" He dropped down beside her, and Alissa drew back, alarmed at the eager light in his eye. "The Keepers carry out the wishes of the Masters in return for being taught magic, right?" he said.

She nodded, edging back from him. "Something like that."

"I heard about Masters at the coast," Strell exclaimed. "The people there are terrified of them. Refused to tell me anything. Every time I asked, they ran me out of town and burned the chair I had been sitting on. They were afraid I'd bring the Masters down upon them. Apparently whenever they show up, they steal the children and leave war in their place. I thought at first they were just stories to scare the children into behaving, but the adults are afraid, too."

"Must be some other Masters," Alissa said, scooting back until Strell was a proper distance away. "The ones my papa told me about were very civilized."

"And they really exist? They live here?" He pointed excitedly to the map, and Alissa nodded uneasily.

"That's what the map says," she offered.

"Hounds," he breathed. "I'm coming with you. I have to see this."

"No, you aren't," she said quickly.

Strell snorted. "What can you do to stop me?"

Alissa closed her eyes in a long blink, wishing she would learn to keep her mouth shut.

Map in hand, Strell rose to his feet and strode forward, seeming to have forgotten she still had her rump in the dirt. Alissa took a breath to rise, letting it slip from her in surprise as he whipped around, striding back to her. "Wait," he said excitedly, waving the map. "You said 'That's what the map says.' You can read this swirly stuff?"

She grimaced, not pleased at all with how things were working out. "My papa taught both my mother and me. Can't you read?" She dropped her eyes and tightened the laces of her lovely boots. She didn't care if she sounded like a spoiled plainsgirl. This wasn't what she had planned.

"I can read," Strell said defensively. "I have a chartered name."

She shrugged. What did she care if he could trace his lineage back four hundred years to the first families who settled the plains? "You can't read that," she said, gesturing at the map.

Strell hesitated, then crouched. "No. But I've never seen writing like that. Anywhere. Can you read this?" Brushing away the leaves, he made a series of scratches with a twig.

Alissa glanced at it, then away. "No." So as not to appear completely brainless, she pointed to the seventh figure. "I recognize that one." It was the figure etched on the hearth tiles at her home. They were Hirdune-made, she thought, stifling a groan. She should have known.

"Good." Smiling, Strell got to his feet. "I like knowing something you don't."

That got to her, and she threw his old hat at him in disgust. He caught it, gave her a slow wink, and threw it back. "Hey!" she exclaimed. "I can read."

"I'm sure you can," Strell drawled, picking up *her* bag.

"That's mine!" Alissa cried, struggling to her feet and snatching it back. How irritating, she thought as she pushed past him to take the lead, but it wasn't long before she was lagging behind as usual. Somehow though, she found her heart wasn't in her sharp words anymore.

10

They found the lake long before sunset, and after a discussion loud enough to set the jays off, decided to camp at the edge of a nearby clearing. Alissa was scuffing up a spot for the fire when there was a thump in the grass. She looked to find Strell with his hand full of stones.

"Magic?" she said, her eyebrows raised.

Strell flushed. "No." A rock was tossed to his left.

She sucked her teeth as a third went to his right. "Really?"

"Really," he said, blowing the dust at her.

"Uh-huh." Plainsmen, she thought. "Is it *safe* now?"

"Unless you brought something in on the bottoms of your boots."

Alissa shook her head in exasperation, intercepting his reach for her water bag. "I'll get it," she offered. "I'm going to take a swim anyway." Strell's bag was nearly full, but they would need more than that to get through the evening.

Strell nodded. "I'll see what I can find for dinner."

Grabbing her soap and spare clothes, Alissa walked to the lake and followed the shoreline until she couldn't see the camp. She prudently went a bit farther, and with a nervous look behind her, she slipped out of her clothes and waded in, gasping at how far she sank into the muck before she found firm ground. It was cold, but it felt so good to be clean that she went deeper, losing track of the time, the soap, and nearly the rock where she had left her clothes. Gooseflesh and a sudden irrational fear of what the dark water might be hiding sent her rushing back to the bank.

As she crouched on a rock checking for unexpected guests between her toes, Strell's music came faintly across the flat purple water. It sounded different than the last time, higher pitched but stronger, richer. Her fingers were clumsy from the cold and her damp skin as she struggled into her fresh shirt and trousers, tying a narrow band of fabric tight around her waist. She liked this outfit. The shirt came down to her knees, and she could at least pretend she was wearing her more customary dress. The water dripped from her hair to make a cold trail down her back, and she shivered, wanting nothing but to get back to the fire. Carrying her boots, Alissa minced through the scrub.

Strell looked up as she entered the ring of light. His eyes widened upon seeing her naked feet, and decidedly red-faced, he quickly averted his gaze. Mortified, Alissa sank down on her bedroll and tugged on her stockings. No one had seen her bare feet since she was five. Ashes, she may as well have come dancing through the trees naked. He must think her an absolute barbarian. Even knowing an entire society of farmers spent days without shoes did nothing to alleviate her disgrace. "Was that your music?" she said into the uncomfortable silence.

With a rueful snort, Strell extended his good hand for the water bag. He filled Alissa's mortar and set it in the outermost flames. "I can manage the easy tunes," he said, "but it's still too tender for anything tricky."

Alissa squinted across the fire. "That's a new pipe, isn't it?"

"Yes—I mean, no." He shrugged. "It's my grandfather's. I don't play it very often."

"Why not? It sounds better than your other one."

"It is," he agreed hastily. "It just that . . ." Strell's mouth shut and he frowned. "I just don't. That's all."

Alissa's predatory instincts stirred. It wasn't sorrow that had closed his mouth, it was embarrassment. "Can I see it?" she asked, and when he actually hesitated to think it over, she knew there was something here he didn't want to admit. She raised her eyebrows in a mocking challenge, and he slowly rocked to his knees to hand the pipe to her.

It was small, about as long as her forearm, but heavier than it looked and finely crafted out of a single length of reddish wood. The faint smell of tart apples and pine seemed to linger about its polished smoothness. It was exquisite, and she could see why he was hovering over, as anxious as a new mother letting a stranger hold her baby. "It's beautiful," she said, handing it back.

His smile as he took possession of it was half relief, half pleasure. "It's been in my family for generations," he said. "Tradition is to lull an ill-tempered baby to sleep with it. My mother says . . ." He hesitated for a heartbeat. "She said it never worked on me. I'd just cry all the more."

Alissa chuckled, not surprised that even as a baby Strell had been too stubborn to succumb to such wiles. "Huh," she said, hoping to worm the truth out of him. "If my pipe was that nice, I'd play it all the time."

"Special occasions or rich takings," he said, not meeting her eyes. "It—ah—gives me a headache if I play it too long."

"A headache?" Expecting her to believe *that* was ridiculous.

In what Alissa thought was distraction, Strell sent a simple melody into the cricket-filled night. She couldn't help but slump into its sound, as mellow and rich as the pipe's color. "That's beautiful," she said with a sigh, not caring if playing it made him break out in purple spots. Strell inclined his head graciously, his music not missing a tick.

By now the water was boiling, and as Alissa put the tea

leaves in to brew, her smile widened. Not only was camp set in good order, but Strell's cooking pot was already full and bubbling. "My," she breathed, noticing he was clean-shaven. "How long was I gone?"

He hit a sour note and lowered his instrument. Grinning, he took a spoon and ladled something thick and steamy into his bowls, handing her the fullest. "Not long. I rushed." He absently rubbed his chin.

Alissa's eyes closed as she took a deep sniff. "Mmmm, smells wonderful." She took a careful bite. "And tastes delicious." Evidently it was the right thing to say, for Strell favored her with one of his expressive grunts before putting all his attention into his bowl. He never talked when he ate, consuming his meals with the seriousness of a beggar counting money.

"This is very good," Alissa said, needing to fill the silence with something other than the scraping of spoons. "It's been ages since someone cooked anything edible for me." She poked at a soft root. "I was eight when I took over the kitchen. My mother never managed to master it."

Strell came up for air with a faint smile. "She was burning the bread when I met her."

"Her bread invariably is." Alissa shuffled the white and brown lumps about in her bowl, looking for something recognizable. Even the taste was unfamiliar. It had an earthy, woody spice. "But this is really good. What is it? A traditional plains dish?"

Strell glanced up and away. "This and that."

"This and that?" Alissa felt a faint stir of unease. That last root was really tender. She hadn't been gone long enough to cook it that soft. "You didn't put any of your—"

"I promise," he interrupted, "I didn't put anything in the pot that ever had feet."

Satisfied, Alissa resumed eating, starting to see Strell's attraction with silent dining. But then she got to thinking. If it wasn't meat, what was it? Her chewing stopped. Her tongue felt around, trying to identify what it was pushing on. Soft. Smooth. Squishy. It wasn't a root.

"Uh, Strell?"

"Don't ask, Alissa." He didn't even look up.

"Strell?" She swallowed hard. "Did—did it ever move on its own?"

His eyes flicked up, then down. "Not very much."

"They're *grubs*!" Alissa shouted, feeling herself go red.

Strell sighed, not meeting her eyes. "What does it matter, if it fills your stomach. Food is food. And they never had feet, Alissa."

She looked at her half-empty bowl. She looked at Strell. Slowly she set the bowl down. Strell chuckled and kept right on eating.

Pulling her blanket up about her ears, Alissa tried to ignore his enthusiasm. She'd heard stories but never believed them. The plains were a harsh place: insufferably hot in the summer, stupefyingly cold in the winter. The people in the foothills spent all their efforts growing or raising all—well, most, apparently—of the food the plains ate, leaving the foothills little time to make necessities. The plains obligingly produced everything from chamber pots to blankets. They traded, cheating each other to the point of no one having enough of anything. Her mother, Alissa mused, treated food with almost a reverence. Alissa had thought it was because she couldn't cook. Now Alissa wondered if it was because she had grown up not having enough.

Deep in thought, Alissa dipped out two cups of tea. Strell finished his bowl, then, without even asking, hers. They sat in a ponderous silence, keeping their thoughts safely to themselves. Strell reached for his cup. Setting it down beside him untasted, he brushed at his coat sleeve. Alissa looked up, half expecting his next words.

"Um—Alissa?" he said. "I—uh—want to apologize for what I said about your ancestry the other night." He dropped his eyes, and Alissa could tell this was something he didn't do often. "I spoke out of ignorance, and it shames me to think I can't admit it when I'm wrong. It's just that—when you're told something long enough, it can't help but become a truth for you."

Alissa's face hardened, and she took a deep breath to inflict a few choice words.

"I'm not done yet," he interrupted, and with a tremendous effort, she held her tongue.

He poked at the fire, his eyes lowered. "My father kept the usual low opinion of hills people, and he took great pains that his children inherited this."

Acutely aware of the practice, Alissa nodded stiffly. The foothills were just as bad, instilling their children with a hatred that stopped just shy of violence.

Catching her eye, Strell held it with a frightening intensity. "Everything you said about the plains is true. We are self-righteous about our skills and ignorant about yours. I'm truly sorry for what I said. I didn't know. I've never known anyone . . . well . . . Can we just begin again?"

Alissa's eyes dropped and her anger vanished in a puff of shame. "Actually, Strell," she said, embarrassed by his honesty into some of her own, "your belief that the foothills are lacking in any skills other than farming is fairly accurate." She looked up, reading his genuine surprise. "The only reason I can sew is because my mother insisted I learn. And how to smooth out a bowl, and pretty much everything else. My papa taught me how to read, bring in a crop, and husband a herd, or rather, he taught my mother, who taught me. There's no question I'm a foothills farmer, but I'm also the daughter of a plainswoman." She swallowed hard, forcing herself to be painfully blunt. "It's obvious I'm a—a half-breed. I'll never be accepted in the plains or foothills." A spark of defiant anger stirred. "The villagers hate me more than they hate my mother. She, at least, doesn't have to pretend to be anything she isn't."

Strell sat before her, stiff and unreadable, and she wondered if he was going to take back his apology. "Is that why you're going to this Hold place?" he finally said.

Alissa looked away, rubbing a faint ache at the back of her neck. "Maybe. Personally, I think my mother sent me because they need someone who can properly weed a garden."

"Beg your pardon?"

Giving him a wan smile, Alissa ran her fingers up her neck and over the back of her skull, following the odd sensation of tingling prickles. "What else would a farmer do? You'd have to be daft to believe the stories about that place."

Strell chuckled then, and she felt her knot of fear loosen,

glad he hadn't started with the expected recriminations. "Yes. The stories," he said. "Tell me one?"

The soft prickling in Alissa's head became a buzz. As she looked up in alarm, her balance left her. She reached out to find the ground, blinking as she struggled to focus.

"Alissa?" came Strell's voice, sounding hollow and distant. "Are you all right? You don't look well."

"Uh—no," she murmured, noticing that the trees seemed to have their leaves again, and that they were green, and that the stars were gone, and she could see daisies in the grass where there should be none. Her vision started to blur. "Listen," she said, struggling to stand. "Can—can you smell apples?" and with that, the clearing and Strell disappeared from her sight.

Meson tossed his apple core into the pine scrub and frowned. His eyes went deep into the empty sky, dropping to the majestic peak looming over the fortress, and then to the Hold itself. Not a clue could he find to explain what he had found.

The outer doors were standing open—as usual. Someone had placed a ward upon them in a long-forgotten incident, and the heavy timbers couldn't be shifted. Beyond them were the exquisitely carved, but no less formidable, inner doors. They had been locked, but it was simple to bypass a ward keyed for general entry. All appeared as it should on the outside; it was the inside that told the story.

The Hold was all but deserted, and that couldn't be.

Yesterday, a mere half-day's journey away, he had sent an unspoken hail to tell those at the Hold of his arrival. No one had answered him. This morning, on this very spot, he had run a mental search of the Hold, catching a wisp of familiar thought. It was Bailic. Meson found him in Talo-Toecan's rooms. Apart from Bailic, there were no other Keepers, students, or Masters. Everyone was gone. Something had gone very, very wrong.

Having learned caution when it came to his "old friend," Meson had spent the earlier part of his day prowling furtively about the Hold and its environs. His exploration of the silent halls and fallow fields had a double purpose. It confirmed his mental search that only Bailic remained, as well as confused his trail as to where he hid the book. Meson was not so innocent that he would bring the book to the very man he feared was behind this utter abandonment.

The wind gusted and dropped, and gusted again. It spun the leaves by the door into a clattering whirlwind, and then, as if tired of the game, it dropped them and ran away. Meson shouldered his pack and strode forward through the late daisies. As he slipped between the tall doors, he felt the tingle of the Hold's truth ward take him.

The Masters of the Hold abhorred lies, though they would willingly stretch the truth or view it from unbelievable angles. Knowing mankind was easily swayed, they had long ago blanketed the Hold from its highest balcony to its rumored, but never seen, dungeon with a truth ward. An entire generation of Masters had reinforced it until it was said the very walls of the Hold would fall in defense upon any who would dare attempt to break it. But that had never stopped Bailic from trying.

Meson stood in the spacious entry hall, his eyes narrowing. It had been stripped. Not a scrap of fabric or stick of furniture relieved the ancient gray walls. The sight had shocked him the first time, now it made him angry. Even the pendulum, a silent witness to the spinning of the earth and the weave of time, was gone. The stairs of yellow stone wound upward in graceful swoops, becoming thin and rough at the base of the tower where the Masters' quarters were. It was said the Masters had no need for aesthetic beauty that men did, but Meson knew better. They found their beauty in other places.

To his left, the tunnels leading to the annexes gaped. They were the Hold's belowground attics, holding everything from bootstraps to strawberries, forever fresh under wards. His eyes rose to the fourth-floor walkway, where, as boys, he and Bailic had dropped feathers from his pillow to see who could control the lightly drifting bit of fluff. Bailic, Meson remembered, always took the friendly contest too seriously, sulking for days if he deemed himself the loser.

Leaning back against the closed door, Meson exchanged his boots for the soft-soled shoes worn behind the Hold's walls. He turned to the stairway and padded on his muffled feet to the small closet he and Bailic had once found hidden under it. Here, among the cobwebs, he placed his pack. There was nothing in it that would help him now. Unencumbered, he began to ascend.

The ninth landing marked the base of the tower, and it was here that Meson stopped at the first of two doors. It was plain and unadorned, opening silently to his touch. Meson slipped inside and shut it behind him. The tall-ceilinged room was lit entirely from the enormous balcony jutting out to overlook the Hold's entrance. He recalled his teacher's rooms as being airy and bright. Now they were dingy, carrying the acrid smell of burnt metal. On a small table sat a teapot and two cups. Evidently his efforts to remain undetected during his search hadn't been as successful as he hoped.

"Meson," a mocking voice broke the hush. "I'm surprised. Rumor had it you became a farmer to cultivate turnips instead of wings." A shadow at the end of the room shifted. "As we both know, wings are notoriously difficult to tend. Tell me, are turnips any easier?"

Meson's unease blossomed into a thick apprehension at the scorn that cold, smooth voice carried. "Bailic." He gave him an incommunicative nod. "How is it that everyone is gone and you're in Talo-Toecan's rooms?"

"Suffice it to say he didn't require them anymore. But they do have a lovely view, don't you agree?" Bailic waved a thin hand to the balcony and turned to regard him.

Dressed in a Keeper's traditional tunic, short vest, and floor-length trousers, he cut a startling figure. He was refined-looking, not yet old, but thin with the sharp look of too many late springs spent in want. Though plains-born, only his height and spare frame would attest to it; his skin was a pale mockery of his true ancestry. As a boy, his severely short-cropped hair had been a transparent white. It had since darkened to a pale yellow. His eyes, too, lacked almost all pigment, and were so pallid, they were almost pink.

It had been this nonconformity that prompted Meson to take the awkward, half-starved, terribly nearsighted plainsman under his wing soon after Bailic arrived at the Hold. Meson had treated him like the brother he never had, and *after reaching an understanding thanks to a black eye and bloody nose, they had become nearly inseparable, banding together to fend off the pranks of rival students. But a great friendship can often turn into an even greater animosity. And so it happened between them over the oldest of reasons: the affections of a young woman.*

Bailic stood with his back to the window. Meson knew the glare was enough to trouble him. His weak eyes saw best when the light fell over his shoulders. "I see the years have been kind to you, old friend," Bailic said. "Perhaps I should have abandoned my duties as well."

Meson stepped closer, staring at the long, puckered scar running from Bailic's left eye and down his neck. "I said, where has everyone gone?" he demanded.

Bailic laughed, choking it back with a rough cough. Slowly he eased himself into a once plush, high-backed chair. His eyes never shifted from Meson. "Somehow," Bailic said sadly, "the Masters got it into their fancy to journey to find the lost colony."

"Lost colony?" Meson said as he recalled the tale they had concocted together as students. "That was a story. Everyone knew it was only a bit of nonsense to whittle away a long winter."

"True." A grin danced about Bailic's thin lips. "But when I 'found' your map of the island, they took it as a truth making itself known through you—the quick and clever Meson."

Meson stiffened, disguising his alarm by taking a step forward. He remembered now. Bailic had encouraged him to illustrate the tale, and he'd willingly obliged. The map had gone missing halfway through the winter. They'd still been friends then.

Seeing his confusion, Bailic sniffed. "My dear, innocent farmer, it takes but a small thing to spark a fatal interest among the bored centennials. At my subtle hints, they flitted away and drowned trying to find your island. How unfortunate," he mocked. "Your tale led nearly all of them to their deaths. You," he scorned, "emptied the Hold."

"No," Meson whispered, knowing it was probably true. But that didn't explain where the Keepers were. "Why?" he said, half to himself. "Why did you do this?"

"Because they wouldn't give it to me!" Bailic shouted. A trace of madness swirled to the forefront of Bailic's eyes, vanishing as he shuddered. Rising with an exaggerated care, Bailic stepped behind his chair to hide the almost imperceptible trembling of his fingers. "It must have been an oversight," he murmured. "One can only imagine?"

Bailic smiled brokenly. "My dear Meson," he crooned. "Did you come all this way empty-handed, or is there something you may have felt a need to return?"

Meson made his face a mask. There was only one thing Bailic could be speaking of. Thank the Hounds he had already hidden it. "Return what?" he asked softly.

"Come now," Bailic cajoled. "You're the only Keeper left. You must have it."

He blanched. All the Keepers dead? Not just gone? Bailic couldn't have killed everyone! "H-have what?" he stammered, feeling the first whispers of the Hold's truth ward rise up about him like hard snow swirling in a late-winter field, cold and unforgiving.

"Don't be foolish," Bailic said sharply. "Talo-Toecan gave the cursed thing to someone. I need it." He crept from behind his chair as if drawn by the thought of the book. "Have you seen the chaos of the foothills and plains lately? It's appalling. They have far too much freedom. They could accomplish so much if they would just swallow their pride and condescend to work together. You haven't noticed how their divided talents lend themselves perfectly to each other? No?" he mocked. "Talo-Toecan didn't either, and when I approached him about it, he forbade me from instigating any such plan. Forbade me!" Bailic caught himself with a steadying hand upon his chair. He took a slow breath.

"That was when I knew I had to do it on my own. All they need is someone to unify them under one rule—to properly guide them, you understand. I'm going to lead them to the future I foresee, even if it takes a war to do it." Shaking his head in mock remorse, Bailic chuckled. "Knowing them, it will. A good fight will teach them the value of solidarity if nothing else. But regardless, I can't control the situation unless I have the First Truth, and you aren't leaving until you tell me where it is."

Meson took a confident step forward. "You can't hold me here. You know that. What the Wolves is wrong with you?"

Waving a careless hand, Bailic gracefully sat before the tea. "Didn't notice when you came in, did you?" he almost sighed. "I worked long to hide the resonance so you wouldn't feel it. Talo-Toecan's doorsill has a ward on it. Unless I wish it, you can't pass the threshold." He leaned back deep into the cushions, smiling. "And I don't. You, my farmer, have caught yourself more securely than a mouse in one of your grain traps. Ripping the truth from you will be easy.

"True." Bailic leaned forward, lowering his voice. "I can't make a ward that subtle and strong. But it's a simple thing, is it not, to bend someone else's handiwork to one's own use?" Bailic looked up, his eyes almost glassy from his greed. "Once you know how?"

Meson took a shaky breath, knowing with an ugly certainty what was going to follow. The Hold's truth ward would force him to speak, and now he couldn't leave to avoid it as he had done before. The phrase "disturbing tendency to paranoia" flitted through him, a muffled comment overheard from behind closed doors when they both had been younger. Talo-Toecan had always dismissed the concerns of the other Masters, rationalizing them away, but now . . .

With a contrived carelessness, Bailic reached for the pot, and the soft, domestic sounds of tea being served filled the room. "After you left, I began my work. A word here, an idea planted there. Soon the Keepers began to leave. Those who refused to be swayed, disappeared. It was really quite disturbing," he said lightly as he set the pot down with a surprising gentleness. "No one could find them. Our benevolent teachers were next." He hummed a regretful tune, sipping at his cup. "All in a watery grave trying to find an island that only existed in your thoughts. The wandering Keepers returned one by one, and one by one they died. It took some time, learning which wards can be easily countered and which ones can't. I'm quite good at those now." He sighed in an easy memory. "You haven't a chance."

A small chortle escaped Bailic, and he choked it back. Setting his cup down, he gestured grandly for Meson to join him, frowning when he didn't move.

Meson tensed, his eyebrows tight. "I'll take out the ward on the door," he threatened.

Bailic laughed. "Try," he crooned. "I can't remove a ward that strong. It was all I could do to bend it to my will. And even if you could, I would simply follow you home. What a splendid idea," he said, simpering. "Family reunions are so-o-o-o endearing."

Meson nearly groaned in despair. The book would be safe, but his family. . . . What did a book mean? Nothing. Escaping Bailic wasn't a victory but a postponement of defeat.

"Your precious Talo-Toecan," Bailic said, "finally got over his sulk and came back."

"He's alive!" Meson cried.

"Yes, alive but quite useless." Bailic rose and strode to the mantel. His fingers drummed together, a nervous habit Meson remembered from their youth. "He's . . . He won't get out," Bailic said stiffly. "I bested him. He can't. It's impossible."

Seeing Bailic standing in his tight panic, Meson finally understood. "By the Wolves," he breathed. "You don't want the book for its wisdom. You want it for protection. You're afraid of him! You killed everyone in the Hold over a book for protection you don't even need!"

"I am not afraid of him!" Bailic shouted, his eyes large and wild. "I'm not afraid of Talo-Toecan! I bested him. Did I tell you that? He surprised me, coming in through the window. But I tricked him, tricked him soundly, and now he's no threat to me." He glared fiercely at Meson, daring him to call him on his slip. Slowly he forced his clenched hand down and away from his scar. "No threat to my plans, I mean."

Meson stared at him. It was worse than he could have imagined. "What happened, Bailic?" he whispered. "This is insane."

"So what!" Bailic strode to the table and snatched up his tea. "I'll be alive when the sun sets tonight. Will you?"

Meson's chest tightened. He had to get out. Edging backward, his fingertips brushed against the door. His breath escaped in a pained hiss from the strength of the warning he only now recognized. Bailic was going to question him, not stopping until every last scrap of lore was ripped away, including his most precious secret playing at home before the fire. "Alissa," he breathed. All thoughts of the book vanished with a gut-wrenching chill. His Alissa would be coming. As a latent Keeper, nothing could stop her, and all she would find here would be Bailic.

The thought of his child caught in Bailic's devices kindled within him a rage fueled by fear and helplessness. Instinctively he set his thoughts to a ward of destruction and lunged. Too late he learned Bailic had been watching and was ready.

The air shattered with a sharp crack! as Meson's ward was nullified—its energy set to burn and entangle, turned to that of sound. Meson found himself paralyzed, having flung himself into Bailic's ward. His momentum propelled him into the table. He hit the floor in a crash of pottery and splintering wood.

Meson cleaved the ward from him, feeling it fall away with the cooling sensation of rain. He lay gasping, clutching his shoulder. Smooth, uncallused hands pulled him up, throwing him, stunned, into a bookcase. "No!" he heard himself scream as fire lanced through his mind. Bailic had thrown him against a ward of his teacher's making. It had been created to guard his books, but it was capable of far more. Agony sang through his mind as it tried to channel the devastating mass of power. He felt his tracings begin to melt to slag, unable to contain the force running through them.

Meson never realized he fell, but suddenly the cold rock was there, soothing his cheek.

"You're the only one left!" Bailic screamed, and a foot slammed into Meson, doubling him up. The salty taste of his blood trickled over his tongue. Again he was pulled up, hearing in his breathing the beginnings of a terrifying gurgle. Something had broken within him. The pain was spotting his sight; he could hardly see Bailic's rage, a hand's width from his eyes. "You must have it," Bailic demanded. "I want it now!"

"I hid it," Meson gasped, struggling to keep his thoughts from where. If he couldn't remember, the Hold's ward couldn't force him to tell. "You'll never find it."

"Aarrrgh!" Bailic cried, throwing him out onto the balcony and into the sun. Meson struck the thick railing, a groan slipping from him. His hands scrabbled for a hold as he strove to pull himself up, to think, to form a ward, anything. But the pain in his chest and the agony in his mind was all there was.

A small part of him realized Bailic was quiet. Meson sprawled awkwardly, focused on keeping his rasping breath moving in and out. Slowly he looked up, seeing Bailic standing tight to the shadow's edge, unwilling to chance burning his skin, knowing he would have his answer whether he beat Meson into a senseless pulp or not. Meson's sight darkened, then cleared as he pulled himself into a crouch, and from there, to an unsteady stand.

"You made me lose my temper," Bailic said stiffly, wiping the sheen of sweat from under his chin with the back of his hand. "That shouldn't have happened."

"No?" Meson wheezed. "Neither of us seem to be having a very good day."

Bailic half turned as if in dismissal, then spun back, his eyes wild. Meson gasped as Bailic's field formed about him, but he was helpless, his tracings burned to ash. He tensed, only to cry out at the cessation of pain. It was a ward of displacement to prevent his mind from recognizing the hurts of his body.

As Meson straightened from his crouch, Bailic smiled patronizingly. He hadn't done it out of compassion but because he didn't want the pain to keep Meson from talking. Even escape by way of his own suffering would be denied him. Bailic had him—body, but not soul. There was a way out. He had a choice—there was always a choice—he just didn't like it.

Meson turned, trying to keep his breathing shallow as he felt his ribs grate. With a sick feeling, he flicked a glance over the edge, spasmodically clutching the railing in a white-knuckled fervor. The wall dropped nine stories in a sheer expanse of stone. But he couldn't jump. To jump would deny him any chance to take Bailic with him.

"Come now, Meson," Bailic cajoled from the edge of the shadows. "I followed your thoughts through every corner of the Hold and pastures. It's here somewhere. You will tell me."

The force of Bailic using his name was a strong compulsion, and Meson began to sweat with fighting it. Unseen, the strength of the Hold rose, thick and cloying, the scent of ice and snow. The scent of truth, of death.

"Meson," Bailic said tensely, seeing him glance past the edge. "Don't be a fool. The fall will kill you more certainly than I. Where," he thundered, "is the First Truth*!"*

Black and cold, Meson's thoughts swirled. Nothing could stop Alissa from coming. But perhaps he could even the odds. He had to believe she would survive given a chance, and that was something he could still give her. She would find the book where he hid it—he wouldn't be here now if she couldn't—but to give her that chance, he had to summon the strength to do the impossible. He must shatter the Masters' truth ward.

The attempt would trigger the Hold's safeguards and cost him his life, but he was already dead. He couldn't let Bailic trap Alissa like he had been. Meson, too, could use the Hold's wards for his benefit. But where would he find the strength to break what a Master created?

He would have to find it, he decided. For the love of his child, he would have to. And with that, he knew. Here at the end of all, he recognized the only entity stronger than any ward, than any Master. And Bailic had none of it, not even for himself.

Bailic watched and waited, sending his elegant laughter to mock him, sure of his victory.

With a muffled groan, Meson grabbed the rail and looked down. A single tear fell, and he watched it vanish from view. "Oh, Alissa," he whispered, "I'm truly sorry. Rema, you deserve so much more." He turned, trembling. Bailic's laughter cut off sharply upon seeing Meson's face soften with an emotion that Bailic could only link to betrayal.

Standing on the balcony, bathed in the warm sun of his mountains, Meson remembered his wife: her joyous abandonment to an early spring morning, her dark whispers in the twilight, the sly smiles when she thought he couldn't see, and then his daughter, instigated by one of those smiles. His child, who delivered his lunch late and half-eaten, knowing he would understand how long the trek had been and forgive her. She, who would fall asleep in his arms to the soft alternating rumble and murmur of her parents' voices in the late dusk of summer. She, who would bring him injured crickets and mice for his inspection and treatment, knowing he could do anything, anything at all, because he was her papa.

All these things he drew close, wrapping them about himself in his thoughts as if they were a mantle of grace, and when he had them both so close, he could almost smell the hot, meadowy sun in their hair, he looked at Bailic, startling him to stillness with the enchanted look in his eyes.

In a clear, centered voice, Meson uttered a single word. "No."

There was a heart-stopping crack. With a terrifying shudder, the balcony collapsed itself in a vain effort to stop Meson's solitary word of defiance. But it was too late. The word had been spoken. The truth ward was shattered, overcome by a force stronger than the truth.

"Stop!" he heard Bailic scream as he lunged to the balcony in a futile attempt to snatch Meson even as he fell. Meson's last sight was of Bailic, but his last thought was of his Alissa. His child had a chance, and sometimes that was the best a papa could do.

You were wrong, Talo-Toecan, he mused as the bare moment before he struck the ground seemed to stretch to infinity. There is a force more potent than that wrought by the mind—that of the heart.

11

Strell watched in astonishment as Alissa turned ashen, blinked twice, and collapsed where she sat. Startled, he simply gaped at her. "Alissa?" he said, leaning forward to give her a shake.

A sudden flurry of wings and beak drove him back.

"Hey!" he shouted. "Daft bird. What the Wolves is wrong with you?"

Hissing like an angry cat, Talon landed next to her mistress's outstretched hand. Strell leaned back, and the bird's warning turned into a worried chitter. "I just want to see if she's all right," he muttered. Slowly he stretched toward Alissa again, his eyes tight to the bird.

Talon began to keen eerily, and he withdrew. He had felt the sting behind her small beak and claws, and was in no hurry to repeat it, not with Alissa unable to stop her. Sinking back on his heels, he grimaced at the tiny predator, not liking to admit he was afraid of something so small.

Alissa didn't look like she was in immediate danger: She was breathing, her skin was again its normal color, there were no convulsions, and she hadn't shown any sign of pain before passing out. And it wasn't anything he had put in their dinner. He had grown up gleaning the desert for food. Finding it in a verdant valley was second nature after his years of travel. The foothills people were wasteful, not eating a third of what was available. She hadn't eaten anything, picky little foothills girl that she was. She probably collapsed from exhaustion. She had no business being out here.

But he couldn't just leave her lying there all twisted and askew.

Strell's eyes slid from the girl to the dark sky. She had better be all right. He wasn't about to cart her out of here, though he might make better time if she were unconscious, seeing as he wouldn't have to listen to her incessant prattle. It was a wonder she ever had any breath for walking. Her mouth never seemed to stop.

He blinked, suddenly realizing Talon was stalking a line between him and Alissa. "Now look, bird," he said with a confidence he didn't feel. "I want to see if she's all right." Despite the odd, unbirdlike growl coming from the kestrel, Strell stretched his hand out. Again there was a whirl of wings. Glowering, he put his knuckle to his mouth. It was throbbing dully, and he wasn't surprised to find it was bleeding from a small scratch. Clearly he would have to win over the bird before he could touch Alissa.

Crouched on his heels, he thought for a moment, then with a soft grunt, he turned to find his dried meat. He had made friends with aggressive dogs in the past. Charming a silly little bird couldn't be any harder. "Hush," he crooned as he had seen Alissa do, reddening in embarrassment. "Have some meat. I won't be eating much of it anymore. Alissa makes such a face when I do." Strell awkwardly extended a piece of meat, and Talon cocked her head. "Hurry up, bird," he whispered, risking a worried glance at Alissa. "Take the meat."

The bird eyed him, then the meat. Temptation became too much, and she cautiously extended her neck and took the tidbit.

"There." Strell sighed in relief, glancing at Alissa. "That wasn't so bad." Shifting closer, he tried once more. This piece was accepted as well, and he continued until, faster than he would have believed possible, he had a plump, content kestrel pinching his hastily cloth-wrapped hand. Strell ran a tentative finger over her markings grayed with age, marveling at the feel of having a piece of the wind perched on his wrist, even if it wasn't his to claim. Then he chuckled, dismissing the odd thought. "I'm glad I'm not the only one who thinks with his stomach," he murmured as he put the bird on the stack of wood and turned to Alissa.

Watching the kestrel for any hint of attack, he tried shaking Alissa, then shouting, all to no effect. Only when Talon chittered a warning as he prepared to douse Alissa with the water sack did he admit defeat. Frowning, he drew her blanket over her and returned to his side of the fire.

His breath came out in a long, puzzled exhalation as he sat. Pulling his pack to him, he dug to find his grandfather's pipe. He pulled it out and unwrapped it, hesitating as he recalled Alissa's unvoiced doubt when he confessed playing it gave him a headache. Not liking how her disbelief had made him feel, he rewrapped it and jammed the pipe deep into his pack. He took up his other instrument instead, polishing it as he stared across the fire at Alissa.

By the Wolves, he thought. What was he supposed to do now? What if she was sick? But it seemed unlikely she was seriously ill. Alissa was fit and strong, and he had never known anyone to heal as astonishingly fast as she did. Her ankle, for instance, should still be too tender to walk on, much less nearly keep up with his pace. But if it was only exhaustion, he should have been able to ge some response from her.

Finished with his polishing, he blew into his pipe. The single note slipped into the evening's mist, shaming the crickets and clattering leaves to a temporary, respectful silence. Talon shifted her feathers in a pleasant hush. "Like that, eh?" Strell leaned to ruffle her feathers. Despite his better judgement, he was beginning to like the little beast.

Strell seldom practiced without a paying audience, but tonight, curious as to how far his still-tender hand would stretch, he was reluctant to put his pipe away. "How about that tune your mistress taught me from across the valley and under raku wings?" he mused, delighting in the head bob Talon made as if she understood him. Carefully, until he knew his limits, Strell reconstructed the melody, finding it easier now that his thoughts had mulled it over.

Soft at first, then even softer, Strell's breath slipped into the rising damp, a vanguard for his wanderlust soul, sending it out with his music, feeling as if it became the mist somehow as soon as it left the circle of light his fire cast. Within him stirred a hushed restlessness, a need to rise, to go. There was a quiet acceptance of loss, an unsettling need for something unknown. He would have to be careful when he performed it, or he would lose his audience. It made him want to wander, to search. It was disturbing. Strell liked it.

He began to modify the tune, shifting notes until he found something better. The results of his tinkering pleased him immensely. The tune had begun odd, but now it was downright eerie. With uncertain descents and unexpected rhythm shifts, he expunged everything but the desperate need to fulfill and become. He shivered, cold for the first time in months.

Strell reached the end and began a third time. He had played it once to learn it, once to modify it, and now he wanted to play it for himself. Captivated by the music, he hardly noticed Talon had become alert and tense, and the crickets had stopped their incessant chorus. He sounded the last desire-filled note and lowered his instrument, rubbing his palm and sighing wistfully. It had been a most satisfying exercise, and he was sorry to end it.

"That was very close to the original, Piper. You seem to have a knack for putting a tune back to its beginnings," came Alissa's voice, sounding unnaturally strong and articulate.

The pipe slipped from his fingers and Strell half rose. He had forgotten she was there. "Alissa?" he breathed, for her accent was strange, even for her. Talon began to hiss.

"No," she sighed, sitting up and blinking at him owlishly. "Alissa is otherwise occupied."

Strell dropped heavily to his seat. Alissa looked decidedly wrong. Her brow was furrowed, and her jaw had an unusual tightness to it. Though never clumsy, Alissa now moved with a smooth, controlled grace he had never seen in her before.

"Restrain that bird before she hurts herself," Alissa said, her blanket slipping from her to pool about her crossed legs as she sat with a ramrod straightness.

Strell unthinkingly reached for the kestrel, earning a new gash on his hand. Quickly he wrapped his hand back in the cloth and gripped Talon's feet, wishing she had jesses. Talon, weaving her head and sputtering, never noticed her new perch.

"A-Alissa?" he stammered. "You passed out. Are you all right?"

She harrumphed, shocking Strell with the rude sound. "I told you, I'm not Alissa. But seeing as I'm useless at the moment, you can call me that."

"The Wolves take me," Strell whispered in sudden understanding. "She's sunstruck."

Alissa's eyes narrowed. "Alissa isn't insane. Trust in that—always," she said, pointing a finger at him. She pulled her hand close to her nose, watching her fingers as she slowly opened and closed her hand, seemingly fascinated by the simple act. "But I thought plainsmen were made of stronger stuff that what you're showing," she said softly. "Catch your wind under you. I gave you a name to call me."

Strell raised a placating hand to the heavens in frustration. "I don't believe this. The little dirt-farmer is sunstruck!"

Ire crossed Alissa's face for a fleeting moment, then, ignoring his outburst, she calmly asked, "Do you have a bit of mirror about you? I haven't seen Alissa since her second season."

"What did I do to deserve this?" Strell shouted to the sky. "Halfway into the mountains before I find out she's mad. I should have known something was wrong when this ignorant bird"—he gave Talon a little shake to try and get her to be still—"attacked me."

"No mirror?" Alissa sighed dramatically. "Pity. Did her eyes remain blue?" She sent her gaze disapprovingly over her attire. "Or did they darken to that absurd shade of her father's?"

Alissa's words finally penetrated, and Strell's mouth shut with a snap. Even in her dreams Alissa wouldn't call herself Useless, and she certainly wouldn't sit calmly by as he shouted insults about her. And Talon was ready to tear her eyes out. Whoever that was, frowning at the tuft of red fur stuck in his old hat, it wasn't Alissa.

Slowly he edged back, ignoring Talon's violent efforts to fly at her mistress. He had always dismissed tales of possession as fantasy, but it seemed all wagers were off tonight. "Useless?" he whispered, and Alissa inclined her head, amusement dancing about her. It was a decidedly masculine greeting, and Strell swallowed hard. "Her eyes are gray in the sun," he said. "Where's Alissa?"

"Burn me to ash, I was afraid of that." Useless sighed. "No matter. He won't see them. She is to turn around and go home."

"Where is Alissa?" Strell demanded, refusing to let his panic gain a foothold.

Useless reached for a stick and rearranged the fire, sending Alissa's fingers perilously close to the flames. Giving a sharp gasp, he snatched Alissa's hand back, looking betrayed. "I told you," he mumbled around the fingers stuck in her mouth. "She's occupied."

"Occupied as in busy, or occupied as in taken over?" Strell said wildly.

"Right," Useless said, eyeing the mild burn with an obvious disgust.

Talon was hissing like a teapot, pinching so hard, she almost drew blood. Wondering if he should just throw a blanket over the bird and be done with it, Strell shouted, "Well, which is it?"

Useless glanced at him through narrowed eyes. "Don't be getting above yourself, my good minstrel. Or I'll sear you as easily as I could that bird."

Strell forced himself to unclench his fist. Talon's screeching dropped to a skin-crawling growl, no doubt responding to Strell's less aggressive posture.

"Oh, don't be foolish," Useless said, frowning at the hole in Alissa's stocking. "I wouldn't burn you. It's a wonder I located you at all. You may rest assured, mender of misplayed melodies, that only when Alissa's thoughts are in the past, may *useless* thoughts enter."

Strell winced. "Is that useless as in inconsequential, or Useless as in your thoughts?"

"Right again." Useless twitched Alissa's face into a wry smile. "Alissa will wake come sunup. I was simply making sure she was secure as she tripped the lines. I'll admit it pleases me she has found someone other than that ill-tempered sparrow to watch over her. I wouldn't have spoken up, but your ancient song was ever one to charm the savage heart. Remember it well, it's been long since it was played correctly."

"Tripped the lines?" Strell said wildly, terrified the conversation might be ending, and terrified it might not be.

Gruff, but with an undertone of sympathy, Useless said, "The reasonings would take more time than we have tonight. Suffice to say that when she wakes, you will take Alissa to her home."

"I'm not taking her home," Strell said. "I won't overwinter in the plains, and the passes will be closed if I have to backtrack."

Useless fixed him with a withering gaze. "I—do—not—care. You will take her home."

Strell's brow furrowed. His panic ebbed, tempered by a grudging hatred of being dictated to. He carried a chartered name. He didn't take orders from any but his father. And if this Useless didn't like it, he could just scratch for sand fleas.

"Now isn't—er—the best time for me to take on a student," Useless was saying, color showing on Alissa's cheeks. "I have sent her among the lines of time to relive the nightmare of her father's death, to frighten her away. Frankly, I'm surprised she's even coming. The pull should be too weak with only myself here."

"Her father's death?" Strell whispered, suddenly cold at the thought.

"I regret the necessity of such harsh wisdom," Useless said, Alissa's stiff posture slumping for the first time. "But it's for her own benefit. She must not continue. The experience should be enough to send her scurrying home in time for supper."

"Not a good time to take on a student. . . ." Strell frowned, then his eyes brightened in understanding. "You're at the Hold."

"She told you of the Hold!" Useless cried, then settled back. "Aye," he said sourly. "I'm here, trapped by a seditious Keeper who deems himself more than he is."

"Well, that's where we're going," Strell said cautiously. Something about Useless's words was giving him the feeling of a clammy noose slipping about his neck. "We can free you, maybe."

"No." Useless sighed, sending Alissa's bangs to dance in her exhaled breath. "Freeing me is a grand thought, but the task is beyond both of you. Even my jailer cannot loose me—if he dared. Just take her home. She can come back when Bailic is no longer of importance. He's getting old. There can't be many years left in him." Useless frowned, pinching Alissa's face into a mask of pain. "I can't allow myself to believe they're all gone. Someone must be left. Someone who can free me. Perhaps they're waiting him out, letting my imprisonment be my penance for allowing such a thing to happen."

"Bailic?" Strell said, feeling the noose tighten. "Who's Bailic?"

Alissa stiffened, and Strell drew back as a wave of fury and hatred washed over her, looking terrifyingly wrong. She shuddered violently, and Useless regained his calm control.

"Bailic?" he murmured. "He's the one who deceived me.

He's the one who sent my kin to their deaths in the name of search. He's the one who systematically committed genocide upon all the Keepers and students. If he realizes who Alissa's sire is, he will slaughter her, too. It will be done out of vengeance, if not for his fear of her potential Keeper status." Useless shook Alissa's head. "Something went wrong with that one. He's afraid. Why is he so afraid?"

Strell's breath came fast, and he began to shove things into his pack as if to leave right then. There it was, right in front of him, the rope he was going to hang himself with. "We can't go there now. It would be a sure death!"

Useless chuckled. "That's what I've been saying. Escort her home and you will be fine. Your only other choice is to destroy Bailic."

An icy wash broke upon him as he mouthed the words, "Destroy Bailic?" He tried to speak, but nothing came out. "Hold it!" Strell exclaimed. "What do you mean, 'destroy Bailic'? You said he's killed people. You expect *us* to get rid of Bailic when you couldn't?"

Useless gave Strell a dark look ripe with impatience and embarrassment. "No. I expect you to take her home. How many times do I have to say it."

"But—but how?" Strell stammered. "I'm just a piper, and Alissa is just—well—Alissa. She's a nice enough girl I suppose," he babbled. "But she won't harm anything. Hounds. She won't even let me eat meat anymore!"

"Take her *home*!" Useless thundered, and Strell winced. Even Talon jumped, her hissing cutting off with a startled peep. In the silence, a lone cricket chirped. Strell heard Useless sigh, and he looked up, his breath catching at wrongness pouring from Alissa. "Just take her home," Useless said quietly.

"What if she doesn't want to go?"

A canny eye focused upon him, then slid away. Useless settled Alissa as if for sleep, bunching the blanket up about her chin as she lay down close to the fire. "Then I expect you will die a miserable, degrading death," he said, and with a happy sigh, he shut Alissa's eyes.

Strell swallowed hard, not trusting Useless was gone. Slowly the crickets began to court the night again. His mind was swirling as he loosened his grip on Talon's feet. The ruffled bird dug in her claws until his eyes widened from the hurt. With a saucy flick of her tail, she leaped at Alissa.

"No!" Strell lunged to stop her attack, but tripped on a root and measured his length on the hard ground. "Oof!" he gasped as the wind was knocked out of him. Landing lightly, Talon looked back as if commenting on his lack of grace. She ran her bill through Alissa's still-damp hair, then, satisfied all was well, she hopped to his shoulder and hunched down for the night.

"Right," Strell wheezed from the ground. "You take the first watch."

There was a spat of chittering, and Talon went still.

Strell brushed the dirt from him and returned to his blankets. He stretched out on his bedroll with his eyes wide open, shifting his attention between the night and the lump that was Alissa. "Take her home, he says," Strell muttered. "I'm not taking her home, and I'm not going to the Hold anymore. I'm going to the coast. There's no reason for me to get involved in this. All I did was haul her out of a ditch. She can find her own way home."

Talon shifted her feathers. The small sound drew Strell's eyes and they settled upon Alissa. Her blanket had slipped, and she was clenched from the cold. Silently he rose and adjusted her cover. Neither the bird nor the girl stirred. For a long time he stood over her, watching the mist eddy to their fire like white shadows, only to dissolve from its warmth. "Oh, Alissa," he whispered, "what have you gotten me into?"

12

"Oh-h," Alissa groaned, pressing her fingers to her head and trying to shade her eyes from the sun. "Ah . . ."

she whined, quieter, as her head felt like it had nearly split apart. She managed to roll over, cracking her nose on the ground. Slivers of fire snaked down her spine.

The pain from her nose helped clear her head, or perhaps it was the smell of the mangled bird a finger's width from her nose, undoubtedly a gift from Talon. Whatever the reason, this time when she tried to move, all her muscles responded and she got into a sitting position.

It was a *bad* idea. The headache doubled its intensity and added a new dimension, nausea. With a desperate whimper, she buried her throbbing head between her knees.

"Alissa?" she heard faintly, followed by the sound of twigs snapping and rapid footsteps. "Alissa!" Strell shouted again, sliding to a halt just before crashing into her. "Are you all right?"

"Stop. . . . Oh, do stop!" she whispered, clenching her hands to her ears, and she nearly passed out from the throbbing waves of thick, muzzy agony that crashed over her.

"Alissa!" he shouted, shaking her. "It's you, isn't it?"

"Oh, just burn me now and get it over with," she groaned, wondering who else he thought might be sitting in their camp. Hounds, it even hurt to breathe. If only he would be still. "Stop," she croaked, trying to figure out why her head hadn't rolled off her shoulders yet.

"What's that?"

"Stop," she moaned, curling up into a tight ball.

"Stop what?"

Her voice barely audible even to herself, she rasped, "Stop—talking."

"Oh."

Finally it was quiet. Alissa stoically waited for things to improve. They couldn't possibly get any worse. As she wallowed in her private purgatory, she felt the oddest sensation, and almost so vague as to be imagined, a voice rumbled through her thoughts, *"Burn me to ash, I forgot. Here, impatient one. Let the excess energy flow thus, otherwise it will block your synapses like the fog blocks the morning sun."*

As if this wasn't surprising enough, Alissa caught a glimpse of a spiderweb-like structure glowing deep in her unconsciousness. Before she could form any conception beyond that, it seemed to wink out of existence taking her headache with it. The pain vanished, absolutely and completely vanished as if it had never existed. Not trusting it was really gone, Alissa blearily looked up to find Strell crouched on his side of the fire, warily watching her.

"Can I talk now?" he said, his eyes wide in worry.

"Uh-huh," she groaned, completely wrung out.

"Are you all right?" he whispered. He hadn't moved. It looked as if he was afraid to.

"I don't know," she said sourly as she uncurled her legs. They were terribly stiff. Her finger, she realized, had a blister. "My head hurt."

"Do—do you want me to find you some snails?"

Alissa looked up. "Snails?"

"For your headache."

Her eyes closed, and she tried not to shudder as she imagined what he intended to do with snails that might cure a headache. "No thanks. It's gone."

He gave her an incredulous grunt, and she nodded. "Yes. Just like that."

Strell settled back. "Ah," he said wisely, "it must be Useless."

"Useless?" Alissa frowned, and with the word echoing in her thoughts, it came back in a sudden implosion of memory. She had relived her papa's death!

Horror stricken, she looked to Strell, desperately wanting it to have only been a dream but knowing it wasn't. Her face went cold and her stomach twisted. Strell scrambled to his feet. "You're not going to do it again, are you!" he cried.

"Oh, Strell," she wailed. "He died to keep me a secret!" and then, with her arms wrapped tightly about her knees, she began to cry, right in front of him, not caring if the ill-mannered flatlander watched or not. There was a soft, hesitant touch on her shoulder and a whispered something. Up to then she might have been able to stop, but his slight show of compassion buried any hope of that, and Alissa clutched at him, pulling him down and sobbing all the harder.

She felt Strell stiffen, then relax. "Who died?" he asked softly, a hesitant hand touching her shoulder.

"My papa!" she cried into his shirt. It was rough against her scraped nose, smelling of hot sand and open spaces. "He left when I was five on one of his mapping trips. We didn't know what happened. He died," Alissa wailed, "so Bailic wouldn't know about *me*." There was another upsurge of tears, and it was some time before she realized Strell had asked her something. "What?" Alissa snuffed blearily up at him. He was kneeling beside her, his arms about her shoulders, keeping her connected to the Now so she wouldn't lose herself to the Then.

He smiled, running a thumb under her eye. "I said, 'so who doesn't find out about you?'"

"Bailic." She turned away. "He used to be my papa's friend."

"Your father was a Keeper of the Hold," Strell said quietly, almost to himself.

"Yes, he was." Alissa looked up in surprise. "How did you guess?"

Strell glanced uneasily to the west. "So, what do you know about him. Bailic, I mean."

Feeling the tightness of threatening tears, Alissa bit her lip and tried to make her voice even. "Bailic wanted the *First Truth*. My papa had it. Bailic tricked the Masters to their deaths for it, then systematically murdered the Keepers and students to discover who possessed it."

"The *First Truth*? What's that?"

"It's a . . ." Alissa, began, then shivered, surprised at the warm upwelling of emotion that filled her at the thought of it, a strong stirring of desire, seeming to be out of place. "It's a book," she whispered, her eyes distant and unseeing. "It's the pinnacle of the Masters' knowledge, given to my papa for safekeeping. I think it was the book I found before he left . . ." Alissa frowned. He couldn't have left because of that, could he? Putting the horrid thought out of her head, she turned to Strell. "So I figure it belongs to me until they ask for it back."

"But you said all the Masters were dead!"

She felt the ghost of a grin on her face. "That's right. All I have to do is find it. My papa said I could. We'll go to the Hold, I'll hunt it up, we leave, you show me the coast this winter, and I'll be home by early summer. What could be easier?" Alissa beamed up at him, her smile freezing as she realized she was nearly in his lap. Strell cleared his throat and loosened his hold.

At that moment, Talon landed in a nearby pine, something furry in her grip. She twittered in a pleased fashion at her catch as she turned to them, seeming to do a double take. The rodent fell forgotten to the moldering needles in a sodden thump. Raising her feathers, she began to hiss.

"Uh, maybe I should . . ." Strell awkwardly stood up.

"Yes," Alissa mumbled, red-faced, though they'd done nothing wrong. "I agree."

Talon dropped to the ground. Yowling as if moonstruck, she stalked toward Strell, a dangerous look in her avian eyes. Strell and Alissa looked blankly at each other, completely dumbfounded. Strell took a wary step back, which only seemed to add to the bird's rage.

"I'm—uh—going to take a walk," he muttered, and he beat a tactful retreat into the morning fog, snatching the empty water bag in passing. Talon watched him go, looking as satisfied as a bird can. Alissa thought that would be the end of it, but as soon as he was out of sight, Talon turned and flew at her.

"Hey!" Alissa shouted, hunching into a quick duck. Her mouth fell open in shock as Talon started scolding her. The bird jumped up and down on her prey, flapping her wings and screaming like the proverbial banshee. First on the mouse, then the bird, then the mouse again. She didn't eat them; she tore them to shreds. When they were scattered over the entire camp, she flew to the dwindling stack of firewood and appeared to deliberately turn her back on Alissa.

The camp went silent. Even the morning chatter of the birds had stilled, stunned by her tantrum. "Talon?" Alissa ventured, and the bird stiffened. "Fine!" Alissa said. "Be that way. He was only trying to help."

Talon turned, cocking her head and glaring as if she understood.

"You relive your papa's death and see if you handle it any better!" Alissa shouted. "I don't have the slightest idea what's going on, and when someone shows the smallest bit of sympathy, you turn into a suspicious nanny! Well, you can just stay on that stick. See if I care!" The tears pricked again, and she spun away to throw her bedroll together.

There was a familiar fluttering, and Talon landed on her wrist looking decidedly subdued. She had her mouse, or what was left of it, and tried to push it into Alissa's clenched fist. Immediately Alissa's anger softened. "That's all right," she said with a sigh, accepting the mangled thing. "You didn't know."

From behind them came a soft fall of footsteps, and Strell called hesitantly, "Is it safe?"

Alissa turned to give him a thin smile. "Yes, just don't expect an apology from her."

Talon stiffened, snatched her mouse, and retreated to the outskirts of the fog. Strell edged back into camp. He silently rummaged in his pack, avoiding Alissa's eyes. It was cold, and she shrugged into her coat, pulling her blanket up around her as she fussed with the fire.

Strell hesitated at the severed wing on his blanket, finally nudging it off. "What under the open skies . . ." he said.

"So, tell me . . ." she said simultaneously.

"You first," he offered, putting her mortar into the coals and filling it with fresh water.

Spotting her lovely, cream-colored boots, Alissa stretched to reach them, struggling to put them on without unwrapping from her blanket. "How long was I out?"

"Just last night. My turn. What was all that about?"

"You mean blacking out? I don't know. But it wasn't my fault," Alissa said defensively. "All I know is I dreamed a memory that was definitely my papa's."

"And it's never happened before?"

"No." Alissa watched the water still, feeling used somehow. She crumpled a travel cake into the bowl, and immediately it began to give off the wonderful smell of apples and nuts. Her thoughts went back to that peculiar dream she'd had the other morning of her papa. "Maybe one other time," she added.

Strell's distant eyes cleared into an unmistakable sympathy. "Want to tell me about it?"

She nodded. Much as it hurt, it would be best to tell him when she was all cried out. As they sat together in the chill morning mist waiting for their breakfast to moisten to an edible softness, she told him about the Hold and Bailic. Through the entire narrative, her thoughts kept returning to that book like bees to a honey tree. Several times Strell brought her wandering attention back as she puzzled over where the thing might be. Now, more than ever, she was determined to get to the Hold. She wanted that book. Bailic couldn't still be there. He'd have to be mad to stay in an empty fortress by himself for fourteen years.

"And your mother let you walk out into the mountains?" Strell exclaimed, handing Alissa her bowl of mush and sitting down beside her.

"She didn't let me. She made me."

Strell stared, and Alissa chuckled. She could understand his confusion. What kind of mother forces her daughter out of the house cold? The usual method involves a wedding. "That nice lady did no such thing," he finally managed.

"Did too. She said that those at the Hold could further my education, whatever that means. Perhaps she meant me becoming a Keeper." Alissa's eyes dropped and she traced a dismal circle in her breakfast with her spoon. "She didn't know the Hold was empty when she sent me away."

She hadn't known why Papa hadn't returned either, Alissa thought morosely.

"Magic?" Strell muttered. He started to shovel his breakfast, his eyes carefully averted.

"There's no such thing as magic," Alissa said quickly.

He glanced up. "Alissa, you saw your father's death. If that's not magic, what is it?"

"I don't know," she said, biting her lip.

Strell stopped chewing and looked up in alarm, "You aren't a shaduf, are you?"

Preoccupied with thoughts of her papa, Alissa shook her head.

"You saw your father's death! Isn't that what they do?"

Annoyed, she gave him a sharp look. "I'm not a shaduf," she said. "It runs in family lines. Mine are clean."

"But your temper—"

"My temper has nothing to do with it!" she shouted. "And the guild finds you right away to start training." Her eyes lowered. "And besides, the first thing a shaduf ever sees is his or her own death, not their papa's. I *relived* his death, not *foresaw* it." Depressed, Alissa pushed her bowl away. "And do you see even one scrap of blue on me?"

He solemnly shook his head. Shadufs always wore blue as a sign of their office; the deeper the blue, the stronger the skill. In reality it was a warning to get out of their way. The deeper the blue, the quicker you moved. They weren't very nice.

Strell's eyes got round. "Maybe you're a septhama!"

Alissa turned away in disgust. What a superstitious milksop, she thought.

"That's it, isn't it!" he cried, drawing back away from her. "Bone and Ash, have you been—doing your septhama thing? And never told me?"

She picked her bowl back up and ignored him. That was insulting. Doing your septhama thing, indeed. But he just sat there with his wide, alarmed eyes, looking at her as if she had a radish growing out of her head. "I thought you didn't believe in magic," she finally said.

"Magic, no. Ghosts?" He shuddered. "Yes."

"Look," she said patiently. "I'm not a septhama. Do you even know what they do?"

Strell shifted awkwardly. "Get rid of ghosts."

"Wrong. They modify the emotion left after a tragedy so it doesn't bother anyone."

"Yes. They get rid of ghosts."

"Strell," she cajoled, "a traumatic event makes an imprint on its surroundings. When an equal level of emotion is reached in the same place, even hundreds of years later, it sets up a resonance that acts like an echo, multiplying the force until people can see it. That's all it is."

"So you *are* a septhama."

Alissa rolled her eyes. "No. I read a book about it. All right?"

Still he sat uneasily. "There are no books on septhamas."

"There are at my house," she muttered, then sighed. "I'm not a septhama. I'm just me. No ghosts, no auras, no foreseeing the future, just me, a girl on her way to a mythical fortress." That sounded absolutely absurd, and Alissa sat and stewed, not knowing what to think anymore. To continue on to the Hold under the inane assumption that she was more than a simple farm girl was ludicrous, but yesterday she would have said the same thing about her papa. *He* hadn't been mad, and he truly believe he—Ashes. What was she thinking? Magic wasn't real.

But there in the tower, reliving her papa's thoughts, she had felt something . . .

Strell wiped his bowl clean and stood, shifting from foot to foot as he looked down at her. Slowly she looked up. "Um—Alissa?" he stammered. "It isn't empty. The Hold, I mean. Useless wants you to turn around and go back home."

Ever so carefully, Alissa set her spoon down. "Who?"

Strell's eyebrows rose. "Useless?"

She stared at him. "Who—is—Useless?"

"I thought you knew." Seeing her blank look, he shrugged. "I don't know either, but he's at the Hold, and he wants you to go home."

"Home!"

"Please, Alissa." Strell stepped back as she scrambled up. "Useless told me—uh—he talked through you when you blacked out—he said it's not safe. That you have to go home."

Watching Strell's anxious face, it suddenly all wove together and Alissa's jaw dropped. That's whom the voice in her head belonged to. She hadn't imagined it. "You're telling me someone who calls himself *Useless* has been poking about in my head, forcing me to relive my papa's death and using me to deliver his messages!"

Strell nodded somberly. "He wants you to go home."

"Well, if that doesn't hatch your hen's eggs!" Alissa started packing, tying the knots with a fierceness she knew she'd regret later. Inside she was shaking, but she wasn't going to let Strell know how scared she was. The idea that someone could make her pass out at will and speak with her voice was frightening. She didn't believe in magic. She wouldn't.

"Uh—Alissa? Just how set are you about going to this Hold?"

Her breath came quickly. She was going to the Hold. If he abandoned her on the trail, so be it, but she was going. Alissa didn't say a word, but continued shoving her things away. Strell watched, shifting nervously. "He's at the Hold," he finally said.

"Good. Then I can tell him what I think of him."

"Not Useless. Bailic."

"Bailic!" Alissa stared up, unable to hide the fear in her voice. "How do you know?"

Strell's eyes were full of worry. "Useless."

Alissa grew very still, pushing her fright down where she knew it would fester, keeping her awake at night. Taking a deep breath, she grabbed her pack and strode to the lake.

"He has Useless trapped somewhere." Strell was half jogging beside her. "Useless told me to take you home. I think I should. Or at least the coast."

Alissa continued forward, afraid if she stopped, her legs would give way. "Nobody tells me what to do," she said, hating the quaver in her voice. "And I'm not going home."

"Alissa." Strell grasped her arm, halting her. Eyes wide, she tugged it free. "Alissa, please. What can you do against Bailic?" His eyes flicked away. "It's too late to go home, but come with me to the coast. You'll be safe. No one will care what you look like there. But if Bailic finds out who your father is, he'll kill you, too."

"Then he'd better not find out," she whispered, turning away in apparent confidence, but she was far from it. She was going to the Hold. She had to have that book. It was hers, she kept telling herself. She wasn't going to have the only thing to remember her papa by be a stinky little bag of who-knew-what around her neck.

And yet, a part of her smelled the smoke from the 'ware fires. It almost seemed as if something was drawing her to the Hold. But by the Navigator's Hounds, it was only a book.

13

"Sand in the west will protect you best," Alissa heard Strell whisper as he blew his handful of dust at the setting sun. She had watched him carefully choose and place his sundry rocks and pebbles. Though he was very subtle about it—nudging a stone with the toe of his boot here, tightening a bootlace and dropping another there—the dust was rather obvious, and his eyes lowered at her questioning look. "I don't believe it really works," he muttered.

She nodded dismally and returned her attention to mending his old hat. Who was she to say anything? Her papa had been able to do magic. Sweet as potatoes, as Strell would have said.

Much earlier, after the usual loud and lengthy "discussion," Strell had chosen to stop at the base of three very large fir trees. Camp had gone up smoothly. Though having traveled together for only a short time, they had already settled into a comfortable routine. Strell would arrange the basics of the camp while Alissa looked for something to eat. He would then make dinner while she finished setting up. It worked well, and they weren't constantly in each other's way. More importantly, Alissa knew exactly what was in the pot.

And so, as the sky darkened and the soothing fog rose, they found themselves content before the fire. Alissa's back was against the largest tree, and she could feel the wind shift it from time to time. The chill deepened as the light faded, and Alissa worked steadily on Strell's nasty old hat. She found cold, like hunger, to be an excellent goad. She had meant it when she said he could have hers, but it looked ridiculous on him. If she could get his old one halfway decent, she was hoping he'd ask to trade back.

Strell was busy with fashioning a pair of jesses. It had taken him all afternoon to convince Alissa they were necessary, but she was again having second thoughts. He had already cut two narrow strips from his scrap cloth and was now trying to fasten them about her unruly bird's feet. Leather, he had claimed, would be better, but the only other practical source besides their coats was the map, and he wouldn't touch that.

"Come on, Talon," he coaxed. "You'll get used to them."

Talon pulled at the unfamiliar binding, biting neatly through the thin material. With a happy chitter, she held it up and gave it a vigorous shake. Enjoying the new game, she dropped it in Strell's lap, eager for him to tie it back on. "It's no use," he sighed as Alissa began to laugh. "She just keeps taking them off." He turned up the bottom hem of his coat and fingered it. Alissa could almost see the thoughts going through his mind. His coat was new, hers was obviously not.

"You're going to have to use *your* coat," she warned him. "I still think jesses are a bad idea. Talon flies free. She'll get tangled."

"It's jesses, or I throw a blanket over her if you black out again. I can't control her."

"Why?" Alissa set her work down to give him a wary look. "Does she go mad?"

"Uh—her claws are awfully sharp." Strell glanced sheepishly at the tender new skin on his hands, and Alissa nodded. Although the healing properties of her mother's salve were inversely proportional to its nauseating stench, pain was still pain.

"Well, I still think it's a bad idea," she said softly.

Strell took his duller knife from his pack, and not bothering to remove his coat, cut the hem free to slice two strips from the bottom. Shaking her head, Alissa bent over her work. *She* wasn't going to hem it back up for him.

"You know," she said, biting off a thread, "for someone who claims to be a minstrel, I haven't heard much music from you."

He gave her his usual grunt, smiling as he looked up. "I don't play when I'm alone."

Alissa gestured in confusion. "So who's alone?"

There was a moment of silence. "You're right," he said, sounding surprised. "I'm usually alone when I travel, so I naturally equate the two."

"Not me." Alissa looked up through the needles at the few stars not yet eclipsed by the nightly fog and sighed contentedly. "Talon has been with me every time I've gone off the farm."

"She must be a comfort," Strell murmured.

Puzzled over his tone, Alissa looked at him, unable to tell if he was being sarcastic or not. "Yes," Alissa said carefully, "she is."

Strell slowly let his breath out. "I've been thinking about your blackout. Do—do you think you can control what you learn when you're unconscious?"

Alissa set her work down to give his question her full attention. "I don't know." She thought back to when Useless showed her how to get rid of that mind-numbing headache. Clearly there was more potential here than at first glance. "Maybe."

"Do you think," he said, fidgeting with the fire, "you might learn something for me?"

"For you?" Alissa raised her eyebrows, wondering just where this was headed.

Strell glanced from her to his empty hands and back again. "I know it's foolish, but I've always wanted to know why I was 'encouraged' to seek my profession away from the family. I wouldn't even ask, but I have no other way of finding out now." His eyes dropped. "It's unheard of for a son to be excluded from the family trade, especially if it's a profitable one."

She stirred uneasily. "I don't know . . ."

"Do me this then," he said before she could refuse him outright. "Think about it? It might be a good way to see just how much control you have."

Put like that, it almost made sense. Almost. "And knowing why you aren't a potter is that important to you?"

"Listen." He leaned forward intently. "My entire family, as far back as can be recalled, has been trained in the craft. Ever since my grandfather Trook resettled in—in the ravine"—he swallowed hard—"no one has left the household. Even my aunts stayed. Their husbands were eager to learn the skills necessary to get by. For them, the opportunity for their children to carry a chartered name far outweighed the loss of their own inheritance."

Pausing, he shifted a log on the fire before it rolled out. "There's lots to do at a potter's stead besides spinning clay," he said softly. "There're pigments to grind, clay to dig, fuel to gather, kilns to tend. If nothing else, there's selling of our wares. Being born to it, I was assured a position regardless of how sorry my crafting was or how many brothers I had."

"How many were there?" Alissa asked, fascinated with this slice of plains culture.

"Five." Strell's face went still.

"Five!" she gasped. "In one house? And you were the youngest?"

"Youngest son. I had three sisters my junior, one senior."

"By the Navigator's puppies. Ten children in one house!" She picked her hat back up.

"No," Strell mumbled. "There were eleven of us at one time. I had an older brother who died of hills pox when I was six." Strell rose and edged away from the fire. "On second thought," he said, his eyes downcast, "why don't you forget the entire thing."

"Mmmm," Alissa said gently. He had just found out about their demise. Bringing them to the forefront of his thoughts probably wasn't wise. She watched in sympathy as his hunched form slowly moved out of the ring of light. For a moment she heard him snapping through the underbrush, then nothing. Talon flew after him in a smattering of feathers. Alissa's hand rose to stop her, but then dropped. The cheeky bird had cheered her up countless times. Perhaps Talon could ease Strell's thoughts a little.

Turning back to his old hat, she thought about what he had proposed. She had been a passive participant last time, but what if she could direct the situation? Deep in thought, she yanked her pack closer, looking for the blueberries left from dinner. By mutual agreement they had combined their stash of provisions into her bag. It was easier that way. She always got hungry before he did.

She dumped the berries into her bowl, promising to save

some for Strell. Settling herself against the tree with the
bowl in her lap, she cast her thoughts back to that morning.
Useless had said her headache was from a blockage across
her—what was it—synapses? He could have called them
windmills for all she cared. It had looked like a simple
enough task to divert the flow of shimmery force to the
proper path, if she could find that maze of lines.

Fumbling for another berry, Alissa closed her eyes, trying
to find that in-between area somewhere in her thoughts. But
the harder she tried, the more ridiculous it sounded. She gave
up, flushing. It had probably all been in her imagination anyway, she thought, leaning her head back against the tree with
a soft thump.

The push of the wind against the boughs was soothing,
and she smiled and shut her eyes again. It reminded her of
when she used to climb the pines behind the house for a better view of the western hills. She had spent almost an entire
fall up in those trees: scraping her palms, getting sap in her
hair—watching for Papa.

Alissa slumped in an unhappy memory, blanking her
mind of everything, unwilling to think about her papa right
now. She and her mother had come to the realization years
ago he must have died, but to know it, to *live it*, made the
hurt as fresh and new as that winter night when a sobbing,
frightened child figured out for herself that Papa wasn't
coming home this time.

"Nothing," Alissa whispered, willing all thoughts from
her with a slow, exhaled breath. "Empty." There was peace
to be found in the lack of thought. "Blackness." She sank
deep into herself, finding that practiced, still-point-of-ab-
sence that her mother taught Alissa to be when she was about
to lose her temper. Idly, Alissa noticed a thin whisper of a
glow. It skirted the edges of her mind's eye, not really there,
and she smiled at her fantasy, eagerly grasping at anything
that wasn't a reminder of her papa.

She let it grow. It blossomed from a smudge, to a smear,
until with a jolt she realized it was really there! Sunk deep in
her unconscious between her thoughts and reality was a luminescent silvery-golden sphere. Her eyes flew open, and it
was gone.

Alissa's breath caught and her heart pounded. It wasn't that glorious, spreading net she had glimpsed this morning. This was something different!

Realizing how this mental exploration worked, she again closed her eyes and unfocused her concentration. The entire process was similar to finding a dim star on a dark night. Look at the star directly and it can't be seen, but by shifting her focus a bit, she might spot it out of the corner of her eye. It took some effort, but soon she found the thin glow again. The light came from a thick tangle of lines weaving among themselves to form a hollow ball. It was the shell that was giving off the light. What, by her papa's ashes, was it, and why hadn't she seen it before?

By her papa's ashes? Alissa thought. Ashes? Or dust? She had never seen the sphere until her mother gave her that bag of dust. The Navigator knew she had spent enough time daydreaming before now to have seen it had it existed. The sphere and the bag of dust had to be one and the same.

It made perfect sense. Her papa wouldn't give her a smelly little bag of dust if it wasn't important.

Curious, Alissa took a pinpoint of thought and focused it upon the glowing sphere. In a trice she lost the entire thing: the sphere, the enclosing lines, even the vague impression of power at rest, were all gone. She bit back a sigh of annoyance and started over. It took a moment, but once she relaxed, the sphere came swimming into existence. With a small shove, she pushed her focus into it.

It was the snick of a key, a jolt of connection, as satisfying and certain as a butterfly bumping into her. Alissa gasped, wildly clamping down on an upwelling excitement. A strand of shimmering silk had shot from the sphere, racing through her thoughts in a graceful S-wave to slam to a startling stop.

Refusing to open her eyes, she stared, watching the glowing stuff pool up, spreading out like cracks in new ice. Her head began to throb, and with some surprise she recognized her headache from this morning. Now she was on familiar ground, and she mentally opened the path to release the force as Useless had. The ribbon of force, or thought perhaps, flowed back to the sphere in an elegant reflection of itself before disappearing back inside. A twisted, crossed loop flowed icily through her mind, forging a connection between her consciousness and the sphere.

"Oh!" she exclaimed in delight, and the grip on her focused impassivity shattered. She was back before the fire with a bowl of blueberries in her hands.

"If you're going to horde the food," came Strell's wry voice, "you should at least eat it."

Shocked, Alissa looked up, finding Strell sitting unnervingly close to her, eating a handful of berries. "How long have you been there?" she blurted, refusing to give in to her urge and shift herself away from him.

"Not long," he said slyly.

"I don't remember you sitting down."

"Didn't think you would." He grinned as if he knew something she didn't. "Well," he drawled, reaching over to take a berry from *her* bowl, "how did it go?"

"What?" she asked.

"How did it go?" he repeated. "Did you find out how to control your blackouts?" Smirking, he took another berry.

"Stop that!" she shouted, pulling the bowl close.

Talon opened her wings and shifted on the stack of firewood. Alissa didn't recall her return either. Her lips pursed in confusion, and Strell had the audacity to smile. He watched in evident delight as her scowl turned into a glare, and then he began to chuckle. "I'm not laughing at you," he asserted between guffaws.

"Would you be so kind," Alissa said tightly, "as to inform me how you got back into camp without my knowledge?"

Beaming, he said, "I walked."

Alissa made as if to throw the berries at him, and he raised his arms in mock fright. She never would, of course. She would eat them. Sometime. In the very near future. She hoped.

"Oh, all right," Strell said, relenting. A trace of worry crossed him. "I thought you had blacked out, but you were sitting up and Useless didn't—uh." He tried to disguise his shudder by stretching his shoulders. "You didn't answer me. I figured you were trying something."

Somewhat relieved, Alissa reached into her bowl to find

there were only three berries left. He had eaten them all. She stiffly extended the bowl. "Want the rest?"

"Yes," he grunted, and her eyes widened as he actually leaned over and took them.

"Why doesn't that surprise me?" she said under her breath. Her concentration must have been so deep that she lost sight of what was going on around her. She didn't like that. Not at all.

"So . . ." Strell twisted to reach Alissa's old floppy hat, and he handed it to her. It was filled with freshly picked blueberries. "What had your attention so tight that I could snitch food from you?"

Alissa's ire melted to a confusing mix of pleased embarrassment, and she fought to keep from blushing as she dumped half the berries into her bowl and passed the rest back. "I'm not sure what I did," she admitted. "You might say I made a link between something and nothing and back again. It surprised me. I lost it."

"Something and nothing, eh?" he teased, popping a berry in his mouth. "Think you could do it again?"

"What, now?"

"Yes. Now."

"Not if you're going to watch." Ashes, she thought, how embarrassing!

"Tell you what. I'll just go over there"—he pointed to his customary side of the fire—"and completely ignore you." He grinned, apparently finding something amusing in the idea.

Alissa frowned, not sure she could concentrate if she thought he might be watching.

"Oh, go ahead," he cajoled, taking the hat with the berries and shifting himself. "Unless you really want to wait until I'm asleep to try again?" Whistling a child's tune about three mice and their ill-fated excursion into a kitchen, he reached into his inner coat pocket and took out his pipe. True to his word, he ignored her and began to polish it.

She eyed him suspiciously, but it wasn't until he began to play a lullaby that she took a slow breath and closed her eyes, trusting him to keep his word. It was easier this time, and Alissa managed to retain the barest perception of camp as the sphere came swimming to the forefront of her thoughts. The individual ribbons of gold, yellow, and white that gave it shape were so intense, it was almost painful. Even more fascinating was that she couldn't focus upon the gaps between the strands. Her attention seemed to slide away.

But she could slip a thought between them, and as she listened to Strell's music, she did. Again the ribbon of force curved through her thoughts. The outgoing channel was open before the incoming flow had a chance to build and give her a headache. It was with great satisfaction that Alissa felt the force return smoothly back to where it had originated, making a crossed loop.

Now she was ready to try something new, but she had no idea where to start. Carefully she withdrew part of her attention from the glittering loop to focus back on her surroundings. Strell's playing and the hiss of the fire became obvious. She could almost feel the thick wool beneath her legs and the flickering, come-and-go warmth of the fire. Confident everything was as it should be, she set her attention back to the loop, hunting for that chaotic maze of lines she'd seen that morning.

As her focus centered into a relaxed still-point, the thin spiderweb of tracings she recalled drifted into existence. The bright glow of the sphere and crossed loop had distracted her from seeing it before. Being empty of anything, the thin lines were nearly impossible to see. They were a blue so dark as to be unseen against the absolute blackness of her mind, and if not for the thin gold tracing they were shot through with, she wouldn't be able to follow them. Sprawling in every conceivable way, they seemed to be solid from only one direction. The tracings touched one another and fragmented like the veins in a leaf, weaving a fantastic pattern in all directions with more junctures than there were stars.

The network was dark and cold, easily overshadowed by the bright glow from the crossed loop and sphere. Alissa studied it, trying to get a better sense of what under the Navigator's Hounds it was for. She was sure she could do *something* by directing the loop of force through the pathways, but which route did what? There were too many possibilities.

Begin with what you know, Lissy, her papa would say, so

with a mental shrug, she found the lines she used to eliminate her headache. She placed a drop of awareness there as a permanent dike to prevent that agony of a headache should she black out again. Terribly pleased, she smiled.

Her contentment was distressingly short-lived.

Waves of anger and surprise broke over her, shocking in their intimacy. They weren't her emotions, and suddenly frightened, she mended the opening she had created in the sphere. Her twisted loop emptied and grew dark in an unheard hiss. Alissa willed her consciousness back to the fire, becoming frantic when she found she couldn't. Someone was holding her in the nether place between her thoughts and reality, and that someone wasn't happy.

Something in her broke then. Anger, hot and potent, filled her. Not the anger of fear or frustration, but of being wronged and knowing there wasn't the slightest consideration she was aware of it. It was Useless. He shouldn't be here. He wouldn't stay. She would get him out!

Revulsion joined her anger, and as if in response, the glow about the sphere intensified. With a sudden, silent explosion, a wave of force shot from the sphere in a flat pulse, looking like a ripple spreading out from a thrown pebble. There was an unheard yelp of surprise and hurt.

"Bone and Ash!" she felt Useless say in her thoughts as he ducked behind a hastily constructed bubble of thought. *"Where the Wolves did that . . . Meson, you fool. You gave her that source? She's going to kill herself."*

Pleasure joined Alissa's anger, silky-smooth and seductive. She was not without recourse. She encouraged a second pulse, feeding her anger with the justification that he had no right to be here. This was hers and hers alone.

A second pulse shot out, seemingly more intense, more controlled. Again, the presence hid. *"Ashes,"* she heard him gasp. *"She's nearly incorporated the cursed thing. What the Wolves did Meson do, tie it over her cradle?"*

There was a tug on her awareness, as if someone yanked her attention in another direction. Immediately a thick blanket of glowing gold obscured the sphere. Alissa felt herself stiffen as she realized Useless was putting a barrier between her and her sphere.

"Hey!" she shrieked into her thoughts. *"What are you doing?"*

"I can . . . hear you," Useless stammered into her thoughts. Shock poured from him, so thick, her anger turned sluggish, overwhelmed by his emotion. *"Can you hear me?"*

"Of course I can hear you," Allisa thought hotly.

"Do you think I'm an idiot?"

Now confusion joined the thick slurry of their emotions. *"No, of course not."* He seemed so dazed, he had to turn to conversation as familiar ground. *"I just . . . No Keeper, much less a latent one, has ever heard me in this fashion before."*

"Get out," Alissa thought coldly, holding her temper just barely.

"Now, see here . . ." he said placatingly.

Furious beyond reason, her anger focused, sending out another pulse. It slammed into the barrier Useless had placed about her sphere, her outrage beating its strength ineffectively out on the golden shield. As if in response, a wave of vertigo shook her to her core, and she fought to keep her awareness intact. The dizziness ebbed, leaving only a frenzied outrage. He had walled her off from her sphere. How dare he!

Alissa flung a quick thought at his barrier to break it. *"No!"* she shrieked as icy hot flames shot from the shield to engulf her thoughts. It was the same pain that had destroyed her papa's mind, and she panicked. But the fire ebbed to nothing before the hurt became permanent. It was a warning, nothing more. She was left huddling within herself. Shock, hurt, and pain swirled through her, but Useless's satisfied huff burned them away like dross, leaving a bright and shiny rage. *"I said, 'get out,'"* Alissa thought at him.

"Child . . ." he said softly, but the emotion that flowed from him was pity, making her all the more angry.

"Get out!"

"Alissa, calm down," he cajoled. *"I've sealed off your source with a ward. Nothing can get in or out, and if you don't stop trying to fry me, you're going to burn your tracings to ash. I have every right to deny you access to your source until you know what you're doing. It was an accident*

that you possess one, and an even bigger misfortune you're cognizant of it."

"Get out!" There was a faint glow about her tracings. It grew, fed from her own spirit, taken from somewhere within, from her own strength, not the sphere's. In an instant, it filled her tracings. A pulse of force exploded in all directions. It lacked the focus the first had, but it was just as effective. Perhaps more so.

The resounding boom of silent thought left Useless shaken. *"Wolves, Alissa. Just listen for a moment."*

"Get out!" Another blistering hot thought shook him. Alissa's tracings were building up again, and she knew Useless saw it as well; he immediately seemed to fade.

"Fine," he seemed to snap. *"I'll leave. But listen to your slippery songsmith and go home. Give Bailic another fifteen years to choke out his last breath. Your instruction must wait until things are settled."* He hesitated. *"Don't bother coming back if you can't control yourself."*

"Fifteen years!" she cried, then, *"More settled! Don't you mean until someone gets you out of your cell?"* But he hadn't heard. He was halfway gone, taking his emotions of anger, surprise, annoyance, and irritation with him. Alissa's own emotions seemed weak and paltry by themselves. But there was something else he took with him, and she frowned as she realized it was amusement.

"Ashes. That went well," she seemed to hear him chuckle. *"How did she figure that out?"*

Quickly Alissa willed herself back to the fire and Strell. Opening her eyes, she blinked in confusion. First she thought the camp had been rearranged, but then realized she was standing on Strell's blankets, her finger pointing at him rather rudely. Talon was nowhere to be seen.

Strell was standing stiffly up against the tree she had been against. He was gripping his pipe with a white-knuckled strength. Alissa's berries had spilled in a cascade of blue upon the brown of her blanket, and the memory of her tracings seemed to put ribbons of gold connecting them until she shook off the last of her mental imagery. "Alissa?" Strell said hesitantly.

"Well, yes," she said, dropping her arm and wondering how she had gotten over there.

Immediately he relaxed. "You—uh—passed out," he said, his eyes dark with emotion, but he wasn't angry at her. "Again."

There was an awkward silence as they exchanged places, each ignoring that something had occurred that Alissa wasn't aware of. Silently she put the berries back into her bowl. Her fury at Useless had been frightening. She had never wanted to hurt anyone before. Now that it was over, it was embarrassing. "How long was I out?" she asked softly.

"A moment or two, but it seemed like forever."

Alissa glanced uneasily across the fire to where Strell sat, unusually still. His hands were empty, and that in itself was strange. Generally he was oiling this, cleaning that, or mending something else. Sitting there, he looked angry and frustrated.

She set her bowl down and sighed. "Useless talked to you?"

Strell nodded, his gaze firmly on the night. "If you want to call it that."

"He was angry?" she guessed.

He nodded again.

"Why? It's not your fault I won't go home."

Strell made a pile of needles with the toe of his boot. "Let's just say I'm beginning to feel like an unwelcome suitor from a poor family." He squashed his hill flat and looked up. "I know you won't, but please, won't you go the coast? Your mother wouldn't have sent you if she had known what happened."

Alissa bit her lip and dropped her eyes, and she heard Strell sigh. The rest of the evening was spent in silence, each on their own side of the fire doing nothing, lost in their respective thoughts they were reluctant to share. Talon returned as Alissa settled herself for sleep, startling both her and Strell with her abrupt entrance. Strell had told her that Talon didn't like Useless. Apparently she had left when he showed up. Now that she felt safe again, the small bird had returned. Alissa wished she could lose her apprehensions so easily.

Strell had long since collapsed on his bed, just staring up at the sky. Alissa, too, found sleep elusive. Slowly the mist deepened, and as she was drifting off, she turned to him and murmured, "It's not magic, Strell."

"I know," Strell said and was silent.

14

Alissa's feet hurt, but she'd let them fall off before admitting it to Strell. Ever since that hard frost two days ago, he had been setting an unreasonably fierce pace. Yesterday he had forced a march late into the dusk, ending it high in the pass to the next valley. Alissa had been too exhausted to start a fire, making it a miserable night, as the fog was unusually thick and clingy. Just before dawn, the mist turned into a light rain. She was awoken quite rudely by the dampness seeping into her bedroll. Despite her strident opinions otherwise, Strell refused to let her take the time to light a fire from the wet wood she found. They had left without a hot breakfast.

Needless to say, they were both out of sorts. Alissa's toes squished, and her boots pinched at every step, but she kept up with Strell's irate strides with a stoic desperation. Clearly he was worried about the rain—it meant autumn was full upon them—and Alissa thought this, more than anything else, was responsible for his sour mood. She was miserable but didn't want Strell to know, afraid he might think she was milksop.

They had nearly reached the floor of the next valley when Strell finally called for a halt. He stood ramrod straight in defiance of the rain, alternately squinting at the map and scowling into the fog. Alissa was exhausted and hungry, still carrying the fatigue of the previous day with her. She leaned heavily against a cold boulder, wiping a cold hand under her cold nose. The damp had seeped into her, making her achy and slow. "Terrible weather," she said, trying to break the silence in as inoffensive a manner as possible.

Strell said nothing. He had hardly said a word all day, and his mood was growing tiresome. Not even acknowledging she had spoken, he continued to glower at the map.

"The rain sure gets into everything, doesn't it?" she asked, trying again for some response.

Absorbed in his scrutinizing, Strell gave her a preoccupied, "M-m-m-m . . ."

Alissa grimaced in defeat and whistled for Talon. At least her bird would talk to her. Talon's gray shadow ghosted out of the rain from up ahead and landed upon her wrist. "Where have you spent your morning?" Alissa whispered, giving Talon a good scratch.

Soft and silky, Talon fluffed her feathers and chittered. Alissa breathed deep, taking in the smell of long, dusty afternoons spent in the hay. A frown passed over her. "Strell," she said tersely, "Talon's feathers are dry."

He turned to her with a frown. "So?"

"It just seems odd," she said. "We're dripping wet, and Talon is as dry as a summer day on the plains."

Starting, he came close to run a careful finger over Talon's markings. "You're right," he exclaimed. The frown he had worn all day softened as the bird chittered deep in her throat, enjoying the attention.

Catching Strell's eye, Alissa smiled hopefully. "Maybe her dry spot is big enough for all three of us. How about it, Talon? Show us where it is?" With an ease born from long practice, Alissa launched the kestrel into the soggy afternoon. Talon disappeared as quickly as she had come. Strell took a step to follow, hesitating when Alissa didn't move.

"Go ahead." She waved him on, not wanting him to see her limping. "My lace is loose. I'll catch you up." Talon's shelter couldn't be far; she had responded very fast to Alissa's whistle. Pretending to tie her lace, she waited until he was out of sight before lurching into painful motion.

Rounding the next outcrop, she spotted them beneath a good-sized ledge of stone. Strell had his head up for the first time all day. One hand supported Talon, the other was on his hip. He cut an unexpected figure, and Alissa blinked, realizing how different he was from the short farmers she had grown up avoiding. His head nearly brushed the ceiling of the shallow, open cave.

"Look at this!" he cried, gesturing with his free hand. There was a surprisingly large patch of dry earth. They would never find a better place to stop. There was even a fallen tree for a fire, only half of which was in the rain. "Let's eat here."

"Good," she said, clenching her teeth as she tried to walk without crinkling her face in pain. Strell shifted to make room as she came under the overhang, and she gratefully eased her pack off. Trying to hide the soreness of her feet, she slowly sank to her knees. If she wasn't careful, her heels were going to blister, and she was so tired, she wanted to cry.

Alissa stared out at the rain with a numb fatigue as Strell set Talon on the fallen tree. If it was up to Alissa, they would stay the night, but she knew Strell would object. She was tired of arguing with him. She never seemed to get her way. It was frustrating.

A contented sigh slipped from Strell as he sat down at the edge of the dampness. Taking his hat off, he hit it against the palm of his hand, trying to shake off the rain.

Maybe, she thought morosely, if she had a fire going, he might want to stay. Slowly, afraid of being noticed, Alissa tugged the dead tree farther in from the rain and began snapping the smaller branches into the proper size for a large fire.

"What are you doing?"

Alissa jumped. "Making a fire," she said softly. She felt her cheeks redden. She didn't want to argue. She just wanted to stop.

"We don't have time," Strell said, and her shoulders tightened. "Only a short break."

She swallowed hard, too weary to be angry. "I'm tired," she whispered. "I know we have to move faster now that the rains have begun. But if one of us gets sick, we are both likely to spend the rest of our very short lives out here halfway to nowhere." She felt the hot pricking of tears and hated herself for them, but she refused to cry from exhaustion. It was humiliating. "I want to stay and dry out our things," she said, working to keep her voice even. "I want a hot meal. I want to rest. All right?" She stared at the unlit fire. "You haven't said one nice thing to me all day, and I'm sick of it."

"Look, Alissa," Strell said tightly. "The weather has turned. We have to move as fast as possible. You know that."

Alissa sent her fingers to arrange her sticks, making room for the dry fluff in her pack to start the fire. Keeping her eyes lowered, she sighed. "I'm not going to move," she said with a quiet resolve. "And you can't make me."

Strell took a breath, and Alissa looked up. His jaw was clenched, and anger had hardened his eyes. She shrugged, too tired to argue, and Strell seemed to collapse with a slow exhalation. "You don't travel well, do you," he said in sudden understanding.

She dropped her gaze. "Not this long."

"All right," Strell said softly. "But we'll have to leave before the sun rises, rain or no."

Alissa looked up, thoroughly confused. "I thought you wanted to go."

Strell got to his feet with a soft groan, looking everywhere but at her. "I do, but it's the first time you ever disagreed with me without shouting. I'm not about to say no." He flashed a grin, and she flushed. "Besides," he finished, "you should put some oil on your boots before they get so wet, they start to leak."

"Yes. I suppose," she mumbled with a flush of guilt.

Strell stood at the edge of the overhang and put his hat back on.

"Where are you going?" she asked, surprised.

"Fungus," he said, striding out into the rain.

"Fungus?" she repeated, but he was already disappearing into the mist. She watched him go, mystified at his change of heart. She had been so sure he would get angry. This calm acceptance left her not knowing what to think.

"At least I don't have to walk anymore," Alissa said glumly to Talon, and the small bird chittered as if in agreement. Immediately Alissa turned her attention back to starting the fire. Now that she wasn't moving, the damp seemed to grip her all the more. The first hint of warmth was like a sunbeam, and she settled back, catching sight of her wet boots. Alissa glanced out past the overhang. Strell was nowhere in sight. Struggling, she tugged on the slimy laces, trying to loosen them. The heavy leather had darkened to a light brown, and it stuck to her like a second skin. Finally her boot came off with a sodden, sucking sound, taking her stocking with it. A small noise of disgust slipped from her, and she glanced at the rain, wanting to get the other boot off before Strell returned to see the mess she had made of her boots.

There was a rustling of wet leaves, and her head shot up. Panicking, she gave a final tug. The second boot popped off, and she hurriedly hid them behind her. Her feet were naked, and she tucked them under her, hoping he wouldn't notice.

"Fungus," he said, his eyes bright as he dropped a handful of mushrooms in Alissa's upturned hat. "There's more. I'll be back."

"Thanks, Strell," she said softly.

He glanced back before returning to the wet. The faint smile he wore made it obvious he knew she hadn't meant for the mushrooms. She watched him go, his back hunching in a sudden flurry of wind and rain. Rivulets were running from the wide brim of her old hat to his shoulders, and she felt a pang of guilt. Strell hated the rain, and she was the one making a fuss.

Their usual roles were reversed that afternoon. Strell hadn't wanted to stop, but once decided, he utilized the time to its utmost. By nightfall they were surrounded by piles of roots, late berries, and other woodsy stuff Strell assured her was edible. She had grown up in the outskirts of the mountains and was amazed at what Strell could find to eat. She wouldn't have given most of it a second glance. The fog was heavy and damp, making the night darker than it should be. It seemed to have encouraged the rain, and it pattered noisily upon the fallen leaves, beating them into a submissive brown. The earthy smell of the leaves was comforting in a way, not yet soured to the bitter decay they would greet the spring with. It mixed pleasantly with the musty smell of drying leather and wool. The night would have been unbearable if not for the overhang. Alissa couldn't help but smile as she worked steadily on the last bit of stitching on her hat. Her aches had disappeared with the warmth of the fire, and her mood was considerably lighter now that she knew they were from the weather and not an illness.

Strell was fussing about with her papa's map, having carefully unrolled it out on his blanket so it wouldn't get dirty. She watched, stifling a stab of envy. "Strell?" she said slowly, tugging her last three stitches tight. "How about a trade?"

He glanced up, his eyes glinting in amusement. "You've nothing worth this map, Alissa."

Pursing her lips, she wedged her needle through the leather. He sounded so much like a plainsmen at market, it was hard to forgive him. "How about my bowl? You said it was good."

His eyebrows rose in an infuriating mix of amusement and confidence. "Not that good."

"Why not?" she said defensively. "I've traded my work lots of times for cloth."

Strell leaned halfway across the fire and whispered, "I gave her a length of silk."

Dismay washed over Alissa. "How much silk?" she asked, not sure whether to be dismayed or proud that her papa's work was worth a scrap of silk.

"Enough to make a skirt—"

Alissa couldn't help her gasp.

"And a long-sleeved shirt," he added, grinning.

Astonished, Alissa set her work down and rubbed her eyes. Her papa's map was worth that much silk? She would never have enough to get it back.

"It was a good trade," Strell said, clearly pleased. "I think I made out the best."

"But you can't even read it," she protested.

"I know enough to use it," he said lightly, returning his attention to the map.

Alissa's lips pursed. "At least let me trade you something for her hair ribbon."

He didn't look up. "No."

"You have no use for it," she cried. Why was he being so difficult?

"You never can tell," he said softly, his eyes distant with an unvoiced thought. "She gave it to me as a token of her motherly affection. It keeps the map from unrolling. I'm keeping it. And besides, you don't need it. You're hair is shorter than the lowest plains' beggar's."

Alissa stiffened. Her hair was cut foothills, as her papa had liked it. She wasn't going to change it for *him*. But maybe . . . "If I let my hair grow long, will you trade it to me?"

"No."

"Why not!" It was practically a shout.

He shrugged. "If you want a hair ribbon, use the one your cup is tied with."

Alissa slumped in temporary defeat. Slowly she picked up her stitching. She would get that map. She could be patient, make something so fabulous, he would beg to trade. He could carry it for a while.

Strell slid closer, map in hand. "Alissa? What does this say?"

Curious, she glanced down. With a breathless thrill, she realized they were almost to the Hold. She was going to get her book, insane Keeper or not! She looked to where Strell was patiently pointing. "It says 'Deep Water,' and do you realize how close we are!"

His eyes dropped, and a sigh escaped him.

Alissa's smile fell. "All we have to do is find my book and leave," she said quickly.

Strell looked at her askance. "Bailic isn't just going to let you walk out with it."

"He will if he doesn't know I have it." She hesitated. "We should find Useless, too. Let him take care of Bailic." Alissa frowned, wondering if she really wanted to. Useless was a domineering, egotistical, ill-mannered idiot. He might think the book was his.

Strell was silent, his eyes on the rain. Finally he nodded, looking as eager as Alissa to find Useless. "Just how helpful," he muttered, "can someone be who calls himself Useless?" Sitting up straighter, he smiled, but it faded quickly, leaving her rather disconcerted. "Here," he said, pointing at the map. He was clearly trying to change the subject. "What does this say?" Strell pointed to an open area next to the Hold.

Squinting in the flickering light, Alissa read the tiny scratchings. " 'Grazing,' and this"—she pointed to the word next to it—"is 'Fields,' and that says 'The Hold.' "

"Really?" Strell bent closer. "They're all in that circle. What does that mean?"

Not bothering to look at the map, she made a tight knot of her thread and bit her needle free. "It means the fields and pastures are part of the Hold's environs."

Strell brought the map close to his nose, turning it sideways. "Are you sure?" he asked, and she nodded. "What about this one?" He pointed to a symbol just outside the Hold's circle. Alissa didn't recognize it, and had been hoping he wouldn't ask.

"I don't know," she admitted sheepishly.

"What do you mean, you don't know? You said you could read that stuff."

Alissa flushed. "It's a proper name. I won't know what it is until someone tells me."

Strell blinked. Embarrassed, she pulled the map closer. "If you want to get specific, that word means 'to be neither,' but this little mark"—she ran a finger over it—"means it's being used as a proper name. Until I hear someone say it, I won't know how to pronounce it."

He stared at her. "You don't know how to pronounce a name until someone tells you?"

"Yes, and I can't write a name until someone shows me what it looks like."

"Even if you know how to say it?" Strell asked incredulously.

She nodded, not liking the way he was looking at her.

"That's a daft way to write," he finally said.

Her eyes narrowed.

"Look here," he said, sliding close with the map, seemingly oblivious to her ire. "See here, how the trail bends back on itself like a slow river?"

Alissa glanced down. Strell had put himself closer than usual, and she felt awkward for him being so close. "Yes."

"I would be willing to wager we could eliminate two days of travel by leaving the trail and cutting across it here." He ran a long finger over his proposed plan, and Alissa puffed in doubt.

"If my papa detoured, there's a reason," she said shortly, going back to her sewing. She jabbed the needle through the leather, wishing he would back up but refusing to move herself.

"Maybe," Strell said. "But it looks to me as if he looped around to go through that neither place. I want to try cutting across. What do you think?"

"I think you ought to give me my papa's map if you can't read it and won't use it."

Strell glanced up, his face turning sly. "You know what?" he said, rolling up the map and edging away. "I don't think you can read at all. Not even that swirly stuff on *my* map."

Alissa's mouth fell open. "What?" she sputtered.

Grinning, he moved farther. "I think you're making the entire thing up. I don't think those squiggles mean anything."

"What about the berries the other day? I told you that's what the map said, and that's what we found."

He smiled indulgently. "Everybody knows berries grow thick on that side of the slope."

"But I said they would be blueberries!"

"Lucky guess."

Alissa stared as his smile grew wider. It was obvious he was teasing her, and it made her all the more frustrated. She fixed her attention on her sewing, desperately hoping he couldn't tell how much it bothered her, but she thought the white-knuckled grip she had on the rim of her hat and the sharp jabs as she stabbed with her needle gave it away.

He leaned around the fire, coming dangerously within reach. "Look, Alissa. See this?" He pointed to the map. "That's where the stars go in the daytime."

She ignored him.

"See here? Snails." He leaned back, adopting an important air. "For your headache."

Her jaw clenched.

"And this one here? See this word? That means you can't cross the river unless you catch a fish for the river spirits first."

Alissa gave him a slow look through narrowed eyes, but it only seemed to encourage him.

"And this one says wolves meet here on the full of the moon to dance by its light."

She glanced down. "It says 'Good Fishing.' Merchant."

"Merchant!" he cried, putting a hand dramatically to his chest. "Oh, you've wounded me to the quick with that." Grinning, he leaned closer. "Look." A finger pointed. "Here's where rakus go to learn to fly."

"Give me that," she exploded, lunging for the map.

"No you don't." Laughing, Strell scrambled out of reach. He rolled the map up, retied it with her mother's ribbon, and tucked it away. Talon seemed to chuckle, settling to doze in the ash-scented warmth of the fire. Alissa gave them both a dark look and returned to her sewing. Any other response would give Strell the idea that it bothered her—which it did.

Apparently deeming she was sufficiently harassed for the evening, Strell took out his pipe and ran through a bit of "Taykell's Adventure" to warm the wood up. The music mixed pleasantly with the dripping branches and the solitary, stalwart cricket. The poor thing sounded decidedly frantic, as if it, too, had noticed the morning frosts. Immediately Alissa softened, eagerly waiting for Strell's next tune.

Strell could sing, too, though it was seldom he sent his resonant voice to shock her with its startling presence. It was obvious he was well-suited for his chosen profession, and she envied him for that. He had a pleasant life before him, confidently making his way wherever he chose. All she had was an inane but steadily growing desire to get her hands on a book. She had no idea what she was doing out here. Their situations were in sharp contrast, but she was oddly content.

The past month had been grand. She was beginning to feel that Strell saw her as a friend despite their different up-bringings. She had always been held at arm's length by the villagers, and a friend was something she never had before or ever thought she would miss—until now.

Strell shifted to a slower-paced melody that Alissa recognized as the one he had been humming the last few days. When she had asked him about it yesterday, he'd muttered something about a new song and that he would stop if it bothered her. She made the mistake of telling him she didn't mind. He had taken that as permission to hum it almost every waking moment.

It had a soothing sound, though, and she felt her restless anticipation ease as she listened to it dip and swoop. It was quickly becoming her favorite, as it seemed to capture the very essence of the mountains they were traveling through. Strell hit a sour note and hesitated, playing the phrase again. Giving a grunt of dissatisfaction, he switched to a light, quick-paced song.

A gasp of vexation slipped from Alissa as she recognized it. It was a child's song regarding a spider in a rainstorm and the virtue of perseverance. Strell's music bobbled as he struggled to keep from laughing at her. "No more music tonight?" he said innocently, setting his pipe down. "How about a story instead? Have you heard the one of the farm girl who couldn't keep her sheep together?"

"Hush, Strell," she warned, putting her eyes back on her needle.

"No really. It's about this girl who—"

"I've heard it!" she exclaimed.

"Well, then . . ." He hesitated. "You tell one. How about the story you told me yesterday?"

"You mean about the raku who wanted to learn how to sail?"

Strell bobbed his head. "Yes. That one."

She stared at him. "I've told it to you twice."

"I'd never heard it until you told me. I'm not sure I have the nuances yet."

Nuances? she thought is disbelief. "It's just one of my papa's silly stories," she protested. "There're no nuances to it."

"Please?" he said, looking so wistful, Alissa sighed, wishing she had never suggested they exchange stories to make the nights pass faster. Secretly, though, she was pleased, and she settled herself to tell him again. As she reached to shift the fire back to light, a buzzing stirred the back of her skull, pulling her to a stiff alarm. It was Useless.

"Burn you to ash, Useless," she cried as her sight began to fade. "I will not be dragged about like this!" But she didn't know how to stop him, and she was pulled unwilling into the darkness. Deep in her thoughts, she sensed the first glittering crossed-loop already glowing. She hadn't done it. As Alissa watched, the better part of her tracings came to life as pathways and channels filled with the cool, hissing energy. She struggled, but the pull was too great, and the tracings began to fade as the blackout took hold. How dare he do this to her again!

Refusing to let Useless think she would meekly accept his mandates, Alissa set her thoughts upon Strell and his question, gambling that was all there was to it. If she had to black out, she would learn something *she* wanted to know, no matter how frivolous it might seem. Alissa relaxed her grip and slid easily into the memory. Her last conscious thought was of Strell and how upset he would be that they wouldn't get that early start he wanted.

From the vantage point of his wagon, Trook Hirdune polished his instrument, keeping a careful eye upon the chaos that was a foothills' market. The sun was low, just beginning to burn away the fog, and he pulled his coat closed. He wasn't used to the cold. A shiver took him, and he wasn't sure if it was from the damp, or that his survival or eventual starvation would be decided today. Trook could smell hunger close. It was hiding under his wagon like a cur.

Anxious his trip this deep into the foothills might be for naught, he scanned the crowd for a scrap of blue. It was insufferably noisy with a month's worth of commerce jammed into one day. Unlike most plainsmen, he didn't mind rubbing elbows with the short, sweaty, down-to-earth farmers smelling of sheep and grain. If it weren't for his new wife, he would be content to settle on the outskirts despite the low status it would confer upon him.

Trook ran a quick hand under his hat and through his hair

in worry. It was thinning already. He was going to lose it all, just like his grandfather, he thought in a bittersweet sadness. May he rest at last. Trook tugged his hat lower, shading his scandalous blue eyes. They gave evidence that somewhere in his past was the blood of the mountain folk who now surrounded him. It was never admitted in pleasant company, but behind his back he knew it was gossiped that his nonconformity was at the root of his current misfortune.

A blue-robed figure broke through the throng to vanish behind a display of rugs. Trook started, feeling his chest tighten. A shaduf. Jumping to his feet, he hurriedly tucked his pipe into his belt, shouted to his unhappy wife that he would be back, and slipped over the side of the wagon. His height gave him a clear advantage, and he had no trouble tracking the hooded man over the shorter farmers. The streets were busy at this hour, and his fast, long-legged gait earned him angry stares as he hurried to catch up. Finally he was close enough to be heard, and he called, "Please wait. . . . Excuse me! I have a question."

The figure turned. Trook blinked in surprise as their eyes met. It was a woman. A single finger beckoned, and he followed her to an abandoned wagon. The cart was covered, indicating its contents had already been sold.

Silently the shaduf regarded Trook. He couldn't tell if she was a well-preserved old woman or a young woman prematurely worn down by a hard life. It was difficult to guess what was concealed under the robes she wore, but they lent a grace that was undeniably attractive. She wasn't tall enough for a proper plainsmen or short enough to be from the hills, and her eyes were a neutral hazel. There was no way to know where she had originally come from, but this, too, was typical. She was a shaduf, and so belonged to both, and neither.

"You have a question?" she said, her voice giving no clue as to her age.

"Um—yes," he stammered. "My name is Trook Hirdune. I'm a potter by trade."

She inclined her head, but didn't offer a name in return.

Ignoring this small lack of courtesy, Trook continued. "The plague that decimated my family has left me home-

less," he said with a practiced calm. "My wares will not sell. People distrust my clay, saying it may contain the seeds of a new sickness. I have had to abandon my home in search of a new one. If I wander much longer, the name Hirdune will be unknown. What I ask is simple."

Trook took an uneasy breath. He had thought long about the wording of his question. Dealing with a shaduf was like dealing with a demon. They always spoke the truth, but often twisted the words so they were meaningless until looking through hindsight. By then it was too late. "Tell me," he said, "where to settle in order to bring the name Hirdune back to greatness."

"There's one way to reach what you ask." Her face was blank and her eyes unfocused. "But it's not without grief." As if blowing out a candle, her expression cleared, becoming greedy. "What can you pay me?"

"What do you want?" he countered. And this was the sticky part. All his possessions were on the wagon, and there wasn't much: six weeks of food, the tools of his trade, and a woman who was willing to risk starvation for the chance he might regain the security his name once had. His worth was in his work. The only thing anyone might want was his instrument, and that he wouldn't let go. The pipe had been in his family for centuries, passed down each generation to the child most skilled in the art of spinning clay. It served as a carrot to entice the young to practice the family craft; whoever held it had earned the legal right to guide the profits of the entire clan's work. Trook had nothing else left of his vast inheritance besides his skill and the chartered status of his name. Nearly everything had been burned as a source of the plague.

The woman eyed Trook up and down, undoubtedly assessing what she could get out of him. With a cold, contemptuous look, she destroyed her graceful countenance. "You have nothing I want," she snapped, turning in a whirl of skirts.

Now Trook knew she was young. An old woman couldn't move that fast, or be that cruel. "Wait," he cried desperately. "There must be something!"

She stopped and turned, considering him again. Smiling

coyly, she swayed back. Trook wondered what had made her look so becoming at first. She was distasteful now. "You've nothing I want," she repeated demurely from beneath half-closed eyes, "but if you promise . . ."

He took a distrusting step back.

"Such pretty eyes," she murmured. "I'll answer you, my handsome plainsman, but you must promise you will take my advice." She ran a finger across and down his shoulder.

Trook stiffened at her touch, and the shaduf turned sullen.

"Do you want my help or not?" she demanded. "I have more important people to see."

This wasn't what he had expected. He had planned on taking her counsel. It would be as if he were getting something for nothing. If he had learned anything from his father, it was to be suspicious of a deal that was decidedly in your favor; there was something you overlooked. "You know where I should settle to make Hirdune pottery famous?" he asked again.

"I know where you should settle in order to bring the name Hirdune back to greatness," she quoted, tapping her foot. "Well? Do you swear to take my guidance?"

Trook shifted uneasily. This woman wasn't going to help him out of the kindness of her heart. Still, her advice was why he was here, and he didn't have much choice. Her robes were so blue as to be almost black; her counsel would be the best he could get. He had to save his name. It was all he had left to keep the cur from his belly. Terribly uncomfortable, he said, "I swear it."

"Oh, grand!" she said, her mouth twisting into a patronizing smile. "There's a canyon a good two days' walk northeast of here with a snowmelt-fed stream running the length of it. You will find water and clay for your work. Unless you settle there, the name Hirdune will soon fall below the basest of clay works."

"Thank you," Trook said, bowing his head to take his leave, which he was eager to do. This woman made him feel unclean.

"I'm not done yet," she said with a snigger. "For my casting to remain unchanged, your youngest grandson can't be allowed to remain among the family."

Trook's head came up. There it was, the ugly condition
that had enticed her to drop her fee. It was unthinkable for a
boy born to a chartered name to leave. Daughters generally
left, but sons never, unless the wife-to-be came from a very
wealthy house indeed.

"If he stays," she simpered, delighting in the mischief she
knew she was creating, "the name Hirdune will be lost, but
if he leaves in time, Hirdune will never be forgotten."

Not bothering to see his reaction, she turned and flounced
away, seemingly confident he would do as she advised. Trook
shook his head and watched her disappear into the crowd.
How, he wondered, could he have mistaken her for a man?

As he stood in his dismayed quandary, the owner of the
wagon returned, glaring until Trook noticed and left. Slowly
he made his way through the crush, deep in thought. Why
was his family's success contingent upon his grandson leaving the Hirdune home, a grandson whose father had yet to be
born? Even more worrisome was the shaduf waiving her fee.
He would like to think the opportunity to make trouble was
the sole reason, but it seemed unlikely. He had missed something, but for better or worse, he had committed himself and
his youngest grandson. At least, he thought dryly, he knew he
and his wife would have one child.

Trook swung aboard his wagon and lightly slapped the
reins to get the placid horses moving. The rolling motion
brought his pretty bride out from the back, where she had
been hiding. She detested foothills people and had flatly refused to show her face. Evidently her curiosity was stronger
than her dislike, and she blinked in the bright sun.

"Did he give you an answer then?" she said, clearly glad
to be moving again.

"Yes, she did," Trook replied, his eyes forward and his
brow furrowed.

"She!" his wife exclaimed. "Fancy that." There was a
long pause. When it became apparent no more information
would be volunteered, she cleared her throat. "What did she
say?"

"She told me of a ravine."

"Marvelous!" There was a pointed hesitation. "What did
it cost?"

Trook was silent, guiding the patient beasts out of the market and into the open fields. "I have no idea," he finally whispered, leaving his wife only slightly more confused than he.

15

Talon chittered as Alissa's eyes rolled up and she collapsed into a painful-looking heap. "Easy, old one," Strell said, reaching to ruffle the bird's feathers. "I think she's all right," he said through a sigh. Curse that Useless. That early start he had planned was now looking highly improbable. Setting his pipe down, Strell stood, stretched, and blew in mild frustration.

He knelt before Alissa, taking her in his arms like a sleeping child to shift her to a more comfortable position. Her head thumped into his chest as he lurched to his feet, and Strell hesitated, noticing how Alissa's hair was nothing like his sisters'. So straight and fair. The color of an autumn meadow. He breathed deep, his eyes going distant at the warm scent of lace flowers that clung to her. A sudden pang of grief took him, and he closed his eyes as his chest tightened. He was all alone. Everyone in his family was gone. Nothing could replace them. Nothing.

Refusing to acknowledge the lump in his throat, Strell settled Alissa on her bedroll and pulled her blanket up tight to her chin the way he knew she liked it. The small satchel she wore about her neck, the one she tried to hide from him, had fallen from behind her shirt. Strell eyed it, wondering if she would tell him what it was if he asked.

His old hat was caught under her, and he tugged it free, grunting in surprise as he looked it over. Alissa had worked decorative stitches in with the mending ones to make the appearance of a stalk of wheat running around the expanse of the rim. He had been thinking about asking if she wanted to trade back once she mended his old one, but he wouldn't ask now. She had put so much work into it. He carefully set the hat down and put her needle and thread away. Satisfied, he looked at Talon for approval. The canny bird was staring at Alissa as if ready to attack.

Lunging to his pack, Strell frantically dug for the jesses. "Wolves! Where are they!" he swore. "What good are jesses if they aren't on the bird? Alissa must have hidden them!"

"Aye," came Alissa's voice, full of dark irony. "What good are any preparations when they're interfered with?"

Strell spun to take Talon forcibly, but the small bird was gone! "Where's Talon?" he cried, finding Alissa sitting cross-legged upon her bed, her fingers steepled in a scholarly fashion. But it wasn't Alissa; her eyes had gone ancient with an unguessed wisdom—it was Useless.

"I sent her away lest she harm herself," Useless intoned. "*She* is in no danger. *She* listens to me. *You* however. . . ."

Never taking his eyes from Alissa, Strell stiffly sank down on his bedroll, not liking this at all. "What do you want?" he said belligerently.

"You're closer to the Hold," Useless said in disbelief. "I thought the plains instilled more honor than that. Putting your wants above the life of another is cowardly."

Strell's eyes narrowed, and he felt his anger trickle into something more enduring. The first time Useless had appeared, the shock left him afraid. The second time, Useless railed upon him, making him feel like an untutored drudge. Strell wasn't afraid now, and he wouldn't tolerate the man's domineering attitude. "You think I haven't tried?" he exclaimed. "Alissa does the first thing that comes into her head, and only the first thing. She won't listen to me."

"A little bit of a thing like this?" Useless mocked, gesturing dramatically to himself, or Alissa, rather. "You could just carry her out."

"You haven't done any better." Strell adjusted his coat with a self-righteous huff. "Making her relive her father's death was cruel. She doesn't care about Bailic. Thinks he won't know who she is until it's too late. She wants her father's book."

"It's *my* book," Useless protested with an unexpected vehemence. "I only let him hold it! And what, by my sire's ashes, does she want with the *First Truth*?" Then he sent Alissa's eyes to close in a slow blink, shivering. "Does—does she know where it is?" he asked softly, making a poor show of concealing his eagerness.

"No," Strell said from between gritted teeth. "Only that it's at the Hold where she can find it and Bailic can't." He jabbed at the fire to try and slow his anger. The conversation wasn't going the way he wanted. He had given a lot of thought to what he would say if Useless showed himself again, and as much as it rankled him, Strell was going to try to get the man out of his cell—if he couldn't convince Alissa to go to the coast. "Look," he said. "Just tell me where you are and we'll get you out. Then you can take care of Bailic."

Disbelief and a mocking surprise flowed over Alissa's face. It was so familiar to the looks Alissa had once given him, it was eerie. "You think you can get me out?" Useless said. "Fine. I'm in the cellar. The passage starts from a hidden closet under the stair. The door there can only be unlocked by a full Keeper. If you get past that, there's a gate made impassable by a ward only a skilled Master can break. Are you a Master, poet?"

"What stairway?" Strell said, undeterred. Useless's disbelief didn't bother him. The man's mocking tone did.

"In the great hall, but don't be foolish. You can't free me. Take her home." Useless sent a quick hand over Alissa's head, grunting in surprise when he touched her hair. "What I want to know," he said tightly, "is how she got it into her head to seek out a memory belonging to your line. I set for her a pattern of thought that would frighten the wind from the hills, and she's shifted it to some—frivolous—no account path that's—*absolutely worthless*!"

Strell struggled to keep his breath even and his hands unclenched. Drawing himself up, he looked across the fire, proud for some inane reason that Alissa had succeeded in defying Useless. "I asked her to," he said boldly. "She said she wouldn't be dragged about any longer."

"Dragged about!" Useless choked. "*Dragged about!* I try to save her miserable hide, and she complains of being dragged about!"

In a single, fluid motion, Alissa rose and began to pace the edge of the overhang, keeping just shy of the rain. Strell scrambled to his feet, unwilling to let Useless have the high ground. But Useless seemed to be angry at Alissa, not him. "Burn her to ash," Useless said in a whisper. "I can't send her among the lines again. She might jump to one that's not compatible with the pattern I set. She was lucky I found a congruent septhama point this time."

"Septhama?" Strell's hostility vanished in an icy wash and he swallowed hard. "You mean like—a ghost?"

Alissa turned from the rain in astonishment. "Ghost! *Ashes, no.* A septhama point. A memory fixed in an object rather than a person."

Strell felt himself go pale. Angry voices taking over young women were one thing. Ghosts were something else.

"I found it on a piece of Mirthwood, no less," Useless said, unnoticing or, more likely, uncaring of Strell's increasing panic. "Where," he accused, "did you get a piece of Mirthwood?"

"Me?" Strell said, wincing at how high the word came out. "I don't have any Mirthwood." He hesitated. "What's Mirthwood?"

Alissa ceased her pacing and sat on her bedroll as if made of stone. Her gray eyes looked almost black in the dim light of the fire as Useless drew Alissa's features into a tight knot and fumed. "Reddish wood. Heavy. Smells like—like Mirthwood," he said irately. "I know Alissa doesn't have any. And the memory was fixed by someone in your line about sixty years ago." He stared up at Strell. "How did a sliver of Mirthwood get into the plains sixty years ago?"

Strell slowly sank to the ground, his thoughts swirling. His grandfather's pipe. He had asked Alissa to see why he was forced to leave his family. It couldn't have been his grandfather! Slowly, Strell brought out his second pipe from his pack, watching as if his hands belonged to someone else, hoping that Useless wouldn't confirm his suspicions.

"That's it!" Useless shouted, snatching the pipe from

Strell. Alissa's eyes went round. "Bone and Ash. It's worked wood," he whispered, gazing at him in undisguised wonder. "How did you come by a piece of worked Mirthwood?"

"It's my grandfather's." Feeling betrayed, Strell stiffly extended his hand for his pipe. Not his grandfather, he thought. Anyone but him.

Useless slowly gave the pipe back, watching Strell tuck it into a shirt pocket. "Who are your sire and dame," Useless murmured calmly, and Strell started. "Your family name," he prompted. "Though having no unusual properties other than being exceedingly dense, Mirthwood is hard to come by. I haven't seen a worked piece that large since—in a long time."

"My family name means nothing anymore," Strell said tightly. "They're all dead."

Useless blinked. "You're from a culled line? From the plains? Which one?"

Strell caught his breath, refusing to speak. *Culled line!* Had their deaths been arranged?

Useless pointed an angry finger at him as if to demand an answer, then seemed to reconsider. "Fine," he snapped. "It doesn't matter. If you can't turn Alissa from the Hold, you'll soon be dead with the rest of your kin." He glanced deeply into the pattering rain. "I'm leaving. I can't save you if you insist on killing yourself." He sent his gaze back to Strell. "I wash my hands of you. Both of you."

Alissa collapsed where she sat into a crumpled heap.

Trembling in anger, Strell stood looking down at Alissa. "And I wash my hands of you as well—Useless."

16

Oh, no! Alissa thought, horrified, as she set her empty breakfast bowl down. Her boots! What did he do to her beautiful boots! Trying hard not to cry, she met Strell's proud smile. "Thank you, Strell," she murmured. "I'm sure they will keep my feet dry now."

"Uh," Strell grunted, his morning grump brightening with a flash of satisfied embarrassment. Scrubbing a hand over his face, he stumbled to his feet and scattered the last of their fire.

Alissa swallowed hard, gazing at the most *ugly* pair of boots she ever had the misfortune to own. It had been three days since she'd soaked them. Rightly deciding she was going to tempt fate by not oiling them, Strell had taken it upon himself—waiting until she fell asleep last night. Obviously he had meant it as a surprise. It was.

She knew she should have oiled her boots at the first sign of rain—they had been stuck in that storage chest for ages—but all Strell had was that vile dark grease. Alissa guessed it would turn her lovely cream-colored boots to brown. She had been right. "Vanity," she whispered, "your last name is pain."

"What's that?" Strell said as he tossed his shaving water away.

"I said, 'thank goodness there's no more rain.'"

He tied his bedroll to his pack, his fingers moving slowly as if the small task took all his mental strength. "Yes. Clear skies. It's going to be hot again." He glanced into the pale haze of blue. "I could do with a bit of frost right now."

"Strell!" she warned. "Shut your mouth!"

"What?" he said around a yawn.

Alissa looked nervously at the cloudless sky. Mountain weather was as unpredictable as a new bride's supper. "Why did you go and say that? Now it might . . ." She hesitated. Saying the word would bring it on that much sooner.

"Snow?" he said, a wisp of a smile appearing as he tossed the hat back.

"Be still!" she shouted, snatching her boots and cramming her feet into them as if the clouds were massing already. She paused, startled at how soft the brown leather was now and how her heel slid into place with a satisfying ease.

"And you think I'm the superstitious one?" he said.

Giving him a severe frown, Alissa folded her coat, wedging it between her pack and her bedroll like Strell had shown her so she wouldn't have to wear the thick leather. His wish for frost, though dangerous, was understood. It had turned exceedingly hot and sticky for late fall. The sun was barely above the horizon, and already the heat pressed down like a physical sensation. The scrub they had been forcing their way through for the last three days was high and thick, blocking any cooling wind that might have existed and slowing their pace to a crawl. What should have taken a day to traverse was taking three. Strell's shortcut was anything but.

Alissa sighed. She was quite proud of how well she had held her tongue for three entire days, never saying a word as the briars caught at her legs and the vines tripped her. Oddly enough, she had found not saying anything was nearly as effective as rubbing Strell's nose in it. He had become positively guilt-ridden, making an obvious effort to make her path easier. But she couldn't resist saying something, now that the tangle seemed to be at last thinning.

Her eyes strayed to his pack, and she hid a smile as an idea struck her. She might not have to say anything after all. "Strell? Can I see the map?" She kept her eyes wide with mock innocence. "I want to add this path to it."

Looking distrustful, he dug it out of his pack, untied the ribbon, and handed the roll of leather to her. Alissa tried not to smile as she took a sharp rock and etched the path and two symbols onto the map. She went over it with a bit of charcoal to make it semipermanent. "There," she said, handing it back. "Now it's accurate."

"What does it say?" he asked suspiciously.

"'Strell's Shortcut,'" she answered as she bent over her boots.

His defensive attitude seemed to vanish as he brought the map close to his nose. "That's how you would write my name?" Strell eagerly ran a finger around the first symbol.

"It is now."

He thought for a moment, his stance becoming wary. "You said proper names are written as everyday words. What word is this?"

"That's the word for stone," she said, hiding a smile as she looked away. He resumed his packing, seeming to be relived. "As in hard head," she added to herself.

"Kind of like firm and substantial," Strell said, clearly pleased.

"Or dense," she added, grinning at him.

"No. I like it," he said shortly, putting the map in his pack. "What word is your name written as?"

"Mine?" she said, surprised. It wasn't polite to ask, but he didn't know that. "Mine is written as luck."

He bobbed his head. "Somehow, I'm not surprised." He got to his feet, standing as stoic as a mule at the plow as she finished tightening her ugly boots. Ashes, she thought sourly. She didn't care if her boots did fit better, he had ruined them. Perhaps this was her penance for Talon tearing his coat. It would be pointless to tell him what she thought of his hand-iwork now. Besides, it was nice seeing even that small glimmer of a smile. Though not unhappy, Strell had been decidedly subdued since she told him how his grandfather purchased his family's fleeting success with Strell's expulsion from the Hirdune home.

Odd, she mused, how an erratic spring flood proved the shaduf wrong. Typically, they were infallible. But how could his family name become forever known now? He was the only Hirdune left, and he wasn't even a potter anymore. Perhaps he hadn't left soon enough.

"Uh, Strell?" Alissa said, wondering if it was a mistake to bring it up. "Why didn't your parents just tell you about your grandfather's agreement with the shaduf?"

Strell sighed, squinting into the sky. His eyes traced an arc in the haze, and she knew he had spotted Talon riding the breezy end of the updraft, leaving them to slog through the stagnant bottom end alone. "It's shameful to deny the family trade to a son, even on the advice of a shaduf," he said somberly. "I don't fault them for not telling me. I always assumed my grandfather wanted me to follow his second love, music. That's one of the reasons I'm a piper." Strell's eyes went distant as he touched the shirt pocket where he had taken to keeping his grandfather's pipe. "I liked him," he said softly. "We spent a lot of time together before he died."

A faint smile stole over him. "Apparently I look like he did when he was my age—except for his blue eyes." Strell extended a hand to help Alissa up.

"You do, especially your hair."

"He had hair?" Strell's eyes went wide and wondering.

Grinning, Alissa needlessly adjusted his hat. "Oh, yes. As dark and unruly as yours."

"He had hair!" Strell exclaimed. Then his smile faded, and he put a slow, hesitant hand to his head, running his fingers under his hat and through his dark mop, checking to see if anything came away with them. Seeing her laughing eyes, he shrugged sheepishly. "It usually skips a generation," he muttered, turning away to start their slow slog forward.

Alissa followed, her steps marginally easier for being behind him. The chore precluded their usual conversation, leaving her to her own devices. It was a dangerous enough situation on the best of days, but lately it had been more so. She was dreadfully uneasy with the thought of going nearly comatose every time she wanted to see her source or tracings. The last few days, in the mornings when Strell was the most incommunicative, she had been practicing dividing her attention to find her source *and* retain her awareness of her surroundings. The first time she had tried, it was a disaster. The temptation to lose herself entirely to her inner sight and slip into a light trance was nearly irresistible.

Fortunately, or rather unfortunately, every time she did, she was yanked back to her surroundings rather painfully as her toe hit an outcrop of stone or she slipped on a loose rock and fell. Sure as flowers spring from sheep dung, she would misplace her inner sight completely and have to start over. Strell's concern over her stumbles had quickly faded, and now her every slip was followed by his barely audible, "Bone and Ash. Again?" It was really hard, on the thoughts as well as the shins, but yesterday Alissa thought she had finally begun to see some improvement.

Today, Strell stayed unusually closemouthed, silent even during their infrequent breaks. Alissa took advantage of his mood to practice long after she usually quit. By late afternoon she was successfully visualizing the sphere while simultaneously watching her feet. Yes, she thought with a nod, it was definitely getting easier. Her pleased smile lasted all of three heartbeats—until she ran into Strell. "Sorry," she muttered, rubbing her nose and backing up.

He half turned, grinning back at her. "Are you still stumbling about back there? We've been out of those vines for ages. If you're that tired, we can stop and make camp."

She looked up, seeing for the first time all day more than the small circle her feet were in. The brambles and burs were gone. They were in a mature forest, on what looked like an overgrown road. "For the night?" she said, shocked. "The sun is still high." She spun in a slow circle, looking behind them in a growing excitement. "Is this a road? You think it leads to the Hold?"

Strell grinned, pushing his hat up to glance at the sky. "For the night? Yes. Is this a road? Yes. We've been on it since you last tripped. Does it lead to the Hold? I would bet my last pipe on it."

"Then why stop!" Alissa cried, suddenly overwhelmed with her mixed feelings of anticipation and apprehension. "Let's get there. Tonight!"

Swinging his pack down from his shoulders, Strell took out his map. "I think we're here," he said, pointing. "We won't be able to make the Hold by sunset. Let's cut today short. That way I have a chance to fix the hem of my coat, have a good meal." He hesitated. "Do some thinking."

Alissa watched him glance to the west and down the road. Clearly tidying up wasn't the reason he wanted to stop early. He was uneasy.

"Besides," he said, looking up through the empty branches to the sky. "Not a cloud up there. We have time. No snow for a while yet. Maybe a week."

Alissa's heart gave a sharp pound. "Ashes, Strell!" she cried. "Would you stop that!"

He gave her a lopsided smile as he moved off the grass-covered road and settled himself with a heavy sigh. "What?" He paused, gathering his breath. "Snow?" he drawled.

She shook her head as she moved to join him. He had said the word three times. It was going to snow for sure.

17

It was the cold that woke her, just as the morning sun spilled over the rim of the earth. The chill pricked the inside of Alissa's nose, seeming to burn. She looked to find Strell with his mouth open, his light snores sending streams of moist breath into the sharp frost. Last night the frigid air from the vast ice sheets in the north had spilled from valley to valley like a river between rocks, filling the mountains with winter. It was cold. Very cold. Alissa didn't think she had ever been this cold. It was almost an ache.

Rising up on an elbow, she poked at the fire's ash until a small tongue of flame awoke. It was difficult building up the fire without leaving her blanket, but she managed. A thin layer of rime sparkled on the surrounding trees in the growing light. Talon was absent, no doubt in search of whatever the silent forest had to offer. With an ease born from her mornings of practice in the brambles, Alissa visualized her source to see if by some miracle Useless's ward was gone. It wasn't. The thin gauze obscuring the brilliant sphere remained. Alissa went still in thought. Slowly she pulled the small pouch of dust from behind her shirt and looked at it. The two had to be the same thing. Hoping that perhaps this time Useless's ward would let her pass, she gripped the sack tightly and edged a tiny thought closer to her source. She held her breath. Closer . . . closer . . .

"Ow," she said under her breath as a bolt of liquid fire raced through her, shocking her fully awake. "Cursed ward," she muttered. Glancing at Strell, she tucked the rank-

smelling bag back behind her shirt and turned her attention
to making breakfast.

Urged on by the cold, Alissa finished breakfast preparations long before Strell showed the slightest indication of
waking. This past week he had been rising slower and slower,
and grumpier and grumpier. When they began to travel together, he hadn't been so bad. Clearly his previous temperament had been a front that continued to deteriorate to an
unknown, dismal depth. But she wasn't complaining. Watching him try to wake up was amusing.

"Strell?" she called softly. No answer. She wasn't surprised.

"Strell," she said louder. He grumbled and rolled over.

"Strell!" she shouted.

This produced the desired effect, and he blearily rolled
back toward the fire. "Tea?" he croaked as he sat up and extended a rumpled arm.

Sniggering, Alissa handed him his cup. He obviously
didn't appreciate daybreak.

"The water bag is half frozen," she said as she handed
him his share of breakfast. "It's good we'll be indoors
tonight."

"Yes, but will we be in the guest rooms or the dungeon?"

Alissa was so surprised he had managed a complete
thought, it took her a moment to answer. "D-dungeon?" she
finally stammered.

He blinked groggily. "Are you forgetting Bailic?"

"Of course not!" she protested, having done just that.

Strell grimaced, and anticipating another argument, she
set her cup down with a firm thump. Tea slopped to make a
steaming puddle that seemed to freeze even as Alissa
watched. Strell sipped cautiously at his drink, ignoring her
show of temper. "Well, it's not like we could get through the
mountains any other way now," he said.

Tugging her coat closer, Alissa silently agreed. "Ashes,
Strell," she grumbled. "Bailic won't know who I am. I don't
look anything like my papa."

Strell's eyebrows rose, and Alissa looked into her tea, refusing to meet his eyes. "I don't like Useless any more than
you do," she said softly. "But we have to try to get him out."

"From behind two locked doors?" Strell said. "Besides, what makes you think Bailic won't simply put him right back there?"

Alissa's breath slipped from her in a slow, measured sigh. She was sure the closet under the stairs Strell told her about was the same her papa hid his pack in. There hadn't been a passage leading from it, though. Perhaps Useless meant another stairway with another closet. Even so, she was sure they could find a way past the locks. Then Useless would take care of Bailic.

Strell stretched, collapsing into a lump with a soft moan, clearly wanting to drop the subject. "I suggest we spend the morning inventing a plausible story as to why two people would be ignorant enough to be caught in the mountains this late in the season."

Alissa swallowed her last spoonful of breakfast, surprised at how coherent his thoughts were this morning. Obviously he had been giving it a lot of thought. "Any ideas?"

He shrugged. "I'd stay with the truth as far as my presence is concerned. A lost bard isn't that uncommon, but to have two traveling together is unusual."

"Is it?" she murmured, knowing little of these things.

"My craft doesn't lend itself to competition. It doesn't pay as well as you might think. The only time I have seen it is when the two involved are siblings."

"Why can't we tell him that then?"

Strell gave her a curious, sideways look. "I don't look anything like you. Besides, our accents are different. Anyone older than three could tell."

"Oh," she whispered. Glancing up through the black branches, Alissa noticed a thin line of clouds on the horizon. If they weren't snow clouds, she was a plainsman's mule. It was going to be a miserable night, one that could prove deadly if they didn't have shelter.

Talon returned empty-handed as they were packing up. Apparently all her potential prey was absent or hiding from the looming storm. "Here, Talon," Alissa called, extending the last of the dried meat. "You should have something." Chittering her thanks, Talon daintily accepted the tidbits until her belly began to bulge.

"Hold on." Strell cautiously knocked the fire apart. "She won't be able to fly if you give her that much."

"When does she ever fly anymore?" Alissa said dryly, and sure enough, the moment their packs were slung, Talon flew rather heavily to Alissa's battered hat and settled herself to nap. "See?" Alissa complained, and Strell grinned. "Get off!" she shouted, suddenly embarrassed, snatching her hat from her head. Talon flew up, then down to land upon her shoulder. It was marginally more dignified, so Alissa let her stay, frowning at Strell's thinly veiled chuckle.

Alissa's past hope of getting her original hat back was gone. Strell had shown no interest in his old one, even with the decorative stitches. All that work wasted. She was stuck with his ancient monstrosity and he with her floppy one. Knowing him, he would eventually slather that awful grease on it, turning it a horrid dark brown to match her boots.

They strode quickly under the graying skies, making a fast pace over the road. The farther they traveled along it, the more grass-covered it became. But it was always clear where it ran, straight as a beeline, to the Hold. The morning slowly turned into a drab afternoon, and they were still no closer to inventing a reasonable story to explain her presence.

"I don't see why we can't use the idea of siblings," Alissa complained as they walked through the woods.

Strell sighed. "It just won't work. You're almost tall enough, and the sun has turned you nearly as dark as I am, and your fair hair and eyes could be excused as bad breeding—ah—no offense. But your accent is a dead giveaway, not to mention the way you butcher your hair. If you sounded more like a plainsman, we might manage it, but you don't, and that's that." He marched stoically forward, his brow tightening. The Hold couldn't be far ahead, and they still were no closer to agreeing on a plan.

Almost unnoticed at first, the threatened snow began to fall. It sifted down in gradually thickening bands to darken the sky and turn the trunks of the trees to gray shadows. Winter had finally come, just as they feared. Strell was silent, frowning as he ignored the snow and Alissa both. In an unexpected flash of empathy, Alissa decided not to point out that he had been the one to call it down. He glanced up at her unusual silence, and she shrugged. The lines in his face smoothed and his pace slowed as he realized she wasn't going to say "I told you so."

"You know, Strell," Alissa said, pleased she had held her tongue, "your accent isn't as thick as you might like to believe. Your travel has softened it."

"Your mother knew I was from the plains," he said, brushing the snow from her shoulders.

"She would. The plains are her heritage as much as yours."

"Thought so," he boasted. "She didn't sound it at first, but her looks give her away."

"Her family is from deep plains," Alissa continued. "But she was sent to the foothills to study the art of diplomacy at Finster's School for Fine Ladies."

"Diplomacy?" Strell peered at her, clearly trying to decide if she was joking, and Alissa nodded. "I've never heard of a school teaching diplomacy," he said warily.

Alissa glanced behind them into the heavily falling snow. It was beginning to build, and they were leaving prints. "Well," she said, turning back to Strell, "it never promoted itself that way, but that's what Mother said it was."

She watched Strell eye her. She could tell he didn't believe her and was too smart to come right out and say so. Wise man, she thought. Curious as to how he would broach the subject, Alissa kept silent.

"Uh, don't take this the wrong way," he said slowly, "but why did she school for diplomacy only to become just a farmer's wife?"

"What do you mean by *just a farmer's wife*?" Alissa cried, stopping dead in her tracks.

"That's not a slur, Alissa," he said with a wide-eyed bravery. "That's what she is. And from what I could tell, she's very good at it."

Slowly Alissa's pressed lips loosened as his eyes held no scorn. "M-m-m," she said. "But that's not what her father had intended."

"I can imagine." Strell smiled softly as they began to move forward again. "She's a very gracious lady. You can't learn grace like that, you're born with it. I bet her father wanted to use her to make ties with another family."

"Use is exactly right," Alissa muttered, conversant with the plains' barbaric custom of arranged marriages. They never married for love. A mother chose her daughter's husband with a sharp eye on the purse strings. "That was why my mother was sent away to school," Alissa continued. "She was supposed to learn how to live with someone she couldn't tolerate. Instead she found the strength inside herself to say no. Her father was so incensed, he sent her back to the hills in disgrace. He expected she would repent and beg to return. She never did."

Alissa stomped her boots to shake off the snow. Looking down at the ugly brown leather, she sighed. "And that," she said, "is where she met my papa." Alissa smiled sadly. "He used to tease her, telling me he found her chained to a post in the hills. I suppose in a way she was."

"Huh," Strell grunted. "How long did your mother stay?"

"At the school? I'm not sure, six years maybe?"

"Do you suppose . . ." He hesitated. "Do you suppose that in those six years, her accent could have shifted so she might sound as if born to the hills?"

Alissa felt a trace of a grin as she followed his thoughts. "I do believe that in six years, she might have lost her accent completely."

"A school in the foothills could account for your hair, too." Strell nodded to himself. "And you're sure Bailic has no idea you exist?"

"Very sure," she whispered, her eyes on the ground as she remembered how costly that protection had been.

"Then that's what we will do," Strell said firmly. "We can't use my name; the Hirdunes are potters, not minstrels. But my mother's name used to be Marnet. It's common enough." He hesitated. "That is—if you've no objections?

"Alissa?" he called, but she wasn't listening. She had stopped and was staring in openmouthed awe at the massive stone structure that had loomed suddenly out of the swirling snow.

They had arrived.

18

Strell dragged Alissa's numb feet across the frozen ground to stand wide-eyed before the huge entryway of the Hold. Even after having seen it through her papa's eyes, it was impressive. The outer set of doors still hung open, and snow had collected against the thick, rough timbers. Standing taller than two men, the doors would have covered a space wide enough for three carts to pass. The doors looked frighteningly substantial, and she wondered why they weren't closed.

It had been left to the decorative set of doors to keep the Hold secure. They were made of the same black wood, but were heavily bound with metal on all edges. The precious stuff was tooled, softening the harsh, blackened silver with the look of twining ivy leaves. Between the two sets of doors hung a huge bell. Shrugging, Strell grasped the frayed cord and gave a firm tug.

Even expecting it, the harsh clank made Alissa jump. The snow seemed to swallow the sound, and she fidgeted as her pulse slowed. It seemed to take forever until the doors opened and they were greeted by a pale figure clenched with cold under a long, elegantly trimmed housecoat.

"Burn me to ash," Alissa whispered, her eyes going wide and her knees threatening to give. Her papa's memory hadn't been a dream. This man standing before her had killed him. The last few weeks hadn't been a nightmare but a demented reality. She was a Keeper. Useless was real, and she might be able to do—magic?

He didn't know her. He didn't know her. He didn't know her, Alissa repeated to herself in a half-mad litany to keep from bolting. The fierce grip Strell had on her elbow helped, too. Her pulse pounded as Bailic frowned up into the snow and hurriedly gestured. They stumbled over the threshold and the door thundered shut.

The silence was almost palpable as the candle he held flickered, threatening to go out, then burned steady. Her eyes darted nervously to the stairway. The closet's door was hidden on the opposite side, but she knew it was there.

"What luck," Bailic said, his soft voice shockingly smooth. "To find shelter just as the storm began. You must be a favorite of the Navigator." He stood ramrod still, unmoving as he looked them over. There was the same hard tightness to him that Alissa remembered, and she felt her stomach knot. Why hadn't she just agreed to go to the coast?

"Not too much of a favorite, I hope," Strell said lightly, a grin pasted on his face. "Could you ask your master if we might stay the night?"

Bailic shook his head. "I'm the master, and I don't think you will be staying just the night. I do believe it will be all winter." He seemed to soften as a slow, almost predatory smile came over him. Something had shifted. Alissa felt her chest tighten. What the devil was she doing here?

"Weren't you warned?" Bailic said. With a shake of his housecoat, he lost the last of his sharp demeanor, extruding a warm welcome instead. "Once it starts to snow in the mountains, it doesn't stop." He turned to Alissa, his smile freezing and the barest hint of disgust flicking over him as he realized she was of mixed blood. Again he hid his emotions behind a smile, and Alissa's eyes dropped in a shame she hated herself for feeling. "It's cold in the great hall, my dear," he said, bending solicitously close. "Let's go to the kitchen to discuss the terms of your stay."

His steps light, Bailic turned and began walking to a small door. *"Bailic?"* Strell's eyes seemed to say, and Alissa nodded, reaching to touch Talon's feet reassuringly planted upon her shoulder. Bailic's pale eyes and even paler features made a startling contrast with the rich blackness of his coat. Despite his refined polish, he looked all wrong. He was tall, even for the plains, topping Strell by nearly a head. Thin, almost gaunt, he exuded the proud arrogance that comes from growing up in the desert. His coloring, though, was wholly

from the foothills, with his unnaturally white skin paler than
the most pampered farm girl's. His hair was hardly there, it
was cut so short. Even so, it suited him very well. If not for
being nearly white, he wouldn't look more than a decade
older than Alissa remembered her papa being when he had
left.

As they followed him across the echoing expanse to a
narrow door, all the doubts Alissa had ignored the last few
weeks rose up. This won't work, she thought as her breath
quickened. He had to know who they were. They would
never get Useless out. She would never find her papa's book.
She was risking her life for a *book,* and she didn't even know
why!

Alissa was near panic when Strell bent close. Speaking
loud enough for Bailic to hear, he whispered, "Relax. I've
done this lots of times. I don't see any domestic help. If we
aren't hired as entertainers, we can surely stay as kitchen
drudges." He gave her shoulder a firm squeeze then, but she
wasn't sure if it was in encouragement or in warning to keep
her mouth shut.

The small door opened to a dimly lit kitchen. Bailic
pushed a tarnished kettle over the fire, and after stirring the
flames to brightness, he sat at the head of one of the three tables. Strell and Alissa sat at the foot. A hard gleam seemed
to come into Strell's eye at the prospect of haggling the terms
of their stay—his plains upbringing coming to the forefront—and Alissa would admit she ignored them as she
looked around in astonishment.

Simply put, it was the largest kitchen she could ever
imagine. The ceiling went up at least two stories so the heat
wouldn't become unbearable, even in the last days of summer. Chandeliers, their candles gray from disuse, hung from
thick support beams that crisscrossed where the ceiling
ought to be. An amazing three hearths took up the north wall;
only the smallest was in use. Formidable metal doors were
set in the stonework between them, telling of ovens large
enough for a whole sheep. An entire wall was devoted to
utensils, some of which Alissa couldn't begin to guess their
use. One corner—it was the size of her kitchen at home—

had herbs making a low, once-fragrant ceiling. Now they looked brittle and tasteless in their forgotten age.

"Sounds fair," Strell said loudly, breaking into her reverie. "What do you think, Salissa?"

"I'm sorry. I wasn't listening." She blushed, too flustered to be annoyed with him mangling her name. Then she recalled the plains custom of naming children with the same first sound.

Bailic leaned forward, and she struggled not to stiffen. "You implied she was your sister," he said, a contrived confusion in his voice. "Your accents are different."

"So they are," Strell hastily agreed. "She's my half sister—at least, that's Father's best guess." Smirking, he slumped conspiratorially toward Bailic. "Just between us, she isn't much of a musician. Father thought to marry her off, and when she refused, he exiled her to Finster's School for Fine Ladies to find some manners. It's on the edge of the foothills. *That's* where she picked up that barbaric accent."

Bailic glanced from Strell to her, his eyebrows raised. "So why is she with you?"

"Alas," Strell sighed, "she's too stubborn. Even the good ladies at the seminary could do nothing with her. No looks, no talent, what was Father to do?"

Despite her fear, Alissa's face began to burn.

"She's my favorite sister despite her—shall we say?—questionable origin," Strell said, "and rather than let her rot at Finster's any longer, I pleaded with Father to allow me to take over her care as I traveled for new material. She'd been there since she was thirteen. Obviously, the banishment wasn't working, but perhaps if she found how miserable life could be, she would be more amenable to marriage. Besides"—he grinned—"it was less expensive than keeping her in that cell of a school. And so I'm stuck with her!" Strell merrily gave her a whack on the back, pretending not to see her frown. "It's a shame about that hideous accent," he said. "I think she picked it up out of spite. If not for that bird of hers, I wouldn't have bothered rescuing her."

"Bird?" Bailic said uneasily. "What bird?"

Strell hesitated. Alissa could understand his confusion. Talon was surprisingly quiet and had apparently been missed, seeing as she was pressed up against Alissa's neck, hiding amongst her hair. "Why—she's a kestrel," Strell said. "Can it be such a worthy man as yourself doesn't know the least of the falcons?"

"I know them," Bailic said tightly. "I just didn't see her." His pleasant demeanor slipped as he rubbed the scar running from his ear to across and down his neck. The gesture gave Alissa a chill. Then he slumped, hiding his ire behind a friendly smile. He leaned forward, and Alissa held her breath, struggling not to shirk away.

"Be easy, my dear," Bailic said, apparently recognizing her fear. "I'm not a bad man. I won't throw you out into the snow to perish. You're welcome to stay the winter."

Though it was meant to be reassuring, the soft threat behind his words rang clear in Alissa's thoughts, and she swallowed hard.

Strell exhaled in a slow puff. "We accept your fine offer," he said formally, "and ask that we have until tomorrow to assume our new duties."

Bailic stood abruptly, startling Talon and Alissa both. "Done and done," he said, all business again. "You may stay in the kitchen, if you like. I don't know if there're any rooms suited to habitation anymore besides my own."

"Might we look about regardless?" Strell asked. "We've been sleeping on dirt for ages."

Bailic inclined his head graciously. "I would ask you don't go above the level of my chambers, then. That would be the ninth floor." He paused, then still smiling, added, "That's where the stairs become narrow and rough. It's the beginning of the tower, and the stairs can be treacherous."

Pulling his coat close, he nodded his good-night and headed for a large open archway. Alissa and Strell exchanged relieved looks. Then Bailic paused, turning on a slow heel, his head cocked in thought. Alissa dropped her eyes, and she felt him shift his attention from one of them to the other. "She isn't your sister, is she," he murmured, and Alissa's heart seemed to stop.

Bailic ghosted closer in the sudden silence. Alissa thought he seemed dangerously lost in his own musings, not recognizing they were still there. "No," he said with a sigh.

"Any child born to the plains who looked like that would be run out long before she reached thirteen." He placed his palms on the table before Alissa to make a stark outline on the table. "I would know."

"That's why the school," Strell said smoothly.

Bailic jerked to alertness. "Oh, do stop," he said jovially. "Just admit you're a flesh-runner. I don't care. But I *am* surprised. Have things become so bad in the lowlands that a well-bred plainsman such as yourself needs to take on a bit of flotsam to make ends meet?" His honey-smooth voice did nothing to make his accusation any less foul than it was.

Alissa struggled to keep her breath even as her panic shifted to a nauseating mix of relief and childhood fright. Bailic thought her family had paid Strell to take her away so as not to shame their name with her existence.

Strell said nothing; his hands hidden below the table were clenched.

"You're wise in taking her to the coast," Bailic was saying. "With that hair of hers, they might give you a fair purse—if she can gut a fish."

"Salissa is my responsibility, not my property," Strell said stiffly, and Bailic chuckled.

"I imagine not." He smiled, showing even, white teeth as Alissa glanced up. "But you're safe. I won't turn you in. The way I see it, there's no better way to keep half-breeds out from societies' tender eyes. Your profession is admirable—in a way." Bailic loosened his coat, adjusting it carefully. A short vest the color of slate, reminiscent of her papa's favorite outfit, peeped from behind the coat flaps. "You really can tell a story and play a tune?"

Strell nodded a slow, controlled nod.

"Good. My offer stands. I'll find you tomorrow." Without another word, he left.

Alissa's stomach churned as she stared at the table, struggling to rebury the irrational fears that Bailic had pulled from behind her hard-won barriers and fervent denials of reality. She had always been loved. True, the surrounding villagers barely tolerated her, but her mother had always dried her tears, hotly insisting that *they* were the ones with the problem, not her. But there were children who weren't so lucky—children, who, if they didn't die outright from neglect, grew up as guilty family secrets, kept from the sun and neighbors' eyes until the exorbitant fee to lure someone into taking them away could be raised. Such children carried with them an enduring self-incrimination, and all for nothing more than their appearance. It could have been her.

"Wolves," Strell swore. "That didn't go very well."

"No," she agreed softly. "But we're here." She stood with a sigh, and Talon made a quick flight to the rafters. Feeling miserable and lost, Alissa hung her dripping coat and hat by the fire and knelt to build it up. She was cold. "Thanks, Strell," she murmured to the warm ash.

"For what?" He was brushing the snow from their packs, keeping the puddles in the corner.

Alissa bit her lip. "For telling him—for saying I wasn't . . ." She hesitated. "For not thinking I'm . . ." She stopped, and her gaze dropped. She couldn't say thanks for not thinking she was less than nothing, fit only to be sold to a reluctant bidder as if she was a wagonload of half-rotted potatoes to be hauled out to the edge of town and dumped.

Strell grimaced. "I should have punched him in the mouth."

"And we would be back in the snow," she said, smiling thinly.

"Better part of valor and all, eh? But I don't like it. What do you think of Bailic?"

Alissa grew still, refusing to meet his eyes. He scared the breath from her, but she didn't want to admit it.

Seeming to understand, Strell dropped their packs and came over to peek into the kettle. Anxious to change the subject, they put their heads together and gazed at the unidentifiable chunks bobbing in the thick, greasy-looking soup.

Alissa's nose wrinkled at the sour smell drifting up. "What is it?"

"I'm not sure, some sort of stew?" Strell poked at it with the ladle, making a face as a sticky bubble broke.

"I'm not going to eat that," they said in unison.

They both forced a laugh, trying to dispel the last of their unease. Alissa turned away and began to hunt for something edible. Strell began investigating the cupboards, humming a tune about a woman and her hungry dog. Behind a small door, Alissa found what she thought was a kitchen garden. It was complete with a refuse pile, and that was where she was going to dump the stew until Strell convinced her she shouldn't.

She lingered in the softly falling snow looking for fresh herbs, enjoying the chill now that she knew she could return to the kitchen's fire when she wanted. They had done it, or at least the first step. Now if only they didn't slip up, they would free Useless, or at the very least, sneak away with her book. Even if Useless couldn't stop Bailic, he ought to be of some help.

Alissa would be the first to admit the presence of the garden had a lot to do with easing her fear. She was a farm girl. It was hard for her to stay anxious with so many familiar herbs and trees around her, still recognizable in their overgrown disarray beneath the slowly accumulating snow. The garden seemed to stretch the entire length of the Hold, its end lost behind the tangle of vegetation and lazily drifting white. What she could see was more of a slice of wood and field than a true garden, and Alissa loved it even before she saw its entirety. The distant walls rose higher than she could reach, blocking the worst of winter's bite. But it was still cold, and with one arm wrapped tightly about herself, she turned to find the way back with a handful of overgrown chives.

"Can you believe this kitchen?" she said, shutting the garden door tightly.

"I was hoping you'd like it." Strell looked up from a large pile of onions. "I found the larder." His eyes grew wide. "You can walk right into it! It's bigger than the whole kitchen was at my home. And the shelves are all full!"

"It's early winter. Why wouldn't they be?" Then she became suspicious. "Just why were you hoping I'd like the kitchen?"

Strell sniffed from the onions. "Part of the arrangement was that we would prepare three meals a day for him as well as us."

Alissa's eyebrows rose. Normally she might be upset at playing cook for a madman who would do nasty things if he knew whose child she was, but after seeing what he had been eating, it sounded like a good idea. He wouldn't need any special strength to be rid of her, just make her eat his cooking. "Our choice of menu, or his?"

"I never thought to ask." Strell set his knife down in thought. Then he smirked. "I don't think he will care what we put in front of him if he ate that stew. What do you think is in it?"

Alissa shuddered, settling herself across from Strell and taking an onion in hand. "I don't even want to guess."

19

Dinner preparation was a leisurely affair, and by the time they sat down, it was nearly dark. It was the first meal they had eaten together at a table, and they couldn't help but feel rather festive. The tight, anxious look Strell had been wearing the last day or so eased, and he cracked joke after bad joke about Bailic's dietary habits. Alissa found herself humming as she finished the superb meal that she and Strell had prepared together.

"So," she drawled, comfortably full of potatoes, carrots, and biscuits. "You never did say what our other tasks are."

Strell sighed and pushed his empty dishes away. He'd eaten more than Alissa believed could be stuffed into a person. Wrapping his hands around his mug of tea, he leaned back with a contented air. "We have all the food we can eat, shelter, and most of our time to ourselves. In return we keep up the wood for the kitchen hearth and any other we want." Strell smirked. "He told me to take it from the nearby woods and not that garden you found."

"What about his fire?" Alissa asked.

Strell shrugged. "He didn't say, but since he's got enough

food in that pantry of his to last all three of us until spring, I imagine he has wood stashed somewhere for himself. Apart from that, there's only some light entertainment."

She felt a frown drift over her. "You'll take care of that, right?"

"Nuh-uh." He grinned. "I help cook. You help entertain."

"Come on, Strell," she pleaded. "Can't you tell him I'm no good?"

"I already did," he said cheerily. "And besides, you'll make up for your lack of experience in enthusiasm!" He drained his mug with a noisy slurp. "Let's go," he said as he stood and took his coat and hat. "I want to see if that door under the stairs is still locked."

"I told you," Alissa said, rising to her feet. "There are no passages from that closet. Useless must have meant some other set of stairs. But maybe we could find my book tonight."

Strell grunted doubtfully, and she agreed. Bailic had spent the last fourteen years searching and hadn't found it. Besides, they had time. In all likelihood, they were snowbound already. The storm was from the northwest. It wouldn't stop until the snow was so deep they couldn't get down the mountain.

A stirring of excitement filled Alissa as she shrugged into her coat and took up a candle. Leaving the rinsed dishes, they headed to the great hall by way of the dining room. They had taken a quick peek at the dining hall as they prepared dinner, but the barren room held little: several long black tables, their accompanying hard-backed chairs, thick red drapes covering a wall, and an enormous hearth, black and empty. Together they passed through the archway into the echoing darkness of the great hall. Their candles did little to light the four-story-tall room.

Impatient with Strell's cautious pace, Alissa strode to the far wall supporting the stairs. At first glance, the wall looked like solid rock. She peered closer, the memory of her papa helping her find the outline of a door. "Here," she said, running a finger across the hairline cracks in the rock. "This is where my papa hid his pack."

Strell was silent as he came up beside her, his eyes on the

yellow stone. His brow furrowed, he set his candle down and tried to wedge a fingertip into a crack. The stones fit too closely for anything more than a thumbnail. "Useless said the closet under the stair in the great hall," he whispered. "Do you think there might be a hall bigger than this?" Then he turned to Alissa and smiled. "What did your father do to unlock it?"

Alissa's eyes widened. "You think I could do it?"

"Why not?"

Her heart gave a heavy thump, and she handed her candle to Strell. Nervous, she stood before the door and steadied herself. "He put his hand like this," she said, cautiously extending her palm until it touched the stone. The rock was cold, and she stood poised, waiting for something to happen. She suddenly felt foolish, and she dropped her arm and stepped back.

"There must be something more to it," Strell said, not a trace of amusement in his voice.

Alissa flushed. Had he actually believed she might be able to shift the stone door? Magic, she scoffed. How could she have even thought it was real?

"Too bad," Strell said. "Bailic probably already took your father's pack."

"Probably," Alissa whispered, more disappointed than she thought she would be.

"Do you think Useless meant those tunnels?" Strell whispered.

Alissa turned to where they were gaping a darker black. She was tired and didn't want to explore them tonight, especially in the dark. Her papa had said they were for storage. "I don't think so," she said softly, heartsick at the reminder of him. "Why don't we find a place to sleep? We can start searching tomorrow."

Strell nodded, and they headed for the stairs. Alissa had been sleeping outside for nearly a month and was sick of sticks in her hair and fires that wouldn't last the night. A warm bed was worth more right now than just about anything. Cold and tired, she followed Strell up the impressive stone stairway to the second floor. The first room they came to was large and empty, sporting several unshuttered windows. Wondering why the snow swirled outside, yet didn't come in, Alissa leaned out into the shadow-gray of the snow-induced twilight.

"Alissa!" Strell cried. "Don't!"

"What's that?" She smiled innocently, leaning out farther. A tingle hummed through her fingers, seeming to cramp them where she touched the sill. Surprised, she jerked herself back in.

"Don't do that!" Strell said. "You might fall out," he added, dropping his eyes.

Ignoring Strell's dramatic gestures, Alissa leaned out to run her fingers over the sill again. This time the tingle was a sting, and she snatched her hand back. "There's a ward on the window," she said, wringing her throbbing fingers.

"A what?" Strell came close. She couldn't tell if he was anxious about her fingers or if he wanted to be sure she wouldn't lean out again.

"A ward," Alissa repeated. "You know, the same thing that's keeping me from—from my source," she whispered. She looked up to see understanding fill him. "It's cold in here," she said, "but not as cold as it should be. I think the ward is to keep the snow out and the heat in."

Strell frowned in worry. "That, and empty-headed farmers who don't have enough sense to keep from falling out." Seeing her still rubbing her fingers, he bent closer. "Here, let me," he offered as he took her hand and carefully studied her fingertips. "You should know better than to stick your fingers in a boiling pot," he murmured, his words a warm breath on her skin.

Alissa froze, and Strell arched his eyebrows, refusing to let go under her slight tug. Disconcerted, she yanked her hand away and crammed it into a pocket. "I didn't think it would strengthen as I tested it," she said, the hurt in her fingers and the confusion in her thoughts making her voice harsher than she intended.

"Come on." Strell chuckled. "Unless you want to stay and not burn your other hand?"

With an indignant "harrumph," Alissa snatched her candle and strode to the next room. They found it much the same. All the rooms on the second, third, and fourth floor were oddly empty. She was beginning to despair of ever finding a place to lay her head, when on the fifth floor they found abused-looking cot frames running in two tidy rows down a long, narrow room. "Want me to get the packs?" Strell asked, and Alissa winced.

"I don't know," she hedged, thinking the room wasn't much better than a cave. "There's bound to be something better," she said, and they retreated.

But they found the entire floor the same, as were the next two. The only difference was that the rooms became smaller and the unmade beds fewer. Alissa followed Strell, her gloom deepening with every barren room they found, but as her feet reached the eighth level, she straightened with a faint sense of purpose. Perhaps it was a fragment of memory from her papa, but she knew where to go. "This way," she said eagerly, and turning left at the top of the stair, she skimmed past all the closely set doors until she found the last one. Her hand jerked back at the slight tingle as she touched the door, but it creaked under her small pressure. Wiser now, Alissa pushed it open with her foot.

"This is better!" Strell exclaimed, following her in. The small corner room had surprisingly large windows facing south and east, so it would receive sun almost all day. There was a single low bed accompanied by a rickety-looking table. The west wall held a small hearth. An orderly pile of ancient-looking wood was stacked next to it. A large, over-stuffed chair was pulled up to the hearthstones, its fabric so worn, the pattern could only be guessed at. Over the top of the fireplace were empty shelves. Although there was no fire, the wards on the window made it feel warm after weeks of being outside. It looked as if the last occupant had just walked away—a decade ago. This, she decided, was where she would stay if Strell could find something equally nice nearby.

"It even has curtains." Alissa smiled as she fingered the heavy yellow cloth, "and a rug." She pulled the drape against the night and turned, absolutely beaming. It was the first bit of warmth and comfort they had found, and she wanted to keep it.

Strell grinned. "You want this one, huh?"

"Are potatoes sweet?" Alissa set her candle on the mantel and plunked herself possessively into the chair, sinking deep into the musty cushions.

"I'll see what's down the hall. Maybe the next is bigger." Still chuckling, he left.

Settling further into her chair, she decided she didn't care if it was. This room was perfect. It even felt like home. There was only one presence needed to make it complete, and Alissa whistled. If Talon heard it, she would come. Not moving from her chair, she whistled again. It would probably take three calls before Talon found her. After all, there were eight floors to be bypassed. Alissa took a breath to whistle a third time when Strell's rapid footsteps echoed in the hall and he skidded to a halt before the door. "What! What's wrong?" he cried.

She stared at him in astonishment, then grinned as she figured it out. "Sorry." She laughed, pleased he had dropped everything to see if she was all right. "I was calling Talon."

"You don't sound very sorry," he muttered, shooting a furtive glance behind him into the dark hall. "Give a person some warning next time, all right?"

"Strell," Alissa whispered, her eyes dancing.

"What?"

"I'm going to whistle."

Grunting, he gave her a sour look and set his candle down to plug his ears. Alissa gave a shrill blast, and Talon winged in to settle neatly on the back of her chair. Not bothering to rise, Alissa sightlessly reached up to ruffle Talon's feathers.

Strell puffed in resignation, but then his brow furrowed. "Do you hear something?"

Alissa shook her head, hesitated, then nodded. Beginning as a low rumble, it grew unsettlingly fast into a loud, irate roar. It was Bailic, thundering down the hall, hollering something unintelligible. Alissa jumped to her feet in alarm. What, she wondered, had she done now?

"Who made that beastly noise, and how did you open that room?" Bailic's shout echoed as his shoes whispered to a halt in the hall. His housecoat was open, revealing a black shirt whose fabric and stitching was of an astounding quality. The gray vest was an exquisite fit, accenting his pale coloring, making him look all the more elegant. He held his candle high to see them.

"We apologize," Strell said with a slight, formal bow, stepping between her and Bailic. "It was a whistle to call our bird."

Bailic took a huge breath as if to shout at them, and Alissa cringed. But then his wrath evaporated, and his face went frighteningly still as he slowly exhaled, his eyes narrowing almost imperceptibly. His icy control was reminiscent of the moments before her papa fell to his death. Alissa's fear tightened. "I see," he said lightly. "There will be no more such disturbances."

There was a tiny pull on Alissa's thoughts, as if someone had tugged on her skirt or sleeve. She jumped, covering the motion with soothing Talon. The small bird was glaring at Bailic, a faint whine coming from her. The feeling was very much like the one when Useless had invoked that bothersome ward to block her access to her sphere. Immediately she slipped a peek at the dark, still pattern in her thoughts. Although no force had flown for weeks, there was a dim glow from her tracings.

Alissa bit back a gasp as she realized Bailic had his own tracings, and when he shunted force into it, he must have created a ward. It seemed to have set up a resonance to cause her own pathways to glow. Hounds! she thought. She was a Keeper!

"I expect you to keep quiet, especially after sundown," Bailic said, trying to disguise his earlier anger with a stiff smile. "I've been here alone for some time. I'm used to the silence."

"Of course," Strell agreed, interrupting him.

Bailic's smile faltered. "And how did you get in here? The door was locked."

"Why, it was open when I crossed the threshold," Strell said with a wide-eyed innocence. "Shouldn't we be here? This is the eighth floor, isn't it?"

Alissa's exuberance evaporated, and she went cold as Bailic's face tightened. He said nothing for a moment, studying Strell from the tip of Alissa's old hat to the toes of his brown boots. Strell was walking a fine line between being a simpleton and being belligerent, and she thought Bailic knew it.

"The door was open?" he asked softly, his eyebrows raised.

Strell gave a pensive nod. He looked none too eager to push Bailic any further.

"Curious," the tall man drawled from the hallway. "I had thought all these doors locked." He leaned forward, and Talon began to hiss. "Tell me, most fortunate of tale-tellers," he said, "did you open more?"

"I hadn't the chance to try," Strell said boldly, but Alissa could see his hidden tension.

Bailic nodded, his eyes distant in thought. "Any of the rooms on the eighth floor are acceptable," he said smoothly, ignoring Talon's noise. "I have decided that for tomorrow's entertainment I would hear the story of how you found my doorstep."

"Oh," Strell protested. "It's a dull tale. Wouldn't you rather hear of a giant fish and the men who braved the sea to catch her?"

"No," Bailic said. He turned to smile at Alissa, and though he did it very well, she couldn't help her shudder. Seeing it, Bailic stiffened. "We will hear your story tomorrow, bard," Bailic said with a forced politeness, and with a disparaging glance at Talon, he spun away, his open coat snapping about his ankles.

His footsteps padded down the dark hallway, and Alissa shivered, trying to rid herself of the last of his presence. Thank the Navigator he hadn't actually come in. The only good thing was realizing she really was a Keeper. Bailic had set up a ward, and she had seen it.

Alissa caught her breath at an uncomfortable thought. "Strell, try to whistle."

"Don't you think we're in enough trouble?" he said sharply.

"It doesn't have to be loud," she said. "Just try."

Strell obligingly pursed his lips. As she expected, nothing came out. Thoroughly confused, he frowned and tried again.

"You can't," Alissa said glumly, then brightened. "I saw it. I saw how he did it!"

"Did what?" Strell asked, blowing all the harder. "And what do you mean I can't?"

"Make the ward, of course."

Strell's eyes went wide. "Wait. You saw how he made a ward, and it keeps me from whistling?"

She nodded, kneeling to light the fire, only to remember all her equipment was in the kitchen. Her eyes rose to the mantel, where her mother had kept the kindling in the event the fire went stone cold. A pleased smile came over her as she saw a basket of fluff and striker rocks exactly where they'd be at home. Taking them, she arranged a small fire with the crumbling wood.

"Sweet as potatoes," Strell grumped, collapsing in *her* chair. Talon chittered sharply at him, pecking softly at his hat.

Alissa turned from the hearth, settling herself more comfortably. It would need close attention for a while; besides, it was warmer. "He suspects, doesn't he?" she said, looking at her boots. They were due another oiling, but she wasn't going to do it. She scuffed them on the hearth, drooping as Strell shifted in the chair.

"Probably. I don't think he even believes his version of the truth anymore, much less ours." His eyes slid away. "I don't want to be your brother, but I'd rather be that than a— than what he thinks. Let's hold to our story. But even so"— he smiled faintly—"you'll notice I'm the one silenced, not you."

Alissa's eyes widened. "He thinks you're the threat. Strell! You can't be my scapegoat."

"You may also note that I'm still here, and you have possession of a nice room. Obviously he isn't sure, or he thinks he can use me to his advantage."

She stifled a tremor. Bailic could wring every last thought from Strell and find nothing he wanted. What Bailic would do then was anyone's guess. "You can't do this, Strell," she pleaded. "Right now he's playing the pleasant host, but he could turn in the flick of an eyelash."

"I know," he said lightly, "but I'd rather have him watching me than you."

"But—"

"Let me finish," Strell said, holding up a hand. "Three reasons. One: No offense, but you aren't that good at friendly deception. I can draw attention from you and any other mistakes that happen, like unlocking a door that won't open for me."

"Oh," she said, just now realizing the significance of that tingle. Perhaps she ought to try the door under the stair again.

"Two: If he's watching me, you at least can poke around to find that book of yours."

Alissa nodded. "And number three?" she prompted.

"Uh," he said, dropping his eyes. "If he's watching me, he won't be likely to look at you."

It was nearly the same thing he had just said, but the way he said it caught her attention. "Sorry?" she asked, a slight smile hovering about her. "I didn't quite hear that."

Strell got to his feet. "Your fire is almost out." Grabbing his candle, he walked into the hall. "I'll get your pack," he shouted from the dark.

Her smile widened as she watched the thin glow in the hall slowly fade. Didn't want Bailic looking at her, indeed, she thought. Bailic was almost as old as her papa.

The fire was well set by the time Strell made his way back with their packs, and once they had a pot of water on for tea, they went to see what the other doors offered. "Were all of them locked?" Alissa asked, not comfortable in the least that one of them had opened itself for her.

"All I tried," Strell said as he wrung the handle of the door next to hers. It wouldn't budge, and with an exaggerated gesture, he motioned for her to try. Not expecting her luck to be any different, she warily touched the door. It creaked open with a whisper of tingles in her fingers. Alissa fought with the twin feelings of elation and alarm, finally deciding to pretend it hadn't happened.

Curious, they stuck their heads in. It was almost a mirror image of her room, without the west window, of course. The chair didn't look nearly as comfortable, but the rug was newer. There was a faint, stale smell that disappeared even as they stood there. Strell spun in a slow circle, his arms outstretched. "What do you think?"

"It's not any bigger than mine."

He sighed in mock sadness. "I suppose some concessions must be made."

Alissa watched in astonishment as Strell knelt before the hearth and craned his neck to look up the chimney. "That's what I thought," he said as he got up and dusted his knees.

"What are you talking about?"

Strell nodded at the fireplace. "See where the hearth is in relation to yours? The flues are joined."

"So?" Alissa said, not seeing the significance.

"So I hope you don't snore."

Alissa let her breath out in a huff. Grabbing the back of the chair, Strell started to drag it to the door. "What are you doing?" she cried, jumping out of the way.

"You don't think I'm going to sit on the floor do you?" he grumbled, lugging the chair into the hall and to her room.

"Well—no, I guess not." She followed Strell to find he had already arranged their chairs companionably before the fire.

"Sit," he commanded. "*I* will make the tea."

Alissa gratefully sank into the fire-warmed cushions, and as the night deepened, they talked, enjoying the novelty of four walls and a hearth. It was Strell's belief that her "talent," as he called it, had unlocked the doors. He had no idea why Bailic had reacted so strongly to her whistle. It was, in his words, "not that loud," and according to him, it was painfully clear Bailic knew they weren't simply travelers lost in the snow. Strell believed he was playing a cruel game of cat and mouse. Maybe, Strell thought, they were simply some serendipitous entertainment for him. Maybe he didn't want to eat his own cooking.

It was with thoughts of potatoes in white sauce that Alissa fell asleep, not meaning to, of course, in her lovely chair before the fire. Strell must have covered her with her blanket, because much later she found it draped about her when she woke as the fire shifted. Smiling, she snuggled deeper under the prickly wool. She had spent the better part of a month sleeping on dirt. Her chair was large enough to curl up in and an absolute delight.

The embers of the fire glowed, shedding enough light to

see Strell, still slumped in his chair, snoring lightly, his gangly legs outstretched almost to the coals. He, too, had succumbed to the drowsy effects of a full stomach and warm fire before reaching his cot. Glancing up to Talon, Alissa was surprised to find her awake. Peering down at her, Talon raised her feathers and murmured comforting noises.

"Keeping watch, old girl?" Alissa whispered and closed her eyes, too comfortable to move, satisfied to spend her first night in the Hold right where she was.

20

Bailic sat brooding in his rooms. The hour was late. A trio of candles set behind him lit the page he was studying, and he leaned closer, squinting to see the swirling print. It was the third time he had read the page, and he still didn't remember what it contained. Manipulating a closed population for a desired trait was by no means beyond him, but Keribdis had written it. Her tight scrawl was hard for him to decipher.

Leaning back, Bailic stretched his shoulders painfully. He would try again in the morning when there was more light. The bright glare would hurt his eyes, but he needed the sun to see as much as any man—maybe more. Bailic set the book aside. He knew the real reason he couldn't concentrate was that his thoughts were on other, more pressing matters.

As he sat, he cast his thoughts inward, down through the Hold's abandoned halls in a halfhearted search for the last object of any importance left to him. He had known for years the *First Truth* was close, and it was his habit to listen for its sirenlike call at this hour. The empty space between sunset and sunrise, when all men's minds were still, had always been the easiest time for him to search. Someday, he thought bitterly, the book would be his.

He had once been counted as a Keeper and was confident he could use its knowledge. Its borrowed wisdom would give him the strength to claim the souls of Ese' Nawoer. The abandoned city had once fallen under the shadow of the Hold, its commerce and population supporting the burgeoning needs of the fortress. It had lain abandoned for four hundred years, populated by the ghosts born from a single man's tragic decision.

With the book he would demand their support and overwhelm any opposition to his plans. He would be free of the Hold, now both his protection and prison. He could claim anything he desired, which, he admitted, might be more than many would willingly give. But more importantly, he could govern the miserable denizens of the plains and foothills. Bailic huffed in contempt. They had, in his opinion, far too much freedom.

But first, he mused, slipping easily into the familiar thought, he would instigate a conflict to throw their two highly structured but stagnant societies into chaos. It shouldn't take much with the strength of the book to help. They already despised each other. Open hostility wouldn't be hard to instigate. Keeping safe in the background, he would manipulate both sides to insure there would never be a victor, just continuous losses. Only when he deemed they had beaten themselves sufficiently would he arise as the great peacemaker, bringing his will upon the dirt-eaters and foothills squatters. "You will welcome me," he whispered, "and praise me. I will forge you into the image *I* desire, and no one will think to question me." He couldn't help his smile, but it faltered as a small tug of doubt took him. Against his will, his eyes were pulled to a high shelf where a Keepers' wide-brimmed hat, old and work-stained, sat like a silent accusation.

"Isn't that right, Meson?" Bailic said mockingly, shoving the unwelcome feeling away. He rose and strode across the room to snatch up the hat. Forgotten notes hidden under it sifted down on top of him. Bailic set the hat on his desk and stooped to gather the papers. Another smile, this time of satisfaction, eased over him as drew near the fire to put them back in order. The sheets were old, written when he had begun his self-taught lessons of how to cripple another Keeper with wards, something their Masters diligently conditioned them against.

It had been nearly fourteen years since the last entry. "Today Meson settled our argument that pushing the Masters' truth ward too far could kill you," Bailic read. "He lies at the base of the tower." Still looking at his shakily written words, Bailic set the paper on the desk, and taking a quill, he added in a slow, careful script: "Meson was the last of the Keepers."

Growing unexplainably wary, Bailic set his notes aside and looked at the yellow hat again. It had been sitting atop that shelf all these years, unnoticed until his "guests" arrived. He had forgotten he even had it until he saw the plainsman's hat. The plainsman's *Keeper* hat, Bailic added soundlessly, not sure if his pulse had increased from fear or anticipation.

It was increasingly obvious one of his guests was a latent Keeper. Long before Bailic's time, great pains had been taken to insure there were other, easier ways through the mountains. No one found the Hold unless he was drawn to it, and no student Keepers had stumbled in since the Masters drowned in the western sea. Even more compelling was that the ancient wards of the fortress were waking. Only someone who truly belonged could account for it.

Having renounced his title of Keeper, he was no longer recognized by the warming wards. They had slowly diminished until it was like winter inside, even during the brief mountain summer. Since the two passed the threshold, the icy grip had loosened. Soon fires would be unnecessary except for light. It would make for a more comfortable winter, but the idea of another Keeper in the Hold made him uneasy. Even a latent Keeper could alter his plans, especially if he knew of his potential status.

"What do you think, Meson?" he said, again taking the hat into his hands. The yellow leather was dry and needed oiling. "Is the unfortunate innocent of his skills, as I was when I found the Hold, or aware of them, as you were?"

Bailic tossed the hat to his balcony chair and turned to a small cabinet. His fingers ran lightly over the sundry containers, hunting more by feel than sight, for a jar of oil. "I think," he muttered as he searched, "that it's likely the latent Keeper knows of his dormant abilities and is here to find the *First Truth*." Bailic straightened with a large jar of black animal grease from the plains. Frowning, he replaced it, taking a jar of light, watery oil instead, made from a foothills grain. Now that the Masters were gone, the book was probably the only way for a Keeper to learn how to use the complicated pattern of tracings that lay unused in his or her thoughts.

Striding to his worktable, Bailic took one of the rags he used to bathe his eyes and returned to his high-backed chair before the balcony. The appearance of a latent Keeper could work well for him if he balanced it right. The untutored mind lacked wholly in discipline and was therefore frustratingly sensitive. "You could find that book for me," he said as he tugged a small table closer to his chair. "I need only to claim it for my own then," he said, pleased at the thought. But he couldn't let on he knew they were looking for the book. Forewarned is forearmed. Once they were on their guard, he'd never be sure if or when they found it. They might even leave, preferring to risk perishing in the snow then allowing him to claim it.

If Bailic didn't believe brute strength was the resort of a feeble mind, he would simply pin them both with a ward, make his demands, and threaten one with death until the other found the book, but why? Bailic was a realist. Bloody experience proved holding and utilizing hostages was difficult and messy, especially for the long period finding the book would necessitate. Far better to leave well enough alone until they found the book for him. Besides, the idea of spending another winter by himself when he could have two guests to torment seemed like such a waste.

He would be taking a definite chance in allowing a latent Keeper the run of the Hold unchaperoned. Knowing whom to watch would greatly reduce the risk. It would add just enough spice to the game. And he could keep track of the person easily enough. Yes, he thought, twisting the cap out of the jar of oil. His gamble would be almost nothing if he knew who was the Keeper. His personal risk would be reduced as well, and Bailic preferred his battles won before begun.

Oddly enough, untaught Keepers were surprising in their strength, their abilities not yet shackled by wisdom and restraint. This was exactly why they weren't granted a source until attaining a certain level of control. All Keepers, latent or not, could send out a pulse of force when under great stress. It wouldn't do to get his tracings burnt from a knee-jerk reaction. It hurt, not to mention it would leave him unable to implement the smallest ward until his tracings healed.

He needed to discover who the Keeper was. The man was the more likely candidate, but Bailic refused to chance burning his tracings on the advice of a hat. A Master would simply take an unsanctioned peek at the pattern of tracings sprawled through their minds. The difference between Keeper and commoner was ludicrously distinctive. Bailic, though, had only a Keeper's skills to draw upon. He couldn't see anyone's tracings but his own unless invited or the subject was all but dead.

Getting one of them to respond to wordless speech would tell him who the latent Keeper was, but either Bailic or his "guests" would have to leave the Hold to bypass its ward of silence. Bailic wasn't going to abandon the iron-clad protection the Hold provided, and he wasn't going to let them off the grounds either. Although the ward was a hindrance now, it had been a blessing when the Hold was alive with Keepers. Just imagining the multitudes of silent conversations stretching from one end of the Hold to the other gave Bailic a headache. He didn't think the Masters had been bound by this ward. News had traveled very quickly in the past.

Conversations between Keeper and Master had been, without fail, verbal. Never had Bailic heard of an exception to this. It seemed the mighty beings wouldn't, or more likely couldn't, speak silently to any but themselves. It was rumored the thought patterns were so different between Keeper and Master that no common ground could be found with which to communicate. When wishing to converse, and that had been often, the great scholars shifted to their more conventional form—the one capable of speech. The only other way was to borrow the unconscious tongue of another. The occupied fool never recalled what transpired as he slept, animated by the thoughts and words of another.

Bailic began to dab the oil onto the hat, being careful to keep the rag clear of his clothes. The snare he had crafted and utilized with such ease in the past was useless—now that Meson had broken the Hold's truth ward. Bailic might still lure and trap his prey in his rooms, but they would be under no compulsion to say anything, much less the truth.

Finding the hints in their conversation as to who had a Keeper parent was his best option, a parent he probably killed. He would have to weigh their words carefully; they were already lying to him. The fear on their faces when he challenged their story of siblings had been real as was their relief when he labeled the plainsman as a flesh-runner. There shouldn't have been relief. Alarm or cockiness? Yes. But not relief.

"Not even here an hour," he mused with a false regret, "and lying already."

At least part of their story rang true. Finster's "school" was well-known, and while looks alone claimed they weren't siblings, there was an ease between them that spoke of a long association. Perhaps they grew up together, and the man was taking her to the coast as a personal favor. Almost, though, it seemed as if he were courting her, and the thought of *that* sickened him.

Bailic sneered as he continued to oil the hat, turning the yellow leather a darker shade with short, abrupt motions. "Disgusting," he said aloud. "The man's a full-blooded plainsman. He can do better than a *half-breed*." Even taking a foothills whore was better than a half-breed. The man had actually tried to shield her from his sight when he found them in Meson's old room.

"And I don't like them opening your door, Meson," he muttered as he turned the hat over and began oiling the inside. But Meson had been a trusting fool. Never more than a simple ward on his sill. Anyone with good intentions could bypass the threshold. "Besides," he said with a snigger, "you were warned not to have any children. You wouldn't have chanced it, *old friend*."

It was rare that a Keeper had a child when the Masters advised against it. Usually the pattern of tracings degraded rather than improved. The result was a network with only bits and pieces in working order, capable of oddities even their parents weren't able to mimic, hence, the shadufs and septhamas. Their disjointed tracings gave off a half-resonance, sending their Keeper parent into a dizzy nausea at the mere touch.

Finished, Bailic set Meson's hat down and carefully corked the oil jar. The yellow leather was several shades darker but would regain its usual color in a few hours. Meson had been particular about the color of his hat. "Why the Wolves am I oiling his hat?" he said suddenly. "It's not as if Meson can browbeat me over letting it dry-rot." He stood, and with a small thought, he severed the window ward stretching thinly over the broken balcony. Snow blew in from the dark, small hard pellets that would continue to fall for days. He snatched Meson's hat. His arm cocked, tensing, preparing to throw the hat into the black, only to hesitate. "Curse you, Meson," he swore under his breath as his arm dropped. "Why can't I be rid of you?"

But he knew. Deep in his soul he knew. Bailic couldn't sever his last connection to Meson, to finally end it, and he flushed with anger and self-loathing. From the day they met as boys, Meson had accepted him—a tall, thin plainsman with skin and hair like a hills farmer—when no one else would. "I am a pure blood," Bailic said fervently, feeling his chest tighten. But for all his claims, he looked like the half-breeds he despised, and Meson had been the only one in his entire life who hadn't cared. Except for Rema.

Bailic closed his eyes, taking a long, pained breath as his fists clenched. Rema didn't count, he avowed as he exhaled. When push had come to shove, she'd spurned him as well, abandoning him just like everyone else. Bailic replaced the window ward, snapping it into place with an unusual abruptness. He threw the hat into the chair, refusing to look at it.

The hat was all Bailic had been able to pull from beneath the pile of rock Meson had buried himself under. For weeks the wolves had complained, able to smell but not reach what they considered theirs by right. Everyone else,

Keeper and student, had been given to the wary scavengers. "But not *you,* Meson," Bailic said harshly. "You buried yourself under rock where I couldn't reach you." He clutched his coat closer in the chill he had let into his rooms.

Bailic crouched before the fire to stir it up. "I would have given you a proper funeral pyre," he whispered to the bright flames. "You were too good for wolf fodder."

Slowly he placed the hat back on its shelf and returned to slump into his chair. He listlessly wiped his fingers on the rag, only now realizing he had ruined one of his best eye towels. Smoothing his brow, he took a practiced, calming breath, trying to rid himself of his heavy mood. His eyes fell upon Meson's hat again, and angry, he rose and strode to his door. He was too restless to sleep and would visit his cellar as he did when his thoughts weighed heavily upon him.

Shunning a light, he padded down to the great hall and the door hidden in the wall supporting the stairway. He placed his palm to unlock it, and once through, firmly shut it behind him, sealing himself in a damp pitch blacker than a moonless night. By feel alone, he edged past his stack of torches and the dusty lump of Meson's warded satchel to peer down the dank hole and the cramped stair spiraling down.

A chill breeze eddied about his ankles like the breath of a giant beast. It had been this ever-present draft that led him and Meson to find the hidden door in the stairway's wall. As a boy, Meson had pointed out that, when left to their own devices, the feathers of his pillow shifted about the floor of the great hall as if pushed by an unseen wind. Through trial and error they found the secret room. It wasn't until long after Bailic had begun his conquest that he discovered the second door in the floor leading to the much gossiped about but never seen dungeon.

Bailic grasped a torch and set his thoughts to light it. Flame burst into existence to throw flickering shadows against the close walls. He nervously licked his lips and started down.

The mountain seemed to press heavily against him, filling his senses with the biting smell of wet rock. His flickering torch sent smoke to sting his eyes and dry his throat. It was cold, and he was glad for his coat. At the end of the long stairway, he edged unhesitatingly into the narrow passage before him. The ceiling was so low, he had to walk almost double, cramping his back and legs. He knew the passage would eventually open up into a small room just off the spacious cell buried under the Hold. Though only a few body lengths wide, the anteroom would allow him to taunt his prisoner and remain at a reasonable, if not safe, distance.

He had been in the larger of the two caverns but twice. It was a prison no matter how smooth the floors had been worked or how stately the pillars holding up the distant ceiling were—and it made him uneasy even though it couldn't hold him. Again he wondered why the owners of the Hold had crafted such a place. It had only one discernible purpose: to confine a Master. It could bind no other. It was rumored some skills the Masters pursued carried a risk of insanity. Perhaps this was where they put them until they recovered their wits. Bailic smiled. It seemed to fit. He had lured and trapped Talo-Toecan down here by telling him his beloved Keribdis had returned and lay wounded, calling for him.

There was only one other way out besides the narrow crack he now shuffled down, and that was the west gate. It was more of an enormous barred window than anything else, revealing the steep drop-off that was the western exposure of the mountain. It gave Bailic a perverse pleasure knowing his old instructor could see his freedom, yet not partake of it.

Bailic heard the plinking of water long before the tunnel ended. Tonight it was accompanied by a low warning rumble. The light from his torch fell upon nothing, and he slowly stood, feeling his back crack. He remained by the tunnel's entrance, squinting at the large, irregular shape behind the widely spaced metal bars. Two yellow eyes, each as big as his head, glittered in the shadow-light. Apparently his presence tonight had been anticipated. His permanent guest was already waiting. There was a glint of torchlight on teeth. They were as long as Bailic's arm.

"You've been very quiet lately, Talo," Bailic murmured, not moving from the tunnel's mouth. "Can it be," he mocked, "that you are beginning to enjoy your accommodations? Acquired a taste for rats, perhaps?"

There was no answer but the rumble and the measured

drips of water, echoing in the distance. At the edge of the light, the blunt tip of a long tail wove.

"Come now," Bailic coaxed patronizingly. "I would lighten your evening with a bit of friendly conversation. Arrange yourself to speak with me." He stepped closer, trusting the thick bars imbued with ancient strength to protect him. The rods were far enough apart that he could easily slip between them, and although mere metal couldn't contain his prisoner, the wards that accompanied the bars would. It was a one-way gate, much like the ward on his own door.

A shimmer of gray swirled behind the gate. The huge eyes vanished, and the great shadow shrank. "Be very careful, Bailic," a voice grated, replacing the warning growl. "Come much closer and I'll try the Hold's strength despite the pain."

"Optimistic words, don't you think?" Bailic said with a sneer. "Especially from one who hasn't been under the sky for—what is it now a—decade and a half?"

"Fifteen summers and fourteen winters," the dangerous voice said wistfully, and a figure of a man moved into the light. The torch did nothing to illuminate his features, lost as they were in the darkness. It was clear, though, his frame was thin and spare, and that he should have no trouble slipping through the bars to his freedom. The shadowy figure took a breath, and lunged as if to do just that, halting shy of the bars, knowing to a hairsbreadth how close he could come.

Bailic scrambled back, slamming into the wall with enough force to knock the wind from him. The torch fell to roll and sputter on the flagstone. "Curse you!" he wheezed, bent double as he gasped for air. His heart pounded and his sudden sweat turned cold, even as he hated himself for his reaction. He knew he was reasonably safe. Talo-Toecan couldn't set a ward past the gate.

Rendering a Master powerless was nearly impossible, but the wards on the gate came close. As long as Talo-Toecan was imprisoned, the Hold, its abandoned city Ese' Nawoer, and everything in between were completely exempt from his wards. This was to help minimize the possibility of the imprisoned Master joining the thoughts of another, using their tracings to leapfrog his wards farther than was normally pos-

sible. To ask to extend this blanket of protection farther than
the city was ludicrous, as it would take more strength than
even an assembly of Masters could produce. Crafting such a
defense was beyond Bailic, but fortunately he didn't have to.
Still, Bailic thought bitterly as he straightened, it must have
given the insufferable beast a small bit of pleasure to watch
his jailer awkwardly backpedal into the wall in fear.

"Can something be the matter, Bailic?" Talo-Toecan rumbled, a trace of amusement in his deep voice. "You never
come a-visiting unless you're displeased."

"Nothing is wrong." Bailic haughtily adjusted his coat.
Snatching his torch from the smooth floor, he jammed it into
a wall bracket. "I came to tell you of my progress is all."

Talo-Toecan turned as if to go.

"Stay," Bailic shouted, "or it will go badly for our
guests!"

"Very well." Talo-Toecan sighed. "Talk." The thin figure
returned to the light's edge.

Bailic leaned closer. "One of them is a latent Keeper in
search of his birthright."

Talo-Toecan shrugged dismally.

"The *First Truth* and its knowledge will soon be mine,"
he gloated. "Surely such an innocent will respond just the
tiniest bit to the book's call, enough to find its hiding spot
before I could, enough to serve my purposes." Bailic smiled,
pleased with the thought. "Soon I will know which is the unlucky fortunate, and I will squeeze the other to get what I
want."

The Master started. "You don't know? Didn't you
see . . ." He caught his breath, and a thin chuckle slipped
from him. "You don't know who it is, do you."

"Didn't I see what?" Bailic said, angry his nearsighted-
ness might be held accountable for any of his failures. He
didn't need to see well to succeed. He was clever and quick.
But the Master only raised a mocking eyebrow. "See what!"
he demanded as Talo-Toecan turned away. There was another shimmer of gray, and his tall figure was gone. Again
the low rumble of discontent shifted the chill, damp air.

"You don't know anything," Bailic said, suddenly afraid.
"You're nothing but an archaic remnant of an extinct sect,

and you'll never again be anything more. Hear me, Talo! Nothing!"

The rumbled warning ceased. Bailic froze, then frantically flung himself back. But he was too slow. With a crack that reverberated in the cavern behind the bars, he was struck by a thin, whiplike coil. Reeling, he scrambled on all fours to the safety of the low archway. Bailic touched his cheek. His hand came away wet with blood. He stared at it in disbelief as the pain blossomed and continued to grow. There was an accompanying retort of agony from behind the bars as the ward sent a pulse of pain faster than thought along Talo-Toecan's tracings. The beast had been lucky to have slipped even his tail past the ward and not seizured from the pain.

"Your attempts to stop me will be forever useless," Bailic all but snarled, and he spun about; the meeting was over. Too fearful to retrieve his torch, he left it behind. For a time it glowed, reflecting off the angry eyes as he crept up the thin tunnel, back to the Hold's upper rooms.

What, Bailic seethed, had he missed?

21

A ribbon of sun stabbed through the narrow windows, snaking its way down the steps, showing with a glaring harshness all the nicks and imperfections the hard stone had acquired through its centuries of use. The damage ought not to have been as bad here, above the ninth floor, but the native stone the tower was constructed of was softer than the marble used in the lower floors. Bailic sat and fidgeted on the uppermost step, his back against the railing. Perhaps he ought to abandon his attempt to search their rooms this morning. But there was bound to be something there that would reveal who had a Keeper parent, and they had to make the noon meal soon.

He edged farther down the step to pull his slippered foot out of the moving band of sun. A wash of irritation passed through him, and he sent a small tendril of thought down the long Keepers' hall at the foot of the stairs to seek out his two guests. It was difficult to find them, situated as they were in the very center of the Hold's strength. For although the Masters built it, the Keepers had dwelt here the most, making the Hold their own. Finally he detected a whisper of presence. He narrowed his concentration and placed them still in her room.

A faint, laughing jest shattered the silence, and he straightened. He hadn't really needed to do a mental search of the Hold to find them, arguing as they were. Bailic caught a few words and smiled, sure his wait was almost over. If the girl got her way, they would be having carrot stew for supper. If the piper won, it would be potatoes.

Bailic took a quick breath, releasing it slowly to steady himself. He was used to waiting, but waiting on two such fools was aggravating. Giving in to his jitters, he dabbed a cloth at the new welt on his cheek. Though it was nearly half a day since he acquired the whip mark, it was still oozing. Raku score was tenacious. It probably wouldn't heal until spring. The thought of wearing another scar inflicted by Talo-Toecan rankled him to no end.

The noise in the hallway increased. Bailic tucked the cloth away and stood. He glanced upward, wondering if he ought to go farther up and let the stairway hide him, but his eyes narrowed as he reconsidered. They wouldn't see him unless they started up the stairs, and he had told them not to. Besides, it was his Hold. He could be anywhere he pleased.

The girl's voice grew steadily closer, and Bailic tugged his vest down and straightened his sleeves. They turned the corner and continued on downstairs, her prattle interspersed with the plainsman's laugh as he gently teased her. Slowly the sound of them faded. Still Bailic waited, listening until even the memory of their voices was gone.

"Good," he whispered, ghosting down the stairs. He ought to have taken the ward off Meson's room a long time ago. But there had been no reason. He knew the book wasn't there. Meson hadn't visited the Keepers' hall on his last day on earth.

Reasonably sure they wouldn't be coming back any time soon, he strode confidently down the hall to Meson's old room. Bailic's pulse pounded in his ears, and he felt a flash of annoyance with himself. This small theft of knowledge was nothing compared to what he had done to his fellow Keepers in the past. He must have been alone too long. His steps slowed as he neared the last door. With a quick glance behind him, he settled himself. He would save the piper's room for last.

Bailic reached out and pushed open the door. It swung into her room without a sound. The ward was in the sill, not the door. The rule had been hammered into them, only the Navigator knew why. Bailic peeked in, finding the room much the same as when Meson had called it his own. The drapes were open and the fire was banked. One of the two fireside chairs was dangerously close to the hearth in his opinion. Satisfied that the girl's bird wasn't present, Bailic closed his eyes and settled himself. Modifying Meson's wards had always been difficult for him.

Taking three practiced breaths, he forced his tension away, finding a calm, relaxed state. His source and tracings seemed to drift into existence, and Bailic settled into the light trance he always found helpful. The first crossed loop of power was quickly put into play, and he calmed himself further. He had thought long on how to modify this particular ward. Bailic was confident he knew the pattern Meson had set. All he needed was to duplicate it exactly, then add a juncture or two to break the flow and hence the effectiveness of the ward.

"Simple stuff," Bailic murmured, allowing his source's energy to fill the proper pathways. Satisfaction eased through him as his ward settled into place. It was an exact fit. He had guessed properly. Not releasing the ward from his mind, Bailic opened a channel to break the perfect pattern. Immediately he felt the change. Now, instead of burning him, the humming flow of force would be harmlessly directed away. This was a skill he had honed while ripping wisdom from his fellow Keepers. It was laughably easy to do when there wasn't someone trying to incinerate him at the same time. "I should have done this ages ago," he muttered, squinting into the girl's room.

The sunlit chamber looked vulnerable. Everything she had was in this room. It was his for the taking. Squinting from the sun, Bailic strode forward. The nullified ward buzzed a warning, and he ignored it. The ward hadn't been removed, only modified. It was powerless to affect him now.

Bailic's foot touched the floor.

Sharp pain shot up his leg, exploding into his skull. "No!" he cried, instinctively jerking himself backward. His balance gone, he stumbled, falling back through the door. There was a dull thunk as his head hit the far wall. He clawed at his head, trying to free the fire that seemed to consume him from inside. Reeling, he slipped to the floor. Agony raced through his tracings, burning him. There had been a second ward.

Bailic lay on the floor, gasping, waiting it out. There was nothing he could do. Slowly the fire retreated until all that remained was the pain from knocking himself into the wall. "The Wolves should hunt you," he gasped, his head pounding.

Slowly Bailic pulled himself up to a sitting position. Before him lay the girl's room. The door was still open in invitation, and he gritted his teeth in anger. How could he have been so foolish. There had been a *second ward*. Its warning buzz had been shrouded by the first. The skill needed to balance one ward within another should have made it impossible.

"I'll remember that little trick," Bailic groaned. Moving like an old man, he slowly rolled to his knees. A harsh buzzing between his ears ebbed and flowed with his motion. He rested on all fours for a moment, catching his breath. Unsteadily, he gained his feet, leaning heavily upon the wall. He cautiously reached to feel the back of his head. There was a lump but no blood.

"Curse you, Meson," he rasped, glancing back into the untouched room.

Bailic staggered to the stairway and laboriously climbed the single flight to his room. Stumbling in, he pushed his door shut and collapsed in his chair before the balcony. The drapes were open, and he turned from the glare. Only now, safe in his room, was he bold enough to examine his tracings. His chest tightened in fear as he imagined the worst. Closing his eyes, Bailic unfocused his concentration.

"Wolves," he whispered, feeling his breath slip from him. It was worse than he imagined. He had never been burned this badly before. Black against black, coated in ash stood his tracings. Nothing would flow through them until they healed, and nothing could hurry the process.

There was a story of a Keeper who had fallen unconscious while under a ward of such magnitude. The burn had never healed, leaving the man as a commoner. Bailic froze where he sat, wondering if this was to be his fate. He took a deliberate breath, steeling himself to try to use his tracings, to determine if he had burned them into an unusable tangle of nothing.

Carefully he made the smallest ribbon of thought to connect his source to his blackened tracings. Agony thundered through his head as the incoming force pooled up, unable to flow through accustomed channels. He gasped and closed his eyes in a dizzy nausea, reaching out to find the chair arm. "Bone and Ash," he breathed, stoically waiting for the pain to ease. He had known it would hurt, but this was almost unendurable.

His limbs begin to tremble as he mended the opening in his source and the inflow of power stopped. Taking a slow breath to settle himself, he watched intently as the pool of force gradually slipped into his tracings to seep away. Bailic slumped in relief. They were still usable, or would be in time. He would heal. He hadn't damaged his tracings beyond repair.

"Fool," he muttered as his mood turned to one of self-recrimination. "Great skill isn't much good if you can't use it." What was he going to do now? Never had he burned his tracings so deeply. He didn't know if it would be days or weeks before his pathways were clear and he had the use of his skills again. His disastrous assumption at Meson's door had reduced him back to his first tools of cunning and trickery. It didn't matter, Bailic thought darkly. He would have his answer in the end. And the sweet simplicity of a well-planned deception was often more satisfying than brute force.

Bailic rose to close the curtains. The need for the dark's comfort overrode his need to see. His body protested, and feeling ill, he shuffled over to pull them shut. Slowly he collapsed back into his chair. Sure now his fatigue had its roots in the burn across his tracings, he wondered if he could leave his guests alone while he recuperated, reluctantly deciding he couldn't. Losing his ability to use his tracings would set him back soundly. He wouldn't compound his mistake by ignoring them.

His spying would be severely curtailed. If he wanted to know where his guests were, he would have to laboriously track them down on foot. Also forfeit was the ability to create wards. This was a hard blow, as he relied heavily upon knowing he could dominate any situation with a quick thought. Fortunately the wards he had crafted or turned to his use over the years would hold as a matter of principle, and that was what happened to him.

"Curse you," Bailic repeated softly, his fingertips falling from his temples. His eyes rose to where Meson's hat sat on its shelf, mocking him. How could he have guessed how devious Meson had been? "But I gained one of your secrets," he added. Though it had cost him dearly, he finished silently.

It wasn't fair, Bailic thought bitterly. The Masters had never taught *him* it was possible to balance wards within one another. "You've been dead for fourteen years, Meson," he said. "Leave me alone."

22

"Salissa?" Strell called from the far side of the warm kitchen. "Toss me a few of those apples, will you?"

Alissa looked up from her biscuits in mild irritation. He knew she hated him mangling her name. "You must wait until my hands are full before you ask for things," she said. Wiping the flour from her fingers, she stretched to reach the bowl of small, yellow fruit.

His eyes glinted merrily as he held up an apple. "Wait up. I guess I have enough."

"No, you don't." Grinning, Alissa threw three in quick succession at him. Hard.

Strell ducked in mock fear, and the apples sailed over his head to hit the floor in a series of conspicuous thumps, spinning out through the archway and into the dining hall. Silently laughing, they continued their dinner preparations. Neither of them would go retrieve them. It would be an admission of guilt. Besides, Alissa thought, Bailic would probably be there, and they kept their contact with him to a minimum despite his efforts to insinuate himself in their lives.

Much to Alissa's surprise, Bailic was lavish in his praise of their cooking talents. She honestly believed his thin frame was filling out. His morning and noon meals he took in his room, so they suffered his presence only at dinner unless he came down to spy upon them—which was often. Dinner was in the barren hall off the kitchen. It could have been a pleasant spot, as it had a view of the garden through the tall windows behind the wall of drapes. The expansive openings were completely unshuttered. They let in an enormous amount of light when Alissa discovered them and pulled the drapes, but no cold. Clearly there was a ward at work.

If Bailic ever wondered about their lack of curiosity as to how the heat remained inside with the windows unshuttered, he never let on. It was like early summer in the Hold, and it still shocked Alissa to find snow whenever she looked past the curtains. Bailic steadfastly ignored this incongruity with them, making no comment the night he slipped into his dinner chair without his usual housecoat. His lack of explanation of the Hold's unusual warmth was suspicious at best.

Strell slid his pan of baked apples into the oven. Turning, he clapped his hands, making Alissa jump. "That's done," he said loudly. "How are your biscuits coming?" Leaning over her shoulder, he feigned a grab at the dough with one hand and snitched some with the other.

"Stop it!" she cried. She couldn't say why it bothered her, but it did, and clearly Strell knew it. He moved as if to sneak another bit, and grinning, she brandished a wooden spoon.

Giving up, he levered himself up onto a tabletop with a dramatic sigh to made a big show of scraping the bowl of the last crumbs. "I'm going to tell one of your new stories tonight."

"Really?" Alissa smiled, delighted he thought them good enough. "But they aren't new. Just because you haven't heard them, it doesn't follow that Bailic hasn't."

"True." Strell set the bowl down with a clatter. "But it's a good wager he hasn't."

Pleased, Alissa slipped into the dining hall for the apples, returning to dump them into the slop bucket.

"Hey!" Strell elbowed her out of the way and plucked them free. "Those are still good."

She stared at him. "They're bruised."

"Applesauce."

Her eyes rolled. "We've plenty. I don't want to make more."

Strell carefully polished the apples—worthless things by Alissa's account—and set them on the counter. "I'll do it."

Alissa shook her head. This was not new. Strell never threw anything out if it was remotely edible. He was annoyingly careful with food.

"How long till your biscuits are done?" he asked as he leaned to stir the soup.

"Few moments. The only thing left is your baked apples."

"Then we will say they're dessert." Breathing deeply of the steam, he ladled the soup into a large tureen. Striding to the archway to the dining hall, he hesitated, carefully balancing the tureen in one hand as she checked on her baking. "Ready?"

"Almost. Go on. I'll be right there." Alissa smiled, eager to have a moment to herself.

With a sharp nod and a happy hum, Strell vanished into the dining hall. She started as she recognized his tune. It was of a man who couldn't eat meat, but whose wife could, and sighing at the jibe at their meatless diet, Alissa collapsed in a nearby chair. Strell was a bit trying at times.

Bailic's smooth voice broke the peaceful stillness. "Are you tired already, my dear?"

She jumped to her feet and spun around, finding his tall, unmoving shadow by an unused table. By the Hounds of the Navigator, she thought, how did he get in here? She was facing the archway to the dining room! Then she remembered the seldom-used passage directly off the great hall. Somehow Alissa felt guilty, and she had done nothing wrong.

She glanced up, her eyes sliding from the angry welt he sported across a cheek. It had appeared the day after they arrived, and it still looked raw and painful, a week later.

"Bailic isn't downstairs yet!" Strell shouted from the dining hall, and she felt herself flush.

Strell appeared in the archway with a clatter of booted footsteps. Silently he turned from Bailic to her downcast eyes. "I'll finish here, Salissa," he said tightly. "Why don't you go check on the fire?"

Alissa slipped gratefully out between the two men. Talon chittered a welcome from the mantel, and Alissa ruffled her feathers in passing. Safe in the empty dining hall, she leaned her forehead against the cool stone of a tall window and looked morosely out past the drapes. The fire sent a thin rectangle of light into the herb garden. Snow was sedately sifting down in an inaudible hush, gentling a thicker blanket over the dormant herbs and fragrant grasses. The snow never seemed to stop. She sent her finger to intersect the window ward, intentionally instigating its warning jolt in an effort to distract herself.

When they first arrived, she had been eager for spring and the chance to make the extensive garden as it should be, fool that she was, she thought sourly. Seeing her papa's murderer hadn't grown any easier; she was just getting used to it. Alissa wasn't ashamed to admit she had been using Strell as a buffer, a task he seemed to readily accept and take very seriously.

There was a small scuff and she stiffened, steeling her face into a bland expression. She turned expecting Bailic, slumping in relief to find it was Strell. "I hate it when he does that," he murmured uneasily.

"So do I," she whispered as Bailic entered close on Strell's heels.

Dinner was quieter than usual. Only Strell persisted in trying to bring a sense of normalcy to the evening. Alissa knew he was beginning to despise Bailic as much as she, and she appreciated Strell's efforts. His flagrant behavior let her fade into the background, something she never would have dreamed she would ever want to do. But Strell was a consummate actor, and by the time the fire had settled to a steady warmth, even she wondered if he didn't enjoy Bailic's company. Bailic was, she admitted, quite the conversationalist, having the most interesting views and ideas. Being sharp in wit and quick to laugh at Strell's jests, she could understand why her papa had liked him. It was frighteningly easy to forget who he was.

As Alissa cleared the baked apples from the table, Strell rose with a stretch, resettling himself at his usual performing spot upon the hearth. A dark, uneasy tune lifted from his pipe to set the mood, and Alissa blew out the candles to further it, leaving only the fire to light the room. Bailic eagerly moved his thin frame to the uncomfortable-looking high-backed chair that had appeared without comment before the hearth their second night there. Alissa settled herself at her usual spot at the table and worked on mending a hole in her stocking. Contrary to Strell's claim she was to help entertain, he had never insisted, something she was extremely grateful for.

The fire whooshed as it resettled itself, and the sparks outlined Strell in a glittering shimmer. Except for his music it was silent, almost as if the stones were listening. Talon left the mantel to settle on the back of Alissa's chair. From where Alissa sat, she could see only Bailic's feet from beneath his seat. In her imagination he was gone and Strell was playing only for her.

It was always a pleasure to listen to Strell perform, Alissa mused as his music eased her slight tension away. His entire demeanor changed as he became involved with the emotional context of his art. And it was an art, whether it was piping or telling a story. It wasn't what he said but how he said it that made the difference, adding details and emotion that turned a story she had heard all her life into something that rang of truth and forgotten history.

Ceasing the eerie music, he took a slow breath, closing his eyes in a long blink. When they opened, he seemed like another person, older and careworn, half slumped against the hearth as if weary of the world. His eyes were riveted to the past as he began to speak.

"Far, far back in time, so far that even the memory of their once-proud name is lost, there was a wise and joyful people. They lived apart from all in a great city that fulfilled their every need. Even today, no one can guess if they dwelt on the plains, hills, or perhaps even the coast. But it matters not from whence they came, for they stepped from time itself, fading under a shroud of mystery. It is of this people I would tell you, and of a great battle which they did not fight, but endured, a conflict so magnificent that its memory stands where their name does not. They held they had no choice, and held true to their beliefs.

"It was so that a plague covered the land. Not a plague of the flesh, but of the mind, one that stole the thought and reason from all it touched. It begot a carnage on the plains, in the foothills, and by the coast. People became as beasts, preying upon each other in a rage that excluded little, and those who survived could not say why, only that a fever burned in their mind with the soft thought of killing keeping them from sleep. Confusion and death were a welcome state.

"Only one group of people was spared this plague of madness, if indeed it could be said they did. When the first hint of the illness and the futility of combating it reached them, their beloved Warden consulted his finest shaduf and built a tremendous wall about his city to keep the sickness at bay. Some say it was of earth from the plains, others of stone from the mountains, and yet others of wood from the coast, but all agree it was thick and tall.

"Many were the young mothers who traveled far to the supposed sanctuary after word of it reached them. Some say it was through the dunes of the plains, others through the wilds of the hills, and yet others through the swamps of the coast, but all admit they were lead to their deaths by Amaa.

"To her shock, Amaa found walls about the city of her birth, a friend barring the gate. With feet stained from travel and arms weary from the weight of children, Amaa implored her Warden, 'Let me in. We are not ill. Take my children. They can do you no harm.' She pleaded to no avail. The gates remained closed—her cries, ignored. In shame, the Warden turned a deaf ear to her entreaties. He held he had no choice and remained true to his beliefs.

"A great wailing rose on both sides of the wall as the madness came upon those gathered outside, the seeds of the sickness they carried finally ripening on to their deadly end. Amaa wept as she destroyed her children, and still begging for mercy, she turned upon herself.

"The proud people hid behind their wall and waited for time to sweep the danger away. But after the pitiful screams and mournful cries of the children and women slipped uneasily into the past, a new danger threatened. The illness, having spent itself upon the surrounding lands, left behind a world mourning the loss of two thirds of its people. The survivors looked for someone to blame. The walled city had suffered no casualties. In the survivor's sight, it deserved to be punished.

"Thousands of men racked with grief descended upon the beautiful land, finding a leader to give direction for their separate pain. The coast calls him Keppren, the hills call him Keperen, the plains simply call him Kren, but all call him betrayed as he stood outside the city he had once called his own to find the blood of his wife and children upon the threshold and his friend safe within.

"Kren camped upon the nearby grounds, and as he

stood unmoving, his men hammered upon the gates with the next generation's supply of winter heat. For months, drumbeats set a counterpoint to the pounding of boots and the striking of the gates. But the walls remained true and did not succumb.

"With the passage of time, the heartache of the survivors lessened. Realizing the folly of trying to assuage their pain by inflicting it upon another, they left as they had come, abandoning the untouched city, returning to the plains, coast, and hills. Only Kren remained, a ragged man shattered in mind and spirit.

"Kren wept and pummeled his fists against the barred gates, imprisoning an entire city with only his words. 'Warden!' he cried, filling the sky with the sound of his grief. 'Why have you shut me out? Why have you killed my Amaa?'

"And the Warden answered from atop his walls, 'Kren, my friend, why have you laid siege to me? I must protect my people. I'm their servant. I have no choice.'

"'There's always a choice!' Kren screamed. 'And I am stained with the blood of the ones who looked to me for protection.' Kren raised his hands stiffly to the sky. 'I will not take the blame for this! I *choose* to not accept the responsibility for the deaths of Amaa and our children. Do you hear me, Warden! I give my guilt to you and all who hide behind these walls of shame and fear!'

"The air trembled, stirred by a force so low, it could only be felt, and Kren stood as if made of stone. 'You!' Kren said as an ebony glow enveloped his upraised fists. 'You will be cursed, though you should live for a thousand years, Warden. My anguish and shame are my gifts to you, and you will not rest until, as a people, you prove yourself worthy of the name!'

"Kren's raised hands became lost in a darkness even the sun couldn't penetrate. A wild cry of rage escaped him, and as it reached its peak, the blackness exploded from his hands to cover the sun. Then the blackness was gone. Kren slumped where he stood, shattered and drained. A gentle rumbling began within the earth. Feeding upon itself, it grew to a great unrest as the very ground protested the curse. With a mighty shudder and crash, the gates fell, outraged at the strength of the curse set upon those it once sheltered. Kren didn't look back, turning east to never be recorded in tale or song again.

"The city was untouched, but not unchanged. All who hid behind its walls were deeply ashamed and dishonored. They realized that to have ignored the cries for pity and succor of their kinsmen and to have allowed such violence upon their doorstep was more inhumane than anything done in the throes of a fevered brain.

"The city sent great envoys to the plague-torn lands to heal what remained of those they turned away. Some said it was to avoid Kren's curse, others said it was to ease their shame. After many years the lands of the plains, foothills, and coast grew sound again. Laughter and song were heard as the scars were buried beneath the smiles of the newly born. The walled city thrived as well, becoming more influential and beautiful than before. All appeared well; the city's inhabitants, content. But as the years passed and a new generation replaced the old, the meaning of Kren's curse grew evident, and they became afraid. After fifty turnings of the earth about the sun, it could no longer be denied.

"The souls of the frightened people who built and hid behind the wall were not at rest. They continued in silence, filling the night with their tremulous presence. For they still regretted their choice so long ago and even in death tried to make amends. But it could never be enough, and to this day they roam the empty streets of their abandoned homeland. For, who could remain in a city of ghosts, no matter how gentle and kind they were?

"And so Amaa became Amaa the Innocent, and Kren, Kren the Betrayed. And of the one who built the walls there is no name, be he remembered by the coast, plains, or hills, condemned to be known by his title alone. For the Warden held he had no choice, and remained true to his beliefs."

Strell's head dropped, and Alissa shut her eyes against a tear. It was a story she had heard uncounted times as a child, but Strell, as usual, told it so much better. His haunted eyes met hers as she opened them and she smiled weakly. Talon made a contented chitter deep in her throat.

"That was an excellent rendition," Bailic said, and Alissa stiffened, having forgotten he was there. "Tell me. Where did you learn it?"

Suddenly nervous, Alissa bent over her mending. Though Bailic often questioned Strell about his stories, there was an intent eagerness in his tone she had never heard before. And she had begun to distrust anything different when it came to Bailic.

"It's something Salissa and I shared when we were younger," Strell said softly, his vacant eyes showing he hadn't yet shaken his mood. "She asked to hear it endlessly. It's one of her favorites."

And this was true. She had related the tale to Strell when they were younger, only three weeks younger, but younger. And Strell knew it was one of her favorites. She had told him of how she used to sit on the hearth and shiver despite the fire's warmth as her papa whispered the tale to her, his eyes dark and terrible in the cold shadow of a winter's night. Imagining the distraught man hammering at the gates, and the empty houses populated by ghosts, hundreds of years later, always sent a delicious chill through her.

Bailic leaned around his chair to see her. "You both know the history of Ese' Nawoer?"

"Ese' Nawoer?" Alissa whispered, slowly mouthing the unfamiliar name. "It really existed? It's not just a story?"

Bailic smiled indulgently. "Of course it existed. It still does—in a manner of speaking. Rare is the tale that lacks a grain of truth. Didn't you find the walled city on your way here? It lies only a morning's walk from the Hold. The history texts say—"

"You mean the stories," Strell interrupted, and Bailic's eyes narrowed imperceptibly.

"No. The history texts." Bailic rose to his feet, going to stand before the fire where he could see them both. "You really didn't find it? It's said you can see the walls from the top of the tower." He hesitated, his gaze going distant. "When the sky is clear."

"Strell took a shortcut," Alissa murmured, almost to herself. She felt a stirring of excitement. Ese' Nawoer, she thought. That had to be the mysterious symbol on her papa's map. It was an abandoned city, the same in her papa's tale, and it was called Ese' Nawoer.

Bailic's expression cleared into what Alissa thought was an uncanny sharpness. "The tale of how Ese' Nawoer acquired her walls is well-known to me, but you"—he pointed to Strell—"left out the most interesting part."

Alissa frowned as he faulted what she deemed a perfect rendition.

"Your face tells me you disagree." All sweetness and honey, Bailic chuckled. "Don't be surprised," he said with a mocking smile. "Most are reluctant to speak the truth to little girls."

He said the last patronizingly, and she struggled to hide her anger. Hesitating, he steepled his fingers in a shocking mimicry of her papa, and she waited, confident Bailic would continue. As much as he couched his words with pleasantries, he enjoyed belittling them, and dispensing information seemed to give him a sense of control. He smiled benevolently as he came to where Alissa sat, settling himself beside her on one of the hard-backed chairs. Talon protested with a short hiss, and from the hearth, Strell stirred uneasily. Alissa and he exchanged worried looks.

"I'll tell you the rest," Bailic whispered to her alone, his pale eyebrows looking almost nonexistent in the shadow light, "not because you deserve it, but because it pleases me for you to know how the world will change itself to satisfy me."

Satisfy him? Alissa wondered, raising her eyes. Bailic locked his gaze on hers and the force of his will slammed into her. She took a frightened breath, shocked to find herself confronted with the madness within him. This was the man who destroyed her papa, the Hold, and all who had claimed a place within it. If he guessed who she was, he would use her as he had countless others, discarding what he didn't need. There was nothing she could do to stop him if he knew. Ashen-faced, she sat, drained of all emotions but one. Fear.

From the hearth came a rough scraping as Strell got to his feet. Talon began to hiss in earnest. Alissa's eyes darted to Strell and back again. Her eyes met Bailic's, and he simpered, apparently not caring that Strell was white with anger. "Good," Bailic said, settling back. He glanced at Strell as if in dismissal. "I see we have reached an understanding."

Again he leaned forward, and Alissa couldn't help but shirk away. "Know this then," he continued. "It's written the souls of Ese' Nawoer are obliged to rise and absolve their guilt by serving the one who calls them from their perpetual unrest. When I gain what I need, I will claim them. They will be my first minions, the ones I use to set a new order." Barely audible, his words were a sigh upon on her ear. "My order." Slowly, he leaned back and she began to breathe again. "The souls of the abandoned city will bring the foothills and plains to heel. If not, they will bring a return to the plague of madness. Think on that, my dear, and upon which side you wish to be counted." He rose without a sound, his eyes never leaving the kestrel. "It was an excellent tale, Piper. Quite enlightening." And in a hush of sippered feet, he was gone.

Numb, Alissa stared at Bailic's empty chair. Set a new order, she thought. Gain what he needed? Bailic wanted to shatter the tenuous peace between the foothills and plains. And now she knew why he hadn't thrown them out into the snow. He had killed her papa for the book of *First Truth*. That must be what he meant by "When I gain what I need." Bone and Ash, she nearly moaned. It was just as she thought. Bailic knew they were searching for it.

"What the Hounds is wrong with him tonight?" Strell said tightly as he left the hearth and came to stand beside her.

"Don't you get it, Strell?" Alissa said. "He expects us to find my papa's book for him." She looked miserably up at him. "And if he knows when I find it, he'll take it away."

Strell's gaze darted to the black archway to the great hall. "Shhh," he whispered urgently. "He might be by the door."

Alissa pressed her lips together and shook her head, glancing up to Talon contentedly preening on the back of her chair. The clever bird always knew when Bailic was within earshot. Several times when they were searching the Hold, she had alerted them to his spying. He always had an excuse when they doubled back to confront him, but it was terribly obvious. Lately he had given up—or learned Talon's range of detection.

"But he said he was going to use the ghosts," Strell said as he eased down in the seat Bailic had left. "The ones at that city. What did he call it?" He shifted his shoulders to try and disguise his unease.

"Ese' Nawoer." Alissa picked nervously at her stitching. "I think he needs the book to claim them, and what's keeping us out of the snow is him not knowing who can find it."

Strell was silent. Not meeting her eyes, he rose and went to the hearth. Slowly the bright flames began to disappear under the ash. "So why hasn't he put a ward on us and asked?"

Alissa gathered up her stitching, ignoring how scared she was. Strell waited until she relit a candle before he carefully placed the last shovel of ash on the fire. The flame quivered in response to her hand, and she hated herself for it. Her eyes flicked up to him in the new darkness. "I don't know. But I'm not leaving without my book. And Bailic will take it as soon as I find it."

"We can't overpower Bailic," Strell said softly. His face turned sour, and he sighed as if in resignation. "Not if he's killed all those Keepers. We have to find a way to open that door and get Useless out." The fire irons clattered as they were replaced, and he stood, looking frustrated.

Useless, Alissa brooded. What good was he? Frowning, she rose and followed Strell into the kitchen where the dishes waited. The crockery was already stacked in the sink, and she smiled her thanks as Strell thoughtfully warmed the basin with a portion of water slated for their evening tea. He stood ready to dry her efforts with an annoying mix of expectancy and impatience. Alissa hastily reached for a bowl.

"So," Strell said as he held out a hand, "where do we look tomorrow?"

"I don't know," she said listlessly over the harsh scraping of the plates. They had already searched the first eight floors, finding rooms so empty, even the dust was missing. It had all been a boring repetition except for the Keepers' rooms. Most looked as if their owners had simply walked away. Then it went from boring to alarming as she found each and every ward they had left protecting their things, warning her away with a threat of tingling hums. Only the tower had they left unsearched, as her papa hadn't gone that high before he confronted Bailic the day he died. Still, it might be worth a look if they could come up with an excuse. "Do you think we might sneak up to the tower and see that walled city?" she mused aloud, hinting.

Strell's shoulders shifted as he exhaled. "Maybe, but perhaps we should search the annexes again first." He held out a hand, and she gave him the last plate.

"I suppose, but I don't think my papa hid the book there."

Strell placed the last cup away and hung the towel by the fire. "If we can't find the book, we might find a couple of new stockings for you." Chuckling, he lit a candle and banked the fire.

"Harrumph," Alissa snorted, and after a sharp look around the tidy kitchen, she went to fetch her mending where she had left it in the dining hall. Strell followed with the brewing pot of tea, and they made their way through the dark into the great hall and up the stairs. A swift shadow darted over them as Talon led the way, eerily finding her path even in the darkness.

If tonight were like any other, they would take their evening tea together while Strell planned out tomorrow's entertainment. They would then say their good-nights and he would retire to his room. It was nearly the same pleasant pattern they began on their journey here, and Alissa had been pleased when it continued unabated. Tonight he had promised to play something of her choosing, and she was looking forward to it.

"Anything?" she said as she settled into her chair, not really believing his offer.

"Anything."

"And it won't cost me a thing?"

"Absolutely nothing."

"Well," she said wisely, "that's rather magnanimous of you."

Strell invariably chose what he would play, when he would play, and how long he would play it. Whenever she suggested a tune, he would grin, informing her in a rather irritating fashion that it would cost her, and how much coin did she have? It was his mercenary plainsmen side showing, and the one time she took him to task over it, he had laughed, telling her this was his profession, and he would be compensated for any such tasks. But now she could choose. The decision was easy. "Your new one," she said, setting her cup down in anticipation.

"New one?" Strell gave her a blank look.

"The one you were humming endlessly a while back," she coaxed. As the words left her, she realized she hadn't heard it since they arrived. He had to know the one she meant, though.

"Oh, that one!" Strell pushed at the air is if driving the very idea away. "You don't want to hear that. It's not done yet. How about that ballad about the raku, the fish, and the apple?"

"No," she replied mildly, feeling her ire rise. He had asked what she wanted to hear. Why was he being so difficult?

"Well then, how about—"

"No," she said, her voice as hard as a rock and as soft as a feather. Talon chattered and opened her wings nervously.

Strell shifted in his chair, glancing from Talon to the pipe in his hands. "I can't hit the low notes with this," he said. Standing up, he took his grandfather's pipe from behind him, hidden in the cushions. "I'm going to have to use this one."

"Won't it give you a headache?" she teased lightly.

"One tune won't hurt," he said sheepishly. A few bars of "Taykell's Adventure" briefly filled the air as Strell warmed the wood, and Alissa smiled, remembering the first time she had heard him play it. He paused, and once satisfied all was as it should be, he began to play.

The ethereal melody drifted forth, simple and true, untainted and free from the day's uncertainty. With a heavy smile, Alissa allowed her eyes to close. The very essence of the mountains seemed to be distilled into his music. It was almost too easy to envision the clear autumn skies, pale and washed out from the summer's relentless heat. She snuggled deeper into the cushions of her chair, feeling in their aged smoothness the remembrance of the silken caress of a late evening breeze, damp with the moisture of a coming rain.

Masterfully and from his heart, Strell played, and Alissa let the music flow through her, erasing all the fear and doubt Bailic had instilled. Strell held the last note as long as possible, and she opened her eyes drowsily as it faded into nothing. "That was lovely," she sighed, too far gone to say more. It often seemed Strell's music lulled her into an almost irresistible urge to sleep.

Strell gave her one of his expressive grunts, but she could tell he was pleased. "Good night, Alissa," he said as he stood.

She smiled her farewell, satisfied to remain where she was. Maybe someday she would make it to the bed against the wall. So far, every night had been spent in peaceful slumber curled up in her large, overstuffed chair before the fire. With another nod, Strell left, softly closing the door behind him. Utterly content, Alissa shut her eyes and slipped into an easy sleep.

23

"You decide which one. It was your idea," Alissa said. She glanced past Talon perched on her shoulder to Strell with a faint feeling of exasperation. They stood in the stark entryway of the Hold staring at the six tunnels leading to the separate, underground annexes. The tunnels were dark, but the great hall was filled by the early-morning light that streamed in through the huge windows that lined the eastern wall above the door.

Strell handed her a lit candle. "Well, if you don't care, let's look in the first one again."

"The livery?" she said, looking up to where the word was etched into the stone atop the arch. "Why would my papa have hidden it in the stables? There's nothing but dust down there."

"Oh," he teased. "So you *do* have an opinion."

Alissa sighed. They had found the inscriptions the first time they investigated the annexes, labeling the tunnels in the script she understood. Finding exactly what she expected at the end of the passages went a long way in proving to Strell she could read. His hesitant admission made her think he had believed it all the time. He simply enjoyed teasing her too much to admit it.

They had found the stables dark, musty, and empty. The tunnel labeled Quarters held only row upon row of sad-looking cots. The kitchens were just what they said, but lacked even the smallest spoon. It wasn't until they investigated the archway marked "Perishables" that they found anything worthwhile. The storage room contained more food than an entire fortress could eat in a year, all preserved under wards that dissolved upon touch and left the food susceptible to spoilage. Bailic had said nothing the night the bowl of strawberries appeared on the table. Now they had vegetables and fruit every meal.

Alissa had found the last two tunnels, dry goods and castoffs, to be the most interesting. "Dry goods?" she said, remembering the stacks of leather and linen. She thought searching the annexes were a waste of time, but perhaps she could find something she could use. Strell was right. Her stockings had been mended so often, they were getting rather useless.

"Dry goods sounds fine," Strell said, striding to the last open archway.

Talon chittered sharply from Alissa's shoulder as they stepped under the first arch. The passage led slightly down, its floor worn smooth from use, and they hesitated as their eyes adjusted. Alissa was glad for the candles and their warm glow reflecting off the low curve of the roof. She squinted as the draft shifted her hair into her eyes. It had grown annoyingly long, almost to her shoulders, and needed to be cut.

A faint light at the end beckoned, and soon their boots were edging the sunlight. Together they stood at the opening of the belowground closet, taking it all in. Stretched before them was a narrow, tall room, lit by thin slits in the distant stone ceiling. There were four levels, all of which opened up in wide balconies overlooking a central, narrow work area on the ground floor.

The first floor was devoted to paper and anything one would need to use or make it. There were baskets of ink pots, brushes, quills, and barrels of scrap cloth in various stages of processing. Off to the side were several tall cupboards containing stacks of the precious paper stored out of the sun. The ward that was keeping the Hold dust-free was working here, too.

The three other levels were divided into low-ceilinged alcoves filled with leather and fabric. At the highest point hung a huge block and tackle affair, presumably to raise and lower bundles too large or awkward for the shallow stairs snaking up one wall.

Alissa reached for Strell's candle, blowing it and hers out. Talon abandoned her as she crouched to set the candles by the archway. The small bird flew to the highest balcony, her sharp calls echoing against the curved roof. Alissa slowly followed Strell as he jumped down the few steps to the first floor. The sun streamed in to warm the storage room, but not enough to prevent the small shiver that ran through her. It was chilly, as if the window wards weren't present.

"There are enough goods here for three markets," Strell exclaimed as he jogged up the steps to the second floor.

"Mmmm," she said dismally. Somehow she knew her papa's book wasn't in the dry goods, but if Strell insisted they search, it would take all winter. Alissa followed him up the stairs. It was dark the last time they were here, and she wanted to take a closer look at the leather she had found. There was no reason she had to waste the winter. She could make some clothes. Besides, she rationalized, she needed to. Hers hadn't been designed for the abuse she had been subjecting them to, and were positively threadbare. She was beginning to feel like a beggar next to Bailic's exquisitely tailored clothes.

Sniffing deeply for the warm scent of leather, she followed her nose past bales of linen and wool until she found it. Her hands dove to her favorite shade, a rich cream, and a small sigh escaped her. It was as soft as a puddle of sun-warmed water. Very little good leather ever made it as deep into the foothills as her parent's farm. Her mother's boots were the exception, but now sporting that dismal brown, they had lost much of their appeal.

"Have you ever seen so much good leather?" she said in awe as Strell came close.

"Market," he said, critically eyeing the swath she held up.

"This good?" she questioned.

"Not a foothills market, a plains market."

There was a trace of pride in his voice, and Alissa set the leather back. "I didn't know the plains had their own markets."

Strell headed up the stairs to the third floor. "Only the wealthier families—those with a chartered name—are granted the right by the council to trade for food. It goes from a foothills market to a plains, where anyone can trade for it."

"Why can't everyone trade for food?"

Strell disappeared up the stairs, clearly uncomfortable. "It's safer that way."

Alissa opened her mouth to ask for an explanation, but he was gone. Talon dropped from the rafters, bouncing across the leather as if inspecting it as well. Seeing a good-sized piece of the cream, Alissa draped it over her shoulder. Perhaps she could make a new pair of boots from it. It couldn't be *that* hard. Her fingers caressed a swath of green leather so dark as to be almost black. "Strell would look good in that," she whispered, draping it over her shoulder.

Alissa wandered through the tall stacks and bales of cloth, her awe growing at every turn. "Look at how good this stuff is," she breathed to Talon, pulling out a bolt of blue and holding it up to herself. No wonder Bailic was so well-dressed, she thought. Even the heavyweights designed for hard labor were of an astounding quality. Never had she had the chance to choose the cloth for her clothes, and never had it been this good. Always it had been what was left. Spying a bolt of linen that matched her leather, she tossed the blue away and unrolled the cream. "This is nice," she said admiringly to her uncaring bird.

Fingering the tight, unblemished fabric, Alissa broke into a delighted grin. She didn't need to make trousers. She could make a skirt! They weren't traveling anymore, so her hated pants weren't necessary. Terribly pleased, Alissa measured out enough for *two* skirts and a knee-length blouse, cutting the fabric with a knife hanging from a string on a nearby support post.

Alissa bent close to the faded swirl of paint under the nail as she replaced the knife. "Fail to return my knife, and you will be bringing me my morning trays for a month," Alissa whispered, frowning at the signature, "Keribdis." Glancing uneasily about the empty room, Alissa rolled up the leftover and tossed the bolt aside.

"Strell?" she called. "Have you seen any thread?"

"No," came his faint shout from what sounded like the fourth and last level.

Curiosity pulled her to the stairway. Halfway up to the third floor she spotted the heavy spindles. "You passed right by it!" she shouted.

"Really?" He sounded as if he didn't even care.

Hounds! she thought in delight when she reached it. There were more shades than spoons in her mother's cupboard. Humming happily, she chose the proper weight for her leather and cloth. Alissa wrapped everything up in a messy bundle, eager to get back to the Hold's upper rooms and get started. Her thoughts were deep into flamboyant styles and unheard-of lengths when she noticed the angle of the sun. It had grown late. Nearly afternoon. "Strell?" she called. "Where are you?"

"Right behind you."

She jumped, her pulse pounding as she spun around to

find him grinning. "Where were you?" she accused, not liking the delight in his eyes for having startled her.

"Ropes, nets, and stuff," he said. "Fourth floor is for the men. Want me to take that?"

"Yes. Thanks," she said, handing him the leather.

"A lady shouldn't carry her own bundles at market," Strell said lightly, taking it all.

She flushed, turning away in embarrassment. "We should probably get Bailic his noon meal," she said, eager to change the subject. "Before he comes looking for it."

Strell grunted his agreement, and they headed down the stairway, single file. Trying to avoid the confusion Strell's last words started, Alissa turned her thoughts to her new fabric. She couldn't wait to get started stitching. Her lips pursed as she tried to figure out how she was going to prepare Bailic's meal and still have enough light to plan out how to use all that fabric.

"Tell you what," Strell said as they reached the first floor and he came up alongside of her. "Why don't I make up Bailic's tray today? I don't mind. That way you can get started."

Alissa smiled sheepishly. "Is it that obvious?"

His eyes softened. "I had four sisters, Alissa. You aren't much different from them."

"Thanks, Strell," she said, suddenly shy. "Talon?" she called, looking for a distraction. "Come on, silly bird. You can catch mice in the kitchen." Swooping so low, she brushed Alissa's hair with a careless wing tip, her bird flew up the corridor.

"Just don't go cutting into anything until I ask Bailic if there's anything we might do to trade for your—purchases," Strell said as they entered the dark tunnel.

Alissa's eyes went wide in alarm. "Oh, I forgot. Maybe I ought to put it back."

Strell shook his head, barely visible in the light coming from the great hall up ahead. "Let me ask him. There must be something we can do or give him to trade."

"Whatever it takes," Alissa said fervently. "I've got to have some of that fabric."

Strell smiled in understanding. "Do you know how to make anything special in the kitchen? Maybe a sweet?"

A slow smile came over Alissa. Men were men. "How about candied apples?" she said, recalling how her papa hovered about the kitchen when her mother had taken the effort and time to make them. They took three days.

Strell nearly stumbled, so quick did he look at her. "You know how to make candied apples?" He hesitated. "Think you could make it a double batch?"

"That depends," she said, feeling herself in a position of power for the first time in ages. "What will you give me?"

24

The early afternoon sun shone bright upon the Hold's grounds, reflecting off the snowfield in a blinding glare. A thin sliver still found its way into Bailic's room, where he sat in his chair before his shattered balcony, brooding. It had been nearly two weeks since he had burned himself. Trying to use his ash-clogged tracings still gave him headaches, and worse, he was no closer to finding out which one of his "guests" was the potential Keeper. It was irritating, Bailic thought as he set his book and quill aside. He was more clever than both of them put together.

Soon the plainsman would knock softly at his door and leave the tray. It was a ritual that began shortly after their arrival and showed no sign of changing. Bailic stood, moving to look out over the black-branched woods between him and the cursed city Ese' Nawoer. The sun was bright, making everything a blur of brown, white, and blue. His eyes began to water in hurt, and cursing himself, he backed up into the shadow.

The ward on the window was thin here, not having been

designed to stretch over the larger opening Meson had made, and he felt a slight draft. Odd, he mused. The draft had never bothered him before. He must be getting accustomed to the comforts he had been indulging in lately. Bailic rubbed gently at the welt on his cheek, still as sore and ugly as if he had acquired it yesterday. Three meals a day in addition to the conversation, stilted as it was, had become quite pleasant.

The sound of the piper's heavy boots on the stair came clear from behind his door. There a was the traditional soft knock followed by a surprising, "Bailic? If I might? I have a question."

Bailic turned with raised eyebrows. "Come in," he called, not moving from the balcony.

There was a moment of hesitation, and the door swung inward. The piper stood awkwardly on the sill, seeming reluctant to cross it. He had Bailic's noon tray in his hands.

"Here," Bailic said, remembering to be pleasant and hospitable. "Let me take that from you." Striding forward, Bailic took the tray, setting it on his nearby worktable.

The tall plainsman shifted from foot to foot and took a bundle of cloth from under his arm.

"It smells wonderful as always," Bailic said, disguising his impatience by pouring himself a glass of water. He leaned back against his worktable, glass in hand. "Please," he said graciously, gesturing for the man to continue.

"Salissa and I have been in the tunnels," the plainsman said, his eyes fixed to the balcony,

"The annexes," Bailic prompted, feeling his pulse rise. They had been busy.

"Yes," the man said quickly. "I would propose a bargain with you."

Bailic's breath quickened. You wish to search for something, possibly?" A book, perhaps? he added silently in his thoughts.

"Fabric, leather, and such material," the man said. "Salissa would like to make a few things to prepare for our departure in the spring."

Bailic nodded. This plainsman was clever, dancing around his words. It would make Bailic's victory all the sweeter when he brought him down. "What can you trade?" he said in a mock sadness. "I already have your services."

The man's eyes grew intent. "I have these sundry items," he said, stepping into the room and laying open his bundle of cloth upon the worktable.

Bailic leaned close, struggling not to sneer at the pathetic display: a pouch of salt, a knife, a set of dice, a tied bit of string, two shells, a cracked mirror, a capped jar made of stone, and an anklet bell from the coast, not worth the metal it was made from this far from the coast. Trinkets. He hoped the plainsman was holding something back, because this was nothing.

"Knives and knots I have, fine though these are," Bailic said softly, his fingers rifling through the clutter. "Is there anything else you might . . ." He froze, his fingertips on the stone jar. There was a hint of loose power there, a whisper, no more. A source?

Swallowing his excitement, Bailic picked up the jar and brought it close to his eyes. "Tell me of this," he breathed, looking up in irritation as the plainsman plucked it out of his grasp.

"This?" the man said, slipping into the pattern of words and phrases used when bargaining. "This poorly crafted container is a trifle. The worst of the lot. Good for nothing more than holding horse liniment, perhaps."

Bailic placed his hands behind him, refusing to give in to his desire to take the jar as the piper offered it back. The indulgent smile the plainsman wore was infuriating. Bailic knew he'd lost whatever edge he had. He had allowed his emotions sway. But he had to have that jar.

"Right now it stores an ointment," the piper was saying. "Worthless stuff from the foothills. I couldn't let you have the jar until I empty it. Give me a moment to throw it—"

"No!" Bailic exclaimed, drawing his hands back with a fierce determination. "No," he said quietly. "I'll take it as it is. What did you say you wanted?" He didn't care that his hands trembled in eagerness as the man put the jar into grasp.

"Fabric and leather." There was a hesitation. "As much as she can use."

Bailic looked up. Allowing the plainsman to think he could have anything was intolerable. "None of the silk."

The man nodded, wrapping up his trash and tucking the package under his arm. "Done and done," he said.

"Done and done," Bailic agreed, ushering the piper out with an absent gesture.

Not even waiting for the door to shut, Bailic strode to the shrinking sliver of sun. He dragged his chair into it, sitting down with the jar in the light. He would pay for it later with red, tender skin, but he had to see the container clearly.

The lid grated off, and he sniffed warily at the ointment. Wrinkling his nose at the stench of burnt skies and lightning, he gingerly dabbed a bit onto his finger. Yes, he thought in growing excitement as his fingers cramped with a humming sensation. There was the scent of loosed power, almost a catch in his throat more than a smell. The source was gone, but enough remained in the stone to have seeped back into the salve. Eagerly he slathered the ointment onto his cheek, his eyes closing in bliss as a warm tingle spread from the angry line, taking the last of the pain with it.

A sigh escaped him as he slumped back, smiling as he failed to feel the familiar pull of pain across his cheek. His score would probably heal overnight with only a ghost-line to mark it rather than the expected thick welt. Bailic reverently capped the jar and held it up. "Plains-made," he whispered. "Common enough." It had to have been an accident. Source was too precious to use this way, even if it was highly effective in the healing of raku score. It was far more likely the jar had simply held a source at some time. It was rather tenacious stuff, soaking into anything surrounding it. Once the container was emptied of its precious cargo, the residual power in the stone could have seeped back into the salve. But why store so much source in the first place?

The strength it contained could be drawn upon as long as it was close, but it was unheard of not to meld it into one's inner-being when one had the chance. It was too risky to leave it lying about where a rival Keeper could happen upon it and commandeer it for himself, supplementing his strength with another's. Source was a very rare substance. The Masters of the Hold were uncharacteristically uncommunicative from whence it came.

A wash of anger flooded through him at the thought of them. Rising, he strode across the room to set the jar on his desk with a thump. "They will see," he directed to Meson's hat as he sullenly sat on his desktop. "I'm deserving, and I will have that cursed book! I'd have it now if you hadn't been so *stubborn*." Noticing his fingers drumming upon his crossed arms, he took a methodical, calming breath, dispelling his anger with an iron will and three practiced breaths.

His slow investigations were getting him nowhere, he thought darkly. He had to know more. There had to be a way to discover what he needed without using the power of his tracings. He had gotten soft relying upon the strength of his source rather than his wit. This lack of progress was his own fault.

Bailic reached across his desk and pulled his midday tray closer. His eyes upon the bright rectangle of the balcony window, his fingers sifted through a bowl nuts. They dropped into their wooden bowl with a soft clatter, the repetitious patter calming him.

"So which one of them is the latent Keeper?" he said with a sigh. Taking a handful of nuts, he rose to find two other bowls: a deep, musty green and a brilliant gold. He set them all on the table beside his balcony chair and sank down, deep in thought.

"The piper knows the history of Ese' Nawoer," he said, gently placing a nut into the green bowl. The story was kept unknown outside the Hold, a carefully held history. Only if Strell was a Keeper's child would he have heard it. "But the girl knew it as well." And he tossed a nut into the gold one. There was no help here.

Bailic ran his fingers over his shortly cropped hair as he considered the sparse information he had managed to pry from her over the last two weeks. It wasn't much, but it was patently obvious they weren't siblings, and the piper didn't treat the girl with the disdain flesh-runners usually heaped upon their unwanted burdens. It seemed likely the strange duo had grown up together, probably in the plains, as they both knew the subtleties of its customs: The tea was almost chokingly strong, the cups and plates were laid out upside down to keep the sand from them, and he had seen both of them sitting cross-legged upon their chairs as all good children from the plains are taught to keep the snakes from their ankles.

Their diet, however, had been distressingly free of meat, speaking of a foothills upbringing. It didn't seem to bother either of them. Perhaps they were simply too lazy to go out and hunt anything. Nothing seemed to fit, and it was making him increasingly uneasy.

Spinning from excessive force, a second nut slammed into the green bowl. "The piper opened Meson's room," he said with a snarl. Or did he? Bailic frowned. Perhaps the girl opened it. She was in possession of the room. "No," he whispered. It was far more likely the piper opened it, then offered what he thought was the best chamber to her. Many concessions were made in the name of courtship, and that was exactly what the piper was doing.

Bailic's lips twisted in distaste. The fool was so far gone, he wasn't even aware he was wooing the empty-headed half-breed girl. More proof they weren't siblings. It was a disgrace. The man was clearly pure plains. He ranked better than she. And the nut remained where it lay.

Then there was the piper's hat. The wide brim and loose cut was identical to the distinctive dress of a Keeper. There was little chance the piper would have it unless raised by one of them. Battles were won or lost over such details, and with a crack, a third nut landed in the green bowl.

Sending his gaze into the blur past the balcony, Bailic considered the more nebulous facts at hand. The temperament of the two weighed surprisingly heavily in his decision. Keepers were notoriously willful, seldom suffering themselves to be told what to do, especially when it was in their best interests. The annoying trait was linked to their highly ordered tracings, and therefore, control of one's temper was the first and hardest lesson the Masters taught. It was too dangerous to allow the enormous power of a source to flow through a mind unfettered with restraint. But it was ironic that the fieriest tempers led to the coolest of manners under the Masters' tuition.

The girl was decidedly reticent. Often he would only see

her during their too-brief dinners. She would invariably scurry off to the kitchen after the piper's performance. Once he had followed her, only to be driven away by her bedeviled bird. Who could think with all that hissing? His efforts to question her concerning her background always seemed to be intercepted by the piper. Bailic frowned. At times it seemed as if the man was purposely trying to annoy him.

Bailic shifted in his chair, his thoughts turning to the plainsman. The piper had the flamboyant, easy way with people that most Keepers had possessed. And he had a strong will, Bailic mused, tapping a nut on the table. Taking two nuts, Bailic put his hand over the green bowl. Hesitating, he dropped one.

"And the salve," he said, rubbing a finger over his cheek, relishing the lack of pain. His hand dropped and he reached for a nut. The piper had mentioned the salve, therefore it must be his. A nut clattered into his bowl. Five against the girl's one.

Bailic's eyes narrowed in vexation. The piper's bowl was decidedly the fullest, but something didn't feel right. He had to know more, especially about the girl. A slow smile eased over him. Yes, he would spend the interim while his tracings healed focusing his attention on her. And when he had the full use of the power within his source again, he would act on his findings. He had waited decades; he could bide a bit longer—but only a bit.

25

"Ouch," Alissa whispered as her needle slipped. Setting aside her stitching, she stuck the side of her thumb in her mouth, then checked to see if it was bleeding. It was. The morning sun streamed in to light the dining hall, and she gazed out the windows, enjoying the sensation of seeing snow and not being cold.

Strell glanced up from the fire, where he was contentedly stringing apple slices on a bit of twine. "Why don't you use a thimble?" he asked, a teasing lilt to his voice.

"It's harder to control the needle when I'm wearing it," she grumbled.

"It has to be better than stabbing yourself six times before dinner."

She looked at her thumb again. Deciding to put something on it, she stood and stretched. A smile eased over her as she set her stitching down. If all went as she expected, she ought to be done with it by next week. Then she could turn her attention to Strell's outfit. She had already marked what she thought was a good fit from a handsome green cloth, patterning it after what she could recall from her papa's attire, her sole model. She wanted it to be a surprise. A little bit every night after he left her room ought to get it done in time for the solstice.

Strell's head came up as she moved to the arch. "Where are you going?"

"My room. I want to put something on my thumb."

"Like a thimble?" he teased.

Alissa grinned. "No. Have you seen my jar of salve? I seem to have misplaced it."

Strell stood and draped his string of apples across the mantel. "Oh! I forgot to tell you," he said as he sat back down and arranged himself among his apples and twine again. "That's what Bailic wanted."

Alissa stopped in the archway to the great hall, blinking in astonishment. "For what?"

"The fabric," he said quickly. "You ran back to the annexes before I could tell you, and then I forgot. That's what did the trick. The salve for all the fabric you could use." Strell looked up, smiling uncertainly. "Done and done."

Alissa shut her mouth with a snap. "That was my salve."

"And now that's your fabric. You said you'd give anything to have it."

"My mother's salve?" Alissa felt her warm. "What am I supposed to use when Talon scratches me?"

Strell picked up a handful of sliced apples. "When was the last time she scratched you?"

"That's not the point," she said, not understanding why he was being so cavalier.

"Well, what is the point?"

Alissa gestured in exasperation. "You gave Bailic my salve. My mother made it. I've been looking for it for three days! Just when were you going to tell me you gave it away?"

"I told you, I forgot." His face was reddening.

"Well, why didn't you ask me first?"

Strell glanced up. His brow was furrowed. "I thought I already had. Look. I'm sorry. You said you'd give anything for that fabric. I thought that was what you meant."

"But it was mine!"

"And now you have anything you want in the dry goods." Strell lowered his head, jabbing his thick needle through an apple slice, His shoulders were tense, and he looked cross.

"Everything except for the silk," she muttered, leaning against the arch.

Strell sighed. "Ashes. I think I made a good trade for you. Besides," he added darkly, "Bailic didn't want anything of mine. It seems I don't have anything of value."

Alissa's jaw stiffened. "What about one of your pipes! You don't even play the one."

His eyes narrowed, and Strell leaned back in his chair. "That's how I make my living, Alissa. And you're the one who's going to use the fabric, not me."

Alissa pulled herself away from the arch. "You know what I think?" she said tightly. "I think you're jealous I had something he wanted, and you didn't."

"Don't be daft." His voice was hard.

"That's it, isn't it!" she said triumphantly. "So you gave him the only thing I had that belonged to my mother."

Strell's brow furrowed. "That's not true. You have lots of things to remind you of your mother. I don't have anything from mine. I don't have anything at all. I think I traded well for you. It was only a jar. Look what you got for it!"

Anger overwhelmed her, and she crossed her arms aggressively. "Well you know what? Your grandfather once said if you make a deal that's decidedly in your favor, you've probably overlooked something."

Strell's jaw clenched. Without a word, he stood up and stalked out of the room, brushing past her without a glance.

Alissa followed him out into the great hall. "I'm not done yet!" she called after him. "Where are you going?"

"Somewhere you aren't," Strell shouted over his shoulder.

"Fine," Alissa cried at his back. "Go hide in your smelly stables. See if I care!" He disappeared into the first tunnel. She was alone.

Alissa took a shuddering breath. "How dare he give my salve away without asking," she muttered, flopping back in her chair and pushing her threads into a messy pile. "What kind of fool takes someone else's things and trades them away?" Even if it was for all the fabric she could use, she admitted, feeling a flush of guilt. The finest fabric she ever had the chance to work with.

Her anger slowed in a pang of regret, and she looked the empty room over. It was quiet. She didn't like it. Deep down she knew Strell had made an excellent trade. Bailic had no need for a tenth of what the annex contained. Her salve was probably the only thing he didn't have. And she had said she would give anything.

Alissa sat in the silent dining hall, her pulse slowing. She felt ill. Perhaps, she thought as her eyes lowered, she ought to apologize. It was the surprise that got to her, she rationalized as she rose to her feet. That, and his indifferent attitude. Her temper had gotten the better of her again, letting her mouth run amuck, uncaring of any hurt it might cause. Bringing his family into it had been unfair. Strell had only done what she'd asked. Ashes, she thought. She was a fool.

Her breath slipped from her in a slow puff. She hated apologizing, but she could see no other way. Calmer, but not feeling any less foolish, she followed Strell to the stables. Sure enough, she heard his voice raised in anger before she was halfway down the long passage.

"What an idiotic, sand-for-brains fool!" His voice was harsh, and it jerked her to a halt just shy of the end of the tunnel. "Never again," she heard him vow cholerically, "never will I let that happen again." There was a yelp of surprise. "Cursed ward!" he shouted. "What's a ward doing down here?" There was a short pause. "By the Navigator's Wolves, you've known her too long to forgive that kind of behavior. How is it possible to act that childishly?"

Her pulse quickened and her temper rushed back. She remained where she was, fuming.

"Well," he said, his voice virulently bitter, "I'm going back up there and tell her—"

Strell came out of a box stall then, nearly running her down. "Alissa!" he blurted, his fierce expression changing to one of surprise. "How long—"

"Long enough!" she shouted. "Maybe I can save you a trip. The idiotic, sand-for-brains fool heard every word!"

"But . . . I was coming up to tell you—"

"What! Tell me what? That I'm acting childishly? I heard you the first time!" And with that, she spun about and stormed back up the passage.

Now she was done.

26

"Milksop," she muttered. "Hiding in the stables all day. I can take Bailic's tray all by myself." Alissa stomped up the stairs. It was late afternoon, almost too late for a noon meal. She had prepared the tray ages ago, setting it and herself at one of the kitchen tables, waiting for Strell to come and take it to Bailic. He hadn't, and now she was boiling mad. Rather than risk Bailic coming down in search of his meal, she was going to have to deliver it.

She took the stairs fast, anger adding to her speed. By the time she reached the ninth landing, she was out of breath. Strell once said Bailic's door was the first one, and she pursed her lips and kicked at it. Her eyes widened at the scuff mark, but then her resolve firmed. So what, she thought defiantly, it's not really his room anyway.

Bailic flung open the door and blinked down at her in astonishment. Alissa glared at him, forgetting for a moment where she was.

This was where her papa had fallen to his death.

Her eyes dropped. "Here is your noon meal," she said softly, recalling the long, empty years her mother had waited for her papa's return.

"Thank you, my dear," Bailic said, trying to cover his surprise with a honeyed smoothness. "I'm pleased you finally found the way to my room. Won't you come in? We so seldom have a chance to talk." He leaned forward, his features easing into a false smile. "I just realized the other morning I know nothing at all about you."

She lowered her eyes and shook her head. The hands taking the tray were smooth and pale. He couldn't have done a decent day's work in his life, she thought, her gaze flitting over his new attire.

Draping over his narrow shoulders in a smooth wave of black was a long sleeveless vest. It was bound tight about his waist with a wide gold scarf. Both the scarf and vest went nearly to the floor, lending him a more elegant air than usual. His shirt underneath was a softer black, with wide, expansive sleeves big enough to serve as pockets. He looked like refinement incarnate, and Alissa turned, eager to leave the unhappy place.

"Just one question, then?" he said, smiling warmly, and she halted, edging the stair. "Recently your piper exchanged a jar of salve for material. You know the one?"

Her piper? Alissa thought, taking a nervous step back as he moved into the hall. Strell wasn't *her* piper. Her heel hung over the first stair, and she couldn't distance herself any further without looking obvious. "Yes," she admitted, unable to keep the hurt from her voice.

Bailic hesitated, clearly waiting for more. When it became apparent Alissa wouldn't volunteer anything, Bailic waved a hand carelessly. "It worked wonders on my . . ." He paused, rubbing a slow finger across the faint scar on his cheek. It seemed to have healed in a day. "Do you have any more?"

"No," Alissa said shortly, her face reddening.

"That's a shame. Tell me what you need to make it." His smiled turned conspiratorial. "There's a bolt or two of silk down there. Perhaps we could come to an agreement of our own? There's no need for you to be shy. Women often make the shrewdest of bargains."

Alissa's head rose, her jaw stiffening. "Strell does all my bargaining," she said sharply. Somehow Bailic knew she had an argument with Strell and was trying to worsen it. The horrid thing was that she was nearly willing to agree just to get back at Strell.

"Is there a problem?" Bailic crooned, his put-on charms failing miserably. "I couldn't help but overhear an argument earlier."

"No," Alissa said, managing to sound surprised. "No problem at all."

"Really." The pale, washed-out orbs of his eyes narrowed and he leaned forward.

It was much too close, and she couldn't help but take a step down the stairs. "I have to start dinner," she said quickly, turning leave. She practically ran down the stairs, the noise of her boots clattering against the hard walls. It was the most she had said to Bailic at any one time, and it left her feeling ill. Strell had always taken the trays, and now she thought she knew why.

"What a hinny I've been," Alissa said, her pace slowing as she neared the next landing. Strell had done nothing but help her since the day he pulled her out of that ravine. And for what? There was nothing for him to gain by being here. He owed her nothing, and she had repaid his kindness with her sharp words and quick temper.

Guilt and feelings of remorse slowed her steps. Immediately she resolved to find Strell and apologize. She hesitated at the landing, then deciding he couldn't still be in the stables, she turned and headed for his room. All the way down the hall she tried to think of something to say that would make it better, but the only thing she could think of was: "I'm sorry. You were right."

By the time she reached his door, she had worked herself into a splendid state of remorse. How, she wondered, could she have been so stubborn? Strell had only been being his usual helpful self. Alissa drew to a stop before his door, hesitating as she realized it was cracked open.

"Strell?" she said quietly, pushing the door inward. He wasn't there, but her face went cold as she saw what was. His chair. Strell had taken his chair from her hearth.

Hoping she was mistaken and that he had just gotten a second chair, Alissa opened her door. Only one chair sat before her hearth. Hers. Strell's was gone. He had taken it, leaving her hearth empty and deserted. Stunned, Alissa stood in her doorway and blinked in confusion. They argued lots of times, she thought desperately, but he had never done this! He knew it wouldn't be long before she would cool off and apologize. She must have really hurt him.

"Oh, Strell," she whispered, "I'm so sorry." Any apology would certainly fall upon deaf ears now, she thought miserably. Her cursed temper had dealt her a cruel blow, and she could only blame herself.

27

Bailic eased down the stairs in the great hall. His new Master's vest and sash hissed against the steps, marking his passage in a pleasing sound. He had found the ensemble in a trunk years ago, but never thought to wear it until yesterday. The long, robe-like vest suited his height very well. Even the girl had noticed, despite her mood.

He paused at the foot of the stairs to lean against the railing. It was quiet. Only a few motes of dust that the Hold's nightly sweep had missed could be seen, dancing in the bands of early afternoon sun. He listened, trying to find his guests using his ears alone. There had been a falling out yesterday. He wasn't sure where things stood, or even where they were.

Last night's meal was far from the high standards he had become increasingly used to. The acrid smell of burnt bread had hung thick in the lower levels of the Hold. The potatoes were undercooked and distressingly hard. But the carrots were the worst of the lot, almost a paste.

He hadn't cared. The food was of less interest than the two of them. They were far more entertaining than the sticky-sweet love story the piper stumbled his way through after dinner. Bailic ceased listening soon after the piper began it, preferring to gauge the girl's reactions. He had to turn his heavy chair from the fire to do so, but it was well worth the effort. It was the second chair he had moved yesterday—and by far the easiest.

A frown passed over him as he recalled his frustrating attempts to get the piper's chair out of Meson's old room without crossing the threshold. Eventually he had to throw weighted ropes at it. Once in the hall, he had spun the chair into the piper's room, not caring to tempt fate further. He was lucky he hadn't been caught. The noise he had made was considerable.

He squinted from the small bit of sun as his eyes turned to the annexes. There was an ornate table outside his door to hold his tray that had come from one of them. And their bland fare had improved as well. Rare was the night that a small bit of fresh vegetable or fruit didn't appear with their potatoes or rice. Perhaps he ought to go down and bring up some of the wine. He might get a few answers once tongues were loosened. And tongues needed to loosen if he was to make any progress before the snow melted and his prison became less secure.

An anxious pang went through him. Bailic crushed it, reassuring himself that he had time. If his efforts to worsen their tiff succeeded, he was sure one of them would begin to confide in him. Bailic turned back to the tunnels. But no one was saying anything right now.

Bailic halfheartedly sent his awareness to drift among the passages to search them out using his mind, and today, after weeks of failure he received a soft, garbled response. His tracings were almost healed.

"Finally!" he breathed. An icy thrill of delight sang through him. Bailic unfocused his awareness and looked with his mind's eye to see his network. It was still ash-covered, but when he allowed the connection between it and his source, he was pleased to find its strength raggedly slipping through the lines again. A soft whisper of a headache accompanied it. The flow wasn't true yet. He daren't use his tracings until fully healed. Perhaps as soon as tonight.

Bailic whirled about and took the stairs two at a time, intent on reaching his room. There were scores of ways to loosen tongues. His last two weeks of forced patience hadn't been spent idly. He had a plan, one more certain than wine, more cunning than flattery, and more secure than force. And now he could begin.

28

"You look terrible," Alissa whispered to her reflection in the small mirror on her hearth shelves. She took a deep breath, letting it slowly slip from her. Gray eyes aren't at all attractive when red from crying. Her clothes had thin patches, and though clean, had clearly seen better days. Her hair? It was nearly to her shoulders, and she hated it.

The dimming light told her it was nearly time to make dinner. The very idea tightened her stomach until she felt ill. Last night Strell had been tight-lipped, never looking at her as they prepared dinner together. She had been close to tears, not knowing what to say for fear of making things worse. She was hoping tonight she might find the courage to apologize and Strell would forgive her.

"Yes," Alissa said bitterly, "when the Navigator's Wolves

come to earth to hunt rabbits." She hadn't seen Strell all day. That told her more clearly than words that time had done nothing to soften him.

Alissa turned from her reflection with a feeling of gloom. She couldn't go downstairs looking like a beggar. Perhaps she should wear her new skirt. She had finished it this morning, having hidden herself in her room and buried herself in work. It was her opinion that the cloth was too fine for everyday use, but why make it if she wasn't going to wear it?

Her eyes slid to the fabric she had chosen for Strell. "I may as well toss you out the window," she said. She couldn't buy Strell's friendship back. He probably wouldn't even accept it now. Biting her lip to keep from crying, she wadded the soft fabric up and stuffed it under the bed. Ever the frugal farm girl, she would find a use for it later.

Alissa struggled to keep her breath even, to keep the tears from brimming, to loosen the horrid tightness in her chest. Snatching up her skirt, she quickly changed. She hadn't worn a skirt in ages, and her boots looked odd peeping out from under her hem. A quick brush through her hair and she was ready. She was no less unhappy, but at least she didn't look like something Talon might bring back for her. At the last moment she tied her hair back with a scrap of green she had planned on using for Strell's outfit.

The appealing aroma of Strell's cooking was thick in the hall as Alissa pulled her door shut behind her. "Now you've done it," she whispered, feeling a stab of guilt. Sure Strell would use her absence as fuel for his anger, she hurried to the end of the hall and down the stairs. Bailic's voice shattered the quiet as she reached the landing above the great hall, and she froze.

"What do you mean she's indisposed, Piper," he shouted, his voice carrying well. Alissa almost turned around, but she couldn't leave Strell to face his wrath alone. So crossing her fingers for luck, she ghosted down the stairs and stepped into the dining hall.

"Ah, there you are, my dear." Bailic's anger vanished at the sound of her appearance. He rose from his chair, and she maneuvered quickly to avoid his outstretched hands. His ire showed for an instant until he hid it behind that false smile he had been favoring her with.

"Please," Bailic cajoled, "sit down." He gestured grandly to the table, conspicuous with only two place settings. Silently Alissa blushed.

"Here." Strell was suddenly at her elbow. "Take my spot."

"No," Bailic interrupted smoothly. "Do me the honor."

Alissa hesitated, wondering if she should go to the kitchen for her own place setting.

"I insist," grated Bailic, straightening to his full height.

Helpless to refuse, Alissa reluctantly moved to the head of the table. Bailic assisted her with her chair and turned her cup and plate right-side up. He chuckled as he sat down beside her. Sneaking a glance at Strell, Alissa was startled by the absolute blankness on his face.

"Piper!" Bailic barked, making both Strell and Alissa jump. "Would you please," he continued quietly, "get me a new place setting?"

Strell gulped and vanished into the kitchen. Alissa stared at her plate as she waited for his return. The fire was higher than she allowed herself to keep it, and the room was blessedly warm. Out of the corner of her sight she could see Bailic's fingers drumming, silently drumming, upon the table. Their absolute whiteness was marred by new red-rimmed scratches and the grime of soot.

"Your new attire suits you, my dear," he said, and she stiffened, wishing now she hadn't changed. "You show much skill with a needle. Tell me, Piper," he demanded as a plate slid before Bailic, "my eyes are weary tonight. Is the cloth our companion selected, by chance, gray?"

"No," Strell answered in a strained voice, sitting at the far end of the table at Alissa's usual spot. "It's a blue-gray, much as the bottom of clouds that herald a violent summer storm."

"Really," Bailic said sharply.

Surprised at the emotion in Strell's voice, Alissa pulled her gaze from the table, shocked at the distress she read in him. Even Bailic couldn't fail to recognize the effect his question had upon Strell. Maybe, she thought with a faint stirring of hope. Maybe he wasn't as angry as she thought.

Maybe he would listen to her. She smiled in encouragement, and Strell stared blankly at her for a moment before dropping his eyes.

"I would know," Bailic said as he filled first his glass, then Alissa's, "if you are finding my home to your liking?"

"Yes, of course," she said meekly, as his question was clearly directed at her.

"Of course you do," he repeated firmly. "*Do* have some raspberries, my dear. They're probably older than you and me put together, but fresh as the day they were picked. I'm so pleased you found the foodstuffs." Bailic ladled an enormous helping of berries onto her plate, and she froze. Glancing between Strell, Alissa, and the berries, he ran an introspective finger across the base of the old scar running down and across his neck. Alissa shot a nervous look at Strell, and he shrugged almost imperceptibly.

"Your bird is absent tonight, is she not?" Bailic murmured as he rubbed his reddened knuckles, and before she could answer, he smiled in a fatherly fashion. "Have you chanced a walk in the garden recently? The snow is uncommonly deep this year. I *do* hope it doesn't mean floods in the spring. We will be safe here on the top of the world, so don't worry yourselves."

Bailic generally held himself to one topic while they ate, nitpicking over the smallest point of conversation. Tonight he took over the discussion with such a bewildering array of subjects, it left her breathless. Alissa was continually left fumbling, not knowing what to say. Bailic didn't seem to notice he was doing all the talking and that most of his questions were going unanswered.

Looking miserable and lost, Strell stared blankly into the fire, ignoring everything. It wasn't like him. Alissa wondered if Bailic had set a ward upon him but decided she would have felt it. Strell must simply be as dazed as she by the rapidly changing subjects.

But the fire was warm, much warmer than she allowed herself to have it, and soothing.

Bailic's low, pleasant speech never slowed, and despite her efforts to follow his train of thought, it became increasingly difficult. She found it easier to ignore him and watch the flames dance and leap. A soft lassitude slipped over her, and she yawned, drowsy with the heat.

"Yes," she heard Bailic say. "That's a fine beginning. Let's see if we can't improve it even more. Piper? If you would be so kind? No story tonight. It would be my desire to hear such music that would gentle a petulant child down to sleep."

Alissa watched Strell slip his pipe from his shirt pocket. She wanted to turn to see if he was wearing the same blank stare he had earlier, but the flames would shift and weave so . . . and it wasn't worth her effort.

The dishes, she thought distantly. The dishes should be in the kitchen. Strell was going to play. They should be in the kitchen. "The kitchen," she murmured, then lost her thought. She shifted, confused. There was something she should be doing. She couldn't remember what.

"Hush," a dark voice crooned, and her plate disappeared. With a languorous sigh, Alissa slumped back and lost herself in the fire. Whatever had disturbed her was gone. She could rest.

Strell's music flowed forth, reassuring and soft. It had been so long since he played his grandfather's pipe. Perhaps he *wasn't* angry with her anymore. Alissa felt her eyelids droop.

"Yes," a low, comforting voice whispered, "this is much better, much to my liking. You play well, Piper. Pray, continue for but a little more."

She drowsed, content to simply exist, not caring what happened as long as the music and the dancing flames continued. With a final sigh, she allowed her eyes to close. She was warm and comfortable. Strell was playing for her. She couldn't help it. She didn't care.

"So," she heard softly, "let's see what we may learn, now that you are—comfortable."

The sound of the fire hissing and music, gentle music, came from somewhere. She felt as if she should recognize it. A distant, irritating plinking began to intrude into her contentment. From the soft gray that was her world, the soothing, persuasive voice whispered, "A Keeper lacks the skill for a ward of truth, even I, but there are other, more mundane ways to hear it spoken."

A small part of her realized the heat from the fire was blocked again, but she could hear the flames. It was enough to satisfy her.

"It's an old technique, my dear," came the voice right before her, "older than the Hold itself, and anyone can learn, be he Keeper or commoner."

The plinking grew louder. Annoyed at the disturbance, she focused upon it.

"The only problem," the voice crooned, "is that the technique seldom works on the wary—so let's make this as productive an evening as possible, shall we?"

Once more she felt the heat of the fire. She relaxed further, letting the warmth soak deep into her old bones. Old bones? she mused. What an odd thing to think.

The gray shroud that cocooned her seemed to thin, and the plinking came to the forefront of her awareness. Where was she? she thought in confusion, and then, who was she, for she couldn't form any clear concepts at the moment. But the gray shadow had asked her something.

"I'm sorry," she heard herself say lazily. "What's that?"

"Quite all right, my dear," the voice said kindly. "I know it's hard to concentrate, but you must. Soon, you can rest."

"Yes, rest," her voice said wearily.

"Yes . . ." the gray voice crooned, "but first tell me, why are you here?"

"Hush," a new voice whispered into her thoughts. *"I'll answer for you."* She gratefully acceded to the warm presence, allowing it to enfold her in its comforting strength.

"The need was great, and I can't abandon that which needs me," she heard herself say, but they weren't her words. The music had stopped, leaving only the chilly sound of dripping water.

"Hum . . ." the gray voice murmured. "Where's your home?"

"Home is where I am," the warm presence said through her.

"Really," the gray shadow mused. "I see I will have to be more specific with you."

There was a space before her. She could sense it now. It was an enormous room, almost as big as being outside. The thick cloud obscuring her thoughts was clearing, and she began to remember. *"Alissa,"* she thought. *"Yes, that's who I am, and I'm at the Hold to find my book."*

"Your book?" the warm thoughts spoke to her alone. *"I think not!"*

"Where is the *First Truth*?" the gray voice demanded.

"I don't know. But it calls," the presence said using her voice.

"That's right!" Alissa blurted into the warm thoughts. *"But I can't tell from where, exactly"* And why, she wondered, was someone speaking for her?

"I said be quiet!" the warm thought scolded. *"It's hard when you try to answer as well."*

She suddenly realized she had her eyes shut, so she opened them. The familiar dining hall flashed before her. She glimpsed Strell, seemingly asleep in his chair and Bailic glowering and pacing. Then the room vanished, replaced by a vision of impossibly high ceilings and dark pillars.

"Close your eyes, you fool!" the presence admonished, and she immediately did. The double vision was confusing. Besides, she could sense a source, twin to her own, glittering golden in their shared thoughts. Suddenly she understood it was Useless speaking for her, just as he had before. But why was she still conscious? She wasn't reliving anyone's memory.

"Useless?" Alissa thought hesitantly, not sure if she should be pleased or angry.

"Be still," he hissed into her thoughts. *"I'm trying to save your life. Ungrateful brat."*

All right, she decided. She would be angry. But Useless was too distracted to notice her huff. It was only then that Alissa realized she was in *Useless's* thoughts. He wasn't in hers. That horrible feeling of violation was nonexistent, and her hostility melted away in fascination. She looked at her source shimmering faintly under its ward, then at the other, free and unfettered.

"Are you a Keeper's child?" Bailic asked. Alissa recognized him now. He had been asking the questions all along.

"Yes," Alissa thought absently.

"No," Useless said through her.

"Then whose child are you?" Bailic asked warily. Alissa could tell he was right in front of her, even with her eyes closed, and she struggled not to shudder.

"I am a child of the sun and earth, and sibling to the wind," she told him, but of course she wasn't. She was Meson and Rema's daughter. Useless answered for her, and she didn't care.

Struck by an idea, she made a point of awareness and slyly moved it to the unfettered sphere before her. It was irresistible, and she felt like a small child going for a forbidden sweet, and just like an errant child, she was scolded.

"Stop that!" Useless snapped. *"Insolent little . . . Don't touch anything! You're making this impossible. Deem yourself lucky. No Keeper, much less a student Keeper, has been permitted to remember this technique."*

Alissa's point dissolved with a frightening suddenness under his will. Embarrassed, she turned her attention to Bailic. He was speaking again, and he didn't sound happy at her answers.

"Where," he spat, "did you come from?"

"I was here before you," Useless intoned, "and I will remain when your soul is rent and scattered to the winds of time."

"Who, under the Wolves of the Navigator, are you?" Bailic whispered.

"I'm your death, Bailic," Alissa heard herself say, the words sounding cold and alien falling from her lips, and she shivered. "I'm your death, waiting to be loosed, and I will be loosed, have no doubt. Then we will finish our game."

"Talo-Toecan!" Bailic exploded.

Alissa opened her eyes. She couldn't help it. She had to know, to see what was going on. The double sight was confusing, but the dark cavern quickly faded. Talo-Toecan? Alissa remembered in astonishment. That was the name her father had given his teacher. Useless was a Master? There was one left? Wolves, she thought near panic. It was her book. She wouldn't give it back!

Bailic had backed up almost to the fire. "But . . . how can you speak through . . ." he stammered.

"You made it possible yourself by putting her so close to unconsciousness," Useless said through her. "Leave her alone. She knows nothing of this," and then to Alissa, *"It's too hard now that you're fully awake. If you value your hide don't tell him of me or what you've seen tonight."* Alissa felt him sigh. *"Burn you to ash, why didn't you just go home?"*

"No! Wait! she cried. *"We can't get past the closet door!"*

"I know. I told that piper of yours you couldn't," he said dryly. *"I'm surprised Bailic hasn't seen the obvious and killed you yet."* And then he was gone. Alissa was alone among her thoughts. Bailic's trance was broken, and no, she wouldn't fall for it again. It was only her ignorance that had allowed it the first time.

Alissa knew Bailic saw awareness return to her eyes, mindful that the presence he named Talo-Toecan was gone. All trace of congenial host had evaporated. Again he was the insane, murderous Keeper Alissa recalled from her papa's memories. Terrified, she scrambled up to keep the table between them.

"You," he shouted, pointing a trembling finger at her, "are rapidly becoming more trouble than you're worth!" Bailic lunged, and she darted back in fear. With a shudder, he halted, and they faced each other across the wide table. He smiled then, and Alissa shivered. "You fell asleep, my dear," he said softly, his pale eyes glinting in the low light of the neglected fire. "Did you dream?"

"No," Alissa said tightly, her breath shallow and her heart pounding. What, she wondered, had Useless meant by, see the "obvious"?

"I hope I didn't frighten you," Bailic said. He stepped back from the table and tugged his short vest straight, regaining his usual, poised elegance. "Take no notice of my moods. You're always welcome to stay, even past the spring."

"Thank you," she said, her eyes riveted to his.

"Good night then," Bailic said, and he spun about, the

long sleeves of his shirt billowing as he stalked into the darkness beyond the archway and into the great hall.

29

Alissa took a shuddering breath, listening until she heard the hushed, impatient sound of Bailic's soft shoes on the stair before going to Strell. He looked for all the world as if he were sleeping. "Strell?" she called hesitantly as she bent close. "Are you awake?"

"I don't know," he answered, his eyes closed.

A quick shiver went through her. "Strell, wake up."

He sighed and stirred, and it was in great relief that she watched his eyes open. Another deep breath and awareness filled his eyes. Suddenly nervous, she backed up. He glanced at his pipe in his hands, then at the empty room. "Did I . . . What happened?" he asked.

Alissa swallowed. Perhaps now he would talk to her. "Bailic," she said softly. "He put us in a trance, tried to get me to tell him who my parents were."

"What?" It was a horrified gasp.

"Ashes, I was a fool," Alissa said, half turning away. "I should have seen it coming."

Strell's eyes went vacant. "I saw that at market once. What did I—"

"He never asked you anything," Alissa interrupted. "I would have told him everything, but Useless spoke with my voice, just like before, and answered his questions." She smiled faintly, thankful Strell didn't seem angry at her. "Bailic was furious. You should have seen him."

Strell froze, and Alissa's smile faltered as a thousand thoughts seemed to flit behind his eyes. "We're going," he said suddenly, standing up and taking her elbow. "Right now."

Shocked, she pulled away. "Strell, relax. Bailic doesn't know anything. It's all right."

"It's not all right," he said forcefully. "I nearly got you killed."

For a moment Alissa could only stare. "But nothing happened," she stated as he took her arm and started to pull her to the door. "Why are you so upset?"

"It could have," he said, his expression so intent, it was frightening. "I helped him. I'm supposed to be protecting you, and if it wasn't for my music, you never would have fallen under his sway. It was my fault." He hesitated, seeming to search for words. "I can't protect you from him," he finally said. "I was a fool to think I could."

Alissa stumbled after him into the great hall, too shocked to protest. "But he can't do it again. I know what to watch for. It's all right."

Strell stopped and turned to face her. The hall was cool with moonlight. "What will he do next? He stopped me from whistling. What if he stops you from breathing."

Alissa's lips parted, unable to answer him. Strell nodded sharply as understanding filled her. "You have to pack," he said, pulling her back into motion. "We're going. Now."

Her feet touched the steps, and Alissa pulled away, frightened. "I'm not leaving, Strell. There's snow out there, if you haven't noticed."

He hesitated for only a moment. "Yes," he said quickly. "We'll go first light."

"Strell! It's the winter. The coast is three weeks away, in good weather!"

"I'd rather take my chances in the snow." Clearly frustrated, he stood still, his anger melting into helplessness. "Ashes, Alissa. I almost got you killed. I can't protect you from him. Can't you see that?"

Alissa swallowed hard. "I never asked you to," she whispered.

Strell took a breath, then let it out. "We're going," he said, turning to ascend the steps.

"I'm not leaving!" she said, refusing to move from the stair.

Strell spun, his face in the moonlight full of a frightening shadow. Alissa watched in shock as he raised his pipe between his hands and brought it down hard and fast against his knee. There was a sharp crack, and his grandfather's pipe was sundered in two. The pieces slipped through his grip to clatter down upon the polished steps. "*That's* how much good your magic is," he whispered fiercely. "*That's* how long your deception will last, and *that's* what Bailic will do to you when he figures it out. And he will figure it out, Alissa." He took a breath. "Go pack your things. We leave tomorrow after breakfast. He won't look for us until nearly dinner. By then we will be too far for him to follow."

"Or we'll be dead!" she shouted after him as he stormed up the stairs. Strell never acknowledged he heard her but continued up until she couldn't hear him anymore.

"Burn it to ash, Strell," Alissa said softly as she bent to retrieve the pieces of his grandfather's pipe. "It's not worth this much grief." It never had been, she thought. None of it. The Wolves take her. She had been a fool. She would let Strell be for tonight—talking to him now would be worse than talking to a river—and tomorrow she would make him see reason.

Somehow the polished wood felt lighter now that it was broken, and Alissa carried Strell's pipe up past the empty halls and chambers, past the mirror on the landing, and past his room. Not a sound could she hear as she ghosted to her door and quietly shut it behind her.

"Where's Talon?" she wondered aloud as she glanced about her room. Alissa hadn't seen her since noon. It was very unlike her bird to be gone that long. A flash of worry crossed Alissa until she remembered the kestrel always made herself scarce when Useless appeared. The silly bird would return when she felt safe again.

It could be worse, Alissa thought dismally. Bailic still didn't know who was here to find the book and who was the distraction. And he never will, she vowed, reverently placing the remains of Strell's pipe on her mantel. Strell was being unreasonable.

Sinking down upon the hearth, she poked the fire back to life with one of the legs from Strell's old tripod. There were rusty fire irons propped in their customary spot, but she preferred to use the unwieldy length of metal. It was a subtle reminder to always think before reaching.

"Just like I didn't when trying for Useless's source," she murmured, and recalling his stinging thoughts, harsh with impatience, she blushed. She was worse than a child—no restraint at all. But she learned a lot from the encounter and now had an idea of how she might rid herself of his annoying ward.

Alissa built the fire up and composed herself on the floor, wrapping the blanket about her. She was warm enough but needed some comfort. The blanket was a talisman of home, a reminder of safety, contentment, and long, quiet evenings. Tonight she had lost herself in a trance, been rescued, scolded, threatened, then abandoned by friend and bird alike. She wanted something to hold. The blanket would have to do. Breathing deeply through the thick wool, Alissa imagined she could smell burnt bread. Smiling, she added a new log and leaned back against the seat of her chair.

Useless's unspoken thoughts had confirmed her suspicions that her sphere was nothing less than unaltered power. The sphere only appeared empty, as it was almost impossible for limit-bound thoughts to wrap around anything as large as near infinity. The shimmering ward Useless had encased around her source was created from force, and so, she reasoned, it could be changed. The question was, how? Every time she sent her thoughts near his ward, she received that cursed, sharp warning. It was painful, but not debilitating.

What if, she supposed, she provoked a response and wrapped the force that usually burned her in a bubble of thought, catching it as it were? Her eyes slid her share of the tripod, and she resolved to think about the possible results. One: She would get burned as Useless had warned. It hurt, but it wasn't bad. She had been getting pokes from it for weeks now and was none the worse. Two: It would work, and she would have captured some of the ward's strength.

Do this enough times, and the ward would be gone. It would be like dipping water from a bucket. It may not look like much is removed, but eventually the bucket is empty. Three: There was no three she could think of, so she would try it. The worst she could do was get burned.

Pleased she had taken the time to think it through, Alissa shifted excitedly on the warm flagstones. Her practice in the burrs and thorns paid off and she found her source without even closing her eyes. Only slightly distracted by the fire, she formed a bubble of thought as Useless had done when she tried to drive him from her mind. Slowly Alissa moved it forward until . . .

"Ow," she hissed as a small burst of pain raced through her existence and was gone. Grimacing, she took a deep breath and shut her eyes. It was easier to concentrate that way. This time, she made the bubble thicker. Again she pushed the bubble to her source.

With a sharp snap, Alissa caught the tiniest bit of power and wrapped it up in a safe package. Her breath caught at the feel of it, white-hot and still, all potential, just waiting for direction. It had been surprisingly easy. She could use this, she thought smugly, run it through her pattern, much as she did the strength from her own source. But she didn't. Where would it go when done? Alissa doubted she could loop it back into her source, not with Useless's ward still there blocking anything from going in or out. Only the smallest fraction of his ward was held tight in her thoughts. The barrier was still there. She would have to dump the force somewhere.

"But where?" Alissa whispered, not sure this was such a good idea anymore. She couldn't just carry it around. What if she sneezed or something? She might lose it!

Alissa looked at her bubble glowing a luminescent gold from the power it contained. It was a singularly enchanting sight, shining like a theoretical dewdrop against the blackness of her mind. But it was wearisome holding her attention for so long. Perhaps she ought to put it back.

Disappointed, Alissa drew the bubble back to the ward. As soon as she crossed the unseen safe line, a flash of light erupted and was drawn into her bubble. She watched in horror as her bubble doubled in size as more and more force was pulled into it.

Stop! she thought frantically, finding it difficult to pull away. It was as if the stuff was attracted to itself. Finally she managed to draw the bubble back, and she shivered in relief as the flow ceased. She could feel the bubble tug toward Useless's ward, and she had to exert a constant pull to keep it still.

Alissa heaved a sigh of annoyance as she found out what the third possible result was. "Three," she said tightly. "Get yourself into a spot you can't get out of." It had sounded so easy at first. Catch it, and toss it. But where? This wasn't working. Perhaps she could change it to something that wouldn't attract the ward's power. Gently pushing the bubble around in her thoughts, she mulled it over. It was worth trying.

Full of a new determination, Alissa focused fully upon her bubble. *"You,"* she said in her thoughts, hoping all it took was the will to want it as it had in reliving memories, *"are no longer power, but solid."*

The fire shifted. Alissa heard it quite distinctly. One of the logs hadn't looked quite safe when she began her ill-fated experiment. She carefully divided her attention to hold her bubble and check on the fire simultaneously. Slowly she opened her eyes.

"What under the Eight Wolves . . ." she gasped. There, suspended in space not an arm's length away, was a small spot of shimmering glory. Her bubble of thought. "Oh, my . . ." she breathed, incapable of anything more intelligent. It looked about the size of a star on a clear night, and it was just as bright, too, glowing in the semidarkness of the low fire. Alissa's breath hissed through her teeth as she realized the tiny thing was casting shadows!

"Bone and Ash," she whispered, reaching for it. "No," she said, drawing her hand back. She didn't know what it was yet.

She cautiously shut her eyes from the fascinating sight, and with another shock, found that her bubble was no longer mirrored in her thoughts. She had actually moved it. How, she marveled, had she managed that? Alissa gazed in satisfaction at the tiny spot of glittering sunshine.

"I think," she decided, "I could let go of that bubble now." It was growing wearisome, containing its contents. The constant pressure was noticeably stronger. There should be no problem in releasing it, seeing as it was nowhere near her source anymore. Alissa sighed contentedly, pleased she had found a way to nullify the bothersome ward. Soon she would remove it all, but not tonight. She had done enough. With a smile, she dissolved her bubble of thought.

"Noooo!" Alissa screamed in agony as a white-hot iron lanced through her mind. Searing terror erupted along all her tracings, burning, and burning, and burning. It raged, an inescapable inferno, drowning her in pain until pain was her entire world. But she found a place to hide.

There was nothing else.

There had never been anything else.

There would never be anything else.

30

Strell strode up the stone staircase, the twin feelings of failure and helplessness making him feel ill. He had to get her out of here. She thought she was safe. She still didn't see the danger, and the thought of that frightened him more than Bailic. Upon reaching his door, he flung it open and entered his room.

"I should have known what he was doing," he whispered harshly. "I should have stayed awake." His empty pack lay abandoned in a corner, and upon seeing it, frustration filled him. "I couldn't stop my music," he said roughly. "I didn't want to stop." He had been so intent on telling her he was sorry, trying to use his music instead of words, that he lost himself. If not for Useless, they would have been found out.

"I thought I was so clever," he said bitterly. "I thought I could keep her safe. I'm nothing. *I helped him.*" His eyes fell upon his chair, ignored since its appearance yesterday. He liked to pretend it wasn't there, that it might return to its rightful place at Alissa hearth. Now Strell reached out, and with a single finger, he touched the worn fabric. "I failed her."

With a new determination he turned back to his abandoned pack. There was no possible way he could keep Alissa safe from Bailic. Trickery wasn't enough. Guile wasn't enough. The Keeper dealt in magic. How could he protect her against that?

Strell's frustration thickened. He had to convince her to leave. Turning away, he quickly gathered his things in a small pile on the bed. "We are going," he said urgently. "If I have to tie her feet and carry her all the way to the coast." It was a death sentence to leave mid-winter, but Strell would rather take his chances with the cold than Bailic. At least their death would be peaceful in the snow.

Everything disappeared into his pack; only his map, his coat, and Alissa's old hat remained. He snatched up his coat, stuffing his long arms into the sleeves. Her old hat went on his head. He would go down yet tonight to the cold annexes and steal some blankets. With enough blankets and leather, they might make it. He picked up his map, spreading it on the hearth table. Perhaps there was a shorter way out of these cursed mountains that he had missed. The fire was too low to see, and he knelt to build it up.

Coward, he thought, throwing piece after piece of wood onto the growing flames. He was a complete coward, dragging Alissa away to die in the snow instead of finding a way to make her safe here. "No," he said through clenched jaws. "He's a Keeper. There's nothing I can do against that. There's nothing stronger than magic."

Higher and higher the flames grew until the heat billowed out into the room. They were leaving. Alissa could fuss all she wanted. He wasn't going to give her any sway this time.

Strell leaned over the map, studying it for a way to the coast that he might have missed.

"Noooo!" he heard Alissa scream in absolute terror, muffled little by the thick wall between them. It ripped through him like an icy wind, and he froze, stunned as the force of it seemed to reach the very pit of his soul.

"Alissa," he whispered, his face gone cold, and he heard a small *pop* from her room.

Strell was picked up as if by a giant fist and flung into the far wall as a wave of force expanded into his room through his and Alissa's shared chimney. His ears were stunned by the immense pressure, feeling more than hearing the tremendous boom that rocked the corner of the ancient fortress to echo and tremble down to the very roots of the mountain.

He slid to the floor with a muffed groan as the fire went dead, blown apart from the explosion. Barely conscious, he slumped in a heap amid the charred wood and sifting ash. A deathly cold and bitter wind flowed through the window. It pooled on the floor, almost visible as it steadily displaced the warmer air escaping into the night. Like a fog, it streamed out, taking the life-sustaining warmth of the room. The protecting wards were gone, completely overwhelmed by a force they were never intended to endure.

His thoughts swirled to a confused blur, as if the blackness of the room had invaded his thoughts. Slowly a comforting warmth suffused his limbs, then nothing.

31

Bailic reached the top of the stairs and savagely kicked the small table outside his door. It was heavy and well-made. All he accomplished was to hurt his foot. Enraged, he took the table in hand it to push it down the stairwell. Thinking better of it, he contented himself with slamming his door instead. It made a satisfying crash as the thick wood met the stone doorjamb.

"Talo-Toecan," he snarled between clenched teeth, "I should have killed you when I had the chance!" It was a boastful claim, but he felt better having said it. Deep in his soul he knew he could never destroy the Master. It had only been by luck and planning that he managed to pin the beast in his own dungeon, enticed by the thought Keribdis had returned and lay ill. Bailic had thought himself safe from Talo-Toecan's interference, but obviously this wasn't so. The insidious scholar had found a way around the rules again.

"You will rot down there," Bailic vowed vehemently. He swept his arm across his worktable. Paper flew in a whirlwind to settle in quiet squares. The ink pots were next, crashing into the wall to shatter into stains that dripped evil-looking puddles on the uncaring floor.

"All my plans for naught!" he raged, kicking papers and quills from his path to stand at the edge of the balcony. The dangerous fall often calmed him, but it held no peace tonight. Glaring into the dark, he held his anger still, letting it grow. Only his fingers moved, silently drumming upon his arm.

It had been an excellent idea, he fumed. A deep trance had always yielded a wealth of information, as his subject willingly complied to almost every suggestion. But he had learned nothing. Nothing! He had never even considered that his plan wouldn't work. The hardest part was getting rid of that demon-spawned bird. Knowing it would shatter his carefully contrived mood of contentment, Bailic had thrown her into the snow, shutting the door behind her.

"I could know who the Keeper is right now," Bailic rasped. He spun, storming to his chair. Throwing himself into his chair, his fingers tapped a steady rhythm on the musty fabric. In his zeal, Bailic had forgotten an unconscious person was open to serving as a Master's mouthpiece. And while the girl hadn't really been unconscious, she was apparently close enough. He hadn't been interrogating her. He had been questioning his prisoner still deep within his cell! "Child of the sun and earth," he said with a sneer, stilling his hand's motion.

Bailic rose and paced to his shelves. He was after the salve. The bird had attacked him, marking his hands as he tried to fix a ward of stillness about her darting shape this afternoon.

At least he hadn't shattered his story of concerned host too badly, he thought with a derisive scorn. A person serving as a speaker for a Master invariably awoke with no recollection of it. And the piper, Bailic snorted, had lost his volition before the girl. He shouldn't remember anything at all. It would be foolish to believe they didn't suspect he was up to something, but he was confident his desire for the *First Truth* was still his secret. The entire evening, though, had been an absolute waste.

Bailic stretched to the highest shelf. All the others had been warded by Talo-Toecan, and he couldn't touch a thing on them. Unable to see the top, he lightly brushed his fingers across it searching for the small jar of potent cream. If it healed raku score, it would certainly help his scratches. He was on awkward tiptoe when a muffled boom shifted the warm, still air. "By the Hounds . . ." he muttered, and then the floor trembled, knocking him off balance.

Bailic struggled to catch himself without touching the warded shelves, bumping the salve jar. It tipped and rolled noisily down the shelf until, upon reaching the end, it rolled gracefully off. Bailic reached out with his thoughts to catch it. He failed to get a fix on it in time, and it hit the floor with a sickening crack and shattered.

"Wolves," he cursed. The precious cream was laced with slivers of stone. Worthless. Then he froze. "Talo-Toecan," he whispered, suddenly afraid. "What have you done?"

Only a sudden release of great power could account for the disturbance. Only Talo-Toecan would have dared to try and control such a release. But why? His wards were powerless to act upon anyone or anything within the Hold while he was imprisoned.

Had he escaped? Bailic wondered, and he stood unmoving, testing the moonlit night for any new threats of death.

With a shudder that rocked him, he shook off his fear, drawing his borrowed Master's vest tighter. If there was a way past the bars, the slippery beast would have found it ages ago. "So what are you doing down there, old lizard?" he said. All traces of his anger were gone, replaced by a worried frown. "Perhaps I should find out what and remind you of your new position in life."

Stepping carefully around the broken pottery and scattered paper, Bailic slipped into the hall. Down he went until he stood peering into the damp hole in the floor under the stair. Wiping his neck free of his sudden sweat, he paused, listening. Nothing met his questing senses. Reassured Talo-Toecan wasn't coming up by some miracle, he lit a torch with a quick thought and started his descent.

Bailic's knot of tension loosened as he reached the small anteroom and found his prisoner's massive form waiting behind the black gates, a coiled shadow of wing and hide whose yellow eyes reflected the light from Bailic's torch. They blinked slowly as Bailic edged to the wall socket holding the expired torch from his last visit. There was no sound but the water dripping and the small echoes of his scuffling feet.

He paused at the slight tremor in the air, blanching as he realized it was coming from his captive. The raku was rumbling so low that it couldn't be heard, only felt shifting the damp air. Deciding he would rather hold the torch than cross in front of the raku, Bailic retreated until he was almost back in the tunnel. His eyes never left the beast, motionless but for the slow weaving of the tip of his blunt tail.

"I am pleased," Bailic said softly, "to see you—old teacher. I had thought that perhaps you decided to leave."

The immense shape simmered, shrank, and became the smaller form Bailic also recognized as Talo-Toecan. Eyes designed to detect prey and claws for rending flesh shifted to those capable of focusing on paper and turning a page. "You still breathe, Bailic?" came Talo-Toecan's low voice. "Then I'm still here."

Bailic drew himself up in a show of bravado. "So you are." Braver now that Talo-Toecan was in his human guise, he edged closer. "I came to see what you were up to," he

said, lifting his torch to see if there were any physical mani-
festations of the energy release he had felt.

"Allow me," Talo-Toecan muttered, and a brilliant light
exploded into existence.

"Wolves!" Bailic swore as he threw himself to the floor
and rolled, his hand refusing to let go of the torch. Flat upon
the stone, his eyes narrowed and his face tightened as Talo-
Toecan's scornful laughter filled the small space. Too late
Bailic realized what had happened. Furious, he stood and
awkwardly brushed the imagined dirt from his clothes, glaring at the raku. He knew he was safe from Talo-Toecan's
wards on this side of the gate, but it was hard to control one's
reactions around the devious scholar.

For reasons unknown, Talo-Toecan had created a light
brighter than the sun under the ponderous weight of the
mountain. The wily raku had never done so before. He must
have a reason now, Bailic surmised spitefully, other than
watching him skitter like a dog from beneath a swinging
foot, but at least he could see.

Bailic leaned close, flushing as Talo-Toecan's eyebrows
mocked his stolen Master's vest. The beast hadn't changed
in sixteen years, Bailic thought in wonder.

Talo-Toecan was dressed in the traditional, floor-length
sleeveless vest of a Master of the Hold. The gold-colored
fabric flowed to the ground, bound tight to his waist with a
long scarf of ebony, the ends of which brushed the floor. It
contrasted gently with his yellow wide-sleeved shirt. With a
start, Bailic realized the Master's attire was in direct opposition to his own borrowed clothes, with the colors being reversed.

His complexion was dark despite his long confinement.
Clearly Talo-Toecan spent much time at the far gate facing
the open sky and western sun, looking at his unattainable
freedom. The figure gave the impression of timeless maturity
as he stood straight and unbowed, glaring at him. Straight
and sharp, his features had few wrinkles, but his closely
cropped hair was a stark white. His hands were hidden within
his wide sleeves, but Bailic knew Talo-Toecan's fingers were
abnormally long and thin. It was a characteristic all the Masters had shared along with their unnaturally amber eyes. It

seemed their shift to human form couldn't hide all their raku attributes. For a silent moment they appraised each other. Nowhere was there any hint of distress caused by the massive release of force Bailic had felt.

"What," Bailic sighed, "have you been up to?"

"I!" Talo-Toecan shouted, his cool demeanor shattering with that one word. "*I?* You dare come taunt me with your lies? What have you done!"

His eyes wide, Bailic took an involuntary step back. Never had he, or anyone else, seen a Master of the Hold lose his temper—and live to tell of it. They always had command of their emotions. Angry? Yes. Annoyed? Often. But enraged to the point of losing control? Never.

Talo-Toecan stood stock-still before Bailic, his fists clenched. His shout echoed in the immense space behind him, temporarily drowning out the measured drips of water. "Tell me, you cursed, ill-begot effluent of a corpse worm. What have you done to them!"

It almost seemed as if Talo-Toecan cared, and rakus seldom cared about anything. Cities rose and fell. Tyrants raped and plundered. Never did the Masters interfere in the affairs of men, only watched. The sole exception were their Keepers. Even so, they held the knowledge of themselves and their disciples a well-kept secret. There were tales aplenty of rakus, but nothing to link them to anything other than bloodthirsty beasts. Only the Keepers knew the truth.

"I swear," Talo-Toecan rumbled, "if you leave without telling me what you have done, I will carve out your black and twisted soul and personally give it to Mistress Death herself! *Don't* expect me to believe the mountain trembled of her own accord. I felt it even down here." Talo-Toecan drew close to the bars. "Tell me," he whispered, "or I will make your eventual end more agonizing, more painful, than even you could devise in a thousand years, Bailic."

"My, my, my," Bailic said, carefully adjusting his shirt. "What a state you've gotten yourself into. One would think," he simpered, "you cared."

The Master silently lunged, his eyes glinting with a seething hatred. The ward stood silent and quiescent between them, and believing himself to be safe, Bailic stood his ground as the two powerful forces collided. This could be his end, he thought with a perverse thrill, but his trust in the powers of ancestral rakus was vindicated, and he watched in obscene pleasure as, with a pulse of unseen power, Talo-Toecan was thrown back, repelled by a force stronger than he.

Talo-Toecan's light went out, plunging Bailic into a momentary blindness. His grip on his torch clenched, but he forced himself to stand firm as his eyes readjusted. There was the smell of singed metal. By the flickering light of his torch, Bailic watched Talo-Toecan pick himself up, draw himself straight, and shake out his long vest.

Limping, Talo-Toecan took step after careful step until he was so close, the ward buzzed a harsh warning. "What . . ." he breathed raggedly, "have you done to them?"

"I've done nothing," Bailic nearly spat, refusing to step back, though it took all his nerve and hatred. "I came to find out what you had done."

"It wasn't you?" Talo-Toecan whispered, his amber eyes going to the ceiling.

Bailic sneered. "And it wasn't you," he said, only now understanding. "Your new student has gotten herself in a bit of a spot now, hasn't she? Or is it he? Either way, I should find an interesting situation upstairs." Bailic spun around.

"Bailic!" Talo-Toecan called, but Bailic hardly heard him, already deep in thought as to what he might find in the rooms on the eighth floor.

Talo-Toecan leaned wearily against the rockface and watched Bailic creep up the tunnel. Only one thing could account for the amount of energy that could shake the Hold to its foundations. "You tried to break my ward," he said through a sigh. "I warned you, but you didn't listen. Perhaps now it's truly ended." His ancient eyes almost filled with emotion.

In a swirl of gray, the diminutive figure of a tired man shimmered and grew until the sleek bulk of a raku replaced it. The floor was hard and cold, and he felt it less in the form he had been born with. Besides, he thought, the tragedy was

easier to bear this way. Rakus were never known to weep—
as men often do.

32

Cold. It was so cold, Strell thought muzzily. Why was he
so cold? He hadn't been cold for ages. He sat up, gingerly rubbing the back of his head. His fingers found a small
lump, and he winced as it began to throb under his investigations.

"By the wrath of the Navigator, what happened?" he
whispered. There wasn't even the barest glow from the
hearth. The only light came from moonlight spilling in
through his window. He shifted, surprised to find that not
only was he on the floor, but he had on his coat and hat.
Strell fingered the ash-covered leather and tried to remember
how he had gotten there.

As he stumbled to his feet, he discovered why his fire was
out. It was strewn the length and breadth of his room. Strell
rubbed the soot from his face. He stared at the pieces of
charred wood in confusion, coughing at the bitter stink of
ash. The dark outlines of his fallen chair showed before the
lighter darkness of the window, and he grasped the smooth,
polished wood, setting the chair surely before the fireplace
where it belonged.

A frigid breath wafted through his single window, and he
tottered unsteadily to it to look out. Snow-covered woods
stretched below, a study in black and white. Against his better judgment, he leaned out to test if the ward was really
gone. The bitter night air stabbed deep into his lungs, and he
gazed at the stars. They seemed to be shocked by the astounding cold into hard, sparkling jewels. His breath made a
mist obscuring their severity, and he watched as they alter-

nately softened and cleared as he breathed. The silence was absolute.

No, he thought, frowning, he could hear Talon chittering in distress.

Strell turned to Alissa's window. "Alissa . . ." he whispered softly as a bit of cloth fluttered around the edge of her window looking like a living thing, weakly struggling to escape. There was something about Alissa . . .

"Alissa!" He lunged to his door, slipping on the firewood. His ankle turned on a rolling stick, and he crashed to the floor. With a single-minded purpose, he clawed his way to the door, not acknowledging the pain stabbing through his ankle.

She had cried out. He remembered that. The sound of it still seemed to echo in his thoughts, her heart-stopping scream. Using his door as a crutch, he pulled himself up and flung it open, scarcely noticing the warmth of the hall. The three steps to her room seemed to take forever, and he burst in, forgetting they were still at odds.

"Alissa!" he cried as he took in the destruction. Her room looked as if it had been ripped apart. The fire was pushed to the back of the chimney and was nearly out. Her windows, too, had lost their wards. The frigid wind blew in one and out the other. It was frighteningly cold.

"Where are you?" Strell called, his breath steaming, and then he spotted her on the floor as Talon chittered from beside her. He fell to his knees before Alissa and untangled her from the blanket. With shaking hands, he gently rolled her to face him. Her skin was pale and cold. Her hands, as he took them into his own, were blue.

What had happened? he thought, panic blanking his mind. His room. It was warmer there. He could restart the fire. Carefully he wrapped Alissa back in her blanket, picked her up, and much as a wounded animal, returned to the security of his hearth. Talon followed him, and he set Alissa in his chair, watching her breathe for a terrible moment to be sure she was no worse before hobbling back to her room for the still-glowing coals to restart his fire. Nearly frantic, he divided his shattered attention between the fire and Alissa until the former was strong and bright.

Half mad with worry, he knelt at her side, rubbing her hands to warm them. "Alissa? Please, can you hear me?"

There was no answer. Her eyes remained closed. Standing at her head, Talon began to tug on Alissa's hair.

Strell's dread plunged to his belly and twisted. He stiffened, looking at the empty corners of his room for anything to help him, but it held nothing. For the first time in his life he didn't know what to do. She was dying. He was going to lose her. He was going to lose everything, only now knowing he had it!

As he sat frozen in panic, she turned a pasty gray and her breathing became shallow.

"Alissa!" Strell cried, shaking her shoulders. "Alissa, please," he begged, bringing her blue fingers to his lips to warm them. "Please don't." There was no answer but her slow breaths.

Riven with grief, Strell struggled with himself. "Bailic," he whispered. "He can help. I'll give him what he wants." Strell rose, desperately not wanting to leave her. Finally he bent low and whispered, "Wait. I will return to you," and ran awkwardly from the room.

"Bailic!" he shouted as he raced to the end of the hall. "Where are you? Show yourself!" he bellowed, then quietly, brokenly, said, "You conniving, insidious, worm of a man."

At the landing he hesitated, paralyzed in indecision. Up or down? His frenzied state wouldn't let him go either way, and his face grew tight.

"Killy, killy, killy," Talon called, sweeping low over his head and down the dark stairs.

Strell caught his breath in relief as his decision was made for him. He began to descend, leaning heavily on the smooth banister. Talon would know where Bailic was. She always did.

"Too long . . . too long . . ." he agonized, but down he went until he overlooked the great entryway from the fourth-floor walkway.

"Bailic!" he cried. Moonlit silence greeted him. He must be here, Strell thought frantically. He couldn't wait any longer. He had to go back. He couldn't leave her alone, alone to . . . to . . .

"Bailic!" He looked toward his room where she lay. With a moan, he tore his eyes away, sending them to the floor of the great hall. Talon was there, bouncing insanely along the last step. Again he followed the small bird down to the floor of the great hall.

Strell stood at the center of the hall and looked wildly about. A cry of despair slipped from him as Talon took flight and flew swiftly back upstairs. *"Bailic!"* he shouted, the name raging from him in desperation. "Where under the Eight Wolves are you!"

33

"I'm right behind you—Piper," Bailic mocked.

"Hounds," the gangly man cursed as he jumped and turned at the voice. "Salissa." He gulped. "I need your help."

"Yes, I thought as much." Bailic leaned confidently back against the hidden door under the stair. He could understand the piper's confusion. Bailic heard the man bellowing halfway up the cramped, slippery staircase, but had to wait until Strell's back was turned before he could leave the security of the concealed passage.

"You know?" Strell's expression shifted to anger. "You did this to her!"

Bailic's eyes narrowed. "Don't jump to conclusions that may prove deadly," he said sharply, wondering why the man was covered in ash. "I've done nothing."

Strell seemed to slump in relief. "Quick. She's upstairs." Strell grasped at his sleeve. "Hurry. I—"

"Let—go—of me," Bailic said softly, planting his feet on the first step. His ire rose at the plainsman's insolence.

Strell turned on the stair. His eyes were wide in the moonlight, his face suddenly pale as if just now realizing Bailic might not come. "I—I'm sorry," he said. "But she won't wake up." His eye shot to the stairway. "Please," he whispered. "I'll give you anything."

A thin smile eased over Bailic. Anything would do nicely. "I'll come see," he said. "I wouldn't miss this for all the source ever conferred." Pushing past Strell, he deliberately set a slow pace, wanting to irritate him. It was obvious the piper longed to leave him behind and race up the stairs, but didn't, rightly afraid Bailic might conveniently forget where he was headed.

Bailic eyed him slyly. "Are you going somewhere?" He took a leisurely step.

Clearly at a loss, Strell shrugged. They had risen only two flights; his look had become decidedly frenzied.

"Your coat and hat . . ." Bailic pointed out patronizingly.

Strell looked down. "Oh, yes. I mean, no. No. I'm not going anywhere."

Bailic nodded wisely. "I see. It's a lovely hat. Such an unusual style." He smiled, delighting in Strell's anxious reaction to their sedate pace.

The man said nothing, his gaze fixed upon the next landing.

"Have you had it long?" Bailic asked pleasantly.

"What?" Strell barked, turning to face him.

"Your hat. Have you had it long?"

"It seems an eternity."

"Mmm." Unseen in the shadow-light, Bailic smirked. Much as he enjoyed tormenting the man, he remained silent. He held them to their measured pace, though, all the way up until the eighth-floor landing materialized out of the moonlight. Wild with impatience, Strell lurched up the last steps.

Eager to see what lay beyond Meson's door, Bailic met stride for stride Strell's hurried gait as the man limped down the long hallway. Bailic slid to a hasty stop as he realized the piper was no longer with him; he had gone into his own room. Surprised, Bailic backed up and looked past the open door. His mouth dropped open in wonder.

It looked as if the piper's room had been overturned. Aside from the tiny new fire, the fireplace was a black, hollow shell, its previous contents littering the floor. There was an ominous-looking crack running from the ceiling to the room's single window. A cloying pall of ash hung to tickle his throat. Everything was coated in an oily gray with the exception of a slumped, man-shaped silhouette against the far floor and wall.

The piper was kneeling beside the girl propped up in a chair, watching her take slow, tentative breaths. Perched above her was that cursed bird. How, Bailic wondered, did the beast get inside?

"What under the open skies happened?" Bailic whispered, then louder, his voice dripping with sarcasm, "Isn't this pleasant?"

Strell looked up. "Aren't you coming in?"

"Yes." Only now did Bailic step over the threshold. Any wards that may have been hidden in it were neatly nullified, quenched by the piper's haphazard invitation. It was cold, despite the fire, and he wrinkled his nose. "Oh," he said, clicking his tongue, "your window is broken." That, he thought, explained the bird's presence. Ignoring Strell's pained look, he leaned out past the sill and craned his neck to confirm his suspicions. The entire top of the flue had been blown apart, probably at the same time as the ward on the window. His eyes grew wide as he estimated the force of the blast. If it had been any stronger, it would have taken out the wall.

"Bailic . . ." Strell called from the fire.

Pulling himself in, Bailic set up a new window ward. He didn't like the cold. "You're packed?" he said, seeing the full sack lying on the bed.

"She's over here, Bailic," Strell grated.

"So she is." Bailic picked his way through the scattered wood to the trio. This could very well be his only chance to investigate the piper's room, and he wasn't going to squander it. He eyed the bird cautiously, having learned to respect her weapons, small though they were. Bailic's gaze strayed to the hearthstones and he stifled a gasp. There, almost in the flames, was a map, one he had never seen before, but even in this dim light he recognized its craftsmanship. It was Meson's, and it was in the piper's possession!

He snatched it up and shook the film of ash from it. "Is

this yours?" he asked, trying to keep the urgency from his voice. He pulled it close, the soft blur clearing to show the entire mountain range, the way to the Hold boldly mapped out.

"Yes," Strell said through gritted teeth. "You said you would help, Bailic."

"Of course." Bailic carefully spread the map on the rumpled bed. "What does this say? My eyes fail me tonight." He pointed to one of the phrases etched in Meson's handwriting.

Strell stood with a fierce look. "It says 'Treacherous Ravine.' Now about Salissa?" and he held out his hand stiffly.

Slowly Bailic handed the map back, a thrill of satisfaction cutting through him as the plainsman rolled it up and tucked it into a coat pocket. A thin smile replaced Bailic's look of mock puzzlement. "Yes, of course," he said, going to see what state the girl was in. He didn't know what to expect anymore. He had been so sure she was the latent Keeper, but now . . .

He knelt smoothly before the fire, struggling to not show his pleasure at the situation. With the light behind him he could see the piper's reactions better. "Be silent," he warned, "this is exacting." He shut his eyes in sham concentration, confident as long as the piper thought he was doing something, the man would be still about the girl and let him think.

Perhaps the evening hadn't been wasted, he thought gleefully. He could find a way to use this to his advantage. The bowls of nuts *had* been in the piper's favor. Bailic had allowed his intuition to guide him before. But now the annoying man had made a slip so blatant, Bailic could hardly keep from chuckling. Not only did the piper have one of Meson's precious maps, but he could read the Masters' script. It wouldn't be possible for him to know it unless painstakingly taught. It was a dead language, reserved for the seemingly unchanging Masters and their once steady stream of Keepers.

No wonder Talo-Toecan had laughed at him, Bailic thought. It was obvious. Strell was the latent Keeper and Meson's son. The hat, the map, unlocking Meson's door, even his tolerance of half-breeds. The Wolves take him,

Bailic thought in disgust. The piper was a half-breed himself. He looked full plains, but if Meson took to wife whom he thought, then all likeness to Meson would've been masked by the dominate traits of the plains, his accent included.

Bailic's chest tightened and his blood begin to rise as thoughts long and securely padlocked stirred within him. Rema, the hypocritical whore, would have raised her half-breed spawn in the plains when Meson hadn't returned. May the Wolves take her, he thought, seething. She should have chosen him. Meson was foothills. It wasn't natural. How *dare* she spurn him!

But Bailic had killed her beloved Meson, and he was alive—and Rema's child was kneeling before him, begging for his help.

With an almost indistinguishable shudder, Bailic crushed the memory of his exquisite betrayer, unwilling to let anything mar his evening of success. All thoughts of revenge and vindication aside, the question remained, what had caused the explosion?

He stirred as if coming out of a state of intense concentration. "Tell me, my most worthy minstrel," he said, struggling to soften the hard stare he couldn't help but fix upon the piper, "how did she come to this sad state we now find her in?"

Strell's eyes fell. "I don't know. I—I woke on the floor."

"Ah . . . Well, then, by chance did you two exchange words again this evening?" Bailic waited impatiently, damning himself for trying to find a whisper of his back-stabbing charlatan in the piper's eyes. "Come, come," he coaxed, "it's obvious there was a falling out between the two of you. Perhaps there was an attempt at reconciliation, with, shall we say, explosive results?"

Strell's head came up, and he stared at him fiercely.

"Really," Bailic crooned in delight, "I must know if I am to help. You *do* want me to help, don't you?"

"Yes," Strell said shortly.

"Yes, you want me to help, or yes, you had another argument?" Bailic leaned back, enjoying the look of unmitigated hatred pouring from Strell.

"Yes to both. Curse you, Bailic. Just get on with it."

"Patience, bard." He smiled. "A final question and I'll see what I can do. Did you, perhaps, lose your temper?" Bailic held his breath as Strell glanced toward the hearth.

"Yes. Yes, I did," Strell agonized.

"Very good." Bailic bit his cheek in an effort to remain calm. "It's well you told me. It explains a great deal."

And it did. It had happened many times in the past; a tragedy that would work well for him. They had argued, and in a fit of jealous rage, the piper accidentally scorched the very object of his desire, sending her into a state close to, but shy of, death. In all likelihood it had been an unconscious reaction. The piper might not even be aware he'd done it.

Strong emotions elicit strong power, which was why latent Keepers were denied a source until attaining a high level of control. Yet, it had been a quite a backlash, spilling from the mental plane into the physical. He would have believed only someone with a source could produce it.

Bailic turned his attention to the girl. As she was all but dead, he could see her tracings and determine if she was a Keeper or commoner. It mattered little if a commoner was burnt. The pain was just as bad, but when over, it was done. Their tracings were an unusable tangle anyway. What did it matter if the bridge was gone if no one was there to cross the river?

Carefully, delicately, he slipped a tendril of thought into the comatose girl's mind. "By all that's sacred."

"What!" Strell bent close.

"Be still, Piper," he barked, shoving him back. He hadn't known he said the words aloud. Licking his lips, he reluctantly returned his attention to the girl's shattered mind. It was worse than he had thought. The piper's explanation led him to believe she had only been scorched. She hadn't been. Her tracings were ash. The piper had been very thorough.

His stomach churning, Bailic gazed at the charred remains of her pathways in a morbid fascination. There was no way to tell if what he was seeing was the crusted remains of a defunct pattern, once capable of channeling great power, or merely a commoner's random pathways. The damage looked irreparable. Shuddering, Bailic removed his awareness, glad he had never made the awkward man angry. Bailic would have been hard-pressed to counter a backlash such as this without being forewarned. "This could have been me," he whispered in awe.

"What?" Strell pleaded, the concern almost palpable in his voice. "What's wrong?"

Shaking off his disquiet, Bailic met the anxious piper's gaze. "She has been shattered by the same force that blew out your window," he accused. Strell's face went white, and Bailic was satisfied his words had been understood. The piper knew exactly what he had done.

"But will she be all right?" Strell pleaded.

Bailic's pulse quickened. She would make a splendid hostage. "I can clear the way for her return," he said softly, relishing the delicious feeling of power. He held the piper's gaze, not caring if his fierce desire showed. "Let's discuss my fee."

Strell's face went blank. "Pardon me?"

A smile blossomed over Bailic. He quite enjoyed bargaining when he held the high ground. "I want the same thing you do," he all but whispered, leaning over the girl in a rustle of cloth. "I want that book," he said, stifling a shudder as the words passed his lips.

"I don't know where it is," Strell said quickly, despair creasing his face.

"Then I'll leave you to your mourning, Piper." He got to his feet, hardly able to contain his glee. The man knew of the book. It was as good as his.

"No! Wait!" Awkwardly heaving himself to his feet, Strell gazed down at the girl, his indecision clear. Bailic remained, already knowing the outcome. "I—I'll find it," he whispered.

"I thought you might," Bailic drawled. Fool, he thought. This is where compassion leaves you. "So, you agree? The book for the life of your companion?"

Only now did Strell tear his gaze from her to fix him with a venomous stare. The tall man seemed to tense, gathering himself up. Bailic stiffened, laying a protective shield over his thoughts, but the piper was already collapsing in on himself. "Done and done, Bailic," Strell said brokenly. "Alissa for the book when I find it."

"Alissa is it now?" Bailic all but laughed. "I knew she wasn't your sister. Salissa indeed! No, Piper. 'When you find it,' isn't soon enough. I want it by the beginning of winter."

"But that's only five weeks away!" Strell cried.

"Yes, I know." Bailic laughed then—he couldn't help it—but the sound abruptly died. He hadn't yet sealed the bargain. "So, Strell," he said scornfully, using the man's given name for the first time, "done and done?"

Strell's eyes hardened. "No," he said softly. "I want something as well."

Bailic grinned. "Oh, my insolent guest," he said with a chuckle. "You're indeed plains raised if you enjoy the pleasures of haggling so much you would risk the life of another in the doing of it. Take care I don't tire, though, and leave without making any agreement at all." Bailic's eyes narrowed. "What could you possibly want?"

"I want your nightly visitations to end," Strell said roughly. "I'll see you get food, and you can eat it if you dare, but you won't join us for our meals. I will not entertain you anymore."

Bailic's eyebrows rose and dropped. He rather enjoyed the entertainment, but the fare had turned bland lately. Romance and lost loves. If he pushed the issue, Bailic was sure it would worsen. "Is that all?" He smiled.

Strell tugged his coat straight. "You will leave Alissa alone. Don't even talk to her."

"And in return I get . . ." Bailic said with a leer, leaning casually against the mantel.

"You get the book by the winter solstice."

"Fair enough." Bailic shifted suddenly, startling the bird. "But I want to make one thing very clear." He stepped close, and smiling, leaned over the silent figure of Alissa so his softly spoken words would be indisputable. "If the book of *First Truth* fails to reach my grasp by the first of winter, I'll put her right back where she is now. Only this time there won't be anyone to make a path for her to follow back. You will watch her slowly waste away before your eyes." Bailic smirked. "It will take some time for her soul to depart completely. You want to risk it?"

Pale and uncertain, Strell's eyes dropped to Alissa. He nodded and held out his hand, palm up. "Done and done."

Bailic looked on in wonder before stretching his own to cover it to seal the bargain. "Done and done, Strell," he murmured. "You have until the beginning of winter."

In a daze, Bailic turned to leave. He had won, he thought. It couldn't be this easy.

"Bailic?" came Strell's rough call. "You've forgotten something."

"Oh. Yes." Spinning on a heel, he rudely crowded Strell away from the girl's side. Stoically ignoring the charred remains of her tracings, he again slipped carefully into her mind. He would never be able to hear her thoughts—she was a commoner after all—but he could feel her small knot of emotion. "Ah," he sighed. "There you are. Comfortable, are we?"

Bailic blinked in surprise. There was a glimmer of awareness seeping from her, looking like the faint glow of embers from a neglected fire. She was coming out of her stupor on her own. By morning she would be back among the living without his help! This was almost unheard of. Rare was the person who could find a strong enough impetus to return after retreating this far into their unconscious. They generally wandered lost among their thoughts and dreams until their bodies ceased functioning and died. But the deal had been struck, and he would go through the motions to ensure the piper wouldn't slip from their agreement on a technicality. Besides, he was looking forward to hurrying her along.

Taking a slow breath, Bailic removed his thoughts from hers. Glancing at Strell, he shifted to stand directly over her slumped figure. He paused, considering her, then looked slyly at the piper through half-closed eyes. So concerned, he thought snidely. He was going to enjoy this.

Bailic gently brushed a wisp of hair from her face, and bending low, he breathed upon her pale cheek, somehow free of soot. "Wake, my dear. We are all waiting for you," he whispered tenderly. Then, with an incredible suddenness, he drew his hand back and swung it fiercely.

Bailic's open hand met Alissa's face with an astounding crack.

Strell lunged, crashing into Bailic. In a tangle of arms and legs they went down, rolling on the floor. There was an outraged screeching from the bird, and Bailic flung an arm over his head at the sudden smell of feathers and the beating of wings. Claws raked the air over his face. Bailic formed a field and ward about the bird. He would be done with it now.

Then the bird was gone as Strell plucked her from the air and threw her aside. "What the Wolves are you doing?" Strell snarled, pinning him to the floor.

"Get off," Bailic spat, willing to let the assault go unpunished—for now. He wouldn't chance damaging his prize, not now. And on further thought, it wouldn't be very clever to use a ward and possibly teach the man something. Who knew how much unauthorized schooling the piper had? So Bailic contented himself with smiling coldly up at the furious man, recalling how extremely satisfying it had been to slap the girl. "What," he mocked, "did you expect me to do? Wake her with a kiss?"

Livid, Strell grasped Bailic's vest and pulled him up to smash his head into the floor. Bailic crafted a ward to burn the man as deeply as his lady was. This further attack he wouldn't allow. From the hearth came an excited twitter.

"Strell . . ." Alissa mumbled.

"Alissa!" Strell turned and struggled to his feet.

Bailic's head hit the floor with a dull thunk. His eyes narrowed, and he fought with the desire to burn the man anyway. He touched his face to find a small scratch. The bird had reached him after all. Mustering as much grace as he could, Bailic rose and angrily brushed himself off. It seemed he had been doing that a lot lately. It was becoming tiresome.

Strell was kneeling beside the girl, stroking her forehead, whispering something encouraging. Her eyes were closed, and the imprint of Bailic's hand showed an angry red upon her cheek. Even the bird was fussing and crooning, bobbing next to her ear.

"Disgusting," Bailic said with a snarl, and he spun about. The piper was a fool. Throwing away his chance for immeasurable power for the maybe-affections of a common girl. It was asinine. Compassion made you weak and vulnerable.

There was no strength to be found in it. That was an error he would never make again. Once, long ago, had been enough.

Bailic looked back before he crossed the threshold. They were completely oblivious to whether he was there or not. "Fool," he said shortly, and stomped down the hall. No one noticed him leaving.

Somehow his victory was not as sweet as he had imagined it would be.

34

Safe, she thought, but from what, she couldn't remember. *"You will stay?"* a faint memory stirred. It was a summons so old, it stretched back to before her birth. The call had been unheard for nearly twenty years, drowned out by warm breakfasts, skinned knees, and laughter. But now, alone in her thoughts, she could hear it. *"Remember me?"* it whispered seductively. *"Stay."*

"But what of Strell?" she thought in confusion. She couldn't stay, even if it was warm.

"He bides your company no longer," the voice within her whispered. *"You know this."*

"Talon will grieve if I don't return," Alissa insisted.

"Strell will care for her," the whisper said. *"Stay with me?"*

"But my mother," Alissa said, feeling her resolve loosen. *"She's alone and waiting."*

"Be fair to yourself," the voice soothed. *"She doesn't expect your return."*

"Papa," Alissa pleaded, feeling her will to resist fade. *"He gave his life for me."*

"He returned to me before you," the voice insisted. *"Stay with me."*

"Bailic will get my book," she whispered, but her strength was gone.

"Does it matter?" the dark voice said softly, and with a slow thought, Alissa agreed. The voice left her to her hazy, gray world. Alissa snuggled down amid the gentle warmth, drowsing peacefully, waiting for the fog to soothe her to an immutable slumber.

"Wait. I will return to you," a new voice whispered tenderly, shocking through her fog.

Strell? she thought, startled. He was so angry with her. He wouldn't listen to her, wouldn't talk to her. Would he?

Then a sharp pain rocked her. The cloying gray that enfolded her slipped reluctantly away and dissolved, leaving behind only the recollection of its fearsome security, whispering its lies of peace and contentment. Only now as its hold loosened did Alissa realize. It was Mistress Death, here in her thoughts, and as the dark maid gathered the last of her blanket back in her arms, Alissa felt her settle peacefully down to wait. Death had found a comfortable berth in Alissa's thoughts and was content to stay her hand for a time. But Alissa knew she had been marked. Death could claim her at will. Like a middling fool, Alissa had run to her offered security. Her peace was the peace of death, her refuge one of permanent isolation. And Strell had been the one who freed her.

He does care! Alissa thought, and her entire being seemed to resonate with the knowledge. "Strell!" she shouted, but it came out as a croaked whisper, barely audible even to her. There was a distant crash. Somewhere, Talon chittered in anger.

"Strell?" It was better this time, but the tumult continued.

"Strell," Alissa tried again. She sounded terrible, she thought. What had happened? The third time was the charm, though, and she sensed a familiar presence at her shoulder.

"I'm here," he whispered, and Alissa felt the lightest, trembling touch on her forehead.

"I know." She tried to open her eyes, but they seemed dreadfully heavy. Finally she managed to pry them apart to find Strell's relieved smile. He was covered in gray dust. Streaks of clean skin showed underneath. With a happy sigh, she smiled back. Maybe their argument was finally over. A trace of worry crossed him. "What is it?" she asked.

The look vanished. "Nothing." He pulled away but continued to beam down at her. Perhaps she had only imagined his unease. Talon chittered and fussed, demanding attention, and Alissa wiggled free of her blanket and tried to sit up. She frowned as her muscles failed to respond as quickly as they should. A harsh buzzing seemed to echo between her ears, fading away only to start up again at her slightest movement. "This isn't my room," she said. "It's your room. At least I think it's your room."

He gestured weakly. "It used to be."

It was an absolute shambles, reminiscent of the time her goat, Nanny, had gotten into the house when Alissa and her mother were at market. A thin film of greasy ash covered everything. Over the cloying catch of dust was a fresh smell, and Alissa looked to the window to see if it was open before she remembered the ever-present wards. Her eyes widened at the new crack running from the window to the upper corner of the room. It hadn't been there the last time she stole a glance into Strell's chamber. Turning back, she noticed he had on his coat, and then she saw the sack—packed and waiting on the floor.

Alissa felt her throat tighten. "I don't want to leave."

"I know."

His voice was gentle, carrying a soft understanding, and she looked up, relieved. "We can go as soon as I find my book," she promised, stroking Talon to try and calm the excited bird.

Strell's smile froze and he looked away. An uncomfortable silence settled. Alissa glanced over the demolished room, anxious to change the subject. She wanted to rise and stretch, but she wasn't sure her legs would obey her. She was so tired. "What happened?" she asked.

Strell rose and went to sit on his bed. He moved with a lurching, limping motion that made Alissa ill just watching. "I haven't the slightest idea," he said. "There was an explosion of some kind. From the looks of your room, it came through the chimney."

Talon bumped her head under Alissa's fingers, and weary,

she set the bird aside. Not to be dissuaded, Talon hopped back to Alissa's lap, demanding attention. Alissa obligingly ran her fingers over the bird's head, her thoughts going back to her experimentation before her fire. "Uh," she said, feeling a flush of guilt. "I might have done it. I was trying to break that accursed ward." She looked at the wreckage. "But I don't remember any of this." Realizing her cheek was throbbing, she touched it, wincing as it hurt all the more.

Strell looked past her and into the fire. "I heard your cry. Then I was knocked out." Seeing her questioning look, he glanced to where a frightening silhouette of a slumped man lay on the floor. "I woke up over there," he said. "You were so cold when I found you. I thought you were . . . ." He cut his thought short. "You were so cold," he finished lamely. Rising, he limped to the window and stared out into the darkness. His shoulders were stiff and hunched, and Alissa would almost say he was frightened. Watching him, she began to get frightened, too. He spun around, his face hard with determination. "Bailic knows we're looking for that book."

She twisted in her chair, trying to sit up. "We already knew that."

"Yes, but now . . ." He stopped, turning back to the window.

"But what?"

"Nothing," he said shortly, his back to her.

The fire settled with a shower of sparks. Strell cast about for his share of the tripod. Groaning under his breath, he limped across the room to get the metal rod from under the scrunched-up rug. Alissa watched him warily. Clearly he was hiding something.

"What's the matter, Strell?"

He hesitated, his eyes averted. His jaw clenched, and then, as if reaching a decision, he turned and muttered, "Bailic woke you up. Brought you back. Not me. I couldn't do it."

"Bailic!" she exclaimed, not liking he had seen her unawares.

Strell poked at the fire, placing several blackened pieces upon it. "He replaced the ward on my window, too."

Alissa blanched. "I blew out the wards?" she said. But at

least Bailic had replaced them. Maybe he liked the cold even less than she.

A glimmer of Strell's usual smile showed. "Yes, and it gave me a nasty bump." He gingerly rubbed the back of his head, holding his breath as he lowered himself to the hearthstones.

"I'm sorry."

Strell painfully shifted himself closer. "Hush," he admonished with a faint smile. "It's a small thing. What under the open skies were you doing?" He tucked a tendril of her dratted hair behind her ear, the movement so natural and fast that Alissa had only time to blink. He turned away, and she shifted uneasily, disguising the motion as sitting up straighter.

"Well," she said as she pulled her blanket tight, "I provoked Useless's ward and captured some of its strength." Alissa couldn't help her proud smile. It had been so pretty, casting shadows in the darkness of her fire-lit room. "I was going to slowly draw its strength away. Then somehow I changed it, bringing it from my thoughts to reality. I saw it, Strell! Right in front of me! I could've touched it." For a moment, she lost herself in the remembered glories of its existence.

"Then I let it go," she continued. "I thought it was separated from my source. I must have burned myself. I don't remember much after that." She busied her fingers with Talon, avoiding his eyes. "Until you freed me."

Strell stiffened. Taking his leg in his hands, he carefully shifted his foot. "I told you. I didn't bring you back. Bailic did."

"No," she argued softly, "you brought me back. You asked me to wait. That you would return." She didn't care what he said. Strell had given her the will to return; he was the one who deserved her thanks.

Strell looked up. All his ire was gone, replaced by a look so tender and hopeful, it almost hurt to see it, glowing there on his face. His eyes dropped, and he turned away as if embarrassed. "Look, Alissa," he said quietly. "I'm sorry about everything. I know you said you'd give anything for that fabric, but I should have asked about your salve." His words began to spill from him in an unaccustomed rush of confession. "I meant to tell you sooner, but I just kept putting it off, probably because I knew you'd be angry, but Bailic didn't want anything of mine. I only added it to the pile to make it look bigger, and when I did tell you, you got mad. I didn't know it meant that much to you until you threw my chair out of your room. I'm really sorry. If I had known the salve was that important to you, I would have asked." He hesitated. "Or told you sooner."

Amazed by his rush of words, it wasn't until Alissa opened her mouth to apologize herself that she recognized all of them. Her mouth snapped shut in confusion. "I didn't move your chair," she said slowly.

"What?"

Alissa shook her head. "I didn't move your chair. I thought you had. I figured you were so mad at me for making such a fuss, you didn't want to talk to me."

They looked at each other blankly for a moment. Together their confusion melted away.

"Bailic," Strell all but spat, his eyes narrowing.

Alissa sank back into the cushions with a heavy sigh. "Bailic indeed," she repeated. What a black and twisted thing to do, she thought darkly. He had probably hoped to worsen their argument, thinking one of them would give him the book out of revenge. Still, she couldn't blame it all on Bailic. She could have confronted Strell about the chair. Or not become so angry about the salve. It wouldn't have taken much. Her pride and temper had gotten in the way.

Silently Alissa crossed her fingers, vowing to never let her temper keep her from ending an argument properly. Then she uncrossed them, promising she would never let her pride rule her again. It had nearly cost her a friendship. Taking a deep breath, Alissa met Strell's eyes. "I'm sorry for making such a fuss yesterday," she said shyly. "It was a good trade. Thank you."

A slow smile came over Strell. "Yes, it was. And you're welcome."

Alissa busied herself with Talon. The silly bird had finally stopped crooning, and Alissa moved her back to the chair arm. This time the bird stayed. "You have no idea how sorry I am," Alissa said.

"Me too," Strell said. "I can't believe Bailic did that."

"Never again?" Alissa whispered.

"Never again," Strell said firmly. He held out his pinky finger, and with a smile of delight, Alissa linked hers with his in the age-old practice of children making promises. The childhood custom had apparently crossed the border from foothills to plains with no prejudice. The young are often wiser than their elders when it comes to matters of common sense.

"What fools he made us into," Strell said, seeming embarrassed as he dropped his hand. "I ought to thrash him."

Alissa's breath puffed out in understanding. "Perhaps." She winced as she looked at the crack in the wall. "But then I would have to find my book on my own, as you would be nothing but a fond memory. Forget it." She brought her gaze back to him. "It doesn't matter."

She was just in time to catch that same uneasy look racing over him. His attention went back to his ankle, studiously avoiding her. She eyed him warily. "What's the matter, Strell?"

"Nothing," he grunted.

That grunt she knew very well. There was something he didn't want to tell her. Talon shifted her feathers in warning as if having recognized the questionable validity of his words, too. Alissa shifted her gaze from the bird to Strell. "Come on, Strell," she wheedled, "tell me."

He looked up, an obviously innocent expression pasted onto his face. "You're tired. It can wait—for a bit. I want to know if it worked."

"What worked?" Alissa asked in confusion, trying to figure out what under the Eight Hounds he was talking about. It was clear he was trying to change the subject, but her curiosity won out—as usual.

"Removing Useless's ward." He grinned.

Her heart gave a thump, and she nervously tucked a strand of hair behind an ear. "I don't think so," she said cautiously. It didn't seem likely. She remembered a lot of pain.

At Strell's encouraging nod, Alissa licked her lips and set her attention on visualizing her source.

Much to her delight, the glowing sphere swam into existence alone and unfettered. "It's free!" she said in delight, feeling a smile steal over her. "Strell, somehow I did it." Her source shimmered faintly in her mind's eye, again free of Useless's ward. It glowed a soft blue-gold in the darkness of her thoughts. It was hers to do with as she chose. She had done it. Something, though, wasn't right.

The harsh buzzing that had been plaguing her all night became worse, and she turned her attention to where her pattern spread in all its glory. The faint glow of black and purple was gone. She felt herself go ashen and her stomach tighten. "Strell?" she said, hearing her voice quaver in fright as she saw what was once her tracings. "They're gone! My tracings are gone!"

Alissa stared at the destruction, unable to tear her horrified gaze from the charred landscape of carnage in her mind's eye. Where there had once been the delicate blue-black lines of loops and swirls, there was now only twisted, disfigured channels clogged with burnt debris. She had thought them lifeless before when barren of the source's energy. She had been wrong. This ruin with all its black char and ash was truly dead. It was over. She was undone. There was no reason to find the book now, she thought emptily. She wouldn't be able to use it.

Despair thundered down, crushing her. Strell was calling her, but she was helpless, unable to even look away. "Gone," she murmured, then, "Ouch!" as something pinched her ear. It was Talon, bless her little bird-soul.

"Not again, Alissa," came Strell's voice, close and worried. "I can't take it again, not twice in one night."

The pain in her ear pulled Alissa from her inner vision, and the mangled remains of her tracings vanished to all but her memory. The damage was still there. It would probably remain forever, but now that she wasn't looking at it, the shock seemed easier to bear. "They're gone," she repeated, her eyes filling with tears. "There's nothing left!" Then there was only Strell kneeling beside her, holding her as she sobbed, trying to describe what she had seen. He silently listened, his arms tight about her to keep her from losing herself completely.

"I did this," she wept into his shoulder, taking comfort in the honest scent of sand and wind that clung to him even over the smell of ash. "Why," she sobbed, "didn't I leave them alone as I had been told?" Alissa looked up, surprised to see the shared pain in Strell's eyes. "What will I do?" she whispered vacantly. "I'm nothing. I've lost it all."

"First," he said firmly, "you will have some tea."

Alissa looked at him numbly through eyes wet with tears.

"Then," he said, "you will eat, and finally, as it's nearly dawn, you will sleep."

He was half right. She fell asleep before she finished her first warming mug.

35

Strell sighed as he gently removed the tea from Alissa's senseless fingers. "I should have married Matalina," he said in jest, and Talon, perched protectively over her mistress, shifted her feathers as if in agreement. It hardly seemed possible it had been hours, not days, since he prepared dinner alone in the empty kitchen. He thought he had lost her completely as she shunned him again. When she returned to the hall having changed into her new dress for what he thought had been Bailic, he was certain.

Desperate to break their silence, he was going to play her favorite song on his grandfather's pipe. He only made things horrendously worse by helping Bailic lull her into a highly suggestive state. Strell hadn't meant to. He thought himself immune to such tactics, but he fell under Bailic's sway as easily as Alissa. If it hadn't been for Useless, they would both be dead by now.

Strell felt his dislike for the mysterious Useless shift a hitch to gratitude. He had to find a way past that locked door. It was obvious Useless and Bailic despised each other, and that gave Strell a renewed sense of hope. He couldn't allow himself to believe Useless's claim that he couldn't be freed. Once found, he could take care of Bailic. Strell wouldn't even have to tell Alissa of his dark bargain with the pale man.

Strell glanced guilty at Talon as he eased closer to the fire. He was glad the bird couldn't talk. There would be a time to tell Alissa he had promised Bailic her book, but not tonight. Not after she'd nearly killed herself. Not after she saw her future as a Keeper burnt to dust. Strell smiled. Not after realizing he might love her.

With a slow, resigned shake of his head, he turned to his throbbing ankle. The knots on his boot were tight from the swelling. A tug on them nearly sent him to the ceiling as the pain shot from agonizing to excruciating. His stomach twisted as he cut the laces and slipped the boot off. A moan, half pain, half relief, slipped from him. "Wolves," he gasped, looking down to see the swollen purple mass that had once been his ankle. He had torn it to shreds. Better he had broken it cleanly than this. It would never be the same. Strell threw the boot from him in disgust.

They were still leaving, he thought with a frown. As soon as his ankle could bear his weight. Maybe Alissa knew a foothills' remedy. Her ankle had healed in a day. He'd ask her to look at it. Now that she would, he thought, so pleased, he felt as if he would burst.

Strell carefully slid down the hearth to look into her quiet face. Her skin was still woefully pallid but not dangerously so. Her eyes were shut, but he recalled them easily enough. The deep gray was unforgettable. How, he wondered, could he have ever thought them strange? They fit her perfectly.

"I wonder which family her mother comes from," he whispered, knowing he hadn't enough presumption to ask. Alissa seemed adept at so many things, not showing the usual adherence to one skill or task that was so essential in keeping the peace in the plains. She was good at fashioning clothes, but half the population in the plains could do that.

Chipping stone was rather unique, but he had never heard of a chartered family specializing in that. Rema must be from a common line. Alissa once said her mother hailed from deep plains. The only people who managed to survive there were thieves and assassins. Strell knew his mother wouldn't sanction such a union, even if Alissa was plains, and he pushed the thought aside in guilt and grief.

A wisp of hair lay across Alissa's cheek, and he carefully tucked it back behind an ear. Her hair was so different from any he had spent time looking at. Almost like spun gold. "That's it!" he whispered suddenly. "That's what I will make for her." The solstice was nearing, and tradition was to exchange gifts. He had found lots of beautiful things in the annexes, but nothing seemed appropriate. Besides, nothing in the annexes was his to give.

"Perfect," he breathed, wiping the last of the ash from his fingers and gently shifting Alissa's head to slowly pull the thick mass of hair from behind her.

She mumbled, and Strell froze. His gift was to be a surprise, and he couldn't very well ask for a lock of hair. He had to steal it.

He waited impatiently until her breathing slowed, then selected a portion of silky wisps from the nape of her neck where she wouldn't miss it. Eyeing it critically, he frowned. Her hair was still terribly short. Even the lowest plains beggar had more status to wear it longer. But it was smooth and silky. Nicer than what he was used to working with.

Still holding the small bundle, he reached for his knife, his hand slapping into his calf. His shaving blade was in its boot sheath on the other side of the room. Strell sighed. He looked at the boot in the corner, then at Alissa, beginning to frown in her sleep. Finally he looked at Talon. The cagey bird was watching him intently, and she shifted, seeming to shrug. Strell reluctantly allowed the shiny stuff to slip through his fingers. There was no help for it. He would have to cross the room for his knife.

Limping to the pile of leather, he slipped his knife free. As he turned, his swollen foot hit the table leg, flooding him with pain. "Ahhh . . ." he moaned, desperately clamping a hand to his mouth. Suddenly nauseated, he lurched to the flagstones and collapsed.

"Strell?" Alissa mumbled.

Talon appeared to chuckle, and he eyed the bird sourly, failing to find the humor in the situation. "Hush, all is well," he murmured anxiously, and he hummed a lullaby until Alissa was again deeply asleep. He glanced up at Talon as if for permission, then quickly cut free a small bundle of hair, pleased Alissa never woke. "See," he quipped sarcastically, "that wasn't so hard." The falcon fluffed her feathers and closed her eyes, seemingly convinced nothing more of interest could possibly happen.

Strell leaned back against the warm stones running up the hearth. He twisted the bit of silky smoothness into a coil and tucked it away with a distant smile. Later he would weave the hard-won gold into a delicate charm. It was silly, and he didn't believe in such things, but it would make a lovely bit of nonsense, perfect for his desires. All that remained was to decide what kind of charm to weave. It wasn't a hard choice, and he smiled as he decided upon a luck charm. Never would he have believed he would ever use this bit of knowledge. His grandfather Trook, of all people, had taught him this particular skill, and it was as far from pottery as was piping.

As the youngest son, it had often fallen to Strell to "entertain" the old man, although to be more accurate, it was often the other way around. They had spent an entire summer in the shade of a bartok tree making charms from horse hair. He knew them all: luck, fortune, wisdom, contentment, even love.

Oh, that last was a tricky one, and he grinned as he looked toward the ceiling in remembered frustration. He had even tried its potency once as a boy. Of course it had failed. It was only a bit of hair knotted and tied. There was no magic in the intricate absurdity, no magic at all, but it would be a pretty little thing when done.

Tomorrow he would find a way to convince Alissa to abandon her shattered room, but for tonight she was here, safe beside him where she ought to be if he had any say in the matter. Strell shook his head ruefully. He knew he had no say at all. He would simply have to wait until she figured it out for herself. Still, he mused, there was probably enough to make an additional charm for himself—not one of luck, though—and a little insurance never hurt.

36

It was marvelously hot, and she sat in the dappled shade of the birch trees behind the house, working on her walking stick. It seemed she never could get the bothersome thing done. From behind her came the smallest shift of dry pine needles. The honest scent of sheep dung wafted to her on the late afternoon breeze mixing with the laceflower pollen.

"Hello, Papa," Alissa drawled, and she heard him groan.

"How did you know I was there?" he asked, settling himself down beside her upon the split-log bench before the well.

She looked up and wrinkled her nose. "You've been with the sheep."

"Ashes." Taking her stick from her, he looked over the ivy-leaf design. "I haven't been able to frighten you since you were five."

Alissa's eyebrows rose. "Four. Hiding in the tree outside my window and moaning on Allhallows Eve doesn't count."

He harrumphed. "Four, then." Silently he handed the stick back. Taking a pebble, he tossed it into the well. They never had gotten a wall around it, and the perfectly cylindrical hole just begged to be fallen into. "You know . . ." He hesitated, and the cold splunk of the stone finding water came to them. "There are better ways to spend your time."

Alissa flushed and studiously applied an oil-soaked rag to the end of her stick. "I'm looking," she grumbled. "Every day."

"Dillydallying about in the annexes isn't looking."

Her eyes dropped. "I can't use it anymore."

"It's still yours," he said gently.

From inside came her mother's shout of dismay. Apparently they would be having charcoal instead of bread tonight. He stood, and she looked up in alarm. "Wait. Papa."

"Gotta go, Lissy," he said, his gaze fixed almost hungrily upon the house.

"But where is it!"

"You know exactly where it is," he called over his shoulder.

The staff clattered to the ground, and she flung herself after him. "Papa!" Bursting into the empty kitchen, she saw the door to her room thump shut. "Papa, don't go!" She threw her door open and stood in a shocked surprise.

Someone was halfway out her window—and it wasn't her papa.

"Who are you?" Alissa blurted, and the girl turned, looking as embarrassed and awkward as a fifteen-year-old can.

Unhooking her leg from the sill, she stood and fidgeted, her eyes carefully on the floor, her hands clasped behind her back. She was dressed in shades of purple, her tight vest nearly reaching her knees, looking like a feminine version of Bailic's latest outfit. The ends of the yellow sash about her waist brushed the floor. "I like your father," she said. "I don't remember mine."

"But who are you?" Alissa repeated.

"Silla. I'm sorry, was this your dream?" Her eyes rose, shocking Alissa with their unnatural gold color. "Sometimes I can't tell who's the dreamer and who's the dreamed-up."

"Dream?" Alissa mouthed.

Alissa started awake with a gasp.

The soft gray light of a winter's twilight was pooled about her, chill and lonely in the abandoned clutter of the dry-goods annex. "Aw, Wolves," she swore, disentangling herself from the linen she was nestled in. She had fallen asleep again, but at least Strell hadn't caught her this time. Alissa's eyes rose to the ceiling. She was going to be late with Bailic's supper tray. She didn't care. Bailic couldn't frighten her anymore. He practically ignored her, convinced Strell was the latent Keeper. It was the only good to have come from her misery.

"Talon?" she whispered, reluctant to break the hush, but she was alone. She took a deep breath, brushed herself off, and made her slow way up to the kitchen. It was pleasant today, even in the annexes. This morning, the moist coastal air had pushed itself into the first of the mountains in a spiteful tease of heat. Tomorrow it might be so cold as to crack stones, but today was unusually mild. Alissa would like to blame her drowsiness on the unusual warmth, but she had been falling asleep without meaning to all these past three weeks.

A stir of excitement took her as she made her way to the great hall. Tonight Strell was making *her* dinner. He felt bad about his forced immobility from a badly wrenched ankle. Now that he was becoming useful again, he wanted to make up for it. And so Alissa had been cordially invited to dine tonight with the minstrel of her choice. Bailic's tray, though, came first. He took all his meals in his room now. When she had asked Strell about it, he had mumbled something about Bailic being tired of his stories. Alissa didn't care. Delivering Bailic's trays was a small price to pay to have Strell all to herself.

Strell was hunched awkwardly over the fire as she scuffed into the kitchen. "Don't look!" he shouted, lurching to block her view. "The tray is by the door."

Her nose in the air, Alissa sniffed for a hint as to what was on the menu. The kitchen smelled like nothing. Nothing at all. "Is Talon here?" she asked.

"No. Go away! I'm not ready for you yet."

Alissa scrunched her nose in a mock irritation as she took the tray and left. The plate was covered, making dinner a pleasant mystery. She was tempted to peek but didn't, wanting to preserve Strell's surprise, as it obviously meant a lot to him.

Alissa wound her way up through the dusk to Bailic's door without a candle. After weeks of this, the passage was as familiar as the trails on her mother's farm. She intentionally took it slow, but still only rose five flights before she was puffing and blowing. It seemed she tired so easily, but she was much improved from last week, when she rested every third flight. Even so, by the eighth floor she had to stop. She slid Bailic's tray onto the wide windowsill at the landing, and mindful to keep clear of the window ward, she sat, catching sight of herself in the oval mirror.

"Much better," she congratulated herself, nodding at her image, fuzzy in the dim light. Between mourning the loss of her tracings and Strell nearly breaking his ankle, the last three weeks hadn't been easy. She had lost weight she could ill afford to lose. It was coming back, and she wasn't quite so gaunt-looking. She wore a new dress, too. Just for the occasion, not Strell.

"Look at your hair," she said in dismay, rising to move closer to the mirror. Shaking her head, Alissa untied the green ribbon binding. It was brushing her shoulders as Strell flatly refused to cut it. Her mother would be pleased, holding that a proper lady had hair she could sit on, but her papa would be appalled. Strell, she had found, couldn't be shamed, bribed, or bullied into cutting it for her.

Feeling better for the short rest, Alissa returned to Bailic's tray and wearily ascended the last few stairs. As she neared the top, a muffled curse, followed by a foul smell, slipped under Bailic's door in a luminescent, pearly fog. She sidestepped the cold mist, watching it eddy down the stairwell. She could have left the tray by his door, but this was something new, and so ignoring her mother's advice about cats and their fatalistic tendencies, she kicked at the door.

There was the sound of wood scraping and breaking crockery. "A moment!" came Bailic's muffled shout, and the door swung open. "Good evening," he said, looking down at her through sore-looking, red-rimmed eyes. He held a green-stained bowl smelling strongly of mint, and it seemed she had interrupted something.

"Bailic," Alissa said. Calm and serene, she gazed back at his frown. She had seen Mistress Death, been held in her deceiving embrace, and allowed to escape. Her days were tolerable enough, but her nights brought memories of self-inflected agonies. Bailic could do nothing worse to her.

"Would you like to come in?" Bailic suddenly smiled and stepped back.

Curiosity and a longing to be closer to where her papa had once stood caused her to peek in. The smell was horrid. By leaning, Alissa could see the source of the stench frothing in a frosted metal bowl surrounded by candles. A chipped yellow pot rocked slightly on the floor.

"It's so seldom you have seen fit to rap so gently at my door," he continued, his eyebrows raised at the new scuff mark. "Certainly there must be a reason?"

"Not really," Alissa said. "I was curious."

"Curious!" He shoved the gold bowl out of sight under the table with a backward kick. Going to his worktable, he dumped the green-stained bowl into the froth. Immediately the stench faded, overpowered by a sudden rush of mint. "Well, do come in, at least for a moment."

Recalling the ward on his doorsill, Alissa hesitated. She wouldn't be able to cross it again until he allowed it. Then she shrugged. Tempting fate reminded her she was still alive. Besides, the tray was getting heavy.

As if reading her thoughts, Bailic graciously took it, half pulling her into the room. She imagined she felt the tingle of the ward as she stumbled in. Impossible, Alissa thought. She had felt nothing for weeks. Her tracings were ash. Frowning, she reminded herself that just because she couldn't discern a ward, it didn't follow, it wouldn't burn her, and pain was still pain, no matter how meaningless her life seemed. Alissa's eyes went to the balcony, still as shattered as she recalled it from her papa's memory, and she sighed.

"Quite a view, isn't it?" Clearly misreading her small sound, Bailic slipped to the edge of the drop-off and stared into the night. "I'm told when the sun is high and bright, you can see Ese' Nawoer." He grimaced. "My sight seems to worsen every year. I can't even see the ground anymore in this pitch."

He turned suddenly, and Alissa froze. "I have noticed your skill with needle and thread," he said lightly. "You have a fine eye for cloth. Did you know I once studied under a master weaver? Caldera cloth, my family made, in the finest shades of reds. It was too elegant to be traded into the foothills, but there's a bolt or two in dry goods. I could have carried the family name had I not been driven out." He looked back into the dark and his face went still. "I couldn't make it now. I've been too long from the loom. You need a steady hand and a keen eye to keep the threads even and the pattern accurate."

Alissa's eyes flicked from him to the open door, wondering if she should try to leave.

"Tell me," he said softly, "what does the night look like?"

With a last, longing glance at the door, Alissa took a step closer and gazed over the balcony and into the evening. The moon's light spilled over the fields and woods. The black branches of the forest stood sharp, seeming to be lit from behind as the light reflected off the snow behind them. Lower down the mountain, the moonlight spread in a glorious puddle across the top of the fog. It appeared as if they were an island amid a sea of clouds. It was breathtaking.

"Please . . ." Bailic said softly.

Alissa half turned, staring at him. She could tell his wish was genuine, and a stab of what might have been pity went through her. It must be difficult to have lost one's sight, she thought. Bathed in the shadow-light of an early dusk, he seemed like another person. Against her better judgment, she edged closer. "The moon," she said, "is a scant week from full and has yet to reach its highest point."

"No," he whispered urgently. "You misunderstand. What does it *feel* like?"

Shifting to her other foot, Alissa pushed her growing unease away. What had she gotten herself into? "The night is cool and damp with the weight of the snow carried within it," she tried again. "The wind makes a gentle sport with the empty, black branches of the forest, and they shift in complaint of the disturbance." She felt herself smile as her pulse slowed and her breath grew lethargic. "Whispering remnants of the day's fleeting warmth have swirled the fog into a pool of milky-white, eddying about the lower reaches of the Hold. Even now it rises, swallowing the trees one by one until soon, only the Hold will remain above the mist, appearing to float upon a sea of air, glowing from within from the moonlight. Above, only the strongest of stars bear the shining face of the moon, and even these seem to bow to the glory of her presence, allowing her alone to light the night." Slumped against the wall, Alissa sighed contentedly.

"Yes," Bailic murmured, "that's how I would see it as well."

She froze at his voice. Bone and Ash! She had forgotten where she was.

Bailic shifted and looked through her, not seeing her at all. "Wait," he said, slowly moving to his desk and scratching a note. "Take this to your piper. Mind the ink. It's still wet."

Burn it to ash, she thought. He wasn't her piper. But she gingerly took the paper as Bailic extended it. She glanced down and read: "Eggs and toast tomorrow." What did that mean? she wondered, disguising her confusion by waving the paper gently in the air to dry the ink. "I'll take it to him now," she said, taking a step back to distance herself, but Bailic reached out a pale hand, catching her sleeve, stopping her. Staring hard at him, she tugged free, wondering what he wanted now. Perhaps he wished her opinion of the lovely stench he had made on the worktable.

"Once," he said, low and soft, "I offered you the chance to choose what side you wished to be counted upon." He hesitated. Taking a slow breath he continued, his voice terrible in its stark honesty. "That choice is still yours to make."

Alissa drew back as if slapped.

"I see," he continued, not noticing, or perhaps ignoring, her look of disgust and horror, "you have lost your fear of me somewhere. Just as well. It's of no use to me." He stepped to the balcony and turned his back to her. "I wouldn't ask much," he said to the night. "Perhaps your thoughts on an evening rain, or the soft heat of a summer afternoon, hazy and smelling of bees." He sighed without making a sound, his eyes fixed to eternity. "You may go, but think about it, and please knock if you become—curious—again."

She stifled a shudder. Taking his empty afternoon tray, Alissa stepped over the warded sill. Her thoughts and stomach were churning as she made her way down to the kitchen, vowing to not let Bailic's invitation spoil her one night of being pampered. Ashes. What had she done now? Two months ago she had been a half-breed to be kept out from society's eyes. But then, he had been alone for the better part of two decades. Perhaps the companionship of a half-breed girl who could cook was better than none. She tucked the note in a pocket, anxious to show it to Strell and ask his opinion. Bailic's proposition, she would keep to herself.

Much to her surprise she found the dining hall empty and the fire still banked. The kitchen, too, was conspicuously devoid of place settings. In fact, there was no Strell either. Shrugging, Alissa went to inspect the covered pot hanging just shy of the flames.

"No you don't!" The garden door slammed shut behind Strell with a bang.

She spun about, the lid clattering harshly as she dropped it. "Where've you been?" she accused, feeling herself blush.

"Nowhere." Not taking off his coat, he sat down to ease his ankle, sighing as his backside hit the stool. One foot was booted, the other swathed in tight layers of leather.

"So," Alissa said, her eyes wide in anticipation, "where's dinner?"

"Dinner? What dinner?"

"What's that then?" she demanded archly, pointing to the pot.

"That? Oh, that's my socks." Strell looked at the rafters in apparent idleness.

"Mmm," she said, confident that with his hurt ankle, dinner wouldn't be the extravagant production he so enjoyed. She didn't mind. Anything would be welcome, even if it was only soup. "I see," Alissa said saucily. "You won't mind if I peek then?" and she reached for the lid.

"Go ahead." Strell covered a yawn and brushed at his coat.

Tiring of the game, she did just that. It didn't look or smell like soup, but it wasn't until she stuck a spoon into it that she figured it out. "Oh, yuck!" she cried, letting the sodden mass of yarn fall back into his wash water.

"Told you." Grinning, he levered himself up. "Here, put

these on and close your eyes." He extended her coat and boots, and Alissa arched her eyebrows in question.

"Outside?" she asked.

"Now," he commanded playfully, "or you'll go hungry."

With a small gasp of dismay, Alissa shrugged into her coat and boots, and with a last frown at his dancing smile, she closed her eyes as he demanded. Strell took her hands and guided her slowly to the garden door. "Keep 'em shut," he warned as he dropped her hands. Alissa heard the door open and felt the cool night air on her face. "Gently now, there's a step." Alissa awkwardly followed Strell down the garden path. They went slowly, as it was difficult for him to limp backward, especially when he was holding on to her hands the way he was. Baffled by the numerous twists and turns, Alissa had no idea where they were going.

"All right," he finally whispered. "You can look now." She felt her hands drop, and she eagerly opened her eyes.

"Oh, Strell!" Alissa breathed, entranced. A small fire hissed in the center of a large, lowered pit. It was surrounded by a squat, circular stone bench built into the surrounding walls of earth. Strell had covered several of the stone seats with thick blankets to make the cold bearable. Over the fire was a metal-weave table upon which sat covered dishes. The most wonderful smells were coming from them. Soup? Alissa thought in pleasure. This was a banquet!

"Milady?" Strell inclined his head in a gentle invitation.

Happy to play the part, Alissa extended her hand, and Strell "helped" her to her seat.

And so they took their dinner under the moon and open sky. Strell was overly attentive, causing her to be shy and modest. Their gentle voices rose and fell in pleasant conversation to be lost among the scent of iced bracken and wet stone. For a space there was only the two of them: no book, no Hold, no brooding man in the dark hatching plots. It was as if they were still traveling, oblivious to what might be ahead.

How innocent she had been, Alissa mused, sipping at the first hot mug of after-dinner tea. Imagine. Thinking she could walk in, find Useless, take her book, and walk out. She snorted at her past optimism, drawing Strell's attention.

"Was there enough?" He glanced worriedly at the abandoned plates and bowls.

"Goodness, yes. I couldn't eat another thing." Satisfied, Alissa pulled her blanket close against the damp chill. Thaw or not, the snow was still deep, and it was still cold. She shivered, eyeing the fire. "Remind me to take up some wood tonight," she said.

Strell took a slow breath. "Alissa, why don't you find another room? The one down from mine has a window ward on it. There's no reason you have to be cold."

Alissa eyed him. It had quickly become an old argument. "The shutters work fine. I'm not moving." Alissa took a quick sip of tea. He had been badgering her for weeks, trying to persuade her to move to another room. Apparently Bailic never saw the chaos of her room and had assumed only Strell's window was broken. Neither of them would correct his interpretation of what actually happened that night. Alissa had made the shutters herself using the tools and materials she found in the annexes. They were slipshod and ramshackle—she would be the first to admit her carpentry skills were right up there with her attempt at shoemaking—but they kept out most of the winter. Strell had offered to craft them, but his ankle was the size of a squash at the time, and Alissa wouldn't let him stand on it for more than a moment at best.

Seeming to finally give up, Strell slumped beside her with his own cup, and they sat together, enjoying the unseasonably warm night until he smacked his forehead with the palm of his hand. "I forgot my pipe," he groaned. "There was to be music tonight as well." He sighed and began to rise to make the arduous journey upstairs to fetch his last remaining woodwind.

"Wait." Alissa put a hand upon his arm. "Mine is still in my coat pocket. It's been there since we got here." It had been jabbing her in the ribs all through dinner, and she would be glad to be rid of it. Wanting to make him sweat, she demurely looked up until he shifted and dropped his hand. Beckoning him closer, she whispered, "It's going to cost you."

His eyes went wide in mock alarm. "I've no coin to spend."

"You may use your music as currency," she murmured, dropping her gaze back to the fire. He'd know the song she wanted to hear.

Sure enough, he pulled back. "Not that one. It puts you to sleep."

"Oh, all right," she said, knowing it probably would. "But you owe me." Setting her cup aside, Alissa reached awkwardly into her pocket for her pipe, hearing the crackle of Bailic's note. She removed and handed him first her pipe and then, from her skirt pocket, Bailic's message.

"What's this?" he asked, genuinely puzzled. "I can't read this."

"It's from Bailic. It says 'Eggs and toast tomorrow.'"

Strell tilted the paper to the fire, grunted, folded it back up. "It was on the table outside his door, right?"

"No." Slightly irritated at his possessive tone, Alissa stared up into the night. "Perhaps it's what he wants for breakfast," she said. Then her eyes grew round. "I think he's testing to see how much you know. My papa taught me to read, and he was a Keeper."

Strell froze in mid-reach for the teapot. Slowly he sat back. "I think you're right." Appearing to be deep in thought, he tapped his fingers in an awkward rhythm. Suddenly he snapped them and straightened. "I'd wager he saw the writing on your father's map. Bailic asked me what one of the words was. That's why he thinks I can read those frost-tracks."

Alissa smiled at his obvious pleasure for having solved the mystery. "Which word was it?" she asked.

He grinned. "Treacherous Ravine."

Alissa bit her lip with a sudden consternation. "This could be a problem, Strell."

Leaning confidently back against the bench, he swirled his tea, smiling contentedly. "Hmm? How so?"

"Think about it," she cajoled. "What if he asks you to read something else? Something not on the map?"

Still absorbed in finding the bottom of his cup, he

grunted. "I hadn't thought of that." He gave her a sick look. "I guess you'll have to teach me?"

"I guess so," she said unenthusiastically, glad he had been the one to suggest it, not her. "It won't be easy."

"Oh, sand and wind," he scoffed. "How bad can it be? I already know how to read, just not that scratch. You learned it. I can learn it." He drained the last bit of tea from his mug. Smacking his lips, he confidently threw a stick on the fire as if to say: "So there."

"Yes, but I started when I was four." Exasperated with his self-assured air, Alissa reached across him and threw a stick on the fire as well.

"Even so," he said, adding a third, grinning all the while.

"All right then," she challenged him, "how do you write 'good fishing'?"

Still smiling, he smoothed a bit of packed snow. Using a twig, he sketched the proper figure, looking up for her approval.

"Very nice," she grudgingly admitted, "but that was on the map. Now, this"—quickly she wrote an identical form—"is good fishing as you have correctly shown. This"—she made a drastic modification to her character—"is night fishing, and this"—she drew a completely different symbol—"means anyone caught fishing here will be strung up by their own net and left for the crows."

"It doesn't say that!" he exclaimed.

"Well, no," she confessed. "Actually, it says good night."

"But it doesn't look anything like good fishing or night fishing," he complained, staring at the three sketches.

"Yes, I know." Silently Alissa waited as the magnitude of what he proposed sank in. Every word had to be memorized. Each had its own symbol. The pattern they followed couldn't be seen until one knew nearly all of them.

Strell's breath slipped loudly from him as he rubbed out the words and threw the twig on the flames. It slowly caught and began to burn. "You never did say how you got that note."

"Uh," she said unintelligently, caught off guard. Strell wasn't going to like her answer. "Bailic asked me in," she mumbled into her cup.

"And you went?" he cried. "What about that ward on his door?"

Oh, she thought. She had forgotten she told him about that, and no, it hadn't been a good idea, but instead of admitting it, she frowned and said shortly, "I survived."

Absolutely stunned, Strell could do nothing but sputter. "You survived?" he finally managed. "You survived! Alissa, do you have any idea how dangerous that was?"

Her face reddened, and she refused to look at him. "I'm fine, Strell. He's not interested in me. I was in no danger. Bailic doesn't frighten me anymore."

"That's what worries me!" Strell scooted back from her. "He ought to scare you silly!" Frustrated, he shook his hands in the air, searching for words. "Wolves, Alissa. What's happened to you? You aren't the same anymore. You don't care about anything!"

"That's because I'm *not* the same anymore!" she suddenly cried, her sorrow causing words to spill from her. "My tracings are gone! There's nothing left! I'm worthless! I threw everything away." Her breath caught as she finally said the words aloud. It was true. She was worthless, all because of her own stupidity.

She turned away from him. The night was suddenly silent. Alissa bit her lip in her effort not to cry, but the warmth of tears burned her eyes. She had thrown it all away. Everything.

Beside her, Strell shifted uncomfortably. "Alissa?" he said softly. "You aren't worthless. Maybe it was for the best."

"The best!" she cried, struggling to keep the words from turning into a sob. She looked up at him, her sorrow blunted in the expression of hope in Strell's eyes.

"Now," he said as he dropped his eyes from hers, "you can go to the coast with me. You don't have to be a Keeper. You can be anything you want."

The night seemed to hesitate as they sat a bare moment away from each other, an unnamed emotion dancing precariously within reach. Wild and fierce and dangerous—and right. His eyes rose, and Alissa caught her breath. They were dark and fervent, carrying a whisper of something she had never seen before, yet it seemed as if it was there for a long time, hidden, afraid to be recognized.

And then the fire shifted with a frightening pop of sap and they turned away, finding great interest in their empty cups.

Their discussion was dropped by silent agreement. Alissa busied herself arranging the blankets. Strell was silent, pensive even, as he fussed redundantly with the fire, avoiding her eyes. Taking her pipe, he began making soft noises too obscure to be called a tune. Slowly the silence grew comfortable. Alissa settled back, not wanting to leave but unable to keep her thoughts from what might have happened if the fire hadn't shifted. Her heart gave a thump. That look he had could have led to—to anything.

More than a little relieved, Alissa tucked her feet up under her and watched the few stars make their courtly way among the heavens. Slowly the fog seeped out of the earth, rising slowly up the walls of the garden. Strell slipped into a lullaby—not her song, but close enough—and despite her efforts, she fell asleep. At least she thought she fell asleep, because the next time she looked, the stars had shifted and the fire was nearly out. Its dying embers glowed, barely lighting their dinner camp. Talon had found them and was glaring at Alissa from a nearby shrub.

Alissa's eyes opened wide as she realized her head was on Strell's shoulder. She was quite comfortable, though, and didn't stir, sleepily wondering how he had become her pillow. She could hear his heart beat and the gentle give and take of his breath. The scent of hot sand and bright sun filled her senses, warm and secure. Shamming sleep, she watched the mist rise higher, deepening the night. She let a sigh escape her before remembering she was supposed to be sleeping. Miffed at herself, she shifted and stirred, trying to give the impression she had just woken. Smiling softly, Alissa looked up into Strell's contented eyes.

He grinned. "Ready to call it a night?"

She nodded, too embarrassed at having her deception realized to do more. Reluctantly they rose. Leaving everything but the blankets for the morning, they slowly wound their way through the silent, sleeping garden. The fog was thick, and their steps were muffled by its enfolding gray softness.

It had been the most pleasant of evenings.

37

Strell pulled the charm close, squinting at the final knot as he cut the last of the silken strands free. "There," he said, "that should do it." With a pleased smile, he examined the small talisman resting on his knee. The brilliant gold showed strong against the dark green of his new clothes. Alissa had given him the handsome outfit just this morning, complete with a pair of soft-soled shoes. An early solstice gift, she had said as she shyly handed him the bulky package.

It couldn't have been a more thoughtful present, he mused as he fingered the collar of the shirt, so different from any style he'd seen on his wanderings. His reflection had shocked him the first time he saw it. Through some miracle of thread and cut, the short vest and long, wide-sleeved shirt made his awkward height look elegant, pleasing him to no end. There were years left in his old clothes, but they were looking out of place beside Alissa's new and numerous outfits. What he wore hadn't bothered him before—but it did now. Smiling faintly, he looked up.

Strell was perched in the broad sill of the largest window on the fourth floor above the great hall, well back from the window's ward. There was a wonderful view of the southern expanse of the mountain as well as most of the entryway. If there were a cat in the Hold, this was where it would be, able to see everything, yet not be readily seen. A muffled yap drew his attention to the snowy field. A fox, as gray as one from his plains, was hunting mice. Poised, its ears twitched, then it jumped, turning to trot smugly away, its catch in its teeth. Strell frowned, wondering if it was an omen.

He looked toward the kitchen, unseen past the dining hall arch. Alissa was there amid the fires and pots, cooking up something or other for tonight. She had banished him this morning, insisting he would only get in the way. Soon he would go down and indeed get in her way, as much in her way as he possibly could. It was, of course, the day before the winter solstice: the shortest day of the year, the beginning of winter—and the last day to fulfill his agreement with Bailic.

Strell set the charm on the sill, his stomach twisting. The Wolves should take him. He was a coward, sitting in the sun like an old man making charms instead of fighting for her life. But plainsmen don't fight, they bargain, and that had gotten him nowhere. His pleading today to exchange his life for Alissa's had only gained him a lecture on moral ethics.

Taking a ragged breath, Strell held it, denying his body's demand for action—hating himself. His life for hers, he thought bitterly. Since her tracings were burnt, it was as if part of her was already tending the flowers in Mistress Death's garden, but he would give anything to have what was left. He had been so relieved that she was alive, he never considered she would suffer any lasting effects. Now, rather than a wild summer storm, she was a gentle spring mist. She was calm instead of angry, mild instead of irritated, indifferent instead of excitable. But her placid temperament stemmed from her new fatalistic pessimism, and he hated it, even as he treasured what remained of her.

This past week, though, had seen improvement in her strength. He had stood in the stairwell and silently cheered the first time she delivered Bailic's tray without a rest. Alissa hadn't known he was there, hiding a mere flight away. But there was still the odd time she would nod off in the afternoon, and it was almost a guarantee she'd fall asleep in front of her fire long before he wanted to leave her. On those occasions, he lovingly tended her fire and slipped out with a whispered good-night. These were the evenings he enjoyed the most. Once he had purposely lulled her to sleep, not wanting to admit he hadn't studied the words she set him to learn.

Strell nervously adjusted the last of the wraps about his foot. He hadn't yet told her of his bargain with Bailic, and the thought of that kept him up at night. Every day he had put it off made it that much harder. He had slipped into his old pattern of avoidance almost without knowing. To tell her the first night would have been cruel. She was so tired the second day. The third day Talon dropped a dead mouse right in her breakfast. The day after, Alissa spent all afternoon cutting out a new dress only to discover it would be too small. Something, Strell thought, always seemed to interfere. And it was always easier to put it off.

He had spent an entire month telling himself he would be able to free Useless, convinced he wouldn't have to tell Alissa he bought her five weeks of life for the promise of a book he didn't have. It was only now when Alissa's time was measured in hours, not days, would he admit he couldn't get past the closet door. Bailic was going to have to help him. Unknowingly, of course.

The hidden door under the stairs wouldn't open for Alissa—the Navigator knew he had cajoled her into trying enough times—but Bailic's sudden appearance the night Alissa burned herself told Strell that Bailic could. So Strell sat in the sill whenever he was able: watching the door, hoping to catch Bailic using it, pinning his hopes on the whims of a madman.

He hadn't told Alissa of his plan, afraid of what she might do if it turned out to be nothing. Her state of mind was so tenuous of late, he refused to chance getting her hopes up only to smash them. He was betting Bailic would visit his prisoner today, if only to gloat over his upcoming victory in acquiring Alissa's book. He would have to, Strell thought, his stomach churning.

"I can't tell her," he whispered. Their celebration tomorrow of the new year would end when Bailic made his appearance, then his claim. Alissa's look of betrayal would turn to an even more wrenching expression of forgiveness. That would be the last look she ever gave him, the one he would carry echoing in his thoughts for all time.

"I must tell her," he said, and he carefully slid from the sill so as not to jar his foot. With the help of Alissa's staff he hopped expertly downstairs and into the dining hall. He paused at the archway to gather his courage. There was the clatter of Alissa at work, the splashing of water, and—something else. From the great hall came the distinct sound of stone grating against stone.

"Hounds!" Strell breathed in relief as he ran back to the echoing hall. Ignoring the pain, he skidded around the foot of the stairs to see Bailic's robe slip between a crack in the once-solid wall under the stairs. It was almost as if the distasteful man had been waiting for him to leave.

Panicking, Strell lurched the last few steps and jammed his knife into the vanishing crack. It was a move born from countless games of search-and-find with his brothers, who would trap him in a kiln until supper if he wasn't careful. His heart pounded as he waited, frozen. First one moment passed, then another. There was no outcry, no "Good afternoon, Piper." Finally believing he had done it, Strell allowed himself a small sigh. Not a sound came from the crack, and so he slowly pried open the door to find the smell of wet stone and half-burned oil. As his eyes adjusted, he discerned a hole in the floor, a stack of torches, and what looked suspiciously like Alissa's backpack. Strell's breath hissed in over his teeth. It must have belonged to Alissa's father, the pack she had told him about.

Strell retreated. Keeping his body between the door and the frame, he ripped a small length of cloth from his foot wrappings. Rolling it neatly into a tube, he wedged it into a corner of the doorframe and pushed the door back into place, wincing at the slight noise it made. Now all he had to do was wait until Bailic returned. He would not try the evil-looking hole in the floor with the possibility of meeting Bailic coming up. If he was lucky, the pale man wouldn't notice his modification to the door.

Concealing himself in one of the annex tunnels, he crouched down. With a surprised grunt, he found himself humming the ballad of "Beggar Thumbkin" and stilled himself. Slowly the angle of the sunbeams shifted, and he yawned, nearly falling asleep despite the draft on his neck.

A muffled crash from the kitchen followed by a feminine shriek of dismay jolted him awake. Strell lurched to his feet, then grinned as Talon winged frantically out of the dining hall.

"And stay out!" he heard Alissa shout faintly. The unlucky falcon landed upon the railing of the fourth-floor walkway and began to preen wildly. Flour sifted to make a dusty sunbeam. Smirking, Strell painstakingly began to lower himself. Halfway to the floor, the noise of stone on stone gently filled the air, and he froze, weight on his bad foot. Oblivious to the new surge of discomfort in his ankle, he watched Bailic poke his head out from the closet and look directly at the annexes. "Wolves," Strell swore, shrinking back. But the man spun as if in a hurry and pushed the door shut.

"Please, please, please don't notice," Strell whispered, fingering his knife in his boot sheath. He had never killed a man. And what could he do against a Keeper who had emptied an entire fortress? It would be by guile, or not at all.

Bailic paused and looked at the door.

Strell held his breath.

The suspicious man glanced at the tunnels, then backed up to consider the door, his hands on his hips. He reached up to run his fingers over the slight crack.

"Killy, killy, killy," Talon called from the fourth-floor landing, making both men jump. She ruffled herself, and a feather slowly drifted down. Strell watched it, barely breathing, as it made its circuitous journey to the floor.

In a rustle of fabric, Bailic turned. For a moment, man and bird silently regarded each other. Then Talon took flight to vanish up the stairway. "Indeed," Bailic muttered, "that annoying piper will soon find whatever he's looking for in the old kitchens and will be back at his post." With a final, disparaging glance at the tunnels, he spun about and followed Talon upstairs.

Strell slumped in relief as he watched him rise out of his sight, then listened as Bailic's steps whispered into nothing. He felt like the proverbial mouse as he peeked from his tunnel and crossed the open space. Blood thrumming in calm anticipation, he pried the door open and slipped through.

There was a flurry of wings, and Talon landed upon his shoulder. "Curious?" he whispered. The bird had never accompanied him before, and it gave him courage.

Strell reached for a torch, useless without a flame to kindle it. Grimacing, he looked out at the bright hall. He could light it in the kitchen, but Alissa would want to know what he was doing. His eyes flicked uneasily to the pack. Maybe there was a fire kit in it.

With more than a few misgivings, Strell pulled the pack into the thin shaft of light falling through the open door. There was a faint, finger-cramping tingle of a ward that quickly faded. Through painful experience, Strell had found the tingle was a warning that would either fade to nothing or shock him with a bolt of fiery thought. Having recognized and dismissed him, the ward on the satchel had, in effect, given him permission to open it. Rummaging carefully, he found a set of striker rocks. This, he decided, he could borrow without affronting the dead.

His fingers twitching from anticipation, he quickly lit the torch, jammed the kit back into the pack, and returned the sack to its spot. The thick layer of dust he disturbed gave clear indication that someone had been about, but if all went well, it wouldn't matter. A final look at the great hall and he pulled the door shut. The torch flickered in the new darkness, sending eerie shadows to dance upon the walls of the close room. Excitement, fear, and hope swirled together, making Strell ill. He was going to find Useless. He was going to save his Alissa.

The light firmly in one hand and Alissa's staff in the other, he peered down the hole in the floor. The steps glistened wetly, and a small sound of disgust slipped from him. He hated the damp, and the stairs looked slippery. A capstone lay askew nearby, and he frowned, thinking how easy it would be to become trapped. What, he wondered, was he doing here, so far from his dry, arid home? And with that, he stepped into the black.

The way was long and monotonous. The hesitant click-step-step, click-step-step of his passage was the only sound beside his breath, harsh in the tight confines. His elbows kept hitting the walls, each time more painfully than the last,

and his soles were soon wet through the untreated leather of
the makeshift shoes Alissa had made for him. Strell found
the last step with a jar that rattled his teeth, and he squinted
suspiciously at the narrow crack in the wall before him. The
light from his torch burned fitfully in the stronger breeze
coming from it.

"Down there?" he whispered to Talon. This wasn't good.
Descending a staircase was one thing, but this looked like a
sure path to nowhere. From his shoulder came soft croons.

"If Bailic can make it, I can," he muttered. Walking almost sideways in places, he awkwardly followed the gently
sloping tunnel until he thought he heard the sound of water
dripping. With a suddenness that surprised him, the passage
opened up into a small space.

The stonesmiths had been more careful here, and the floor
and low ceiling were even. The plinking of water could be
heard clearly now, the noise echoing about to make its origin
uncertain. All this Strell took in at a glance. What drew and
held his attention was the widely spaced bars running from
floor to ceiling. "I think we found him, old girl," he whispered to Talon, but immediately began to wonder if he had.

"This can't keep any man secure," he said softly, eyeing
the smooth rods. Useless had mentioned a gate, but this
couldn't be it. It would be simple to slip between the rods.
Baffled, he yanked out an expired torch from a hole in the
wall and replaced it with his own. The small sound of the
wood grinding into the stone seemed unnaturally loud, and
he frowned.

"Useless?" he whispered. He looked past the bars into the
distance to where the glow of the noonday sun beckoned.
The light was all but blocked by the huge pillars rising like
gigantic tree trunks.

Talon sprang to life in a startling whirlwind of motion to
vanish beyond the gate. With a caution learned searching in
the tower, Strell reached to touch a bar with a careful finger.
The cramping hum of a ward took his fingers with a surprising vengeance and he jerked away. The tingle rose up almost
to his elbow before it faded to nothing. Strell slumped in relief. Many of the wards in the Hold had been like that, the
encounter invariably ending with him cursing and shaking

his hand, but this ward clearly dismissed him. Confident the bars would let him pass, he followed the bird into the larger room.

Strell's eyes widened. Judging by the echoes, the cavern was enormous. The sense of an ancient wood at twilight was heightened now that he was actually among the thick pillars. He leaned on Alissa's staff, craning his neck to find the ceiling. He couldn't. "Useless?" he called louder, not having much hope the man was here. It didn't look like a cell. It looked like a temple.

His feet scuffed, sending echoes to whisper into the darkness like ill promises made to be broken. Compared to the murky dusk he now walked in, the small anteroom where he had left his torch was warm and bright. The walls of the cavern spread in a smooth unbroken line to either side of the barred gate, their probable end lost in the black. "Useless!" he shouted. "If you're here, show yourself." Strell gave a resigned puff as his words came echoing back. Useless wasn't here. "Otherwise, I'm leaving!" he added for good measure.

There was a guttural rumble, and a great gust of wind from behind nearly knocked him down. Strell spun wildly, almost losing Alissa's staff. He struggled to maintain his balance as, with a gasp, his eyes found the two focused malevolently upon him. They were as large as dinner plates, a good two man-length's above the ground. Strell thought he saw the curve of a long neck and a glint of teeth. His chest tightened, and he took an involuntary step back.

With a rush of feathers, Talon dropped between Strell and the shifting shadow. Already near panic, Strell swung wildly, almost hitting her. Talon screamed, hovering until Strell held up an arm in defense, only to have Talon land politely upon it. A soft growl came from the shadows.

Reminded of the glowing eyes, Strell spun back. His ankle gave way with a stab of pain. This time he did lose his balance. He fell, hitting the floor in a clatter of wood and a sharp cry. Despite the bird's screeches of annoyance and his pain, Strell managed to awkwardly scoot back. His only thought was to distance himself from whatever was lurking in the shadows.

"Strell?" came a slow voice from the black. Shocked, Strell froze.

A soft glow broke over him, gently bathing the shadows to light. The monster was gone. Illuminated by a head-sized globe of light was the figure of a tall man.

38

Sprawled upon the floor, Strell peered up in relief and embarrassment at the indistinct figure standing before him. It had to be Useless. He was dressed like Bailic, in shades of yellow and gold rather than black. His sleeves, though, were so wide, they went halfway to the floor.

Frowning slightly, the man stared back. "How the Wolves did you get down here?" he said, his voice surprisingly deep for such a thin frame.

"I jammed the door behind Bailic," Strell said breathlessly.

The man's eyebrows rose. Tucking the globe of light under an arm, he strode forward. He held out a strong-looking, strangely formed hand to help Strell rise.

Strell hesitated, then extended his own hand, snatching it back as Talon began to hiss.

"Go away, bird," the man said irately. "See to your mistress."

Talon gave a startled peep and winged toward the distant rectangle of light. The man stood still as stone and watched, his eyes never shifting from her until she vanished. A small sigh slipped from him. "Here, let me help you up," he said, and he offered his hand once more.

The two clasped firmly as the man hauled Strell to his feet. "Ah . . ." Strell cried as his ankle, having twisted again when he fell, clamored for attention. His vision grayed as he slipped back to the floor. His eyes closed, and he desperately clasped his ankle with both hands. Burn it to ash, he thought. His ankle was back to where it was last week.

"Oh," the gaunt figure was saying. "Let me help."

There was a warm pressure upon his temple. From there it flowed, as honest and pure as honey in summer, warming him from within. The heat eddied and swirled, concentrating on his ankle until it hurt no more. Then, like water slipping into the sand, the sensation vanished. Strell shuddered. The pain in his ankle had been so long a part of his existence that its absence was almost a tangible impression.

He opened his eyes. Shocking in its nearness was a wise face, lightly wrinkled and tan. Not old, but far from youth, the man exuded a curious blend of quiet peace and bound intensity. It was his eyes, though, that commanded attention. They were tired, but also clear and true. Their color was an astounding, unnatural golden-brown. "Hum-m-m," the man murmured, and he sat down with his legs crossed, silently considering him. The globe of light went on the floor between them like a cooking fire.

Bailic had never made anything like that, Strell thought, extending a finger to see if it was warm. The man cleared his throat, and Strell jerked his hand away. "You . . ." Strell's voice cracked. "You're Useless."

"Not altogether so, but yes," the figure said with a chortle.

Strell's face brightened. "Out!" he cried, beginning to rise. "I've come to get you out!"

Useless shook his head. "If there were a way, I'd be gone."

Nearly standing, he hesitated. "I made it past the bars."

"Well, I wouldn't. They're warded specifically for my kind. There's no escape for me."

With those words, Strell's grand plan of freeing himself and Alissa from Bailic's devices crashed to nothing. He dropped heavily back to the cool stone floor and looked bitterly at the dark green of his damp shoes. How he could have been so foolish to think he could free Useless when Useless couldn't free himself? His gamble to save Alissa had failed. Wolves take him. He was a dreamer staked out in the sun.

In a single, fluid motion, Useless stood and extended a hand. "Forgive me for not meeting you at the front gate. I wasn't expecting you."

"Of course," Strell said absently, his thoughts on Alissa. He only had a day. He would talk to Bailic again, arrange an extension. Anything. Bone and Ash. What was he going to do?

Taking the oddly shaped hand, Strell was pulled to a stand. He shivered at Useless's touch, recalling his panic when his imagination convinced him the man was a beast with glowing eyes. Strell's eyes darted to the black corner where he thought he had first seen the monster.

"There," Useless said, interrupting his uneasy thoughts, "it's warmer over there." He pointed to the glowing rectangle of light. "I know for a fact," he said dryly, "that it is."

As he gingerly put his foot down, Strell's mouth fell open. There was no pain. His ankle was healed! This was the stuff of stories and tales, not reality! "Thank you," he breathed, stomping hard upon the floor to assure himself it was really restored. "Ashes. You completely healed my ankle. How—"

Useless strode to the light. "Completely healed?" he said over his shoulder. "No."

"But the pain—" Strell jumped as the globe winked out of existence.

"Illusionary. The pain has been deadened. But if you keep stomping about like that, you're going to lose the benefit of the three-day accelerated healing I was able to give you, and you'll be in twice the hurt in the morning."

Feeling foolish, Strell hastened to catch up with Useless. "Can you do it again? To give my ankle six days of healing?"

"Not shy about asking for things, are you?" Useless smiled at Strell's embarrassment. "It's a good thought, but you only have so much reserves in your body. To force it to repair itself again so quickly would cause more damage than it would mend."

Not sure he really understood, Strell remained silent as he followed Useless to the patch of sun. As they passed close by one of the pillars, he paused. It was covered with Alissa's script. After a quick glance at Useless's back, he ran a finger over a familiar word. Alissa had been merciless in her tutorial, and he was beginning to wish he had never seen his map, much less traded for it. Strell's finger lightly traced the elegant lines before reluctantly turning away. Perhaps Useless *could* help him in some way, a trinket or bit of information to buy more time.

As the last column fell behind him, his feet faltered and slowed to a stop before the fabulous view. Too large to be called a mere window, the opening began where the floor ended, rising twice as high as he was tall and stretching a full twenty paces wide. Through another set of wide-set bars was the clear blue of a winter sky, unmarked by bird or cloud. The cavern, he realized in astonishment, went entirely through the mountain. He was looking west.

The horizon was utterly flat. There were hills between him and the sea, but they were all dwarfed by the one he now stared from in wonder. In great, undulating waves, the land seemed to flow from his perch to go gray in the distance. The ocean itself was lost in the haze, but he knew it was there.

There was a small scuff and Strell looked to find Useless arranging himself cross-legged upon the stone floor in a patch of sun. The man gestured for Strell to join him, and slowly Strell sank down before him.

"I'm in truth called Talo-Toecan," said Useless, and he held out his hand, palm up.

"That's it?" Strell blurted as he crossed it with his own, starting at how long the man's fingers were.

Useless's eyes narrowed. "My full title has little meaning now."

Strell stiffened. "I'm Strell," he accused. "My family name has little meaning now either—seeing that it has apparently been culled."

"Burn me to ash." Useless scowled and leaned back. "Is that why you glare at me? I spoke out of turn before. We agreed ages ago that there would be no more mass manipulations. Your ancestral line's demise must have been a true accident."

Strell looked at Useless as if he had a bad taste in his mouth, unsure if he should believe him. His family had a disturbing history of rebounding from only one or two members. And what did he mean by "We agreed no more mass manipulations"? Strell was very close to leaving Useless forgotten in his spacious cell when the tall man cleared his throat.

"Why," Useless said tiredly, "didn't you take her home like I said?"

"You don't think I tried!" Strell exclaimed. "Alissa does as she wants! She's—"

"She's alive!" Useless shouted, and Strell jumped. "Please." Useless leaned forward, his eyes bright. "What happened when the mountain shook? Bailic, who has less honor than a trencher worm, tells me nothing." Useless turned a clear eye upon Strell, and his voice lost its eagerness and grew deadly. "He hints and leaves. I no longer trouble to shift myself when he summons me to the east gate to listen to him gloat. When I'm through with him, there will be nothing left to mark his perfidious existence except for a horrific fable to frighten small children into exemplary behavior."

Strell gulped. The hatred pouring from Useless felt strong enough to bend a monarch's knee. Even though it wasn't directed at him now, it made him shudder.

"But you were going to tell me, were you not?" Useless said with a sudden calm.

"Um, yes." Strell shifted, unsettled by the swift mood changes. "Simply put, Alissa grew tired of your constraints."

"She what!" Useless exploded. The deep sound rumbled and echoed, making Strell wince. "Tired of my constraints? They were for her benefit, to prevent a catastrophe, not precipitate one!" Taking a deliberate breath, he raised his eyes to the ceiling for a moment. "Please, continue," he murmured.

Strell licked his lips and tried again. "She caused a terrible explosion."

"That I surmised." A careless hand was tossed into the air, wafting the warm scent of wood ash to Strell. "Is she conscious?"

"Conscious?"

"You say she lives. I wish to assess the damage. Is she truly alive, or trapped in a death state?"

Not liking Useless's cavalier manner, Strell's eyes narrowed. "She lives."

"Ha! Don't sit in judgment of me!" the man guffawed. "I warned her. They all ignore me—once. She will learn not to cross me except under dire need or die from her own ignorance. At the very least it might teach her—restraint."

Strell leaned back and eyed Useless in disgust. "Who," he said, "do you think you are?"

The man drew himself up, letting the question hang dangerously in the air. He leaned forward, and the force of his words hammered at Strell. "I," he said, his voice as brittle and frigid as ice, "am Talo-Toecan, a Master of this Hold and architect of the same."

"So what!" Strell shot back. Flushed, he met the man's wrathful eyes, refusing to back down. *He* didn't have to take this. His clothes might be ragtag, and he might be sleeping in a borrowed bed, but he carried a chartered name, able to trace his lineage back untold generations to the handful of families who first settled the plains. He just didn't rub anyone's nose in it.

For a terrible, long moment Useless stared at him with a stiff outrage. Finally he grimaced and sighed, slumping as his brow smoothed out. "Quite right, Strell," he rumbled. "I forgot your unique position. It has been long since any have been in my Hold who weren't students—or those who once were. Please continue." Appearing to grow drowsy in the sun, he closed his eyes.

The use of his given name was a surprise. Always Strell had been bard, or minstrel, or even mender of misplayed melodies, whatever that was, but seldom his name. Perhaps, Strell thought, he had been accepted as what he was and not an underling to be taught and tutored. Suddenly conscious of how hazardous his words might have been, Strell dropped his eyes. Useless's mood could have easily turned the other way. He was as sensitive as a plainsman with six ugly daughters.

"Alissa grows strong again."

"Really?" Useless's eyes opened. "Not simply alive, but prospering." As if unable to prevent it, he closed his eyes again.

"I wouldn't say that," Strell muttered, walking the thin line of accusation. "Your ward burned her utterly. She refuses to look at her tracings, and from what she described, I don't blame her."

"Does the girl have no sense of circumspection," Useless cried, his eyes open wide, "blathering about things she barely comprehends!"

"The wards on the windows of each of our rooms blew out as well," Strell said, ignoring the continual interruptions.

"Blew out the wards?" Useless blurted. "What under the Eight Wolves did she do?" Then he caught himself and inclined his head. "If I may interrupt?"

Strell nodded stiffly.

"Did she tell you what she attempted?"

Furrowing his brow, Strell tried to remember what Alissa had told him that night. It hadn't been the time to ask questions then, and later it had seemed pointless and cruel. "She said she captured a bit of the ward and tried to change it so as to be able to get rid of it safely." Strell raised a pained expression to Useless, only to be surprised at the deep understanding in his quiet eyes. "She brought it from her thoughts to right in front of her, then let go of it. Then, and this is my idea, as she will say little after that, it exploded like a badly dried bowl in a kiln."

Useless sat back in a stunned silence. "All with no training. How did she manage that?" he directed out the enormous window. "It's a miracle she didn't take the entire Hold with her. No wonder Bailic thought it was me." He turned to Strell. "It was fortunate she was in her father's chamber." Seeing Strell's confused look, he smiled faintly. "Eighth floor, southernmost room?" He nodded at Strell's astonished blink. "Only two hearths in the Keepers' hall share a chimney. I was brought to task over my lapse soon after it was discovered. To placate everyone's sensibilities, I agreed to lodge only my students in those rooms." Shifting slightly to keep the sun full upon him, Useless closed his eyes. "Her choice of rooms was serendipitous in the extreme. It probably saved her life."

Strell cleared his throat, not seeing how a shared chimney could be credited with such importance. Useless didn't bother to open his eyes. "The energy she so flagrantly released had enough egresses to preclude the necessity to create any of its own."

"I don't understand," Strell complained.

"Even so," he said distantly. "You're sure Alissa said she tried to convert the ward's potential energy to a solid state, one capable of being dissociated without triggering a cascading reaction?"

Strell looked at Useless, his face altogether blank.

"She tried to change it?" the solemn figure said.

"That's what she said," Strell grumbled.

"Hmm." Useless steepled his fingers, looking just like Alissa when she explained a bit of foothills lore to him. "And she transposed it from her personal dimension of thought to the shared one of reality?"

"Absolutely," Strell said, staring in fascination at Useless's hands. His fingers all seemed to have an extra joint. Strell had no clue as to what Useless was going on about, but he was tired of looking like an uncouth farmhand.

Useless sighed. "I would wager a season's worth of mirth blossoms she neglected to harmonize its density with that of her surroundings before releasing her maintenance of it. Either that, or she failed to fix it into an immutable state to begin with. Oh, well." He shrugged lightly. "No one showed her the proper methodologies, but how did she guess such a thing was possible, much less get it nearly right?"

"Indeed," Strell interjected wisely. It was an emotion he couldn't truthfully claim he was feeling at the moment.

Glancing up, Useless's eyes went to Strell's. Immediately the Master hid his hands in his sleeves. "I assume she did this while alone. What state did you find her in?"

"Unconscious and dying." Strell looked across the small space between them, his gaze level and untarnished, betraying his strong emotions. "I couldn't convince her to return. Bailic brought her back."

"Bailic!" Useless barked, beginning to rise. "If you seek to mislead me, Piper—"

"I do not!" Strell protested hotly, then quieter, with a stab of guilt, he added, "It was a costly affair."

"I don't doubt it." Useless settled himself again.

"Alissa said I brought her back, but I couldn't." Strell morosely tugged at a lace.

"She would know better than you, Strell," Useless said gently.

"Perhaps." Dropping the lace, Strell cleared his throat. It wasn't a subject he liked to dwell upon. "Bailic believes I'm the threat to his claim on her book."

"My book again?" Useless said. "What, by my sire's ashes, does she want with my book?" He frowned at a sudden thought he wouldn't share, then shook his head as if in denial. "But well done in the deception."

"I think she has begun to accept her tracings are gone and has—"

"Her loss permanent?" Surprise filled the somnolent figure's voice as Useless snapped to full alertness. "Her burn should heal—I think. Tell me, does she sleep the day away?"

Strell straightened, feeling a quickening of hope. "If I let her. She has been very tired."

"Drops off when the sun sets then?"

"Used to. Now she plagues me with words unless I lull her to sleep—unintentionally, of course." He colored slightly.

Useless eyed him suspiciously. "Aye, she's healing. She just doesn't know it. Her slumberous disposition is a survival mechanism to prevent her from instigating a conflict until her tracings heal."

Strell's breath caught and his heart leapt. His sweet Alissa would mend! Soon her indifference would return to the fiery temper he loved, that is, if he could find that cursed book.

"Strell? I say, Strell!"

"What?" Strell blinked, tearing his thoughts from Alissa.

Useless raised his eyebrows. "I asked," he said cagily, "what words?"

"Oh. Bailic thinks I can read, so now I must learn."

"You're a wellborn plainsman. I can tell by your outrageous accent. You should know already. Has the printed word become shunned during my momentary absence from the skies?"

"No," Strell assured him, not wanting to seem like a complete fool. "Not that writing, this." Casting about, he realized there was nothing he could use to demonstrate. Rolling his eyes in frustration, Strell sketched a simple figure on the floor using his finger. Hopefully Useless would make the connection.

He did.

The Master blinked, and a tremor ran through his spare frame. "So the whippet knows how to read," he whispered. "Curse you, Meson, I warned you, but you were always one to listen only to your own counsel. You have put your daughter in tenfold the danger. And here I am . . ." His eyes on the faultless blue of the sky, Useless smoothly rose and stood before the bars. He extended a finger until a low hum followed by a tiny pop was heard indicating the powerful ward had been engaged. "Utterly useless." He casually examined his fingertip.

Still sitting upon the cold stone, Strell turned to face him. "Why is it bad she can read?"

Useless continued to stare into nothing. "The *First Truth* is written in a script she can read. I entrusted it to her father, in part because I was busy dallying—er—because I was busy, and in part because it seemed to have put an imperfect claim upon him. If Bailic secures it, he will comprehend little of its wisdom, but with Alissa's help, willing or otherwise, he might disclose its purpose. It will give him an enormous amount of leverage to make mischief."

"Mischief?" Strell said.

"Yes, bard. Mischief such as the earth has not witnessed in nearly four hundred years."

An uncomfortable silence fell. It was Useless who broke it, his words giving hints as to where his thoughts lay. "He must have begun teaching her before she was five seasons."

"She was four," Strell volunteered.

"Aye, it stands to reason. Meson was always one to do things as he saw fit."

Strell scraped the floor with the toe of his shoe. "His daughter is much the same."

"Aye."

Useless stood at the west gate as unmoving as the mountain he was trapped within, his sight fixed upon some distant point. A cloud passed before the sun, and in its certain chill, he stirred. "You must go before you are missed," he whispered.

"Hounds, yes." Thoughts of Alissa came rushing back, and Strell awkwardly stood, brushing at his clothes. There was that long, cramped passage he had to negotiate alone, then the humiliating chore of pleading for more time, followed by the excruciating task of telling Alissa after Bailic refused. There had to be another way.

Useless turned. "Do nothing to change Bailic's thoughts of your true identity. Although risky for each of you, it seems the most equitable course of action. We must proceed as if nothing has changed, hoping someone skilled enough to free me still exists and hears my calls. If Bailic suspects you have found your way down here, it will force him to act with little subtlety."

Strell shifted awkwardly. If he were going to tell Useless of his bargain and ask for help, now was the time. But as he looked up, Useless began to chuckle. Seeing Strell's questioning scrutiny, Useless explained. "You, Strell, look like a Keeper: the cut of your clothes, your footwear, by my master's Hounds, even your perchance for injury. No wonder Bailic has been misled. Perhaps the situation can be yet made to work for us."

"It would be easier if you were free." Strell grimaced.

"True," Useless agreed mildly. "Bailic would last as long as the morning mist were I to catch him free and unfettered. If I do, I will individually sear each and every path from his neural net one—by—one." Useless sighed in easy anticipation. "One here, another there, and he will exist watching as I methodically strip his knowledge away until he remembers not even how to sneeze. He will subsist for a very—long—time." Useless smiled longingly. "If I can keep him from ending his own wretched life prematurely."

Unable to stop his shudder, Strell turned away. Hearing Useless's warm, rich voice waxing so elegantly in his calm and cultured accent, speaking of the most horrendous acts, left him shaken. Once more he was fervently glad Useless was on his side. "How," Strell asked, "did Bailic ever get you down here?"

Useless stiffened, turning a cold eye upon him. "Do you

really think I will tell you?" he demanded, his eyebrows raised in challenge.

"Uh, no." Reluctant to risk telling Useless of his bargain just yet, Strell looked into the darkness toward the unseen east gate. "If—um—Bailic wanted to free you, what would he do?"

Useless's weary gaze went back to the sky. "He would have to modify the wards on the east gate so I might pass through. But he hasn't the skill. When dealing with matters of this magnitude, it's always easier to implement than to dissociate."

Strell went to the west gate, standing well back from the drop-off as he cautiously looked down. "What about this one?"

"He could do the same, but it would be harder." Useless turned with a dangerous look. "He'd have to get past me first."

Strell swallowed hard. "The bars aren't driven into the stone here as they are on the east gate," he said, eyeing the eight massive hinges embedded into the floor. Each one was as long as his arm. "What holds this gate in place?"

"Oh, an outside lock or latch I suppose," Useless sighed. "I can't see from my viewpoint, and I wasn't privy to its construction. The gates were created far before my time." He turned from Strell's scrutiny of the cold metal. "It doesn't matter, Strell. My arms won't pass between the bars as yours . . . will."

Golden eyes rose to stare at Strell in disbelief.

"Quick," Useless said urgently, striding to him. "How far did the warning on the east gate cramp your fingers?"

Strell took an alarmed step back. "Nearly to my elbow."

"As far as that?" Useless said in surprise, then his eyes cleared. "I'll lift you up and through."

"Up and through!" Strell cried, backing into the shadow.

"Yes," Useless drawled, pantomiming his proposed actions. "I will lift, and you will go through the bars."

"But I'll fall! Maybe I could just climb out around the edge?" Strell hedged, wanting nothing to do with the idea.

Useless fixed him with a hard look. "There are no handholds on either side of the gate, but there's a ledge above it."

Looking for his proposed handholds, Strell reluctantly agreed. The stone had been purposely smoothed. He would have to try for Useless's ledge. "Are you sure it's there?"

"Yes. The sparrows land on it incessantly. You're not much bigger than they."

Strell pulled his eyes from the drop-off. "Let me be sure I know what you want," he said, eyeing the agitated man up and down. "You're going to lift me up—all the way up there—and hold me steady until I pull myself out?"

"If you let me."

Swallowing nervously, Strell peered down through the gate. Below was the mottled blue-white of snow and ice. At his shoulder was Useless looking down as well. "I don't know," Strell mumbled, backing away as his gut tightened. "It's dreadfully far down."

"Yes, it is," Useless asserted patiently, "and if you think it beyond your capabilities . . ." He let the challenge hang.

Anything for Alissa, Strell thought, that's what he had said. But this? This looked like suicide. *Alissa,* his thoughts whispered, and wiping the sudden sweat from his neck, he took a deep breath and nodded.

Useless brought his hands together with a clap that echoed in the unseen cavern behind him. "Yessss," he hissed, striding quickly to the left of the large opening. "Up you go then," and he made a cup of his hands.

Strell stepped back to estimate the height of the window again. It would be close. He might not even be able to reach the top. Pushing his anxiety aside, Strell put himself in Useless's oddly shaped hands and found himself lightly boosted up. Laying a hand on the wall beside the bars, he glanced down. Shuddering, he forced his eyes back to the wall. He steadied himself against it and made the shift to Useless's shoulders. As he had thought, he couldn't touch even the top of the opening, much less the ledge higher up out of sight beyond the bars.

"My hands," rumbled Useless. "Stand upon my hands."

"What!"

"I have been here forever, Strell. Stand on my hands; I won't let you fall."

His head against the rock face, Strell looked down at Useless's upheld hands. In the manner of a street performer, Useless wanted him to stand over his head. "Are you sure?" he asked, not sure how strong the man could be after years of imprisonment.

"Yes."

Gulping, Strell stepped onto one, then the other of Useless's hands. Long fingers curled over his feet, encasing them firmly. Now he was high enough, and with many whispered pleas to the heavens and unchanging stars, Strell walked his hands along the rock above the window until he was before the first gap between the bars. Useless shifted smoothly beneath him, and they moved as one. Before he could even hazard an exploratory feel for the unseen ledge, a flash of fire raced through him. Together he and Useless yelped in pain.

"My apologies," Useless's voice echoed up. "I got too close."

Strell felt a wash of foreboding. "You mean if you touch the bars, we both feel it?"

Useless grunted, not sounding a bit apologetic. "Apparently. Now, Strell," he warned, "don't look down, you might—lose your concentration."

"Don't worry," he wheezed as a gust of cold air hit him. Stretching, he reached through the bars for the ledge. The hum of the ward was almost a physical sensation, angry and fierce at Useless's nearness to it. "This is so foolish," he whispered, then louder, "It's too far." He leaned awkwardly out between the bars to reach higher, gasping as Useless shifted, seeming to nearly drop him. But then the Master's hands gripped him even more strongly, and he found himself lifted a great deal higher. Scrambling frantically for a new, unseen handhold, his questing fingers found the ledge.

"This isn't a ledge," he muttered, "it's a crack in the wall!" But it would suffice, and he levered himself out onto the bare face of the mountain, struggling until his feet found a toehold. He clung to the rock, breathing hard. The bitter wind tugged at him, trying to loosen his grip. His face pressed against the rough stone, Strell looked to his left. "I see it," he shouted, beginning to shiver. "There's a latch holding the gate to the rock. If I can shift it, I think the gate will fall. It's rusted. Wait a moment!" Carefully choosing his holds, he shifted until his feet were on either side of the monstrous slab of metal. A gust of wind rose and buffed him. Strell pressed himself to the frigid rock, willing the assault to end. When it passed, he carefully adjusted his fingers in a crack and stomped firmly upon the catch of the latch. It didn't budge, feeling as solid as the rock he clung to.

Squinting in the frigid wind, he peered down. "It's stuck!" he shouted. "Can you get me Alissa's staff? I'll try to knock it loose."

He waited, wondering if Useless had even heard him. Soon the end of the staff appeared at his feet. Twisting awkwardly, he bent sideways to retrieve it, as only the tip protruded.

"Useless?" he called as he stooped down. "We'll never make it to the east side. It's too cold. Even if I get the gate open, we're stranded here."

"I assure you, Strell, we will make it," floated up Useless's voice, tight with anticipation. "I can arrange an—ah—alternate form of conveyance."

"Alternate form of conveyance?" Strell said, and with an extravagant sigh, he stood, staff in hand. His fingers were going numb, and he couldn't feel his toes jammed into the frozen rock anymore. Regardless of what Useless planned, he knew there was no other way to escape than to climb. Perhaps Useless would make it. The man was surprisingly strong and a master of skills Strell wasn't privy to.

Jamming his fingers back into the crack, Strell struck at the latch at his feet. Heavy wood met metal in a dull thunk. Large red flakes of rust detached themselves to be whipped away in the stiff wind. The metal underneath was shiny and unblemished.

Harder, he struck. *Clang.* More rust followed the first, but no other change.

Again Strell awkwardly raised the staff and brought it down to no avail.

Trembling, he paused to gather what little strength he had left. The brutal wind was quickly robbing him of his strength. It made needles of the bits of snow and ice that it carried, and they stung where his flesh had yet to lose its feeling. His fingers and toes were long gone, and the cold had seeped into his arms and legs, making them heavy and unresponsive. Soon they wouldn't feel the frigid wind at all. Lifting his eyes to the distant summit, Strell realized he would have to shift the lever soon, or . . .

"Or what?" he sighed, pressing his face against the jagged stone. Eyes closed, he thought of Alissa up in the warm kitchen, contentedly fussing over their next meal. Her hair was down today the way he liked it, and it was probably getting in her way. Just the thought of her bustling happily about in their kitchen filled him with a pang of longing to simply be with her. All he had to do was shift the latch, climb to the other side of the mountain, and keep from freezing to death in the interim—and everything would be fine.

Strell's face twisted in pain as he lifted Alissa's staff. Muscles protesting, he slammed it down. Who, he thought as it fell, who will give you your badly needed luck charm, lying abandoned on the sill?

Clang!

"Who," he breathed roughly, "will sing you to sleep when your rest is troubled?"

Clang!

"Who will tease you until you stamp your foot?" he sobbed, his unnoticed tears of frustration freezing on his cheek.

Clang!

"And who," he whispered fiercely, raising Alissa's staff high over his head. "Who will ever love you more than I?"

With a cry of anguish, he brought the smooth shaft down with all the force he could. The staff shattered, the fragments cutting cruelly into his hand. He didn't feel it at all, the wind having turned his hands a dull blue-white. He stared at them and the bright crimson that slowly seeped out to freeze on the rock face.

As if in a dream, he watched the heavy metal gate creak, shift, and majestically fall to crash against the rock face just below. There was a resounding boom as it hit, seeming to make the mountain tremble. It was followed by a tremendous roar. Strell clung to the rock as something large streaked out past the fallen gate. Craning his neck, he spotted it, and his mouth fell open. High above him doing barrel rolls and loops was a raku, yellow and glistening in the early-afternoon sun. It was the first, no, the second he had ever seen.

"Useless?" he called raggedly, his eyes riveted to the beast. "Did you know there was a raku with you in your cell?" But of course, Strell reasoned frantically, that was what he had seen earlier. It hadn't been Useless's eyes that has sent terror through him, it had been his raku's. It made sense that anyone who laid claim to the Hold could control such an animal as this.

"Useless?" he cried with a tinge of fright. "Your raku is loose. Come catch hold of it!" For now the beast had fixed a hungry stare upon him. Strell began to wonder if the man was still alive. Perhaps upon seeing his freedom, his pet had turned upon him. Well, Strell thought, he wasn't going to stay out here with that great carnivore eyeing him.

"Useless!" he called. "Stand back, I'm going to try and swing myself in."

The raku hovered a stone's throw away, his wings beating furiously with the effort to remain stationary. The gusts rocked Strell as he painfully loosened his grip on the stone. Panicking, he forgot his hands, cramped and unresponsive, were also slick with his own blood. Reaching for a once-secure handhold, he gasped, feeling his fingers slip.

"Noooo!" he shouted, flinging his arms desperately. A fingertip snagged a crack. His jaw gritted in the terrible effort, he hung on for a heartbeat. Then another.

The raku, forgotten, snorted.

Strell jumped in surprise. His tenuous grip was lost. He fell, arms outstretched in a final bid for safety. I am done, he thought sadly. The world spread before him, seeming to come no closer as the air rushed passed him. The prospect of his imminent end made him all but delirious.

"I'm falling, falling, falling," he chanted, half mad with the absurdity of his demise. He had always pictured himself dying in bed in an overdone show of doom and gloom surrounded by his children and grandchildren, not falling off a cliff rescuing an imprisoned Master of a legendary fortress. What, he wondered, would his mother have thought?

"I'm falling, down, down, down," he continued witlessly, closing his eyes. Such a long way, he mused. Would he never reach the end? And with a suddenness that made his eyes flash open, there was a swift jerk.

"Falling?" He shook himself free from his crazed state. "I'm not falling, I'm . . ." Strell gulped. "I'm flying?" he quavered. The ground spilled before him still, but the air no longer beat against him. Incredulous, Strell looked up into the molten gold eyes of the raku. A wickedly taloned hind foot was clenched tightly about his middle just under his arms. Like a child's doll, Strell hung completely at the mercy of the enormous beast.

With a huff, the raku turned his attention from Strell and back to the business at hand. They had climbed up almost to the summit of the great peak, the raku clearly laboring from the effort to carry his weight.

"You can drop me here!" Strell quipped, shouting over the wind. He knew he should be scared witless, but failed to be. He had outwitted a murderous Keeper, had his hurts healed in moments, frozen so as to be nearly frostbit, and slipped to his death on his own blood—all before the noon meal. Being rescued by a raku was a small thing.

Giving a snort that seemed almost laughter, the raku turned. Down he streaked in a lazy spiral. There followed a snap that left Strell breathless as the beast pulled up sharply before the fallen gate. Hovering, he delicately reached out a clawed hind foot and grasped the gate still hanging by its lower hinges. Heavy gusts of wind buffeted Strell as the raku struggled to maintain his position.

Metal groaned and shrieked as the raku pulled at the heavy bars; the ward was apparently ineffective now that the gate was no longer standing. Stone rained down until, with a final creak and a tremendous lurch, it came away from the rock face. Strell bit back a cry as they plunged at the sudden dead weight of the gate. Then the raku dropped it, and together they watched it dwindle to nothing. It took a startlingly long time.

"*Onward!*" Strell cried in jest as he dangled helplessly, brandishing a raised fist. "We go to free the fair maiden!" It was just too ridiculous, like one of his tales he told to gathered children. There was a sudden trembling, and the grip he was suspended in tightened spasmodically. The beast, he realized, was laughing.

"You—you understand?" he shouted, craning his neck to look into his eyes, only now recognizing the intelligence in them.

There was an answering rumble of mirth as the raku slowly blinked a single eye.

"Useless!" he cried. "We have to get Useless!" But the raku only laughed all the harder, flying up and around to the east side of the mountain. Far below lay the Hold, tiny with the distance. The abandoned city looked a stone's-throw away from this height. With no warning, the raku fell into a steep dive, nearly stupefying Strell with their speed. The Hold grew large alarmingly fast, but it was not there they were headed. It was to the adjacent forest they fell.

"Up! Pull up!" Strell screamed, the wind of their passage ripping his frantic words away. Closer and larger the dormant woods grew until he could see individual trees, and still they dropped. "Ohhhh noooo . . ." Strell shrieked, closing his eyes in panic, but at the last moment the raku shifted his balance and again they climbed.

Behind them there was the sound of breaking wood and the briefest scent of fir. It seemed his rescuer had snapped off the top of a tree in their passage. Then there was only the clear, winter sky before them spinning madly. The beast was doing more barrel rolls. It was still climbing, too, apparently getting ready for another pass.

"Please," Strell croaked, closing his eyes in misery. "No more, just let me drop."

With a snort of what could only be merriment, the winged monster checked his upward progress and smoothly banked. He descended at a much gentler angle, laughing all the way. At least Strell thought the raku was laughing, and by the time they were again above the trees, Strell had regained part of his composure. It was, unfortunately, not to last.

Roaring in undeniable anger, the raku lashed out with a powerful foot. Grabbing the top of a pine, he beat his wings furiously until, with a groan and the sound of splintering wood, the tree was uprooted. Strell watched in awe as the pine was tossed aside to crash in the distance. Again the foot descended, and again a tree succumbed. A third was ripped from the frozen ground, and finally Strell could see what was happening. His face went cold, and for the first time, he became truly afraid.

Below him among the shattered ground and ice stood two figures. Silent, with faces upraised, they appeared oblivious to the destruction around them. One face was lost in hatred, the other in wonder. "Alissa," he whispered, his heart sinking.

Snapping his wings in a tight, backward flip, the raku landed gracefully in the clearing he had made. Slowly the grip around Strell loosened and was gone. Finding himself under his own power, Strell collapsed with a muffled groan. He blearily tried to rise but failed, having to be content with his view of the dirt-splattered snow. Sprawled before the immense beast, he was ill-prepared for what happened next.

"Stay back, Talo-Toecan!" he heard Bailic scream in fear and anger. "Or I will burn your precious book to ash—and the girl with it!"

39

"And stay out!" Alissa cried after the retreating shadow of her bird. Bone and Ash, she thought darkly. This was all she needed. Flour was everywhere: the table, the floor, even her. Alissa squinted up at the ceiling as more continued to drift down in a sedate shower of dust. It seemed Talon had gotten it into her little avian head to go poking about on the top shelf. Alissa had just shoved the stock sack of flour away, and Talon had shoved it back off. But it was rather heavy. Now that Alissa thought about it, it was far more likely the sack had tipped by itself.

Feeling a well-deserved wash of guilt, Alissa wondered if she should find Talon and apologize, but decided she hadn't the time. She was late with Bailic's tray—again. Unable to leave without picking up the worst of it, Alissa sighed and reached for the broom. By the time the kitchen was halfway decent, it was too late to even change her skirt.

She tried to beat the film of flour from her as she put Bailic's meal of bread and cheese together. It wasn't much, but if he didn't like it, he could throw it out his window. She frowned in consternation as she picked up the tray. It looked terribly empty. Snatching the pot of tea she had been warming, she impulsively set it next to his plate.

"What a mess," Alissa said under her breath as she strode out of the kitchen and through the empty dining hall. Her eyes rose to the south window as she entered the great hall. Strell had been there for weeks working on something or other, but today the sill was empty. A trace of worry crossed her before she dismissed it with a faint smile. Tomorrow was the solstice, a day of pleasant secrets and surprises. She wouldn't rob him of his fun by seeking him out. Besides, his ankle was still very sore. How much trouble could he get into?

Alissa listened closely as she made her way on the stairs. Strell often shadowed her on her way to Bailic's room. It was sweet, really, and she never let on that she knew he was there. But only the slight whisper of her ill-made shoes accompanied her today; her limping shadow was busy on his own errands.

Her steps grew wary as she neared the top of the stairs to find Bailic's door standing open in invitation. Sliding the tray noisily onto the table in the hall, Alissa peered inside, brushing at the flour on her skirt.

"Ah, there you are." Bailic's silky voice filtered into the hall. "Do forgive my forwardness, but it's in your own best interests, I assure you. Come in. We need to talk."

Alissa's eyebrows arched suspiciously, but she took the tray and stepped inside. Bailic turned from the window and motioned to a table and two chairs. Eyeing them uneasily, Alissa put the tray on his cluttered worktable instead, shoving his things carelessly out of the way. "If this is about your previous offer," she said coldly, "I'm not interested."

Bailic chuckled, and her face burned. "I ask again regardless," he said. "And this time, think carefully before you let your answer spill thoughtlessly from your lips. Your very state of mind depends upon it." He turned, and Alissa's next sharp retort died. He was far too confident. Something was seriously wrong.

"You bring me tea this afternoon," he all but purred. "How fortunate, but there are no cups!" The ends of Bailic's sleeves furled elegantly as he spun to rummage in a tall cupboard. "Ah, here they are," he sighed, his fingers lighting upon two tiny cups. "I knew I still had them. They're pretty little things, aren't they? So frail and delicate."

"What is it, Bailic?" Alissa said warily. Something had been bothering Strell this week. Unwilling to mar the otherwise pleasant mood he had been in, Alissa had ignored it. Now she thought Bailic would be the one to break the bad news. He did seem to enjoy it so.

"Your time is up, my dear," and he took the pot of tea and set it squarely on the table. He smoothly sat in one chair and gestured for her to sit in the other.

She shifted uneasily. "I already gave you my answer."

"Oh, no!" he said with a chuckle. "I don't mean your time to answer me is up." His eyes went hard. "I mean *your* time is up."

"I don't understand." Alissa found herself reaching for the support of the chair. Slowly she sat down, not trusting her suddenly cold knees to support her.

"There, isn't this nice?" Beaming, he served the tea in a demented parody of normalcy. Alissa stoically waited for him to get on with it, her hands in her lap. Visions of her papa swirled through her. She had seen this before.

Bailic sampled the tea gingerly. "Oh," he sighed with a mock sadness, "a bit cool, but as you know, it's a long way from the kitchen to my rooms." There was a whisper of a touch on her thoughts, so faint as to be only imagined, and his cup began to steam. It had to be her imagination, Alissa thought. Her tracings were less than nothing.

Easing back in his cushions, Bailic eyed her. He jerked

himself forward, and she fought to remain unmoving. "Oh, try the tea," he simpered. "I won't say another word until you do!"

"What do you want, Bailic?"

"No, no, no," he said in the manner of a spoiled child. "I simply won't hear of it. You must join me in some tea!"

He's mad, she thought. Her papa wouldn't play his game; she wouldn't either. Alissa picked up her cup and dumped the tea back into the pot. The cup went upside down on the table, the click seemingly loud in the silence. She lifted her chin, daring him to continue the travesty.

His eyes narrowed. "Fine," he grated. "I don't have to be pleasant. Your piper has dropped his contention for the book in exchange for my services in bringing you back to the living. If I don't have in my hands the book of *First Truth* by sunset tomorrow, your piper has condemned you back to the death I pulled you from a month ago."

"You didn't . . ." she said hotly, refusing to let Bailic claim responsibility for her rescue, then caught her breath. "Back?" she whispered, feeling her face go white.

Bailic smirked as he turned her cup upright. "Yes," he drawled around the gentle sound of the tea chattering into it. "You remember the gray fog, don't you? So soothing and warm. It's quite nice, as I recall, until you realize what's happening and find you can't get out." He leaned forward. "And you do understand now—don't you?"

Alissa was silent, the memory of the thick, cloying scent of the slow death she had been trapped in swirling high through her.

"I'm not an unfair man," he boasted. "I only do what has to be done. Don't fault me for that. I have no wish to put you back *there* if you can serve a purpose for me *here*."

Blinking, Alissa focused on him, the absurdity of his claim of fairness pulling her from her dark remembrances. Bailic tilted his head toward her and ceremoniously drank. "So you see, your time is up," he said, "unless you wish to enter into my service. Only that would preclude any, shall we say, previous arrangements? The choice is yours. I'll put you back in your pit"—he smiled—"or here at my side."

Choice, Alissa thought wildly. What choice? Either she

align herself with Bailic's demented plans of conquest and revenge, an unwilling slave, or she would die.

Die! she thought in a stark astonishment. She couldn't die. She wasn't done yet! This wasn't fair. Why didn't her papa put the cursed thing where she could find it! Alissa's eyes shot to the balcony where her papa had taken his last breath. The Navigator's Wolves hunt her, she wouldn't help Bailic. She was going to die. Ashes, she had been a fool. But to serve Bailic . . .

Somehow she found herself standing, her dazed eyes fixed on the balcony. Bailic rose as well. Clearly thinking she was going to fling herself from his window in some feminine heroic gesture of foolishness, he placed himself in front of her. "Sorry, m'girl." He shook his head and grinned. "Not that way. Nasty little ward prevents that sort of thing these days."

She wasn't going to jump. One Meson at the base of the tower was enough. But there had to be something she could do. Alissa refused to believe there wasn't another choice.

"You're lying," she whispered, and Bailic gave her a patronizing look.

"There's still some time!" she agonized.

"Of course there is," he crooned. "Lots of time."

Cold in panic, Alissa looked past him toward her unseen home in the foothills. In the distance glinted Ese' Nawoer, the bright sun reflecting off her roofs and walls. Closer, the woods stood—gray and cold and dead. Nearer still, the barren pastures lay smooth and unbroken under the grainy white of old snow. Her eyes were drawn to the edge of the field where, surrounded by birches and pines, a perfectly round circle of black made a sharp outline against the snow.

She stared, looking at that circle of black, recognizing its shape from somewhere, wondering what it was and why she even cared. The angle was wrong to see it from anywhere but a tower room. Ashes, she thought. The answer was so close, dancing out of reach. She almost knew . . . "Help me, Papa," she whispered, not knowing why. "I'm slipping."

Alissa licked her lips; her heart pounded. With a slight gasp, it came to her. It was a well. That black circle beneath the pines was a well! Her eyes flicked to Bailic's. His consuming need to dominate shone from him, lusting that he had command over her decision. "Strell's ankle," she stammered. "I—we need more time."

"There are no excuses," he breathed.

The Wolves hunt her! The book was in that well. She could feel it. Alissa glanced frantically from the well to Bailic. It was there. It was hers! How could she just give it to him? If she could get it without him knowing, but then . . . Alissa felt herself collapse. Oh, what did it matter? She couldn't use it anymore.

"I can get it," she said into the stillness, wondering if Bailic could hear her soul withering.

"He told you where it is!"

With an ethereal tinkling, his cup hit the floor and shattered. The other, still whole, but made useless without its mate, sat on the table.

"Tell me!" Bailic shouted, grabbing her shoulders and spinning her around.

"No!" she cried as she bumped the table and the second cup rolled off the edge. Jerking herself free, her hand lashed out to catch it, and with a light thump, it landed in her palm. This one, she vowed, he would not break.

"Where is it!" Bailic all but screamed.

There at the balcony, a strange sense of inevitability took her. Her decision was absurdly simple. It made no sense to agonize over it. The alternative was her death. "Down there."

"The woods?" he spat, his face turning crimson.

She shrugged.

"It's been under my sight all this time!"

She shrugged again.

"Out," he said, pointing with a trembling finger.

Alissa numbly slipped the cup into a pocket, and they left. Single file they went down the stairs. The familiar path looked different, as if she was seeing it clearly for the first time. Perhaps the last time. At the doors in the great hall, they paused as Alissa put on her coat. Except for Strell's dinner in the garden, she hadn't worn it in weeks, and it was cold and stiff. The laces on her boots were showing the first signs of leather rot, and she gazed down at their sublime ugliness sadly. They had been so grand when she had left home. With a groan, the heavy door opened under Bailic's insistent pushing.

A gust of cold air assailed them, and Alissa hunched into her coat. Pulling her hat down, she stepped into the snow, hearing her feet squeak against its coldness. Bailic wrapped his arms about himself and squinted into the brightly lit world. "Show me," he prompted, grimacing from the sun.

"This way."

In a flurry of sound, Talon appeared in her usual, startling fashion to land upon Alissa's hastily raised arm. The bird's head swiveled wildly as she alternatively scanned the skies and glared at Bailic, chittering madly. "Here now," Alissa crooned. "What has you all atwitter, and how did you get outside?" Alissa's shutters were latched. Strell must have let her out, she decided as she slowly gentled her bird. It didn't explain Talon's frantic state, though. Perhaps she had seen a large hawk or something. Finally the bird allowed Alissa to put her on her shoulder, and with a last frown at Bailic, they started off. He had been pacing and muttering the entire time. It hadn't helped in the least.

It was a gloriously sunny afternoon, and after the initial shock of cold, it was warm enough. Well, Alissa thought, she was warm. Bailic was soaked from his knees down, as he had no boots. She gave him credit though. He doggedly kept up, stomping along behind her, never saying a word, clutching his thin housecoat tight. Slowly Alissa pushed her way through the nearly thigh-deep snow, angling to the pines where the snow was only calf-deep. They moved faster once under the chill shade of the trees, and soon they entered the tiny clearing.

Alissa couldn't help her small smile as she neared the well. It looked like her backyard at home. The evergreens bent low, heavy with their mantle of snow. White birches rose between them, making a pleasing contrast with the almost-black green of the pines. The dark circle marked the well, and it was here she stopped. She breathed deeply, enjoying the stillness and the spicy scent of pine sap and bark.

"Here?" Bailic's shout shattered the peace. "Right under my window?"

Alissa jumped, startled. "Right under your window," she mocked, not caring anymore what happened.

Bailic stiffened. His arm drew back to slap her. Alissa's chin lifted and her eyes narrowed, daring him to try. It wouldn't land. She was too fast for him, given enough warning.

"No," he whispered, checking his motion. "I have a better idea. Perhaps a—demonstration—is in order."

Leaving her to stand by the well, he stepped under the birches and squinted up into the branches. "As I have said," he murmured, "you've lost your healthy sense of fear of me. Cheating death often sends people in one of two directions. You obviously don't fear it anymore. Pity, it made things so much easier. I can't say I really care, but this insolent behavior will stop.

"Ah," he sighed. "There's one." Much to Alissa's astonishment, Bailic whistled, low and coaxing. High up in the trees came an answering twitter. She watched in astonishment as Bailic persuaded a small black and white seed-eater down, but its merry antics that usually gave her joy, now only filled her with dread.

"You," he said, speaking to Alissa, but looking at the bird, "may not fear harm done to yourself, but what of others?" He turned, the bird perched cockily on his milk-white hand. Hearing the warning in his words, a stab of fear iced through her.

"It's a trusting little thing, isn't it?" he said softly. "Not even afraid of its natural enemy on your shoulder."

"Don't do this, Bailic," Alissa said tightly. "I understand."

"Do you?" he said, his eyebrows raised mockingly.

"Leave it alone. It's done nothing."

"But it has!" His voice was rich in surprise. "It has had the misfortune of becoming important to you." Unaware of the danger, the bird chirped merrily, his sharp, black eyes piercing hers. "You irk me. I can't frighten you with harm to yourself. I must find another way."

"Bailic," she implored taking a step closer. "Please, I promise. You're right. I should have held my tongue. I—I won't do it again." Alissa's eyes began to fill as she stood, helpless. Bailic smiled, appearing to enjoy himself. "Please . . ." she begged, tentatively grasping his sleeve. "I understand. You don't have to do this."

"I know," he said, smiling tenderly down at her, "but I want to."

There was a soft tug on her awareness followed by a bright flash and a small pop. Talon launched herself, and crying, flew away. The small bit of black and white was gone. Bailic's hand was empty. Not even a feather remained.

"You're insane," Alissa whispered, only now believing what he was capable of, and she took a shaky step back.

"If you like." He shrugged lightly. "Next time I will choose a closer target." His eyes glowed with his loosed desire. "Now, about that book . . ."

With a soft moan, Alissa turned to the perfect circle that was the mouth of the well. Talon was to be her incentive. She had thought herself safe from him, but she wasn't. Beginning to shake, Alissa knelt and peered down into the darkness. The damp smell of water reached up to soothe her, and she listened as a single tear fell into its unseen depths. "You didn't have to burn it," she whispered.

I know, her memory recalled, *but I want to.*

"The book?" Bailic said harshly.

Fighting the tears, Alissa lay flat upon the snow-covered ground and ran her fingers over the rough stone walls.

"Well?" he prompted.

"Just a moment." She shifted out farther, searching for anything not feeling like rock. "Ah!" she cried, snatching her fingers back and sticking them in her mouth.

"What?" Bailic shouted, his shadow suddenly covering hers.

"Nothing," she mumbled around her fingers. "Just a sharp stone." But it wasn't a stone. It was the book. Stretching, Alissa ran a single digit across the book's spine. Her eyes shut at the blissful warmth that flowed from her fingers to fill her. From the shattered remains of her tracings, there came an answering response. Her eyes flew open.

Bailic forgotten, she looked for her tracings. Dark and still, they glowed a pale indigo in the nether place between her thoughts and reality. Crisp and clean the lines stood out, bolder, deeper, and stronger than before. Her blood pounded through her, and her breath grew fast. She was whole! Her tracings were healed!

"What is it! Have you got it?" Bailic clamored, and her finger slipped free.

"I think it's the book," she lied, sliding out farther.

"Give it to me!" he demanded.

"Stop rushing me or I'll drop it," she snipped. Then her fingers touched the book again, and she lost herself in the slow warmth of late summer. *"You are mine,"* she vowed silently, and with an answering surge of emotion, the book agreed. Softly, the feeling slipped away, and Alissa was left, hanging half in the well, her fingers resting on smooth leather surrounded by the scent of snow and ice.

"Do you have it?" Bailic cried.

Sighing, Alissa tugged on the heavy tome, and it slid easily out of its resting spot. Small stones and bits of snow fell plinking into the unseen water below, and she sat up clutching it to her. Wide-eyed, she stared up at Bailic. The memory of the book's response resounded in her mind, filling her with a deep sense of calm and peace not easily shaken off.

"Give it to me," Bailic demanded, extending a thin hand.

Alissa stiffened, her tranquility shattering. "No."

Bailic wiggled his fingers impatiently. "It's mine by rights. The piper has lost his claim."

"It's Strell I give it to," she said frantically, postponing the inevitable.

"I will burn everything you hold dear," he vowed, taking a heavy step closer.

"Hold on." Alissa scrambled up to put the well between them. "Your arrangement was with Strell, not me."

"You hide behind details!" he raged. "I will have it now!"

"We'll find Strell first."

"Now!" he roared, and Alissa felt her muscles stiffen as if she had forgotten how to move. There was a tug on her awareness and she looked at her tracings. Almost she recognized the pattern her tracings took, then the resonance faded. That cartload of sheep dung! she thought. Bailic had put a ward on her. A curious mix of panic and outrage flooded her as she stood there, helpless before him. Almost giggling, Bailic took a step closer.

A thunderous clap of sound followed by the splintering wood shocked him into immobility. "No!" Bailic cried bitterly, looking skyward. He fell back as a shadow crossed them and was gone.

Grounded to the spot, Alissa stared at the tremendous shape of what could only be a raku hovering above the trees. With an air-shattering roar, he uprooted first one tree, then another. As he reached for the third, she saw Strell, dangling helplessly from a huge hind claw.

"Strell," Alissa whispered, and then, "Strell!" she shrieked, as he appeared lifeless in the raku's grip. Under Bailic's ward she could do little more than that as a third tree was ripped from the earth and was tossed to crash in the distance. Clods of dirt and snow rained down, miraculously missing them both. The great beast soon followed, gracefully settling himself in the opening it had torn.

Her eyes never left Strell as the raku landed upon one foot and supported Strell until his feet again rested on the earth. With a groan she could hear from where she was, Strell collapsed.

"Stay back, Talo-Toecan!" Bailic screamed. "Or I will burn your precious book to ash—and the girl with it!"

Talo-Toecan? Alissa thought in confusion. That was the name Bailic had given Useless, but Useless wasn't a raku—was he? Masters of the Hold were—rakus?

The beast in question rose up on his haunches, arching his long neck as he roared his frustration at the sky. The sound echoed off the far peaks, making the air tremble with his rage.

"Hold!" Bailic shrieked. "I'll do it!" and Alissa felt an arm wrap about her.

"Strell?" she cried, then cursed herself for sounding so weak.

"What makes you think I care?" came a voice whose inflections Alissa recognized from her thoughts. Her eyes lifted from Strell, and she would have collapsed if not for Bailic and his ward holding her fast. There, where the raku had stood, was a man.

"It can't be," Alissa whispered.

"But it is, *my dear,*" Bailic said, cruelly wrenching her arm, "and you'd better hope he heeds my warning, or you will be as dead as that seed-eater." He turned back to the raku, or perhaps it was a man. "I still live, Talo," he shouted. "If I didn't hold anything of value, I would be dead by now."

"True." Useless frowned, seeming to rethink the situation.

"I don't understand," Alissa complained in a small voice.

"Listen, girl," Bailic snarled, "he's a Master of the Hold. He's what he wants to be, sired a raku but with the skill to take the form of a man. Don't let his appearance fool you. He is a beast, and he will kill you with less compulsion than I."

Useless a killer? Alissa wondered. No, not the comforting presence that saved her from Bailic's trance. Useless's ward had left her burnt and broken, but she had been warned. Her stupidity couldn't be set at Useless's feet. Then Alissa remembered the threats that had spilled so easily from her lips the night Useless had answered in her stead. Those hadn't been idle words. Useless would kill, but not without reason, and reason he had. The deaths of all the Keepers and Masters had yet to be accounted for.

"Bailic," Useless sighed tiredly, his curious accent sounding warm and soothing, "it seems we need to talk."

"I can hear you from there," Bailic yelled, "but there's little with which you have to bargain. Go away. Leave me alone."

Grimacing, Useless bent to help Strell rise. "Can you walk yet?" Alissa heard him ask.

Strell shook his head. His eyes met Alissa's. The blankness behind his gaze frightened her even more.

"I can't leave," Useless said, his low voice carrying well. "I have already promised to see your end. It would be difficult to break such a promise, even when only made to myself. Your death is assured, Bailic. The most I can do is—postpone it. Besides," he said, frowning, "what could you possibly concede to me worth your miserable, pathetic, self-absorbed life?"

The grip Bailic had on her tightened, and she felt him shudder. "The book would be intact," he shouted raggedly.

"True." Half supporting Strell, Useless took a sedate step forward. "I couldn't rewrite it. Perhaps it's worth breaking my oath for. Perhaps not. Let's see what we can agree upon."

"I want my life and no interference. And no closer."

"Not the book?" Useless rumbled. "I see the girl has possession of it. Can it be that the book isn't on the table for consideration?"

"The book is already mine," Bailic stated smugly.

Useless's eyes narrowed. "How do you calculate that?"

"Ask your student," Bailic gloated, wrenching her arm again, and she struggled not to cry out, deftly turning her fear to anger so she wouldn't lose control.

Useless turned a quiet gaze upon Strell.

"He's right." Strell shot a furtive, guilt-ridden look at Alissa. "The book is his by the solstice or Alissa dies."

"How can this be?" the elegant figure said, raising his hands in dismay.

"I told you it was a costly affair."

"Aye, costly. So the only thing I have to bargain with is Bailic's life." Useless paused. His fingers drummed together, and Alissa stared. She couldn't tell for sure, but they seemed to have four segments instead of the usual three.

"Very well," Useless admitted sourly. "The book is no longer Strell's to claim. This I accept." He looked at Alissa for the first time, and his pale eyebrows arched in amusement. "It matters little, Bailic," he continued quietly. "*You* cannot open it."

"What's that?" Bailic shouted in her ear, and Alissa winced.

"Try," the figure of a man taunted. He and Strell took a step closer. "I really wish you would. Only a Master, or someone it sets a claim upon, can open it, provided they have enough wisdom to use its lessons. That hasn't happened in, oh, almost a generation."

"No," Bailic breathed loud enough for only Alissa's ears, a hairsbreadth away, to hear.

"Yes, Bailic, and you're found to be lacking."

Behind her, Bailic shifted uneasily. "So where do we stand?" he asked, his voice cracking.

"Let's talk. I assure you I won't kill or maim you—whilst we parley." Useless left Strell to stand a short distance away.

Looking as if his mood were blacker than the inside of a sack, Bailic turned to Alissa. His hands went to snatch the book, and he hesitated. "No," he whispered, glancing over his shoulder at Useless. "You'd like it if I brought the book that close."

Alissa felt a twinge on her awareness, and she was free, stumbling forward to catch herself. Sneaking a peek at her dimly glowing tracings, she noticed which lines were resonating. "Keep hold of my book, girl," Bailic said shortly. "I won't risk taking it that close to him.

"Keep it safe," he added. "If you lose it to him, you'll die." He turned and picked his hesitant way to where Useless waited.

Alissa opened her mouth to protest, then shut it. With a final huff, she tucked her book under her arm and made her way to Strell, forgotten and alone. "Are you all right?" she asked, peering into his haunted eyes.

"I don't know." He blinked vacantly, standing lopsided in the snow without his coat, his new clothes torn and disheveled. Sniffing, he slumped further in a lost bewilderment.

Alissa glanced dismally about the ragged clearing. "Come on. Let's find somewhere to sit." Clumps of frozen dirt and needles littered the ground making muddy splotches on the snow. "Perhaps on my coat," she sighed, reaching for the tie.

"Look," Strell whispered, and Alissa felt a strong tug on her thoughts. "I wish I knew what was going on," he said weakly as Alissa turned to see what he was pointing at. Behind her was a rough wooden bench where none had been before. There was even a blanket on it. With a slight start, she realized that Useless must have made it. How, she wondered, had he done that?

"Really, Talo-Toecan," came Bailic's faint sneer. Useless grumbled something back, and Alissa turned away. Strell was beginning to shiver uncontrollably, and she wanted to get him to sit down.

"Please," he complained as she took his arm and he leaned heavily on her. "I just want to know what's going on."

"Me too." Alissa frowned at the two figures arguing nearby. After setting the book carefully aside on the bench, she helped Strell with the blanket. He tugged it up to his ears as if trying to disappear under it, ignoring everything. He was trembling violently, looking white enough to slip into a stupor. Alissa would have liked to have gone back to the Hold, but it was clear they would be staying until their "betters" decided their fate.

"What happened to your hand?" Alissa gasped, just now seeing it.

"I'm sorry, Alissa," he said softly, eyeing his hand as it poked out from behind the prickly wool. "I broke your staff."

Dreadfully concerned, Alissa sank down beside him. She didn't care how he had managed to break it, but she wanted to keep him talking. "How," she exclaimed, "under the eight puppies did you manage that?" Taking the scrap of fabric holding her hair, she wrapped it about his hand.

Strell began to laugh, admittedly it was a bit ragged, but it was a laugh, and with a huge sense of relief, she knew he'd be all right. "Rescuing Useless," he said.

"Did you know he was—" she began.

"A raku?" Strell finished, almost painful in his confusion. "Not a clue. He looked like that when I first saw him," he said, gesturing to the pair. Bailic was pointing a thin finger accusingly at Useless, who was, in turn, eyeing him with disgust. "No, that's not right," he amended, shuddering as he rubbed his face.

Alissa shifted closer to him. "Have you ever heard of such a thing?" Of course she was referring to Useless's transformation.

"Never," he said, sounding betrayed. "Never in all my travels, or all of my stories, is there a hint rakus are more than the bloodthirsty carnivores they seem to be. I still don't believe it."

"How did you get past the door?" she asked, thinking of all those afternoons with her hands pressed against the cold stone trying to open it.

"Bailic helped," he said, leaving her more confused.

"That's way out of line, Bailic, even for you!" Useless shouted, distracting her. When she turned back, her eyes met Strell's and she smiled. She had been so worried. Aside from Talon, he was all she had in the world. The look he met her with was so fierce with emotion, she drew back in surprise.

"What?" she said.

Trembling, he took a deep breath. His eyes locked on hers, and he slowly exhaled. "Not now," he whispered.

"Tell me?" she pressed, but he turned as a sharp clap of sound filled the air and Useless came striding toward them. Bailic slowly followed, somehow managing to look shaken and confident at the same time. As Useless drew closer, Alissa blinked in astonishment. His eyes were an unreal golden-brown.

"Done!" Useless cried, rubbing his hands. "But I don't like it."

"And you imagine I do?" said Bailic, drawing even with him. Silently they looked down at them, and wonderingly, Strell and Alissa stared back.

"The book?" Bailic prompted.

"But . . ." Alissa stood, snatching the book up from the bench. She knew she had promised, but still. . . . Then a gentle touch on her thoughts silenced her protests. *"Wait,"* she felt. *"You are mine as much as I am yours. It's been nearly four centuries, but I will claim you in due time. Be easy until then. I don't forget."*

Alissa looked quizzically at Useless. It hadn't been his thoughts sliding warmly through hers, and the Navigator knew it hadn't been Bailic's. Seeming to sense her reluctance, Useless frowned. But it was Strell who wearily rose and took the book from her hands, giving it to Bailic. Alissa stood in a horrified shock, feeling herself go gray; its loss felt like an assault.

"Mine!" Bailic chortled, fortunately missing her turmoil.

"Don't gloat, Bailic," Useless muttered uncomfortably. "It's very unbecoming."

Alissa found herself taking a step after it, and Strell grabbed her elbow, drawing her back to his side, feigning the needed support.

"I want to hear you say it again," Bailic demanded, clutching the book to himself.

Useless rolled his eyes and majestically drew himself up. "I swear," he intoned, "I will not contact, or otherwise interfere, with the piper's instruction."

Strell's instruction? Alissa mused, struggling to keep from staring at the book. He still thought Strell was the Keeper?

"And?" Bailic prodded.

"And I will not contrive to thieve the book from your loathsome, grasping clutches."

Bailic paused. "Which book?" he asked, ignoring the gibe.

Useless shrugged like an adolescent caught in deception. "That would be my book of *First Truth*," he admitted, not at all apologetic for his attempted trickery.

"And what else?" Bailic insisted.

"I will see your befouled soul rent and destroyed as soon as inhumanely possible, Bailic."

"That—that's not part of our arrangement," Bailic stammered.

"Yes, it is," Useless said, "if I catch you a stone's throw from the Hold and its environs." Slowly, he took a deep breath. "In return," he continued, "I have your assurance that the both of them—both, Bailic—suffer nothing in mind, body, or spirit from enduring your sorry presence until they choose to leave."

"Or the *First Truth* is opened," Bailic added, and Useless nodded. Bailic seemed to consider this, undoubtedly comparing it to their earlier conversation. "If," he said warily, "he kills himself during his schooling, I won't be held accountable."

"If he does, we will meet to discuss his demise," Useless agreed lightly, not seeing the look of apprehension that Strell and Alissa exchanged. "Accidents happen, but I will be the judge if it was preventable. I still think it dangerous, Bailic. Instruction is the responsibility of a Master, not one such as yourself. Keepers keep. They've never taught."

"I'll risk it," Bailic said, glowering. "I'll not have you

about, interfering with my plans. I can teach him enough so
that the book will open to him. That's all I need."

"Very well. The piper's instruction is yours. I warn you,
though, don't expect much." Blinking in consternation, he
turned with an apologetic smile. "No offense, Strell, but
Bailic doesn't strike me as a very capable teacher." Bailic
stiffened at the thinly veiled insult. "He doesn't have the
knack, I fear," Useless finished indifferently, eyeing the
angry man up and down.

Bailic tugged his vest straight. "I want a tulpa."

"A what!" Useless boomed, and everyone but Strell took
a startled step back. "You insult me again! I gave my word."

"I want it!" Bailic warned, backing away. "Or the agreement is null!"

"Oh, very well," Useless grumbled.

"What's a tulpa?" Strell interrupted, surreptitiously kicking Alissa's shin. She unclenched her hands and tried to stop
fidgeting. Hounds! How could she have just let Strell give it
to him? How could she stand here now and keep from
snatching it back!

Useless flicked what she thought was a warning glance at
her. "A tulpa, Strell, is an object that retains its substance
only as long as its corresponding agreement remains intact.
It reverts back to nothing when the pact is broken. Its purpose is to ease the thoughts of the untrusting that there has
been no premature dissolution of the contract in question."
Useless frowned. "It's something that has never been re-
quested of me in recorded history."

Strell smiled. "I see. Thank you."

"It's my pleasure." Useless grinned, showing startlingly
white teeth. "It's what I'm here for."

Bailic looked positively poisonous. "Are we finished?"

Useless glanced deeply into the sky. "Yes, I believe we
are. May I take a moment to counsel my former student?"

"No."

"No?" Useless turned, poising in mock surprise. "You
won't even grant me that?"

"Leave, Talo-Toecan, or you have broken your word."

"Oh, very well," he mumbled. Alissa understood how he
felt. He was free after a veritable lifetime of confinement.

Even if Bailic got the better half of the deal, which she doubted, Useless was in far too grand a mood to care.

Alissa had listened carefully to the stipulations of their agreement, and one thing was abundantly clear. Even though he was incapable of it, Strell was being schooled to unlock the book, not her. That wouldn't stop her from listening in, though.

"Then I take my leave of you," Useless said, stepping forward and clasping Strell's shoulder. "Thank you for my freedom, Strell. It will bring you luck. Useless is no more."

Strell gave him a sick look. "I hope so, Talo-Toecan. I fear I will need it sorely."

"You must protect her as I cannot," he continued.

"Yes, of course."

Useless needlessly tugged his long vest straight. "I think you will." Strell glanced down before meeting his pleased gaze, and Alissa wondered at their camaraderie. Useless then turned to her. "Don't antagonize him too badly, eh?" he said.

"Me?" Alissa blinked innocently. "Antagonize Bailic?"

"I meant the piper," he muttered.

"Oh."

"We will indubitably speak again sometime," Useless said loudly, engulfing her hand in his. A long finger traced the word "soon" in her palm. Alissa started then, staring wide-eyed into his merrily dancing eyes. This was unexpected.

"Go away," grated Bailic.

"A moment," Useless called in exasperation over his shoulder, then to Alissa, "You will always be my—inspiration." Upon her hand, he sketched the word "student."

"As you will always be mine," she answered dryly as she turned his hand over and traced the word "Useless." For she couldn't call him Talo-Toecan. He was Useless to her, now and forever.

His eyebrows arched up in amusement as he recognized the simple figure. "If you like," he murmured. She dropped his hand, and he stepped back into the clearing. With only the faintest whisper of a touch on her thoughts, he shifted. In a swirl of gray, his elegant shape blurred and grew into the savage form of a raku, glistening gold in the strong afternoon sun.

Useless eyed them for a moment. Then he turned skyward, and with a look of longing even Bailic couldn't fail to recognize, he leapt into the air. Ice and pine needles flew, causing all three of them to shield their faces. When Alissa next looked, he was making circles about the Hold. Then he was gone; the winter sky was empty.

"What of my tulpa!" Bailic shouted, and as if his words had produced it, a tiny carving of a toad fell from the sky to nearly hit him. "Indeed," he snarled, and scooped it up and turned to the Hold, but before he had gone three paces, he spun about.

"You," he snapped at Strell, "will spend your mornings with me. And you . . ." He pointed a shaking finger at Alissa. "I don't care what you do. Just—stay out of my way." Whirling about, he stormed to the empty fortress.

Alissa stood there, unable to move, as the loud boom of the Hold's door closing reached them. Behind her, Strell sighed and sank back down on Useless's bench. "Well," he said mournfully. "I guess my mornings are spoken for."

Alissa's pulse began to quicken, her feet to jitter. It was in the Hold. She could feel it. Ashes. She could feel that cursed book as Bailic took it up the stairs and to his room.

"Alissa?"

Her breath slid in and out, as soft and as easy as the day she was born, and she waited, letting the feeling grow, curious to see what she would do. One step, then another. Her lips were pressed tight. Her eyes were on the Hold's doors.

"Alissa. Where are you going?"

She didn't turn around. "I'm getting my book."

"Alissa! Wait." She felt Strell take her elbow. "Think a moment. You can't even open it yet."

Alissa shrugged him off and kept moving.

"Oh, Hounds. I—I'm really sorry about this," and something heavy crashed into her. Screeching in outrage, she hit the snow. Twisting violently, she realized Strell was sitting on her, pinning her to the ground. "Get *off!*" she shrieked. "Wolves take you, Strell. *Get off of me!*"

"No. Not until you listen."

"It's mine!" she sobbed, beating the uncaring snow and the frozen ground with her fists. Tears of frustration squeezed out, and she hated herself for them. "He has no right! It's mine! It's mine!"

Strell laughed, he actually laughed, and Alissa felt herself go angrier and more desperate than before. "Alissa," he said. "It's not as if you promised him your firstborn."

She quit squirming.

"Actually," he drawled, making his accent thick, as he often did when he wanted to stress his opinion, "you didn't promise him anything."

Alissa lay for a moment, struggling to breathe from Strell's weight. Her breath had melted through the snow, and a clover poked through, brilliant and green, making a startling contrast to the surrounding white.

"We—we will get it back?" she said.

"Yes. We will get it back."

The magical series that's
"sure to appeal to fans of Tamora Pierce or
Robin McKinley." —Patricia Briggs

Dawn Cook

HIDDEN TRUTH

Alissa didn't believe in magic—
not until she was sent on a journey to an
endangered fortress known as The Hold.
Now, an ancient book calls out to Alissa...
and threatens those she loves.

0-441-01003-2

Available wherever books are sold or at
www.penguin.com